MOST LIKELY
TO DIE

MOST LIKELY TO DIE

LISA JACKSON
WENDY CORSI STAUB
BEVERLY BARTON

ZEBRA BOOKS
KENSINGTON PUBLISHING CORP

ZEBRA BOOKS are published by

Kensington Publishing Corp.
850 Third Avenue
New York, NY 10022

ISBN-13: 978-0-7394-7942-1

Printed in the United States of America

Part One

KRISTEN
by
Lisa Jackson

Prologue

St. Valentine's Day Dance 1986
St. Elizabeth's High School
Portland, Oregon

What the hell does she want from me?

Jake Marcott hated to think what her plans might be. Standing in the near-freezing night air, he braced himself for whatever demands she was certain to make.

Bitch!

He didn't know whether he loved her or hated her.

Probably both.

He lit a cigarette with shaky fingers, a residual effect from the car accident that had left his best friend dead and nearly taken his own life.

Ian.

God, he missed that crazy son of a bitch. Things would have turned out so differently if Ian hadn't been thrown through the windshield. If his goddamned neck hadn't been broken. Shit! The crash and spray of glass, the screech of tires, the groan of metal twisting and splitting still echoed through Jake's brain. Ian's face, freckled from too much sun, floated into Jake's mind for just a second before Jake pushed it quickly away. Too many times he'd wondered what would have happened if the tables had been turned, if Ian were still alive and he had been the one to die.

It messed him up to think about it.

Everything seemed washed out and pale now . . . the joy bled from it.

He drew hard on his cigarette and thought about the tranquilizers in his pocket: the prescription that Doc Flanders just kept refilling, barely asking any questions, somehow knowing how deep Jake's pain was, that the little white tablets were a nearly useless balm for the ache splitting his soul.

Get over it, Marcott, he told himself and was pissed that he was here in his damned tuxedo, missing the dance and waiting for her. When would he ever learn?

Clearing his throat, he looked around at this, the eeriest part of St. Elizabeth's campus.

Why this lame, clandestine meeting?

Because she's a psycho. You know it. You've always known it.

Jake took a drag from his cigarette and let smoke stream from his nostrils in the cold night air. He shoved a hand through his hair and glared up at the night-dark heavens. A few stars were visible, not that he cared. He was sick of dealing with the fallout from the accident, his woman problems, and the whole damned world. Eighteen fucking years old and he sometimes felt that his life was a waste.

So where was she?

He glanced around and wondered if she'd show.

Tired of waiting, he tossed what was left of his Marlboro into the darkness, watching the red ember arc, then sizzle and die on the frosty grass. He glanced up at the full moon hanging low in the sky and heard the thrum of a bass guitar throb through the hills. Edgy, his nerves strung tight as the piano wires inside his grandmother's old upright, he paced back and forth in front of the oak tree just as he'd been told. Hidden deep in the maze of hedges, the leafless oak seemed to shiver in the wind, brittle branches reaching upward like skeletal arms scraping the sky.

From deep in the maze he was invisible to anyone. Even a crafty old nun peering out of her third-story window in the hundred-year-old brick building guarding the acres of this campus couldn't see him here.

The place gave him a bad case of the creeps. Throughout the rounded corners and dead ends of the lush labyrinth, benches, fountains, and statues had been placed. Beneath the oak a sculpture of the Madonna stared down beneficently. Arms upraised, she stood silent, white as bleached bones, and surrounded by topiary cut into the shapes of dark creatures that, tonight, seemed sculpted by the devil.

Oh, for Christ's sake, it's just plants, Marcott. Nothin' more.

Angrier by the minute, he glanced at the digital readout of his watch.

She was late. Nearly ten minutes late. So he'd give her another five and then he was gone . . . a ghost.

Besides, he had more important things to do than to waste time on her.

Snap!

He whipped around, toward the sound of a twig breaking.

He saw no one.

"Hey, I'm here," he said in his normal voice.

Nothing . . . no response, just the faraway thrum of music and laughter and the soft whisper of the wind.

A stealthy footstep.

The hairs on his nape lifted.

Surely it was she.

Right?

" 'Bout time you showed up," he said to the inky darkness, his heart pounding a little.

"I was about to give up on you."

Again, she didn't say a word.

Christ, what was the problem with her?

Always playing these damn head games.

At that thought, he smiled . . . maybe that's what she wanted. For him to chase her down. Find her in this maze of clipped shrubbery.

He heard the sound of a footstep again. Closer now. And something else . . . breathing.

Oh, she was close . . .

"I know you're there," he whispered.

He couldn't help the smile that threatened his lips.

Still, she didn't respond.

All the better.

"Have it your way," he said. "I'll find you."

His eyes narrowed in the night and he noticed a dark shape move a bit . . . away from the twisted shadows of the topiary only to fade away again.

So this is what she wanted.

A thrill of anticipation sang through his brain. His blood heated.

Jake Marcott could never back away from a challenge.

* * *

Where the hell is Jake?

He'd been gone for over ten minutes, and Kristen had the first worrisome sensation that she'd been ditched. At the high-school dance. By her new boyfriend. On the two-month anniversary of when they'd started dating. It was like the lyrics of some bad 1950s song.

Don't panic, he said he'd be right back. Just find him, she told herself.

Jake was easy to spot. At six-four, he stood half a head taller than most of the boys and a foot above a lot of the girls, so why couldn't she spot him? "Where are you, Jake?" she muttered to herself. Tall and lean, with wide shoulders, thick brown hair, and an almost shy smile that had caused many a girl's heart to beat triple time, Jake Marcott was definitely a hunk.

Kristen scanned the packed gym, her gaze skating over the knots of students clustered in the corners and crannies of the old gym. A few couples were dancing beneath a canopy of twinkling lights strung from the ancient rafters. Music thrummed, drowning out most conversation, and a fog machine, supplied by the DJ, gave the old building a creepy, intimate ambience. It was late, nearly eleven, and most of the guys had ditched their ties and jackets, but the girls were still dressed in gowns of silk, satin, lace, and chiffon, some sophisticated and sleek, some outrageously frilly, but all far more interesting than the stupid uniforms they wore daily to this, the last all-girls Catholic school in Portland.

Next year St. Lizzy's, the final bastion of separation and education by sex, would, like its brother and sister schools, fall to the sword of coed classes, a nonuniform dress code, and more lay teachers than nuns. Kristen's senior class was, thankfully, the last of its traditional, and in Kristen's estimation, archaic kind. There was even talk of updating the social curriculum enough that the St. Valentine's Day dance wouldn't be held in the creaky old gym where it had been for nearly seventy years, but could conceivably be hosted someplace way cooler, like the Portland Art Museum or on one of the old stern-wheelers that churned their way up and down the Willamette River, or one of the turn-of-the-century hotel ballrooms around Portland—*anywhere* but in this dingy, old gymnasium.

"Hey! Kris!" a female voice yelled over the din, just as a song ended.

Kristen turned to spy Mandy Kim, her jet-black hair coiled

high onto her head, hurrying through the throng. Petite and athletic, she was weaving her way toward her through the knots of
couples. Inwardly Kristen groaned. Mandy was one of those
friends who were quick to point out any flaw in others. An A student who was captain of the soccer team, president of the Honor
Society, and had already been accepted by Stanford, Mandy could
be a real pain. Tonight she was dressed in a sleek black gown that
exposed enough of her back to give Sister Mary Michael connip-
tions. "Where's Jake?"

If only I knew. "Outside, I think," she said, noticing that
Mandy's date, a tall, handsome Asian kid with a stare so unblink-
ing Kristen was certain he was wearing contacts, stood right behind Mandy, looking over her head, one hand cupped over her
shoulder as if he were navigating her.

"Oh." Mandy turned her head to look up at her date. "You
know Boyd."

"Yeah. Hi."

Boyd mumbled a greeting, but his attention seemed keyed on
the spot where the tips of his fingers scraped the smooth skin of
Mandy's nape. His last name was Song and he was forever getting
teased about his name . . . Boyd Song, or Bird Song, Birdie, and
finally Big Bird.

"Maybe Jake's with Nick or Dean," Mandy went on, mentioning Jake's two best friends who also attended Western Catholic, an
all-boys school and the counterpart to St. Elizabeth's. "You know, I
saw them all talking a while ago, near the back doors." She leaned
closer, as if to whisper the darkest of secrets. "Hey, did you see
who Bella brought?" Mandy's dark eyes deepened. "Wyatt Goddard! Remember? He's been kicked out of about a million schools,
including St. Ignatius and Western. Goes to Washington now and
Boyd says he's been suspended twice this year. *Twice.*" She said it
in disbelief, and yet there was the tiniest trace of admiration in her
voice for something that frightened but fascinated her. Boyd nodded. "I'm surprised he was allowed into the dance," Mandy went
on conspiratorially. "What's Bella thinking?"

Who cares? Kristen thought, but kept her opinion to herself,
her eyes searching the crowd for any sign of Jake while Mandy
rambled on and on about the couples on the dance floor.

Kristen just needed to find Jake.

Boyd kept rubbing Mandy's shoulder, gently kneading her
skin. Obviously he was hoping to turn her on as, no doubt, he was
getting off on the simple touch. Mandy didn't act as if she no-

ticed. "So Jake just took off? I wonder if he was looking for Lindsay . . . I saw them talking a while ago, out in the hallway," she said, motioning to the gym's wide double doors that were surrounded by red and white helium-filled balloons and had been forced open.

"I think he wanted to smoke. Outside."

Mandy's eyebrows lifted and there was a bit of a gleam to her gaze, the barest of a disbelieving smile touching her glossed lips. "Sure."

Boyd kept on rubbing, his eyes even more glazed. Geez, he was *really* into it. Kristen didn't dare let her eyes drop for fear she might see evidence of his enjoyment pressing hard against his rented tuxedo pants.

The disc jockey spun "What's Love Got to Do With It" by Tina Turner, and Mandy, grabbing Boyd's hand and breaking his trance, headed for the dance floor.

Kristen was gratefully alone again.

And still no sign of Jake.

Well, crap. Jake had been gone the better part of half an hour and Kristen wasn't the type of girl to stand in a corner and wait. She tried to fight the paranoia that he'd taken off on her, that he'd either hooked up with his ex-girlfriend Lindsay or that he'd ditched her for a chance to get high with his friends.

No way.

Forcing a smile she didn't feel, she eased her way through the tangle of students, recognizing familiar faces, seeing a few new ones but unable in the semidark room to discern who went to St. Elizabeth's, Western Catholic, or Washington. Nor did she care.

She walked past a chaperone in a pink suit and stepped into the cold night through an exterior door.

Lindsay Farrell, her dark hair twisted atop her head, her face seeming wan in the bluish illumination from a security lamp mounted high overhead, nearly ran into Kristen. "Oh, sorry," she whispered and then, recognizing her friend, stopped short. Lindsay's ice blue dress was sleeveless, her arms bare, and she crossed them over her chest, warding off the chill of winter. "It's freezing out here," she said, glancing over her shoulder. "Let's go inside."

"I'm looking for Jake."

"Oh." Lindsay's mouth puckered into a little frown and the air was suddenly charged with unspoken recriminations. Kristen suspected that Lindsay still loved Jake; the reason for their breakup was still a deep secret.

"Have you seen him?"

"Me? No. I mean, not for a while . . ." Lindsay's voice trailed off and she edged toward the open doors.

"Earlier?"

"Yeah, with you."

"Where's Dean?" Kristen asked, the bad feeling that had started in her gut growing deeper.

"Dean and Nick went to check out Chad Belmont's new car." Lindsay shivered and cast a glance up at the moon, which was shining like an icy disc in the sky. "Kind of a weird night, huh?"

Really weird, Kristen thought. No one in her small circle of friends seemed to be with her date. Isn't that what the Valentine's Day dance was all about? Being together? Being in love? Or was she kidding herself? Was she just a stupid, hopeless romantic? Why would one night be any different than any other?

Or was it a night when Jake was having second thoughts? Thoughts about hooking up with his old girlfriend, the one he really did love?

But Lindsay was here, without Jake, wan and tense, acting as if she couldn't wait to disappear. Kristen tried to shake off her worries. Even though Jake and Lindsay had been broken up before Christmas, Kristen still felt a little strange dating him. Her relationship with Lindsay had definitely suffered because of it. "Look, Linds, if this is uncomfortable for you—"

"What?"

"I mean, me being with Jake."

Lindsay scanned the area. "Are you? With him?" she asked, then shook her head impatiently as Kristen's face reddened. "Look, I don't have time for this." She hurried away, silk skirts rustling, heading inside.

Fighting back a burning guilt, Kristen turned toward the parking lot. She was pretty sure she loved Jake, and that made it okay. And Jake hadn't left her. He was here, somewhere, probably with Dean and Nick checking out Chad's new car. Or he could be drinking stolen beers with them . . . or . . . Her gaze skated to the maze behind the cloister, those imposing, thick, impenetrable hedgerows planted in an intricate pattern.

She felt something. A warning. A tiny shift in the atmosphere that caused her scalp to prickle.

Suddenly she was sure something horrible was about to happen.

* * *

Lindsay barely made it to the bathroom. She flew past two girls adding layers of gloss to their lips, stepped into the stall, and ralphed up all of the contents of her stomach into the toilet.

"Oooh . . . yuck . . ." one of the girls said and they both hurried out, muttering about people who shouldn't drink.

As the bathroom door banged shut behind them, sweat broke out on Lindsay's forehead. Her mouth tasted foul, but once she'd retched, she felt immediate relief. Just as all the pamphlets had told her she would.

How she wished her sickness were the result of alcohol!

Oh, Lord, how am I ever going to get through this? she wondered desperately.

One day at a time.

She placed a hand over her flat abdomen and thought about the child growing inside her. All because of one night. One stupid night. How had she been so foolish? What had she been thinking? She, an A student who knew all about the facts of life. Then one night, because she was feeling down, she'd tossed away all of her values and dreams for one evening of passion.

She closed her eyes and drew in a shaky breath. Breathing deeply, she made her way out of the stall. Stumbling to the sink, she splashed cold water over her face. Too bad about her make-up, too bad about college, too bad about the rest of her life. *You're going to be a mother.* Alone in the bathroom, she leaned her head against the cool tiles covering the wall.

So how was she going to tell her parents? Her mother would be heartbroken, her father bitterly disappointed that his only daughter had gotten herself "knocked up." How could she explain it to anyone? She barely understood it herself.

Slowly, she released a tense breath.

She couldn't cower in the restroom all night. She had to go out and face the truth. No more time for pretend. This was real. She looked at her reflection. Dark hair coiled onto her head, sleek blue dress showing off her figure, and an antique diamond necklace her grandmother had bequeathed her—the princess, heiress to the Farrell Timber fortune.

And pregnant.

Wouldn't Nana be proud?

Well, there was more to her than Barbie Doll looks.

It was time to face the damned music.

She had to talk to Jake.

Squaring her shoulders, uncaring that some of her hair had fallen free of the plastered curls, mindless of the fact that her face was nearly devoid of any residual make-up, she hurried outside and into the night.

She'd lied to Kristen a few moments before.

She knew exactly where Jake was.

It was time for a showdown.

Eric Connolly was a boob. An idiot. A cretin! No two ways about it, and Rachel was stuck with him, at least for the remainder of the night. She watched as he, thinking he was so funny, poured a little gin into a cup of punch before taking it over to Sister Clarice . . . oh, Jesus.

Save me, Rachel thought, heading in the opposite direction. She needed some air, some space, and the appearance of not being with Eric when Sister Clarice took a sip, recognized the taste and smell, then grabbed Eric by the back of his scrawny neck and called his folks . . . as well as hers.

Rachel inwardly groaned and glanced at the doors leading to the back parking lot. She'd seen Jake Marcott walk through them not ten minutes ago and he hadn't returned. His date, Kristen, was standing on the edge of the crowd, alternately checking the doors and scanning the dance floor as if she were looking for him, as if he'd ditched her. But Lindsay Farrell had gone outside along with a few other kids. Rachel had seen Jake's sister Bella and Wyatt Goddard slide outside. Nick and Dean, Jake's friends, had exited earlier, and now dateless Aurora Zephyr had wandered outside behind DeLynn Vaughn and Laura Triant.

It was almost as if the party was moving outside.

She bit her lip and thought of Jake. What was he doing? Her heart ached a bit and she reminded herself she was here with Eric the Clown.

Sure, Eric was cute.

Even funny.

But he was just so over the top. So stuck on himself.

She glanced around again and noticed Haylie Swanson bearing down on her.

Oh, God, not now.

Haylie was still in major bereavement mode: black dress; black hair ribbons; black armband; sad, sad eyes. Ever since Ian had died, she'd worn her grief like a noble mantle. But, Rachel knew, hidden in the folds of Haylie's sorrow was a slow, burning, and intense anger, a hatred for the boy who had escaped injury while Ian had given up his life.

Rachel wanted to avoid Haylie, but there was no hope for it.

"I thought I saw you over here," Haylie said, not cracking a smile, her lips painted a dark purple, as if she were some kind of wannabe Goth.

"Hi."

"You with Eric?" Haylie wrinkled her nose a bit.

"Umm-hmm."

"Why?"

"What?"

"Why did you invite him? He's sooo immature."

Rachel lifted a shoulder. Didn't want to be part of this conversation even though Haylie was only echoing her own thoughts.

"You would have been better off to come alone. Since that bastard already has a date."

"That bastard?" Rachel repeated.

Haylie's gaze skewered her. "I know you're in love with Jake," she said, little white lines of fury creasing around a mouth the color of bing cherries. "God, Rach, you wear your heart on your sleeve. Everyone knows."

Rachel cringed. How could *any*one know, much less *every*one? Hadn't she hidden her feelings for him? She thought of Lindsay and Kristen, her two best friends who had both already dated and professed their love for Jake. Did *they* know? Oh, God, this was terrible. Mortified, she felt herself blush a deep, incriminating red.

One of Haylie's eyebrows raised a fraction. She was satisfied by Rachel's reaction . . . so she'd been guessing about Jake. Haylie didn't *know* anything. Nor did anyone else. Haylie had just made a wild stab and had come up with a bull's-eye!

Leaning closer, a slight gleam in those night-dark pupils, Haylie said, "It's just such a waste, Rachel, because he's a loser. A murderer. He killed Ian, y'know."

Oh, Rachel knew. The whole county knew. Haylie made it her mission to make certain that every living soul in the greater Portland area was aware that Jake Marcott had literally gotten away with murder.

"Not now, Haylie," Rachel said.

"Then when? When is he going to pay?"

"The police don't think there was foul play."

"The police are idiots! They've covered it up." Haylie was

nodding now, agreeing with herself. Thankfully the music was loud enough that no one else heard.

"Why would they bother?"

"Because they just don't give a damn."

At that moment Eric returned, smelling of marijuana. Haylie cast Rachel a withering glance as she sniffed loudly, whether to indicate she'd smelled the sweet scent of the wicked weed or because she was into her near-tears act again, Rachel didn't know.

Rachel felt bad about Ian. Everyone did. Especially Jake. But Ian was gone and there was no bringing him back. No amount of accusations, railing at the gods, praying to Jesus, or crying and wringing of hands could return Ian to this earth. There had been memorials, services, and dozens upon dozens of flowers and candles left at the corner where the accident had taken place. Rachel and her classmates had cried buckets of tears, said hourly rosaries, and prayed for Ian and his family. It was sad. Tragic. Horrible. But in Rachel's estimation, there was no conspiracy. It was just an awful accident that would hopefully help everyone learn not to drink and drive.

Ian had been behind the wheel. Like Jake, he'd not been wearing a seat belt. His blood alcohol level had been in the stratosphere and there had been traces of prescription drugs in his blood as well. He'd taken a corner much too fast and paid the ultimate price. Both boys had been thrown from the car; Jake had ended up in intensive care with broken ribs, a fractured shoulder, concussion, and ruptured spleen. But he'd survived. To live with the guilt of knowing somehow he'd been spared.

Everyone mourned Ian Powers, but Haylie's grief had turned to bitter anger. She claimed that Jake, not Ian, had been behind the wheel of Ian's car.

Haylie checked her watch, sent Rachel a final knowing glance, then turned and headed toward the back of the gym.

"Head case," Eric observed as the song ended and he spied Sister Clarice bearing down on him. "Crap!" His gaze darted around the gym. "Look, Rach, I'll be right back. I've, uh, got to go to the john," he said and half jogged through the crowd, trying to lose himself as the nun, like a patient lion stalking prey, slowly but surely followed after him.

Rachel wanted to melt into the floor. Since that was impossible, she turned and headed outside as another song, Springsteen's "Dancing in the Dark," trailed after her into the cold winter night.

She should just call it a night. Make some lame excuse to Eric and find a ride home. Instead, she kept walking, searching the area for Jake.

Geez, how dumb is that? Ditch your date and go looking for a boy who doesn't see you as a girl, only as a "friend" he can use?

A few kids were scattered in the shadows, hidden from the eyes of the chaperones inside. Some were smoking, others drinking, others making out. But nowhere did she see Jake.

Don't try to find him, Rachel, that's a huge mistake. Huge.

She ignored the warnings running through her mind and let her gaze skate away from the few kids hiding for whatever reasons.

Keeping to the shadows, she walked around the corner of the cloister to the gardens, where a hundred-year-old maze of laurel, photinïa, and arborvitae crowded the dark sky and hid the moon.

It was a place to hide.

A place to avoid the people she didn't want to see.

A place to figure out how to find her pride.

Coward, she thought, but wasn't about to risk her shot at a scholarship and graduating with honors because of that dweeb Eric. God, why had she been so foolish, so damned desperate for a date, to invite him? She'd known enough about Eric to realize he relished his role of class clown at Washington High and yet, determined to go with a date, she'd invited the oaf to the dance. Now she was embarrassed as hell. It would have been better to come single. For the love of God, she should have known better. She was a levelheaded girl, the daughter of a cop, for God's sake, and if not a straight-A student, then consistently on the honor roll.

But in her own way, she was as much of a moron as Eric.

Because of Jake.

Always Jake.

Though no one knew it. She fingered the locket at her throat, the one she always wore, the one no one had ever guessed held not only tiny pictures of her mother and father, now divorced, but of Jake as well . . . hidden behind the little heart cutout of her father.

And Jake, she knew, didn't even know she was alive.

How long had she been in love with him? Three years? Four? Since eighth grade at St. Madeline's?

She'd dreamed of him and told no one about her secret fantasies, not even her best friends, Kristen and Lindsay. Because she couldn't. Lindsay had dated Jake for two years and once they'd broken up, he'd turned to Kristen, never once looking at Rachel, his friend, the girl who tutored him when he was failing. The girl who befriended his younger sister, Bella. The girl who took care of his dog when he went hunting. Good old reliable Rachel, who had covered for him when he'd been in the accident over Christmas vacation that had ended Ian Powers's life.

She hadn't *really* lied to anyone. Not really. She just hadn't admitted to seeing Jake earlier that night.

You're a fool, Rachel, she told herself as she marched toward the maze, a great place to hide, a spot where neither Eric Connolly nor anyone else who mattered would find her.

Kicking off her high heels, she sighed. She'd never had much use for killer shoes, and she didn't care that the hem of her dress was dragging along the grass. Too bad. Her mother would be furious, of course; though the dress was a hand-me-down, it was still good and could be used again.

Tough!

What she wouldn't give for her sweats and running shoes. She would be *so* out of here!

And go where, Rach?

She heard her mother's tired voice as if the woman were walking right next to her instead of pulling a double shift at a local diner.

You can't run from your problems.

Rachel turned into the maze, past a statue of the Madonna with her arms stretched and palms turned upward, as if to cradle the next poor soul to pass.

Rachel kept right on walking.

She had to think ahead. Of her future. One definitely without Jake. She had big plans. And nothing, not even her feelings for Jake, was going to stop her.

Kristen headed toward the center of St. Elizabeth's campus, the garden area where a deep, frigid labyrinth of trimmed laurel hedges, pruned trees, benches, and statues separated the school grounds from the convent and chapel where the nuns lived and prayed. Fog was beginning to rise, causing the light from the moon to reflect oddly, as if the silvery orb were fuzzy with some otherworldly halo.

The temperature dropped.

The wind picked up.

Kristen's skin crawled as she passed the weird gargoyles of the topiary and the walls of foliage. Her premonition about something bad about to happen hadn't left her. She turned a corner and darkness suddenly consumed her as she met a dead end. Far in the distance, the music stopped, the background noise of drums and guitars fading into silence.

Where was she going?

Why was she exploring this maze tonight?

She heard a footstep behind her.

She wasn't alone.

Her heart trip-hammered.

Fffttt!

Something sizzled through the night.

And then a gasp, a strangled cry, like a wounded animal, a gurgling, primal groan.

She jumped backward.

What the hell was that?

Her blood turned to ice. She started running along the grassy pathways, guided by the eerie light of the moon. Her high heels fell off, but she raced barefoot, barreling down blind alleys, bouncing off prickly bushes. *Don't panic! Don't panic! Don't panic!*

But she was already frantic, leaves and branches tearing at her arms, her hair falling around her face, her heart pounding out a terrified cadence.

Where was the sound coming from?

She careened around another sharp corner, stubbed her toe on the end of a bench, and yelped as she hurtled through the maze. It was too dark to see the lights from the school—the hedge was too high to peer over—but she kept running. In circles? Toward the center of the labyrinth? Or out of the damned maze?

Blood was oozing from her toe, through the ripped nylon of her panty hose.

Run! Run! Run! Get help!

She tore around a sharp corner just as a scream of pure terror ripped through the shivering shrubbery.

Her heart froze.

"Oh, God," she whispered, her stomach wrenching.

In the weird moon glow she spied Jake Marcott, his body pinned to the trunk of the gnarled oak at the very center of the maze. His face was white, his eyes wide. A crimson stain covered the ruffled shirt of his tux, a thick arrow at its center. Blood dripped from the corners of Jake's mouth and his head hung forward at an impossible angle, his dead eyes wide and staring.

Kristen took a step forward. This was a joke . . . a sick, awful, twisted joke. Jake couldn't be . . . he wasn't. . . "Oh, no . . . oh, no . . ."

Lindsay Farrell, her hands covered in blood, her dress splattered and stained, was crumpled at Jake's feet. Her hair had fallen out of its pins, the long, dark coils curling at her bare shoulders. She lifted her head, her eyes filled with tears that streaked her face with black mascara.

"Why?" she cried as the sounds of shouts and frantic, thundering feet echoed through Kristen's brain.

Help is coming. Maybe it isn't too late. Maybe Jake can be saved! Maybe he isn't dead yet!

She started to run to him, but Lindsay, her face twisted in fury, forced herself clumsily to her feet and barred her path.

"Why, Kristen?" Lindsay demanded again, her voice a razor-sharp whisper, her face twisted in fury and pain. "Why did you kill him?"

Chapter 1

Portland, Oregon, March 2006

"So, I'm stuck, is that what you're saying?" Kristen balanced her cell phone between her ear and shoulder as she leaned back in her desk chair and felt a headache coming on. Though time was definitely running out, she'd held out hope that her friend Aurora had found someone else to be in charge of the damned twenty-year reunion. "No one's willing to take over the job?"

"You were the valedictorian. If you didn't want to head up the reunion, you should have gotten at least one B, okay? Like in PE or calculus or something." Aurora Zephyr laughed at her own joke and Kristen imagined her toothy smile and knowing hazel eyes. Aurora was the one student at St. Elizabeth's that she'd really kept up with over the years.

"If I'd known this was coming up, I would have."

"Fat chance. Now give up the whole glass-is-half-empty thing. It's going to be fun."

"Yeah, right."

"What's got into you? There was a time when you knew how to have a good time. Remember?"

"Good time . . ." Kristen murmured skeptically.

"You're just going to organize a big party for kids you knew way back when. Get into it, would ya?"

Kristen sighed and leaned toward her desk. "It's just that I've tried to avoid anything to do with St. Elizabeth's."

"I know. Because of Jake. We all feel that way. But it's been twenty years, for God's sake. Time to get over it. Bury the past and lighten up."

"I can try."

"Hallelujah and amen, sister," Aurora said and Kristen smiled.

"I've already rounded up quite a few volunteers," Aurora added. "Remember Haylie Swanson?"

That psycho who believed that Jake killed Ian Powers? She wasn't likely to forget. "She'll be there?"

"Yep. And Mandy Kim. Her last name is Stulz now."

Mandy Kim. Another girl Kristen hadn't trusted in high school.

"We've got a few others who will show up. I just told everyone to spread the word. The more people involved, the better. I even called Lindsay Farrell and Rachel Alsace, but they both live too far away to help out."

"I know." Kristen still received annual newsy Christmas cards from the women who were supposed to have been her best friends.

"Lindsay's some hotshot event planner in New York and Rachel's . . . geez, wait a minute . . . I know this . . ."

"She's in Alabama. A cop."

"That's right," Aurora agreed slowly. "Like her old man. He was with the Portland Police Department for years."

Kristen felt the muscles in the back of her neck tense. Mac Alsace had been one of the detectives who had worked on the Jake Marcott murder. Despite his and the Portland Police Department's best efforts, the "Cupid Killer" case had ultimately gone cold. Kristen had heard that Detective Alsace's inability to solve the murder of his kid's friend had driven him to an early retirement.

Jake Marcott's ghost haunted them all.

Kristen hadn't seen either Lindsay or Rachel since graduation. She remembered them in their caps and gowns, all surface smiles and unexplained tears. The day had been warm for June; Kristen had sweated as she waited to give her valedictorian speech and later, accepted her diploma from Sister Neva, the Reverend Mother. After the ceremony, she'd found Lindsay and Rachel. They'd hugged, posed for pictures, and sworn to keep in touch, but they hadn't. Not in that first summer before college, not afterward.

Because of Jake.

So many things had changed, because of Jake.

Kristen leaned forward in her chair to watch the aquarium

screen saver on her computer monitor where an angelfish was being chased through lengths of sea grass by a darting neon tetra.
"Aurora, you should be running this reunion, not me."

"No way. You're not weaseling out of it! I figured I could
jump-start it for you, but the reunion is your baby."

"Fine," Kristen capitulated. "Why not? Believe it or not, I've
done some work. I've got a couple of places who will cater, if we
really elect to have it at St. Elizabeth's."

"It's perfect. We were the last all-girls class to graduate and
now the school is closing. It would be weird to hold it anywhere
else. I did a quick poll of the first few classmates I contacted and
the general consensus is to hold the reunion at the school."

"If you say so."

"Good. I'm sending you an e-mail with an attachment. It's
everything I've done to date. From there on in, you're in charge.
See you in a couple of hours."

"You got it."

Kristen hung up, popped a couple of aspirin for the impending
headache, then buried herself in her work, effectively putting anything to do with St. Elizabeth's out of her head as she polished a
human interest story about a man and dog who had spent a year
walking from Missouri to Oregon via the Oregon Trail. Once
she'd e-mailed the story to her editor, she glanced up from her cubicle. The Elvis clock mounted on the temporary wall over her
desk swivelled its hips. As the clock kept time, the King's hands
moved around the old-fashioned dial. Right now, Elvis was pointing out that it was nearly six and Kristen, as usual, was running
late. She checked her e-mail, found the note from Aurora, and
printed out an Excel file which contained more information than
she'd ever want on her classmates.

Slinging her purse strap over her shoulder, Kristen stood up
and stretched. She'd been allotted this cubicle while one of the
newspaper's more roomy offices was being remodeled. She'd
been with the *Portland Clarion* for fifteen years, long enough to
actually warrant an office—a dubious honor given that it felt as if
the "higher-ups" scarcely noticed her.

"I'm outta here." Kristen closed her laptop, placing it and her
Excel printout inside her computer briefcase.

"Big date tonight?" Sabrina Lacey asked, two cubicles over,
as she tossed back the remainder of her double espresso, then
crumpled the paper cup in her long fingers and discarded the remains into her wastebasket.

"Yeah, right." Kristen scrounged in her purse for her keys and, once the huge ring was found, headed for the door. Sabrina joined her as she wended her way through the labyrinthine desks, tables, and chairs of the *Clarion's* newsroom. It had been her first job out of college, the one she thought she'd use as a stepping stone to bigger and brighter newspapers. Though her position had changed over the years—stretching, evolving, mutating—it said something she wasn't sure she wanted to examine that she was still here.

"You should go out," Sabrina, all big brown eyes, cornrows, and metal jewelry, insisted. "Find a guy. Have some fun."

"I'm married, remember?"

"You're separated, have been for a year, and last I heard, you were going to divorce Ross's ass." Sabrina arched a perfect eyebrow.

"I know, I know. It's just hard."

"Nuh-uh. I've done it three times."

"Maybe it'll get easier after the first one."

"You'll never know unless you try." Sabrina stopped at the hallway leading to the restrooms.

"I've got a kid," Kristen reminded her.

"Who's nearly grown."

Kristen snorted. "Sixteen does not an adult make." '

"You tell her that?"

"Every day. Besides, I do happen to have a date tonight, only it's with half a dozen women I haven't seen in twenty years. I got drafted into heading the damned high-school reunion."

"No way."

"*Drafted*," Kristen stressed. "I didn't volunteer."

Sabrina wrinkled her long nose. "Can't you go AWOL?"

"I'm hoping to pawn the duties off on someone more deserving tonight."

"Good luck." Sabrina laughed and moseyed down the hall.

Kristen shoved open the glass doors of the newspaper offices and a blast of frigid air, smelling of the river and exhaust, rolled toward her. Dark clouds gathered over the spires of Portland's highest buildings, and as she hurried the two blocks to the parking lot where her beat-up Honda was waiting, the sky opened up. Flipping up the hood of her jacket, Kristen made a mad dash to her Honda. The car looked as tired as she felt, and the fun was just beginning.

Kristen shook her head in disbelief. For her, high school had ended that night at the Valentine's Day dance. The remainder of the school year had been a blur that hadn't become clearer with time. But, apparently, one of the perks of being valedictorian of the class was that she got to organize the class reunion.

She'd managed to duck this responsibility for nearly twenty years, but no more. Aurora was making certain that this anniversary of the graduating class of '86 would be celebrated.

The only good news was the hope that she could pass the baton for the next reunion. If there was one . . .

Sliding behind the wheel, she rummaged in her purse for her cell phone. Starting the Honda with one hand, she speed dialed her home number with the other. On the second ring, as she turned on the wipers, her answering machine clicked on. "Lissa?" she said as soon as the recorded message beeped at her. "If you're there, answer, okay?" A pause. Nothing. "Lissa, are you home?" But there was no breathless response; no sound of her daughter's voice. Obviously she wasn't home. "Listen, if you get this, call me back. I should be home in twenty minutes." She clicked off, punched in the number of her daughter's cell phone, and heard, "Hi, this is Lissa. You know what to do. Leave your number and, if you're lucky, I'll call you back."

Kristen hung up. Her daughter was undoubtedly screening her calls. Caller ID could be such a pain. "Great," she muttered under her breath as she nosed her car out of the lot and settled into the slow flow of traffic that oozed out of the downtown area. She was ticked that her daughter wasn't home. Didn't that kid know what "You're grounded" meant? Hopefully, Lissa would show up before Kristen had to leave again, in what? Less than an hour? "Save me," she whispered, thinking of the evening to come and the first of what would probably be a dozen meetings of the reunion committee.

Never reaching a speed even close to twenty miles an hour, Kristen edged west onto Canyon Drive, which sliced through the steep, forested cliffs of the West Hills. Her route cut under the Vista Avenue Viaduct, more commonly referred to as the Suicide Bridge, and each time she passed under that arching eighty-year-old stone span, she thought of those who had leapt to their deaths on the very pavement on which she was driving. Shuddering, she watched the fat drops of rain drizzling down her windshield as she reached the turnoff leading to her house. She punched the accelerator and her little car climbed up the hill, along an impossibly winding side road that snaked through the stand of Douglas fir trees to the crest and the tiny dead-end lane that stopped at her house, a cedar-and-glass "Northwest Contemporary" that had been built in the 1970s and boasted a panoramic view of the city far below.

Tonight she would have loved to throw on her most comfortable sweats, light the fire, and curl up by the windows with a good book. The last thing she wanted was to leave home again to deal with some of her ex-classmates. She could do without their exuberance to connect with friends, enemies, and unknowns after twenty years of virtual silence. Nothing sounded worse.

As she reached her house, she suddenly realized how wrong she'd been: the reunion meeting was not at the top of her "things I don't want to do" list. That first, dreaded spot was reserved for dealing with her soon-to-be ex-husband. And it looked like she was about to have the pleasure of another face-off with him as well. Ross's monster of a black pickup was blocking the drive.

"Give me strength," she silently prayed as she parked her car across the street.

The day was quickly sliding from bad to real bad.

"Perfect," she muttered under her breath. She sent up another quick plea for patience in dealing with the man she'd married during her sophomore year in college. It had been a rash, hasty decision, one she'd come to regret. If not for their only child, the now "out of cell range" Melissa, the entire marriage could be considered a colossal mistake.

She just hadn't had the guts, heart, time, or energy to end it.

Neither, it seemed, had he.

No divorce papers had been filed.

Yet.

"More fun to come," she whispered under her breath as she grabbed the mail from the box. With her orange tabby nearly tripping her, Kristen made her way through the open door of the garage, past the lawnmower, ladders, and recycling tubs to the door leading to her kitchen, where, big as life, Ross was seated at the nook café table, sipping one of her light beers and reading the paper.

Just as he'd done thousands of times during their years together.

Wearing a white shirt with the top two buttons undone, his sleeves rolled up, his tie tossed casually over the back of a chair, he scanned the business section. His wallet and keys were on the table.

"Been here a while?" she asked as he looked up, his gray eyes, as always, assessing.

Her heart did a funny little glitch. Even after all the years, the
fights, the differing paths of their lives, she still found him sexy.
Her downfall.

"I thought I'd take Lissa to dinner. She hasn't shown."

"Just like that?"

"Yeah."

She was stunned. "Did you consider calling?"

"Yep." He took a swallow of his beer and leaned back in his
chair to stare at her. "Thought better of it."

"Why?"

He lifted a shoulder. "I figured you might try to talk me out of
it. Or, if I got your okay, then I'd have to go through the whole
thing all over again. This seemed easier."

"So you just let yourself in?"

"Still own half of the house. Got my own set of keys." Those
damned eyes skewered her, challenging her to argue with him.
Kristen decided not to rise to the bait. She didn't have the time or
energy to argue.

"Where is she?"

"I thought you'd know." He stretched, his shoulders and arms
tugging at the seams of his shirt, the black hair at his nape a little
too long and ruffling over his shirt collar.

Uneasiness crawled through Kristen's blood. "Lissa was supposed to come home straight after school."

"You told her that?"

"Oh, yes." The ugly scene this morning was fresh in her mind.
They'd argued, the gist of it being that Lissa was furious with her
mother for finding the progress reports from the school. Even
though the envelope had been addressed to Mr. and Mrs. Ross
Delmonico, Lissa had considered the contents about her failing
grades to be no one's business but her own. She'd thrown a fit and
refused breakfast. Her eyes, so like her father's, had snapped gray
fire and she'd half run out of the house to catch a ride with her
boyfriend. "I grounded her because of the progress reports from
her school," Kristen explained.

Ross waited, eyebrows raised, for Kristen to continue.

"She's flunking chemistry and German." Kristen picked up
the progress reports from the dining room table and handed them
to him.

"Flunking?" he said, eyeing the page with the teacher comments.

"She claims it's all a big mistake, that the teachers haven't entered a couple of grades, so I told her to get everything fixed and have Mrs. Hanson and Mr. Childers call me, send me notes, or e-mail me. So far, I haven't heard from either teacher, so I figure until the grades are up, she's going nowhere."

"Isn't that a little Dickensian?"

"You got a better idea?" She didn't need a lesson in parenting from a man who for years was a ghost in the marriage, spending all of his waking hours working. When Ross didn't reply, she said, "I didn't think so."

"She still going to school with Zeke?" Kristen nodded, and Ross said maddeningly, "Doesn't sound much like grounding to me."

"I was running late and—" Kristen stopped short, clenching her teeth. She glared at him. "Why am I explaining this to you? It's not like you were around to drive her."

"Your decision, not mine," he reminded her in that irritating way of his. That much was true. She'd asked him to move out and he'd complied. Now he shifted on the chair to face her and she noticed the square cut of his jaw, still as strong as it had been when she'd met him nearly twenty years ago.

"Okay, let's not go there. The blame game doesn't really work."

"Agreed."

Damn the man. Was that a twinkle in his gray eyes? Was he finding some humor in this impossible situation?

Ross stretched out of the chair, pushing it back so hard it screeched against the tile. Shoving his hair from his eyes, he stood and she was reminded again that Ross Delmonico was one heart-stopping hunk of a man. It was no wonder she'd fallen head over heels for him all those years ago. She'd been vulnerable, hurting, even bristly after the end of her senior year of high school. She'd moved to Seattle by the end of June, gotten hired at a clothing store, and with the help of student loans and scholarships had started classes at the University of Washington in the fall.

Ross Delmonico, a graduate student, had been her TA in chemistry for the spring term. He'd taken the time to tutor her personally, and as the term had progressed the study sessions had segued into a series of casual dates. They'd explored the city, drinking coffee on the waterfront, shopping at Pike Street Market, poking through old book and antique shops in Pioneer Square, getting caught in the rain at the locks. They'd taken a ferry across the sound at sunset and watched the sun settle behind the jagged

Olympic Mountains as they'd slowly fallen in love. Somehow she'd passed chemistry before switching her major to journalism. How ironic that their daughter was failing the same subject that had brought them together.

In her mind's eye, Kristen caught a glimpse of Ross as a younger man. His hair had been longer, his clothes leaning toward denim shirts over faded T-shirts, beat-up jeans, and two days' worth of beard darkening that strong jaw. He'd been soft-spoken, thoughtful, and when he smiled, showing off one dimple and strong white teeth that flashed devilishly against his tanned skin, she'd felt her breath catch in the back of her throat. God, she'd fallen hard for him.

He'd filled out a bit in the years since, and the untamed curls at the back of his neck had been clipped into a shorter, cleaner cut. Crow's-feet fanned from the edges of his deep-set eyes, and if she looked hard enough she could see the first hint of gray daring to show in his thick hair. He looked almost citified in his slacks and white shirt, but in the depth of his eyes and the hint of his smile, there lurked the sexy, intelligent man she'd married.

"What?" he asked, drawing her out of her reverie, his expression faintly amused. Almost as if he knew where her thoughts had gone.

Through a partially open window she heard the sound of a car's engine, and within seconds the nose of a battered red Dodge came into view.

Ross's gaze centered on the window. "Looks like the prodigal daughter hath returned."

"Good. Let me handle this."

"No way . . . my turn, remember?"

Kristen really wanted to square off with Lissa. After all, she was the one who had set the rules and the punishment, but maybe it was time for Lissa's father to step up. "Okay, Super Dad, you're on."

Chapter 2

They watched as Lissa leaned across the seat and kissed Zeke with enough open-mouthed fervor to make Kristen's gut clench. Though rain was falling steadily, the drops weren't enough of a curtain to shield the passion in the kiss.

"She's giving him tongue, right here? In front of us in the middle of the day?" Ross sounded incredulous.

"Welcome to my world."

Lissa slid from the SUV's interior and headed toward the house. "If they kiss like that out in the open, what do they do when they're alone?"

"We've had 'the talk.'"

"'The talk'? You mean about sex?"

"Yes, about sex. You know kids today don't think oral sex is any big deal."

"I think it's a very big deal." He looked shaken.

Where had he been for the past decade? Kristen wondered. Had he been hiding his head in the sand and believing the parents' age-old foolish notion of "*My* daughter would never?" If so, it was about time he woke up.

"You're kidding, right?" he asked, but his serious tone indicated he recognized the truth when it was served up to him on a platter.

"Wish I were."

"Has anyone had 'the talk' with Zeke?"

"I didn't take that one on."

"Maybe I will."

"Yeah?"

"You know, scare the shit out of the punk."

"And risk losing your daughter's respect?"

He snorted. "That's already shot to shreds anyway. A little tête-à-tête with Zeke sounds imminent."

Kristen agreed, but said, "You won't gain any points."

"Who cares?"

Exactly. "Then maybe you want to reinforce my position that oral sex at sixteen is not okay."

"Jesus."

Lissa's steps slowed as she finally spotted her father's car. She sent a guilty look toward the kitchen before her shoulders straightened, her chin jutted forward in rebellion, and she strode into the house, her attitude reeking of battle.

She dropped her backpack near the hooks by the door to the garage. Water dripped from her coat and she smelled of rainwater and something else—cigarette smoke? Or worse?

Mascara-rimmed eyes glared up at her father. Her near-black hair, cut short and tipped in shades of pink and gold, was curling and damp. "What're you doing here?"

"Waitin' for you. My night."

"*Your* night?" she said, barely holding in a sneer. "Since when?"

"Since I got back into town and your mom and I worked out a deal."

Kristen was about to speak up. There was no deal, but she caught a warning glance from Ross and held her tongue.

"A deal?" Lissa repeated skeptically as she walked to the refrigerator and opened the door. "About me?"

"Yep."

"Without my consent?" She snagged a Diet Pepsi. "Shouldn't I have been consulted?"

"Informed," he corrected as she closed the fridge with a shoulder. "Which I'm doing right now. Come on, we're going to dinner, then over to my place."

"What? Why?" she demanded, clearly blindsided.

"Just to hang."

"You and me?" She turned big eyes toward her mother as she opened her can of soda. "This is okay with you?"

"It was her idea," Ross said as he reached for his jacket.

"No way!"

Ross moved toward the door. "Come on, grab your stuff. You must have homework."

"Wait a minute. I can't leave. Zeke's coming back and we're watching television together tonight."

"Aren't you grounded?" he asked.

"I'm not supposed to *go* anywhere, but he's coming here," she explained, as if her thinking were entirely logical. "Besides, the whole grounding thing is lame."

"Then you have notes from your teachers for me?" Kristen asked. "Because nothing came through on my e-mail."

"Not exactly. They're working it out."

"Great. When they do, then we'll see."

"God, Mom, this is just so unfair!"

Kristen nodded. "Probably so. Get used to it. And watch your mouth."

"I'll handle this," Ross said, and Kristen decided to let him go for it. Let him deal firsthand with a stubborn, rebellious teenager.

"Good. I'll let you two work it out."

As he shepherded a recalcitrant Lissa out the door, Kristen took the time to lift Marmalade from the ground and pet the cat's soft fur as she walked to the bedroom. She was rewarded with some deep purrs and a wet nose pressed to the inside of her neck. "Yeah, you're a love," Kristen said before the orange tabby started struggling and Kristen dropped her onto the edge of the bed . . . the king-sized bed she'd shared with Ross.

"Don't go there," she warned and wouldn't even guess what Ross was sleeping on now. Maybe just the recliner he'd been so fond of before he'd moved out. "Not your problem."

But she couldn't help smiling when she remembered going bed shopping years earlier and how Ross had flopped onto the expensive mattress, crossed his legs, and patted the pillow top next to him. "Should we try it out first? You know, see if it can stand up to us?" he'd whispered.

Kristen had blushed to the roots of her sun-streaked hair before muttering, "In your dreams, Delmonico."

"All the time," he'd agreed and as she'd dropped onto the mattress, she'd imagined making love to him on that downy soft bed.

He'd read her mind and told the clerk, "Sold. When can you deliver?"

"Next Thursday," the bald salesman had said, checking his delivery chart.

Ross had winked at Kristen. "I guess you'll just have to wait to have your way with me, wife."

Now Kristen touched the edge of a pillow and sighed. "A long time ago," she reminded herself and shut her mind to those dangerous thoughts. There had been a time when Ross had meant everything to her. But that was before he'd started his own construction company and worked increasingly long hours. It had gotten so bad that some nights he wouldn't come home, staying on the job in other cities, making excuses . . . or so it had seemed. She'd wondered if he was having an affair, had asked him about it and he'd scoffed at her. But there was something in his eyes that had belied his quick denial.

She'd never caught him in a lie.

Never picked up a call from another woman.

Never found a receipt he couldn't explain.

And yet . . .

The worst-case scenario was he was a liar and a cheat.

The best case, disinterested in his family.

And what about you? What about his charges that you'd never really gotten over Jake Marcott? Just how much truth is there that his ghost still haunts you, as Ross charged?

She closed her eyes. How much of the failure of their marriage was her fault?

Half?

A quarter?

Did it matter?

In the past few years, Ross had slowly slipped away from her.

Or did you push him?

The headache she'd been fighting flared again, burning behind her eyes. The bottom line was that Ross had nearly disappeared from her life.

But he was here today, wasn't he? And he's with Lissa tonight.

"Too little, too late." She wouldn't forget that deep down Ross lived and breathed for Delmonico Construction. His wife and young daughter had become less and less important until Kristen had felt virtually invisible.

In the past two years, nothing she said or did seemed to sink into the man.

So it was a good thing he was dealing with Lissa. A very good thing.

She walked into the bathroom and stopped short when the closed blinds rattled slightly.

How odd, Kristen thought. The window was never open. Never. And yet . . . She pulled the blinds up and sure enough, there was a space between the sill and the bottom pane. Just wide

enough to stick fingers beneath and push open. Water had col-
lected on the window track, indicating that the window had been
open for some time.

She frowned at the opening, pushed the window shut, and
tried to latch it, but the damned lock, which had always been
loose, didn't click shut.

So who had opened it?

Lissa?

But she never used this bathroom.

Ross?

Nah . . . he was never here.

But he still has keys.

Why would he come into the bathroom . . . her bathroom?

It used to be his, too.

Oh, hell, she couldn't think about this now. She snapped the
window shut, forced the latch closed, and decided to ask Ross and
Lissa about it later.

She only took the time to brush her teeth, pile her hair onto her
head in an untidy knot, and strip out of her work clothes in favor
of jeans, a long-sleeved T-shirt, and battered running shoes. A
dash of lip gloss, then she grabbed her laptop, portable printer,
purse, and keys and was out the door.

As she drove to the committee meeting, she grimaced. Her
job had lost its luster, she was soon to divorce her husband, her
only child acted as if she hated her, and to top things off, it was a
rainy night and she was headed to about the last place she wanted
to go.

Could her life be any more pathetic?

So it's finally *going to happen.*

Twenty long years had passed, twenty years of questions,
twenty years of heartbreak, twenty years of fear.

Jake Marcott's killer smiled inwardly. She had waited a long
time for this, been patient, knowing that eventually the Fates
would work with, rather than against, her and she'd get her chance
to finally settle the score.

After Jake's death there had been a time of fear and panic.
She'd vowed to herself that she had done all that was necessary,
but of course, she'd been wrong. She knew about the reunion
meeting and itched to be there, a mouse in the corner, listening
and planning, knowing that at last it was time to strike again, to
right the very old and bitter wrongs.

Get ready, she thought, tucking her hair into a hat and glancing at the overcast skies. She thought back to that night, to seeing Jake's eyes find her in the moonlight. His teeth had been a slash of amused white, his cocky expression changing as she'd lifted the already-armed crossbow, leveled the heavy weapon at his chest, and let the arrow fly.

Thwack!

Jake Marcott had taken one in the heart.

Right where he deserved it.

She smiled at that memory. Not once in the past twenty years had she regretted Jake's demise.

Better yet, she'd gotten away with it. She'd left the damning weapon at the scene of the crime, but the stolen crossbow could never be connected to anyone at the dance that night.

No one knew.

She smiled as she looked into the mirror.

Jake Marcott's murder had never been solved.

And the class of 1986 had never been the same.

There had been no five-year reunion, or ten. No one had said a word when fifteen years had passed, but now, on the eve of the closure of St. Elizabeth's, the class of '86 was going to meet one more time.

For some, it would be the last.

Chapter 3

Ricardo's Restaurant was a bad trip down memory lane. Located only half a mile from St. Elizabeth's campus, the little eatery was a place where all Kristen's friends had hung out. Though twenty years had passed and the once-red plastic booths had been re-covered in a green faux leather, not much else had changed. The walls were still covered with pictures of softball, basketball, and Little League teams Ricardo's had sponsored over the years, and the aromas of baking bread, tangy marinara sauce, and garlic still emanated from a kitchen hidden behind the main counter.

She saw the cluster of tables pushed together in one corner near the fireplace. Several women were already seated, and Kris felt a tightening in her gut as she recognized Haylie Swanson and Mandy Kim. Mandy's dark hair was shorter and her face had rounded, but Haylie looked as if she hadn't aged or changed one bit since high school. A trim black woman sat near Aurora, probably DeLynn Vaughn, and the other two women . . . Geez, they looked familiar, but who . . . oh, God, the heavyset one was Martina Perez and the other woman looked a lot like April Wright, whose mouse-brown hair had become sun streaked, her glasses long gone, her crooked teeth now capped and white.

Strewn over the tabletops were yearbooks, binders, a legal pad, yellowed copies of the school newspaper, class lists and the like. The women were talking, laughing and sipping either beer, wine, or Diet Coke.

Aurora looked up as Kristen wended her way to the tables. "Kris!" Aurora smiled widely and waved her over. "About time."

"Sorry I'm late. Issues at home."

"Tell me about it," DeLynn Vaughn said, rolling her large brown eyes. "I've got seven-year-old twins . . . One might have to be held back, while his sister will be moved on to second grade. I get it, I really do. I'm a teacher, for God's sake! But that doesn't make it any easier. Oh, I don't want to think about it right now." She flashed a friendly smile. "How have you been, Kris? You're a big-time reporter for the *Clarion*, right?"

"*Editor*," Aurora corrected.

Kristen shook her head and slid into the empty chair between DeLynn and Aurora. "*Associate* editor. Not so big-time. You work there long enough, they figure they have to give you a title of some kind."

"Sure, that's how it works. They pass out promotions with no thought to talent," DeLynn said dryly and Kristen smiled despite herself, only to glance up and find Haylie, sober as a judge, staring at her.

Great, Kristen thought. *Some things never change.* "Hi, Haylie," she greeted her, deciding to break the ice. "Geez, I haven't seen you since graduation."

"You find that odd?" Haylie asked, fingering the stem of an untouched wineglass.

"A little."

"I guess we're all just too busy," Martina said with a shrug. "Jobs, husbands or boyfriends, kids—"

"Yeah, that's it," Haylie muttered with a trace of bitterness.

"So . . ." Kristen dragged out her laptop and switched it on. "Let's get to it. Thankfully, Aurora's done a lot of the preliminary work, but I couldn't bribe her into taking on the job."

Several of the women chuckled. But not Haylie.

"You earned it," Aurora said.

"Don't remind me. Now, let's see what we've got."

What they had was plenty. Aurora and Martina had already started searching the Internet, using Web sites like Classmates .com to collect as many e-mail and regular mail addresses as they could, all of which were merged into a database. Mandy had elected to put together a booklet of bios of the classmates and De-Lynn had contacted the current principal of the school to come up with possible dates for the reunion. They had agreed to make Friday night of the reunion weekend "classmates only" and decided to use Ricardo's as the venue. Husbands and significant others would be invited to a dinner/dance on Saturday night at the school.

So much like the Valentine's Day dance twenty years ago,

Kristen thought, but held back any objections as everyone else seemed excited about the idea.

"You know, I don't know why we haven't had a reunion before," Mandy chirped.

"Yeah, we should have done this after ten years . . . or maybe even five," April agreed.

"That's such a load of crap." Haylie's voice was a dash of cold water. The skin on her cheekbones tightened as she slid her gaze over all the women. "And we all know why."

Everyone grew silent; even the piped-in music and ambient surrounding conversations seemed to fade.

"It's because of Jake Marcott," Haylie stated. "I told myself that if I came to this, I was going to say exactly what I thought, and I figured that we'd all pretend that what happened to Jake and to Ian was all forgotten. Well, it's not."

Kristen said, "I don't think this is the time to discuss Jake."

"Yeah, of course not. It never is. Why don't we pretend it didn't happen? We'll all be as fake as we were the last year of high school."

"Haylie, not now," Kristen said, uncomfortable in her newfound role as the leader of this group.

"Then when, Kris? When?" she asked. "Ian and Jake have been dead twenty years! Longer than they were alive! Don't you think we should at least acknowledge them?"

"At the reunion?"

"Here! Now!" She was visibly shaking, her wine slopping over the rim of her glass.

"Later."

"It *is* later!"

"Oh, no!" April glanced up as another woman headed their way. Kristen's heart dropped as she recognized Bella Marcott, Jake's sister.

"Cool it, Haylie," Aurora said, but Haylie, already incensed and fueled by a couple of glasses of Merlot, turned angry eyes on Bella.

"Something wrong?" Bella asked, then made a sound of acknowledgment. "You were talking about Jake, right?" Before anyone could answer, she skewered Haylie with a look. "And you're upset because you still believe he killed your boyfriend."

"His name was *Ian*. He wasn't just my boyfriend. He was someone's brother and someone's son. And he was a person. Ian Powers." Red-faced, tears sheening in her eyes, Haylie stood abruptly, knocking over her wine in the process. The crimson liquid ran like blood. She barely noticed as April and Martina started mopping up the oozing stain with their napkins. "He would have been thirty-nine right now, like some of us. But he never had the chance to go to college or hold a job or get married or have kids, and the damned shame of it is no one but his family remembers him."

One napkin soaked, another still wicking up the wine, April said, "We get it, Haylie, okay? We're all sorry about Ian."

"No one really is." She sniffed loudly and backed away from the table, colliding with a chair. "I knew this was a mistake," she said. "I should never have come."

"Oh, Haylie, come on." Aurora, always the peacemaker, reached for Haylie's arm. "Let it go."

"I'll never 'let it go.' " Haylie snagged her purse from the floor and took off through the surrounding tables, half running toward the door.

"Should someone go after her?" Bella asked, turning to watch Haylie disappear into the night.

"I will." Kristen was already on her feet. "She shouldn't be driving."

"What a drama queen," April muttered under her breath. "She's fine. Barely touched her wine."

"I'm sorry, Bella," Aurora said, motioning Jake's sister into the chair recently vacated by Haylie. "I'm sure she didn't mean anything she said."

Bella arched an eyebrow, and in that instant she looked so much like her dead brother that Kristen's blood chilled. "I think you're wrong," Bella said, looking through the large window toward the parking lot. "I think she meant every word of it."

Kristen left her laptop and purse at the table and headed outside. She felt the eyes of other patrons following her and silently kicked herself for getting involved in the damned reunion. One meeting and it was as if she'd tumbled back in time. Here she was chasing Haylie Swanson, who, just like in high school, was always upset. She caught up with Haylie in the parking lot. Haylie had unlocked the door to her car and was about to slide behind the wheel.

"Haylie," Kristen called and Haylie hesitated, turning toward Kristen. "Hey, don't go off all upset. I'm sorry about Ian, really. It was a horrible accident, but it's been twenty years."

"So we should just bury it? Forget it?" She was fumbling in her purse, juggling her keys and a pack of cigarettes. Her hands were shaking and there was an edginess to her. She was almost frantic as she shook out a filter tip.

"Look, no one meant Ian any offense."

"Wasn't Jake your date that night?" She lit up, fingers trembling.

"It was a horrible night for all of us."

"See what I mean? Everyone focuses on the dance and Jake's murder. No one gives a damn about Ian." She opened the car door and slid inside. "Good luck, Kristen," she said as she jabbed her keys into the ignition. "I have a feeling you're going to need it." Cigarette clamped between her lips, she twisted her wrist, the engine firing as she slammed shut the door.

Ramming the sports car into reverse, Haylie floored it. She shot backward, her rear tires hitting a curb. As Kristen watched, she hit the accelerator again, barely slowing as she bounced into the street, almost clipping the fender of a passing white Cadillac. The driver of the Caddy swerved and laid on the horn as Haylie sped away.

Kristen sighed, then walked back inside. Her classmates were still seated, all staring out the window. "I think she's losing it," Kristen said.

Bella rolled her eyes. "It's all for show."

"I don't know."

April shook her head. "I used to work with her brother. Years ago when I was clerking for a law firm downtown. Even then Haylie was having problems, seeing a shrink. On and off antidepressants and anxiety drugs."

"Sounds like ninety percent of the adults in America," Martina said as she motioned to the waitress for another drink. "Let's not worry about her now, okay?" She glanced around the table. "We can't let Haylie derail us. Not when we're on a roll. We've got work to do, wine to drink, and pizza to order." The waitress approached, a tall, skinny woman with graying hair and deep-set eyes, and Martina flashed her a smile. "Do you still serve that Mexican pizza with the jalapeños? I used to love those things."

The next hour was spent ordering and eating any and all foods Italian, organizing committee heads, and catching up. Pictures of husbands, kids, and boyfriends were passed around, and Aurora admitted that her oldest daughter had just married and was talking of starting a family. Aurora had married right out of high school, had her first child at nineteen, and her daughter had followed in her mother's footsteps right down the bridal path. Aurora didn't know whether to be elated or horrified. "Don't get me wrong. I love babies, but me, a grandma? I'm waaay too young." She was teased mercilessly, and the general mood at the table turned upbeat.

"What about you, Kris?" Aurora asked. "No pictures?"

Kristen shook her head. "Not with me."

"You've got what? One daughter."

"Mmm. And the usual axiom applies, sixteen going on thirty."

There were murmurs of understanding.

"You're married to Ross Delmonico, right?" April asked, interest evident in her features, a small smile tugging at the corners of her mouth.

Kristen tried to evade the question. Didn't want to cop to the fact that she was separated. "Mmm."

April picked up on the lack of commitment in Kristen's tone. Her eyes sparked in interest. She plucked a breadstick from the basket in the middle of the table and snapped it in two. "So what's the deal?"

Kristen had always been a terrible liar. Besides, there was just no reason to hide the truth. It would come out sooner or later. "Ross and I are separated."

April tossed her lustrous hair over one shoulder. "Are you nuts?" She took a bite from the breadstick. "I met Ross a couple of times when I was working for the law firm. He's what my daughter would call 'a hottie.'" Leaning back in her chair, her expression said clearly that she thought anyone who would let Ross Delmonico slip through her fingers must be brain-dead. She chewed on the breadstick. "So, are you getting a divorce?"

Kristen thought about the papers she had yet to file. "I don't really know," she hedged, surprised at her reaction. Hadn't she just hours before practically told Samantha, her coworker at the *Clarion*, the divorce was a done deal?

"Well, listen," April said, as if she were teasing, "if you get tired of that guy, throw him my way, will ya?" She laughed at the joke, but there was something about her suggestion that made Kristen feel defensive. Oh, God, she wasn't becoming one of those women who thought of a man as "hers," the kind who only held on tighter when another female showed interest, was she? She smiled at April and said lightly, "Who knows?"

"When you figure it out, let me know."

At that moment the waitress returned and the conversation drifted into safer territory. April turned her attention to one of the yearbooks lying open on the table, and after they ordered refills, the business of the reunion was brought to the fore once more.

Martina, who was married to Craig Taylor, a graduate from Western Catholic, suggested that their class invite the boys from Western who had graduated in the same year. "I think we should make this reunion special. It'll be the last of its kind, as St. Elizabeth's will be closing. Wouldn't it be cool to have the boys that we did everything with there?"

"Ya think?" Kristen asked warily. Nostalgia aside, this was a little too eerie. "It seems like—"

"Like we're trying to duplicate the dance where my brother died," Bella said, and everyone grew quiet once again. Her smile had faded and she contemplated the contents of her wineglass. A crease lined her forehead as she thought. "You know, maybe it's what we need. It could be cathartic."

"Probably not for Haylie," DeLynn said.

"Nothing will be." April frowned. "As I said, she needs help. Serious help. But it's not our problem."

Bella glanced over at Kristen. "I'll go along with whatever the group decides. Please don't worry about me, and if we're thinking about Jake, then what would he say? I think he'd tell us to 'go for it' and 'have a bitchin' party.' "

"She's right," Mandy agreed, still writing on her legal pad.

April eyed a bottle of Merlot. "Then why not?" She grinned wickedly. "It'll be fun."

Everyone, aside from Kristen, seemed to concur.

Martina said, "Good. I'll call Laura. Remember her, Laura Triant? She married one of Craig's friends. Chad Belmont. He graduated when we did and was Western's senior class president, I think. Chad keeps in touch with a lot of the guys who graduated from Western." Martina was running with her idea, nodding her head, her black hair gleaming in the dim lights.

They chose a weekend in July that the school had already approved, then they split into committees, each volunteering to oversee the different jobs that needed to be tackled. DeLynn took over contacting classmates, April wanted to work with the caterers, Martina was in charge of dealing with the boys from Western, Kristen, along with being the general coordinator and treasurer, would make certain that the announcements were sent, and Aurora would assist her. Bella was in charge of decorations. No one mentioned Haylie again.

Mandy Kim, the self-appointed secretary, took copious notes, filling in page after yellow page of a legal pad with information. She worked with the same intensity and focus that she'd exhibited when she was listening raptly to one of Sister Clarice's lectures on world history twenty years earlier.

Some things never change, Kristen thought as she made her own observations and memos on her laptop.

The general consensus was to meet in a month, again at Ricardo's, where they all would report their progress. In the meantime they'd be in touch via phone and e-mail.

An hour later the check had been paid and almost everyone had left. Only Kristen and Aurora remained.

"See," Aurora said, as she stuffed her yearbook into a purse large enough to hold a small computer, "admit it, Kris, this went better than you imagined."

"Okay, okay, you're right. Aside from the Haylie meltdown and a few tense moments with Bella, it was okay."

"Better than okay. It was successful. We got a lot of stuff accomplished and we even had some fun, right? I'm thinking the reunion is going to be a blast."

"We'll see," Kristen said.

"It's just too bad that Rachel and Lindsay couldn't have been here." When Kristen didn't respond, Aurora added, "You're still in contact with them?"

"We do the Christmas card thing." Kristen gathered her things. Aurora was right. The meeting had gone better than Kristen had expected and it had been good to see some of her fellow classmates and find out what they'd been doing since graduation. "Hopefully they'll make it to the reunion."

"So why not just call them? You've got their numbers."

"I will." Kristen walked outside with Aurora.

As she shoved her purse and laptop into her Honda she felt a lot more optimistic that the reunion wouldn't be a total disaster. She wasn't convinced that it would be "a blast," but it might have its fun moments.

After all, she thought, as she slid behind the wheel and turned on the ignition, what could possibly go wrong?

Jake Marcott's killer sat in her car, the engine idling. Parked on a darkened side street, she watched the restaurant parking lot unobserved. Tension tightened every muscle in her body and she felt an old, familiar need course through her veins. Her palms sweated and her pulse jumped in anticipation.

Chill out, she silently told herself, then felt her lips twist wryly as the advice, offered so often by Jake Marcott, rang in her ears. "Bastard," she muttered, gaze locked on the front door of Ricardo's. He'd deserved to die, and she again felt the thrill of knowing she'd put him in his grave.

It had been so long.

Though she'd replayed the scene in her mind a thousand times over, the exhilaration she'd once felt had long ago begun to fade. But now, with the reunion on the horizon, the memories had intensified again, the thrill of killing him and getting away with it. She'd waited so long . . . and now, finally, she would get her revenge.

The door to the restaurant swung open and she reached for the gearshift, ready to pull out of the parking spot, when she saw a man hold the door open. A family of four, middle-aged mom and pop with two preteens in tow. The kids were fighting, the girl swatting at her brother, only to have him hit back, making her scream bloody murder.

As they walked to their vehicle, the father said something sharp to his son, then opened the door of a minivan. The pinch-lipped mother, ever the wiser, narrowed knowing eyes on her blond daughter. The girl was playing it up, putting on a beatific, almost angelic smile.

That's it, girlie, play the part. Just like all the hypocritical bitches from St. Elizabeth's.

Caught up in the family's tiny drama, she almost missed the last two alumnae emerge from the restaurant. But she didn't. And she couldn't keep a smile from crawling across her face. Aurora and Kristen, the eager and the reluctant organizers, hiking up the collars of their jackets as rain began to fall.

Showtime, she thought, and her blood pounded in her ears. She hazarded a glance at the passenger seat beside her, at the yearbook, extra photos, and scissors. Some of the pictures had been cut from the pages and she'd been careful as she'd extracted them, wanting to slice each color photo to ribbons. Fury heated her blood. White-hot rage, fermented by twenty years of waiting, raced through her veins.

Stay cool.
Chill out.
Don't blow this.

Not now.

Not when you're so damned close!

You've waited too long to wreck everything now.

She bit hard on her lip. In her mind's eye, she saw herself with the scissors gripped in her hand. Stalking her prey. Chasing her down. Catching her. Then, as the two-faced bitch recognized her attacker, she would panic, beg for mercy, cry out that she was sorry. Her victim would grovel. Promise to do anything the killer wanted to save her pathetic life. She would pretend remorse, but it would all be just an act.

Then the killer would strike.

Quick and fast and deadly.

She would plunge those razor-sharp blades deep into Kristen's chest, piercing her heart.

Not just once.

But again.

And again.

Over and over.

Watching the blood spurt.

Hearing Kristen's gurgling screams.

Feeling her go limp.

Witnessing the light go out of Kristen Daniels's eyes forever.

"You damned bitch," she whispered, then tasted blood where her upper teeth had sunk hard into her lower lip.

So caught up in her fantasy she was shaking, she almost missed Kristen's Honda pull out of the parking lot and onto the side street.

Almost.

Slowly, letting a truck pass, the killer put her car into gear, stepped on the gas, and eased the car away from the curb. She zeroed in on Kristen's vehicle, one back taillight blinking as it turned onto the main road.

Silently, with dark intent, she followed.

Chapter 4

"I think you should break up with Zeke."

"What?" Lissa looked at her father as if he'd just lost what had been left of his obviously feeble mind. They were seated at the bar that separated his small kitchen from the living quarters of his high-rise condominium, the place he'd moved to after Kristen requested him to leave. The eating bar was slab granite, the floor-to-ceiling windows offered a panoramic view of the city, the Willamette River, and snow-capped Mount Hood, and the real estate agent had assured him he would love it.

She'd been wrong.

He hated everything about the place.

The quiet.

The air of sophistication.

The chic pseudo-elegance.

Even the damned view was lost on him.

It seemed a shell, just a place to crash. He'd rented enough furniture that he could sleep and watch television and that was it. He spent as little time here as possible.

"I'm *not* breaking up with Zeke."

"I don't like the way he treats you."

"Wait a minute. You're telling me how someone should treat me, when you're not even around?" Lissa leaned back in her bar stool and ignored the half-eaten hamburger and basket of fries that they'd picked up on the way.

"I was just giving your mother her space."

"Yeah, right." Lissa scowled.

So she didn't buy it. The truth of the matter was that he'd

gladly packed his bags, that he'd thought they both could use a cooling-off period. Kristen had been certain he was cheating on her and he'd thrown it in her face that she'd married him on the rebound, that she'd never gotten over Jake Marcott, the kid who had been killed her senior year of high school. In the time that had followed his death, she had not only made Jack a martyr but a saint as well. Ross had done some digging and, as far as he could see, Marcott hadn't been a candidate for canonization. Whether it had been guilt or love or some other deep, primal emotion, Kristen had never let go of him. Ross had seen it coming, even before they'd married, but he'd been young enough to believe that she would get over the murdered boy and that she would start living. With him. He'd thought he could make her love him because he'd fallen so hard for her: the athletic girl with the red-brown hair, sad hazel eyes, and throaty laugh.

Intellectually Kristen had tried to move on.

But emotionally she'd never let go.

The ghost of Jake Marcott had never quit haunting her. Haunting them. Sometimes, late at night, after they'd made love, he'd catch her staring at the shadows on the ceiling or looking through the diaphanous curtains that moved in the summer breeze.

Maybe now, with the damned reunion, she'd be able to get some closure. He sincerely hoped there was a chance that she could finally be free.

"You can't tell me what to do, okay?" Lissa said, still trying her best to push his buttons.

"No, it's not okay."

"So now you're going all authoritarian on me?" She sighed loudly, tipped her chin down, and glared at him.

"I'm your father."

"Big effin' deal."

"It is."

"Hey. Don't be that guy."

"What guy?"

"The *father* guy. I'm not one of those kids that you have to . . . I don't know, throw a baseball to, or take hiking, or spend"—she made quote marks with her fingers—" 'quality time' with or even relate to. I'm fine. And I'm fine with Zeke." She grabbed her soft drink and chewed on the straw. "You don't even know him."

"I know he doesn't have the respect to walk you to the door, that he's got his hands all over you, and that I haven't heard you've even gone on a real date together."

"A 'real date'? You want me to go on a 'real date'? What? Like where he comes to the door in a suit and tie and smiles at you and Mom and brings me home by ten. *That* kind of date?"

"Sounds about right," Ross said equably.

"Dad, that was fifty years ago, and even you and Mom didn't do anything so stupid. If you haven't noticed, our family is not exactly Aussie and Harriet."

"You mean *Ozzie.*"

"I mean we're more like the Osbournes than the Neilsons."

"Nelsons . . . Oh, I get it. You're putting me on." Beneath her act of boredom, the crazy-colored hair and make-up, was the little girl who had often run to him, her arms in the air, the ribbon in her dark hair always falling out, bandages on her knees. She'd been thrilled to see him and had always announced wildly, "Daddy's home . . . Daddy, put me on your shoulders . . . Daddy!" That girl was still there, just buried in anger, sadness, and too much make-up. "Should I be flattered that you think I'm like Ozzy Osbourne?"

"Why are you doing all this now?" she asked on a huge sigh. "Acting like you care or something."

"I do care."

She snorted her disbelief.

"I mean it, Lissa, and I've missed you."

"Save me," she whispered, arms folding over her chest, chin jutted forward in rebellion.

"Okay, I screwed up. Is that what you want to hear?"

She didn't reply, and he shoved his uneaten food to one side and turned to look her squarely in the eye. "I think we should get something straight, okay? No one in our family is perfect. We've all made mistakes. But I am your father and the adult here. So we're going to figure out why a smart girl like you lets her grades slide into the toilet and hooks up with a guy who hasn't shown me that he has an ounce of respect for her or anyone else."

"You don't even know him!"

"You're right. I don't." He found his cell phone and slid it across the table. "Call him. I think it's time we met."

"What?"

"You know his number, right? Dial him up, tell him I want to meet him."

"Now?"

"No time like the present."

She glanced away. Thinking. "He's probably busy."

"Thought you said he was coming over to your house to watch television. Call him."

"To have him come *here*?" she asked, pointing at the floor.

"Yeah."

"With you?" She was shaking her head. "He won't do it."

"Why not?"

"It would be too weird. With you. You already don't like him."

"So this is his chance to change my mind."

She eyed the phone, then stood up and walked to the couch, where she flopped down. Picking up the remote control, she started flipping through the channels. "You're so lame," she accused.

"Probably. So, since we're not entertaining Zeke, let's figure out what the problem is in chemistry. I can't help you much on the German, but I'm a chemistry ace."

"Lucky for me," she mumbled with more than a touch of sarcasm.

"That's right. This is without a doubt your lucky night." He sat beside her on the couch and cracked open the huge textbook before taking the remote from her reluctant fingers and turning the television off.

"Why can't you just leave me alone?"

He grinned. "Come on Lissa, how much fun would *that* be? I figure I've made a mistake, not being around so much, but I'm changing my ways, turning over a new leaf. So you'd better get used to it."

She probably should have gone straight home.

That would have been the smart thing to do.

It was getting late and she was tired and there was still the issue with Lissa. But after all the talk about St. Elizabeth's and its imminent closure, after seeing a smattering of her classmates and remembering what they were like in high school, after being dragged kicking and screaming to the past, Kristen couldn't help herself.

Maybe it was the reporter in her.

Maybe it was just curiosity.

Or maybe it was because it was time to put to rest some old ghosts.

Whatever the reason, she headed out of town and toward Beaverton. Though her old alma mater and her current home were less than five miles apart as the crow flies, they were separated by hills and canyons and winding roads. She'd never felt any need to visit the old campus. In fact, if she thought about it, she'd studiously avoided returning to St. Elizabeth's.

Until tonight.

The beams from her headlights cut through the night, shimmering against pavement growing wet with new rain. She wound through the steep hills of Douglas fir, oak, and cedar, her wipers slapping slowly. She wasn't completely alone on the county road that ran past the school. Taillights glowed red in the road ahead when she crested small hills, and she met a broken line of oncoming headlights.

How many times had she driven this route during her four years at St. Elizabeth's? At first her mother, a devout Catholic and a widow who owned a bakery/café on Twenty-third Street, had hauled her to school in the Sweet Nothings delivery van. Kristen had been mortified to be dropped off in the rattletrap of a vehicle when Lindsay Farrell arrived in her father's Porsche and even Rachel Alsace alighted from her mom's vintage, but cool, Jeep.

Kristen had saved all the money she'd earned at the bakery, and the minute she turned sixteen and passed her driver's license test, she bought a 1976 Volkswagen Super Beetle convertible with a dent in one fender and ninety thousand miles under its fan belt. Not in the same class as the Mercedes and BMWs that were parked in the school lot, but better than the stupid van. She'd been in heaven. Innocently unaware of what was to come.

Now, as the buildings of St. Elizabeth's campus came into view, she felt a chill as cold as winter. The church was there, a massive stone structure with a high bell tower, and set back a bit, the attached convent, where once the nuns who had taught at the school had lived.

Kristen wondered if any of the sisters still resided beyond the thick gates. What had happened to Sister Clarice with her weak chin, rimless glasses, and bloodless lips? Or Sister Maureen with her apple cheeks and tittery laugh? She'd filled the classroom with flowers and always smelled of lilacs. What about the Reverend Mother, Sister Neva, who had been in her seventies twenty years earlier and had walked with a cane and thankfully had never been able to remember Kristen's name? Were any of them alive? Did they still dwell behind the thick rock walls?

The rain began in earnest, covering the windshield and fogging its interior. Kristen turned the wipers higher and stared through the glass at the school. In the gloom, it seemed miraculously unchanged. Its broad portico, supported by stone pillars, still protected the heavy double doors leading to the main reception area. The building was two stories, faced with the same rock, brick and mortar as the church.

Kristen eased on the gas and inched closer, fighting the sensation that she shouldn't be there, that she was trespassing into a faraway time and place that was no longer hers.

Her car crept forward and she recognized the gym, set back from the rest of the classrooms, its high, domed roof dwarfing the cafeteria next to it.

The gym. Venue to the doomed Valentine's Day dance. She tapped her fingers against the steering wheel and wondered about the maze separating the gymnasium from the cloister. Was it still intact? Or hopelessly overgrown? Had the order had the hedges removed, hacked down to stumps after the tragedy, or had the laurel and arborvitae been shaped and manicured, the topiary sculptured as if nothing horrible had ever happened within the garden walls?

"This is nuts," she told herself as she flipped up the hood of her jacket and grabbed a flashlight from the glove box. She cut the engine and stepped out of the car into the puddles and drizzle of the night, then walked toward the back of the school, stepping over a chain that barricaded the unused gym lot from the delivery alley. The pavement was pockmarked and rutted, but she followed it unerringly to the back of the gym, across a parking lot to the gardens.

The hedge was as she remembered . . . maybe a little less groomed, a few more weeds surrounding it, but it was there. It didn't take too much imagination to remember that night, the music in the background, the smell of cigarette smoke, the horrifying sound of Lindsay's scream and then the sight of Jake, his lifeless body slumped over the heavy arrow pinning him to the tree, the blood everywhere, dark against the trunk of the tree, pooling on the wet grass, staining the front of Jake's tuxedo and smearing over Lindsay's dress.

Oh, God, what was she thinking, coming back here to this dark place? She glanced up at the nunnery and saw a few lights glowing in the tracery windows. She swallowed hard as she saw a silhouette in one window, a movement of the blinds.

So what, Kristen?

Someone lives in that room, probably one of the old nuns. She was just walking past the window, lingering there with her Bible and rosary in hand, for crying out loud!

Why are you doing this? Why are you trying to freak yourself out?

She had no answer to that one, but she cut the beam of her flashlight and looked up at the window where the shadow passed and the lights were suddenly extinguished.

Either the person inside was going to bed, had left the room, or had decided to use the darkness to hide him or herself.

Now you're really getting paranoid. Turn around and go home. Sit by the fire, have a glass of wine or decaf coffee with a shot of Kahlua and a dollop of whipped cream. Treat yourself, you're alone tonight. No motherly responsibilities.

And still she walked forward, switching the flashlight back on, heading through the entrance to the maze where the walls of shrubbery closed in more tightly, the untended branches brushing against her shoulders, the oddly shaped topiary untrimmed and grotesque. The beam of her flashlight bobbed ahead, offering weak illumination.

What're you doing out here? she asked herself, understanding subconsciously that this was simply something she had to do, an urge she couldn't ignore, a driving force that made her squint against the rain and darkness. She caught sight of an old bench, then a fountain, and with each step in the squishy grass, she felt another drip of fear in her blood, an eerie feeling she tried to ignore.

You're just on edge because you know you're trespassing, that someone at the convent could see your light and put in a call to the police. What would you tell them, hmm? That you wanted to visit the place where the boy you loved in high school was murdered?

Turning one corner, she stopped short, a wall of branches cutting off her progress.

Odd, she thought, wondering at her misstep. She was certain she'd followed the correct path. A cold blast of wind cut through the heavy shrubbery and touched the back of her neck.

Turn around and go back to the car. For God's sake, what're you trying to prove?

Her skin was chilled, but she was going to finish this, whatever the hell it was. Shining the light on the ground, she did an about-face, following her own footprints where the grass was mashed down until she came to another forty-five-degree corner that she didn't expect. Walking briskly, she found another dead end, another wall of foliage.

"Crap." She must be more tense than she realized, and now she was more determined than ever. She backtracked again, retracing her steps. At the entrance, she shined her light on the edge of the maze and, seeing slightly smaller, less dense bushes interspersed with the older arborvitae and laurel, realized that the hedge had changed. The maze she'd known by heart had been restructured, and in the darkness, the newer shrubs changing the pathway were already nearly twenty years old and hard to distinguish from the older vegetation.

Perhaps the old tree where Jake had been killed had been cut down. There had been talk of making it a memorial, but Mother Superior had refused the suggestion, not wanting the tragic incident to mar the reputation of the campus or become a destination for the morbidly curious.

"We need to downplay this painful situation and pray for God's understanding," Mother Superior had told the student body on the Monday after Jake's death. "The police have finished their investigation of the grounds and there is no need to sensationalize what happened, nor should we encourage those who are obsessed or curious about the tragedy. Those who want to pay their respects to the poor boy can do so at his grave site . . ."

It all came back to Kristen now as she walked along the hedgerows, trying to second-guess the new pathways. It took her nearly half an hour before she made the right succession of turns. Suddenly, she was in the center of the maze, the old oak tree still standing, branches naked and spreading in the gloomy night.

Kristen's heart squeezed as she shined her light over the ground littered by branches. The statue of the Madonna was unscathed, bleached white as ever, hands lifted as if in supplication to God.

An unworldly chill ran through Kristen's blood as clouds blocked the moon and rain peppered the ground. "Dear God," she whispered, her hands clenching tight. Her throat closed and she felt hot tears mingle with the cold rain sliding down her cheeks. She imagined Jake as she'd last seen him, slumped and dead, dressed in his rented tuxedo, shot through the heart with an arrow, for God's sake.

Cupid's Killer. The newspapers had run that one into the ground.

In her mind's eye, Kristen once again witnessed Lindsay at Jake's feet, her ice blue dress dark with the stain of Jake's blood, her face white with fear, mascara running in black rivulets from her eyes. And then the accusation.

"Why, Kristen? Why did you kill him?"

What had possessed Lindsay that night? Why had she thought Kristen had anything to do with Jake's death?

Lindsay had never given her a straight answer, not even the next week at school when Kristen had asked her about it.

It had been in the senior hallway, a short first-floor and locker-lined corridor that was wedged between the library and the business offices.

Kristen had found Lindsay struggling to open her locker. "Why did you accuse me of having something to do with Jake's death?" When Lindsay didn't immediately respond, she pressed, "Lindsay?"

Lindsay yanked on the combination lock, but the locker held fast. "I . . . I didn't know what I was saying. I was in shock. Crazy." She rattled the locker door more furiously, trying to force the combination lock to spring open. It didn't budge. "I was upset."

"We all were. But that doesn't explain why you blamed me."

"Okay, I know. I'm sorry!" She was twirling the combination wildly again, her fingers trembling. "What do you want from me? I found Jake there in the middle of the maze, an arrow though his *heart*. And blood everywhere. I knew . . . I mean, I *knew* he was dead. It was like"—she stopped tugging at the lock long enough to stare at Kristen with round, panicked eyes—"it was like I saw his soul leave, Kris. Swear to God, the life went out of his eyes as I got to him and . . . and I knew his soul had escaped, right in front of me . . . Oh, God . . . I was so freaked, so scared, so out of my damned mind and you were the next one who showed up and . . . and . . . and he was your date that night. You were supposed to be with him! At the dance. When you knew *I* was still in love with him!"

"You were broken up," Kristen fought back, feeling a little niggle of guilt. "Jake and I had always been friends."

Lindsay made a disparaging sound, then calmed a little. "Apparently you wanted more than that, but . . . Oh, crap, what does it matter? He's dead, isn't he? Nothing's going to change that."

"I had nothing to do with his murder."

Lindsay sighed. Blinked back tears. "As I said, Kris, I went nuts. That's all. I was crazy. Sorry!" Her chin trembled as she turned back to her locker and added in a whisper, "I don't know what more I can say."

Lindsay finally managed to work the combination, the lock sprang, and the door opened. She grabbed her English textbook, but not before Kristen got a glimpse of the inside of the locker door where pictures of Jake Marcott were plastered: snapshots, yearbook photos, his senior picture decorated with ticket stubs and red hearts cut out of shiny red paper.

Shocked, Kristen took a step backward, and the sounds of the normal noises in the hallway between classes, the clatter of shoes on the shiny floors, the clang of slamming lockers, the rumble of laughter and conversation, the buzzing of the tardy bell all were muted, as if those familiar noises came from a very long distance.

Only when Sister Clarice touched her on the shoulder, her black habit rustling with her quick strides, and told her to "get to class, chop-chop," had Kristen snapped back to the present and hustled up the stairs at the end of the hall, hurrying to slide into her seat in the physics lab before cranky old Mrs. Crandall took roll.

Now, years later, standing in the rain, staring at the tree, she felt chilled to the bone. Alone. With no more answers than she had twenty years earlier. She walked to the tree and shined a light on the gnarled trunk.

"Oh, Jake," she whispered when she found the mark in the rough bark and ran her fingers in the groove. "Who did this to you?"

And why?

She closed her eyes, sent up a prayer, and sighed.

Over the drip of the rain she heard a foreign sound, a rustle of leaves in the wind.

She turned and shined her flashlight onto the hedge behind her. Wet, shiny leaves quivered.

She froze. Felt a frisson of fear. Who else was out here? Had someone followed her? Watched her?

Her heart pounded.

It was probably just a raccoon or possum or skunk . . .

The branches stilled.

No tiny bright eyes were caught in the flashlight's beam.

Her pulse pounding in her ears, Kristen moved her small swath of illumination across the wide expanse of greenery, a weak beam of light that seemed to be dimming in the rain. She saw nothing. No movement. Heard no sound other than her own rapid heartbeat and the steady drip of the rain.

No one was here. She was alone. Scared, feeling like she was trespassing, standing in the heavy drizzle in the middle of the night.

Like an idiot.

Quickly, she scanned the area one last time, then turned and made her way out of the labyrinth. She made only one wrong turn, righted herself, and sprinted across the parking lot and over the blemished tarmac of the alley until she found her car parked where she'd left it.

She'd never been so glad to see her little Honda in her life. She unlocked the car with her remote and the Honda's lights flashed. After tossing the flashlight and her purse into the backseat, she slid behind the wheel and flipped off her coat hood.

Rain slid down her neck. She switched on the ignition and the radio came on . . . but she hadn't been listening to it on the way over to the school . . . what the devil? She glanced down at the illuminated dash and realized it wasn't the radio at all, but a cassette, stuffed into its slot in the dash. She heard garbled sounds and laughter and music . . . familiar sounds . . . oh . . . my . . . God . . . The hairs on the back of Kristen's neck raised as she listened. The song was a Springsteen classic. "Dancing in the Dark."

A shudder slid down her spine, and she glanced through the fogging windshield where the wipers were already moving, scraping a pink piece of paper back and forth.

Glancing around, she opened the window and snagged the soggy piece of paper from the glass. The letters on the pink page were faded, the paper nearly torn to shreds, but she recognized it for what it was: the photograph of her and Jake taken at the Valentine's dance two decades earlier. A picture she'd hidden far away in a school scrapbook that she hadn't looked at in years. Her stomach knotted as she stared at their faces, smiling, carefree, innocently unaware of what the horrid night would bring. Worse yet, scrawled across their smiles was a jagged red slash, the color of blood.

Kristen nearly screamed.

But she didn't have to.

Because as Bruce Springsteen's voice faded and the sounds of the dance so long ago disappeared into the night, there was a second of silence, a click, and then the tape issued a scream of pure, unadulterated terror.

Kristen ejected the cassette, stepped on the accelerator, and tore out of the parking lot.

Her entire body shaking, her heart jackhammering in fear, she glanced in the rearview mirror and thought she saw an image, a quicksilver glimpse of a dark figure, running past the darkened windows of the chapel.

She blinked.

The figure was gone.

Just a figment of your imagination.

No way! Someone knew she'd be at the school that night. Someone had either followed her or been waiting.

She glanced at the passenger seat where the wet, garish picture lay beside the damning cassette.

She'd thought the nightmare was over.

Now she realized it was just beginning.

Chapter 5

Run, Kristen. Run as far and as fast as you can. But it won't help. I'll find you. I've waited this long and I'm not going to let you get away now.

Jake Marcott's killer stood in the shadows of the overhang of the school, watching the Honda's retreating taillights as the rain dripped from the overflowing gutters of the portico that was the entrance to good ol' St. Lizzy's.

How many times had she stood right in this spot, eyeing the others, wishing she fit in, listening to all of them talking about Jake Marcott as if he were a god, as if they all owned a piece of him?

Little did they know that Jake had never loved any of them.

Never had . . . never would.

Jesus, they were all such idiots. Kristen, the valedictorian, for God's sake, was the worst. She was supposed to be smart, but in truth, she was as dumb as a stone. And predictable. So damned predictable. Even if she hadn't followed her, she would have guessed that Kristen would return to St. Lizzy's.

All the planning of the reunion would bring back memories of the night of the Valentine's dance and would drive Kristen here, to literally the scene of the crime. She had known it intuitively.

Which all fit into her plans perfectly. She wondered, watching the taillights disappear in the rain, what Kristen had thought when she'd seen the picture the killer had left on the car. Had she understood the message? Did she know what was coming? Did she feel a scratch of fear along her spine as she'd heard the tape of the dance and Lindsay's howling, bone-chilling scream?

Oh, just you wait, Kristen.

It's only going to get worse.

Remember the night Jake was killed? How you found Lindsay? And Jake?

That night had been perfect. From her hiding spot at the end of one hedgerow in the maze, hearing the music and whisper of voices, the killer, still holding the heavy crossbow, had heard frantic footsteps and pulled farther into the shadows. Then, clicking her pocket recorder on again, she'd witnessed Lindsay, her shimmering blue dress catching the moonlight, running into the heart of the maze. The killer had followed a few steps so that she could watch and tape the tall girl's reaction.

And it had been worth it.

Lindsay, murmuring, "Oh, no, oh, no, oh, no!" had run to the tree where Jake was slumped. She'd tried to revive him, to hold him, to force some life into his already-dead body. "Jake, oh, God, no . . . Jake! Jake!" His blood had run down the bodice of the icy-blue gown, staining and smearing the expensive garment as she'd tried to revive him. "Oh, no, oh, no . . . oh . . ." Then, as if she'd finally understood that this was real, not some dream, Lindsay had let out a high-pitched, bloodcurdling scream that had keened mournfully off the West Hills.

The killer had ducked back and started running, not along the maze's intricate paths but through three slits she'd made earlier, tiny spots where she'd folded the branches back and slipped through, cutting across the north side of the maze and down a hillock and around the edge of the property until she could slip into her hiding space in the basement of the school, change quickly into her dress again, then return to the group of kids who, smoking dope and drinking, had never really noticed how long she'd been in "the ladies' room."

It had all worked so smoothly.

She'd even been clustered with the others when she'd seen Lindsay, her face white, her dark hair falling in disarray, her silk dress stained with the purple-red of Jake Marcott's blood, stumbling out of the maze. Lindsay had been zombie-like and sobbing out of control. Kristen Daniels had been ashen faced and starting to shake. Rachel Alsace had been horrified and stunned, but already moving into action. She'd immediately demanded that a stricken-faced Sister Clarice call the police and her father immediately.

The other students, faculty, and chaperones had been in varying degrees of terror and shock. Paranoia had begun slowly and had reigned for the rest of the night.

Oh, it had been so good. So damned good.

And it would be again.

The killer smiled coldly in the damp darkness.

Kristen had ejected the tape, but that horrible scream ricocheted through her brain. Her heart was pounding a mile a minute, her fingers clenching the steering wheel so tightly they showed white as she pushed the speed limit to her house. *Who would do this to me? Who?*

Someone from the reunion committee?

Someone who didn't show but knew about it?

Someone else?

The damned killer?

Everyone at the meeting ran through her head: Mandy, April, Aurora, Bella, DeLynn, Martina, Haylie . . . Were there others invited who hadn't shown? But Haylie was certainly psycho enough, and weird enough, to pull this off. And she'd left early.

Kristen tailgated a car in front of her and checked her rearview mirror continuously. She didn't know what to expect; whoever planted the sick picture and cassette tape could be following her . . . to what? Do her physical harm? But if that were the case, wouldn't he/she/it have waited for her in her car? Or abducted, or hurt, or killed her there at the campus while she was alone?

"Idiot," she berated herself. She knew better. She read the paper every day, watched the news religiously, kept up on world, national, and local events. She knew there were wackos out in the world and she was usually careful. But not tonight.

Her purse lay on the floor in front of the passenger seat, and now she reached for it and while driving with one hand, searched the side pocket for her cell phone with the other.

Her car drifted a little and she eased it back to the middle of the lane, retrieving her phone at that moment. Flipping it open, she wondered whom to call.

Ross! For God's sake, get Ross!

She gritted her teeth. Speed dial #2 would instantly connect her to him, but she hesitated. They were separated. On their almost-amicable way to divorce. She couldn't lean on him.

So call the cops!

And tell them what? That someone left a prank tape and photograph on the car while she was trespassing at St. Elizabeth's? The police had bigger crimes to investigate. She saw the police blotter every day at the offices of the *Clarion*.

Dropping the phone, she let out her breath, easing her car onto the secondary road that led up the hill to her house. She checked the rearview. No one was following her.

But someone intended to scare the hell out of her.

"Mission accomplished," she thought aloud, pushing the button on her remote garage-door opener. She pulled into the garage and didn't get out of her car until the door had ground back down again.

Still shaken, she grabbed her purse, laptop case, the cassette and marred picture, then tried to pull herself together.

"Get a grip," she ordered, but it was no use. Whoever had wanted to freak her out had done a damned good job. *Who would do this and why?* Again, she had no answer. It all came back to someone wanting to scare the bejeezus out of her, someone who didn't want her either working on the reunion committee or like her poking around St. Elizabeth's . . . no, that wasn't right. She'd had no plans to visit the old school when she'd gone to the committee meeting tonight. Someone had to have followed her.

She just didn't know who.

"Psycho bitch," she muttered under her breath, though she couldn't be certain a man wasn't behind this.

Walking into the house, she nearly tripped over Marmalade. "Oops, sorry." She dropped her things on the kitchen table, then scooped up the cat, who wrapped her long, striped tail around Kristen's side and began purring contentedly and pressing a pink nose into the underside of Kristen's chin. "Somebody's lonely." Kristen forced herself to relax a little as she walked through the house, still carrying the cat, and checked every door and window to make sure they were locked, the house secure. She had no alarm system; she'd always felt safe with Ross around. Even in the later years, when he was home less and less, she'd never worried or been frightened. Now, however, she double-checked every possible entrance.

"Safe and sound," she said at last as Marmalade, bored with the attention, squirmed in her arms. Kristen let her hop to the floor, where she took up a favorite position on the back of the couch and began grooming herself. The message light was blinking on the answering machine and Kristen hit the Play button.

"You have two messages," a mechanical voice advised her.

"Hi, Kris, it's Aurora. I called on your cell and left a message there, but I'll tell you again. I think the meeting went well. Wasn't it a hoot to see some of the old gang again? And Haylie . . . puh–leez, what's with her? Anyway, I forgot to mention that I think you should use some of your pull at the paper to advertise, well, for free, of course, the reunion. Maybe we'll reach some classmates who we've lost track of. I'm thinking even if they're still not in town, their parents or grandparents or cousins or somebody might be. And since St. Lizzy's is giving up the ghost, oh, er holy spirit"—she chuckled at her own joke—"it could make some great human interest stories. Maybe you can interview some of the old nuns who were there when we were. Sister Clarice still lives in the convent, can you believe that? And remember Sister Mary Michael? She's there, too. Wouldn't it be great to interview them? Just a thought. Call me later!" She hung up with a click and Kristen deleted the message. The mechanical voice took over again, reminding her of yet another message. The damned thing aggravated her. She'd been threatening to buy a new one but hadn't gotten around to it. "Next message," the automated voice said.

"Mom, please, please, please come get me." Lissa's voice was a desperate whisper and for a millisecond Kristen's muscles tightened in fear for her daughter. "I can't stay here with Dad," Lissa went on. "It's just too weird." She hung up abruptly, probably because her father had walked in on her.

Kristen leaned back against the cupboards, her pulse slowly returning to normal. She was totally spent but she managed a smile. Let the two of them work things out. She wasn't buying into Lissa's heroine-in-peril ploy. She was with her dad, for God's sake. It was time the two of them got reacquainted.

Nerves still a bit jangled, Kristen poured herself a glass of wine, turned on the tap in the tub, added bubble bath, then wound her hair onto her head. After finding her favorite Eagles CD and pushing it into the player, she stripped off her clothes and sank neck deep into warm, frothy water.

She closed her eyes.

Listened to the music.

And, for the moment, pushed all thoughts of Jake Marcott, the marred photograph, the recording of the dance, and anything else that had to do with St. Lizzy's out of her mind.

Tomorrow she'd deal with everything.

Tonight, after all, was supposed to be her night off.

Her heart was pounding out of control, her body drenched in sweat. Where was Jake? Where? The night was black, the moon hidden by clouds, a thin, rising fog dimmed her vision. Branches slapped her in the face, brambles pulled at her dress. Her feet were bare and the grass was cold and frosty. She stepped around the final turn of the maze and she saw him though the mist. He was slumped, drooping from the tree, an arrow glinting as it impaled him and fastened him to the oak's thick trunk. His dark hair spilled over his face; his skin was as white as the marble of the statue of the Madonna placed beneath the spreading, brittle branches of the oak. The statue appeared to be crying, a reddish liquid oozing from her eyes.

"Jake!" Kristen cried, running toward him, nearly tripping on an unseen root.

Blood poured from his wound, stained his clothes, trickled down to pool at his feet.

"Jake, oh, God, Jake, what happened? Answer me, oh, please, please!"

Horrified, she reached his sagging body and yanked on the arrow, her hands slipping with the slick warmth of his blood. "No, no, no," she whispered, pulling harder, her muscles straining.

She heard footsteps. Turned, her hands still clenched over the arrow's unbending shaft. "Help!" she cried. "We need help! Oh, God, somebody help!*"*

Looking wraithlike, Lindsay Farrell stepped from the fog. Her eyes were round as saucers, her pupils wide and dark as the night. "You killed him, Kristen," she accused. "You."

"No, Lindsay . . . Please, he needs help. An ambulance. Call 911."

"This is your fault, Kris, leave him be. I love him. Me.*" She cradled Jake's head in her hands and tenderly kissed his lips. Tears rained from her eyes, mingling with his blood, and he seemed to twitch a little, as if there were still life in him.*

Was it possible? Kristen saw his fingers move and she gasped. Could it be? Could Jake still be alive? She reached for her cell phone, but her purse wasn't with her . . . She'd left it in the car, the car with the awful note on the windshield.

Backing up, scarcely believing her eyes, she stared at Jake. Lindsay ceased kissing him and both of them turned to stare at her. Their blue eyes were black, and blood smeared Lindsay's dress. Jake smiled, that incredible, devilish smile that she'd known since she was a child.

"Why, Kristen?" he asked, as if he weren't in pain, as if nothing were wrong. "Why did you do this to me? I thought we were friends."

"We were . . . are . . . We're all friends." As the words passed her lips, everyone who had been at the dance that night and others

who hadn't appeared in the mist. They walked toward her like
zombies. Rachel, pale as death, was there along with April. Mandy
joined them, her tattered dress falling off her shoulder where a
hand, Boyd's hand, was connected. They were mumbling, whis-
pering, louder and louder until it became a deafening roar, "Why,
Kristen, why?" Chad, Nick, Bella, DeLynn, Martina—all advanc-
ing upon her as if in slow motion, blood on their hands, no life in
their fixed stares. From behind the tree and out of the maze came
more people she knew, all dressed in tuxedos and gowns, their
faces ashen, blood smeared upon cummerbunds and white shirts
and staining red across lace, silk, and satin.

"I didn't . . . Jake, I wouldn't . . . I love you . . ." Kristen said,
backing up as more kids showed up . . . Aurora and Dean . . . then
Haylie, holding hands with a smiling, very pale Ian.

Oh, God, oh, God . . . no, I had nothing to do with this, Kris-
ten tried to say and then she saw Ross . . . oh, thank God, he was
here! She tried to run to him but her feet were stuck and she
couldn't move . . . Only then did she realize she was sinking in a
bog, a mire deep in the maze, and the bog itself was running red
with the blood of all the people closing in on her.

"Ross!" she cried, hoping he would save her. "Ross!"

Kristen's eyes flew open. Panic ripped through her as she
blinked into the darkness before realizing she was in her own bedroom. The digital alarm clock glowed the time in a steady bright
blue, the numbers blinking out the time: five-forty-five in the
morning.

"Oh, Lord," she whispered, realizing she was covered in sweat
though the room was cool. She let out a long tremulous sigh, grateful to have awakened from the dream, relief flooding through her.

"Only a dream, just a damned dream . . . no, only a nightmare," she muttered as she snapped on the bedside lamp and heard
the sound of rainwater running in the gutters. The light made her
wince and she heard a soft meow of protest. Marmalade, who had
been curled on the foot of the bed, lifted her tawny head,
stretched, then inched upward to press her pink nose against Kristen's. The cat usually slept with Lissa but had obviously given up
hope that she would return. Sometime in the night, Marmalade
had slunk into Kristen's room. "Any port in a storm, eh?" Kristen
said, glad for the bit of company. She petted Marmalade's soft fur
as the dream replayed through her mind, all the people, all the accusations, all the guilt. Twenty years of guilt. Once more she

thought about that night and how, if she'd done just one thing differently, the tragedy might have been avoided and Jake would be alive today.

If only she'd looked for Jake sooner.

If only she hadn't let him out of her sight that night.

If only she hadn't asked him to the damned dance in the first place.

"Let it go," she told herself, as she had so often in the past. "Let it go, let it go." She shoved her hair away from her face. Why in the world had she agreed to get involved with the reunion committee? Hadn't she known it would become a mistake of grand proportions? Okay, so she'd been drafted into the position, but she could have done nothing, just as she had at five, ten, and fifteen years. Either Aurora or another gung-ho, rah-rah St. Lizzy's alumna could have taken over the reins or the whole thing could have just never happened. So what if the school was going to close? Who cared?

The cat settled onto the pillow next to Kristen's head. *Ross's pillow.* Marmalade's tiny chin resting on Kristen's shoulder. "Don't get too comfortable," Kristen warned the tabby. "Haven't you heard? There's just no rest for the wicked, and that's you and me, girl. Decidedly wicked. Come on." Kristen moved and flung off the covers. Marmalade scrambled to the side of the bed and hopped onto the floor. Yawning, Kristen headed for the kitchen with the cat following at a trot. "First item on the agenda? Coffee." She filled the basket with ground coffee, poured a full pot of water into the carafe, then punched Mr. Coffee's ON button.

Within seconds, the machine began to gurgle. Kristen wasted no time. While the smell of coffee permeated the first floor and rain ran down the windows, she pulled down the attic ladder in the hallway and climbed to the musty space filled with insulation, cobwebs, Christmas decorations, and baby paraphernalia she'd never had the heart to give away.

This summer, she promised herself. This summer she would clean the attic, divide out Ross's things, have that garage sale she'd been talking about for years, and be done with it. She flicked on the switch and two bare bulbs illuminated the cluttered, unused space. Old furniture, maternity clothes that were fifteen years out of date, beat-up luggage, and boxes were stuffed into the corners.

Wrinkling her nose at the mouse droppings and insect carcasses, she made her way to a part of the attic where her old textbooks, scrapbooks, and high-school memorabilia were tucked away, boxes her mother had packed when she'd converted Kristen's room into a home office years before.

The first three boxes were paperbacks and records, tapes and CDs, but on the fourth she hit pay dirt—all the notes, pictures, awards, report cards, and personal items from her desk and bulletin board. Near the bottom were loose pictures that had never made it into her scrapbook.

The first was one of Kristen, Rachel Alsace, and Lindsay Farrell, three girls beaming for the camera, though their smiles were false. Kristen frowned, pushed the photo aside and picked up the next, which was a group shot in the parking lot of St. Elizabeth's, one corner of the arborvitae maze visible. Mandy, Aurora, Haylie, Bella, DeLynn, and Kristen were huddled together in the rain.

It was weird, Kristen thought, staring at the images. All of them were so young and fresh-faced in the photo. DeLynn had been the only black student at that time and Bella, having skipped fourth grade, had been the youngest. Haylie was glowing and in the picture she was wearing a ring—Ian Powers's class ring. Aurora, ever the cutup, had placed her hand behind Mandy's head, either giving a peace sign or giving Mandy the illusion of having horns. As for Kristen, she was looking at something in the distance, seemingly unaware of the camera.

She remembered. No one else had noticed Jake Marcott driving into the parking lot. But she had. She'd never missed anything that had concerned Jake. "Stupid, stupid girl," she murmured, spying the wistful look on her face in the photo. She'd had a crush on him forever even though she'd only been his "friend," and that was largely through Bella. Lindsay was the one who'd seriously dated him.

To dispel the wave of nostalgia, she quickly flipped through a few more yellowing snapshots before she found the jacket for the photo she was searching for, the one taken of Jake and her at the dance. She opened the paper folder and it was empty.

No picture.

Her heart lurched.

The photo was missing. She searched through the loose pictures again, but it wasn't there. Kristen's brows drew into a frown. She so clearly remembered posing with Jake. They'd stood beneath an arbor of fake roses, their arms around each other, their heads turned toward the camera.

Was the picture that had been plastered over her windshield her *own*? Had someone taken the photo from its jacket? The box didn't appear to be disturbed, but maybe she just couldn't tell. When was the last time she'd seen the photo? When she'd moved these boxes up here fifteen years earlier? Or had she even looked then?

Or was it taken yesterday, while you were at work? The bathroom window was open . . .

"Hello?" Ross's voice boomed from below. "Kris?"

Her first impulse was to run to him and throw herself into his arms. That was how unnerved she felt. Then she caught herself short and looked down at her old flannel pajamas. She hadn't even brushed her teeth yet. Or combed her hair.

"Kris? You here?"

She hurried down the attic stairs and was on the bottom rung when he appeared at the end of the hall. Jesus, he looked good: hair still damp from a shower or the rain, faded denim shirt, battered leather jacket, not unlike the one he wore in college a lifetime ago. "Hey, you okay?" he asked, his intense gray eyes trained on her.

"Yeah, just . . . just getting ready."

His gaze slid up the staircase. "In the attic?"

"Of course not. I . . . I had to get something for the reunion committee."

"Up there?" he asked, motioning to the picture in her hand.

"Yeah. I was looking for my yearbook."

"Find it?"

"I was just looking through the boxes when I heard you." That really wasn't much of a lie. "There's a lot of stuff up there. Some of it's yours."

He wasn't derailed. "Looks like you found something, though," he said, hitching his chin toward the kitchen.

He was already walking down the short hallway and she followed, all the while knowing what was to come. Last night, cold and wet and freaked out, she'd dropped everything she'd been carrying onto the kitchen table. Her purse, laptop, and notes as well as the tape and marred picture she'd found in her car.

Great, she thought, just what she wanted to do, talk it all over with her soon-to-be ex. She asked, "Where's Lissa?"

"I dropped her off at school." He was already pouring two cups of coffee. Unerringly he found the fat-free milk in the fridge, poured a stream of the bluish liquid into her cup, then handed it to her. He drank his black. "She promised to come straight home after school. On the bus." He glanced over at Kristen. "That's a lie, of course. I think she spent half the night talking to that cretin of a boyfriend of hers."

"Did you call him that to her face?"

"Nope." He tested his coffee, looking at Kristen over the rim of his cup. "Want to tell me what's going on?"

"Not really."

"Do it anyway."

"Not this morning. I really don't have time for—"

"Make time." He kicked out a chair and settled into it. "You can be late for work."

"No, I really can't." She didn't want to discuss any of this with him. At least not now.

"Then talk fast." He jabbed a finger at the wet, red-slashed picture of Kristen and Jake. "Where'd you get this photo? At the reunion committee meeting?" He didn't bother hiding the sarcasm in his voice. "Or was it one of your keepsakes?" Before she could answer, he glared at the cassette tape. "And what's this?" Without asking he took the cassette tape, walked into the den, and slid it into the tape deck.

Kristen braced herself.

With a push of a button, the noises from the dance, the music, the talk, the laughter, and then the bone-chilling scream echoed through the house.

Standing barefoot in the kitchen, her cup of coffee untouched in her hands, her heart thudding as hard as it had the night before, she listened to the horror. Old memories surfaced. The nightmare spun again.

Ross listened, his expression turning more grim as the tape played, the lines near the corners of his mouth turning white as the horrible scream filled the house. When the sounds faded away, he flipped the tape out of the deck and turned, staring hard at her. Gone was any trace of humor. In its stead was a confused anger. "Okay, Kris. Time to level with me. What the hell is going on?"

Chapter 6

Against her better judgment Kristen gave Ross the rundown, from the minute she'd driven into Ricardo's parking lot to meeting old friends, Haylie's scene, then the drive to St. Elizabeth's, where she'd found the disturbing picture and blood-chilling tape in her car.

At first she was hesitant, but as she began explaining, she started talking faster and faster, watching his reaction move from anger to concern as he ignored his coffee.

Once she was finished, he shook his head. "What in God's name were you thinking going back to the school, the maze in the middle of the night?"

"I don't know, but it wasn't that someone would follow me or leave me a tape of the dance!" She leaned back in her chair, pushing her hair from her eyes. "What do you think it means?"

"Nothing good. You should go to the police."

"And tell them what? That I was trespassing and that someone left a marked-up picture and cassette tape of the dance in my car? They'd say it was a prank—I mean, I think it is. Right?"

He didn't smile. "I think it's more than a prank. Anything else happen?"

She hesitated, thought of the opened bathroom window.

"Kris?"

"Okay, so yesterday, before the reunion, the bathroom window was left open a crack, but I never open it. I didn't think it was that big a deal; nothing was missing."

"But someone could have been here for hours, searching the place, looking for the picture."

"That's a pretty big gamble. Who knew I had it?"

"Exactly, who did know?"

She shrugged, reached for the photo, and turned it over. Though smudged, the name, phone number, and address of a local photographer were still legible. "Ron Phillips Studio in Beaverton," she said.

"I remember that place."

"Is it still open?"

"I don't know." He shook his head. "Don't think so."

"I think I'll check it out. Nose around a little." What would it hurt to do some digging? Try to locate the owner of the studio.

"I vote for the police. This could be dangerous, Kris," Ross said, leaving his barely touched coffee on the table. "Did you look outside the window, check for footprints?"

"No. It was dark, and to tell you the truth, I didn't think about it."

"Maybe they're still there." He walked to the pantry, grabbed a flashlight, then headed to the front door and pulled it open, letting in a blast of cold, wet air.

"Don't let Marmalade out—"

Too late. The cat, sensing a chance for escape, had slipped through the doorway. Ross didn't seem to notice as he stepped outside.

Kristen finished her coffee and was putting her cup in the dishwasher when he returned, rain wetting his face and dappling the shoulders of his jacket. "Well?" she asked, wiping her hands on a dishtowel.

"Inconclusive. It looks like someone might have walked back there, but that's also near the spot where the cable comes into the house, and it looks like you had some work done."

"Two weeks ago. The cable was out."

"So much for my detecting skills."

"Nancy Drew doesn't have to worry that you'll take her job?" Kristen teased and to her surprise, he lifted a dark eyebrow, surprised at her joke.

"Nancy's safe." He walked toward her, and in her mind's eye she remembered making love on the sandy shore of a lake hidden high in the Cascades. It had been near dusk, mist had risen off the clear water, and as they'd kissed and pulled off each other's clothes, it had seemed that they were the only two people in the universe.

She swallowed hard, licked her lips, and felt her skin flush.

Ross had always had that effect on her. Always. Obviously, it hadn't changed.

"Yeah, but are you?"

"What?" Dear Lord, was she blushing.

"Safe?" He moved close enough that she could smell the rainwater on his skin, hear the creak of leather as he reached around her to place the flashlight on the counter near the sink. The back of his hand brushed against her bare arm and she flinched, as if burned.

"I think we're blowing this all out of proportion," she said, stepping away from him. He leaned a hip against the edge of the stove and stared at her. Damn the man, sometimes she thought he could read her mind. "Look, if anyone really wanted to harm me, I would be dead by now. Someone's just trying to freak me out."

"Why?"

She tossed her towel on the counter, annoyed that her pulse had skyrocketed. "That's a good question. I don't have an answer yet."

"Are you going to talk to members of the committee?"

"Of course. Don't worry, Ross, I'll take it from here."

"I don't like it."

"Well, neither do I, but there it is." She glanced at the clock on the counter. "Geez, I've got to run. I'm gonna be late."

"Kris—"

"Look, if you really want to help," she called over her shoulder, half running down the hall, "find the damned cat and let her in. Otherwise she'll be out in the rain all day."

She shut the bedroom door behind her and waited, shoulders pressed against the panels of the door, her breath held tight in her lungs until she heard him leave. The back door opened and closed, his truck's engine roared to life. She let out a sigh. What was it about Ross that made her so crazy? Thinking sexy thoughts about him one minute, wanting to wring his neck the next? "Because you're an idiot," she muttered, turning on the spray in her shower, then stripping out of her pajamas.

And there's a part of you that still loves him.

That thought hit her hard. Ridiculous. Whatever she'd felt for Ross Delmonico was long, long dead. She stepped under the spray and turned the faucet to allow a blast of cold water to hit her full force.

She gasped as the icy needles of water hit her skin.

She would have no more hot, sensual thoughts of Ross Delmonico even if she had to take a hundred cold showers.

* * *

Ross didn't like what was happening.

Not one little bit.

His family was falling apart.

He turned off the radio, flipped on the windshield wipers, and reluctantly turned his black truck toward the freeway. First there was his daughter. Lissa was on a fast train to trouble with her attitude toward school and that scumbag of a boyfriend of hers. He'd been a horny teenager. He knew what that kid was thinking.

Then there was what was happening with Kristen and the damned reunion. He'd been against the thing from the start, figuring it would just stir up her old, unresolved feelings about Jake Marcott. But he'd had no say in the matter. It was her life, which she'd so angrily pointed out on more than one occasion.

He let it go, deciding he'd fought the ghost of Jake Marcott long enough. But now someone else wasn't letting it lie. Someone else was resurrecting the past.

Ross waited at the ramp signal to northbound I-5, seeing the taillights of thickening traffic, hearing the rush of engines and tires, but driving on automatic, by rote, his mind going over bit by bit what he'd learned in the last twelve hours.

What the hell had Kristen been thinking, going back to the school at night? Alone, for God's sake.

Not alone; someone was definitely following her.

A prankster?

No way. The light turned green and Ross stepped on the accelerator, threading into the steady stream of traffic heading into the Terwilliger Curves, a section of the freeway known for its winding path through the hills. He held the steering wheel so hard his knuckles bleached white.

Someone was messing with his family.

And it was because of the damned reunion.

Remember, Jake Marcott's killer was never located.

Ross braked as a semi beside him eased a little close to his lane. The trucker kept control of his rig and Ross gunned it, moving past the eighteen-wheeler.

He saw the exit for Macadam Avenue and jockeyed into position for the off-ramp. He knew what he had to do.

His daughter wouldn't like it and his wife would throw one helluva hissy fit. But it was just too damned bad. Until this mystery was solved—and maybe even after it was—Ross intended to insert himself back into their lives.

* *· *

"So . . . how did the, what did you call it—'the reunion meeting from hell'? Yeah, that was it. How'd it go?" Sabrina asked once Kristen had settled into her chair. Because of Ross, Kristen was running late. Damn the man. She remembered the concern that etched across his face as he'd stared at the photo and felt warmed.

She had to mentally shake herself. *Don't buy into it. Where was he when you needed him? When Lissa needed him? And who the hell does he think he is that he can just barge into your life and start handing out advice?*

"It went," she said, answering Sabrina's questions. "Not great, but it went." She shoved her purse into a drawer and pressed her computer's ON button.

Sabrina was leaning both hips against the edge of her desk, long legs stretched out in front of her, and pointing a manicured nail in Kristen's direction. "You survived."

"Barely." Kristen rolled her chair away from her computer monitor.

"It couldn't have been that bad."

Kristen thought of Haylie's outburst and the eerie note and tape left in her car. "It was pretty bad."

"But you couldn't pawn off the responsibility of running the thing?"

"Nope. Believe me, I tried."

"Give yourself a chance, you might just have some fun with this," Sabrina said, a slow smile spreading across her face.

"Think so? Well, get this, you might be invited."

"Me?" Her black eyebrows drew together. "I didn't go to St. Lizzy's."

"No, but your husband went to Western. Graduated the same year I did, right? Class of '86?"

Sabrina's grin slowly fell. "What's that got to do with anything?"

"The vote was to ask the Western boys to join us, so, being as you're the spouse, you too could be a part of the festivities. Hey! I could work it out so that you could be in charge of decorations or name tags or—"

Sabrina had pushed herself off the edge of her desk. She held her hands in front of her in the classic "stop" position. "Okay, okay. I get the picture. Don't be signing me up for any commit tees, and don't let anyone talk to Gerard. He's got enough on his plate already."

"I think someone from Western, probably Craig Taylor or Chad Belmont, will be contacting him."

She groaned as her phone rang and she turned her attention back to work.

The rest of the day was uneventful. Kristen polished up a couple of stories, turned them in to the editor, then, when things were at a lull, thought more about the tape, marred photo, and the night of Jake Marcott's death. Surely the newspaper had articles about what had happened that night, the murder and subsequent investigation. She only had to look. At four o'clock, she began searching all the old computer records, but the information went back only twelve years. Eventually, she made her way downstairs and into the basement. In a windowless room with the fluorescent lights humming overhead, she sat on a stool at a small desk and stared into the viewer until she found the first story on Jake's murder, printed the day after the dance.

Her skin crawled as she read the account, a clinical, facts-only report of the killing at a private school. So much was left out: the human emotion, the pain, the heartache.

Setting her jaw, she worked forward, searching the following editions, looking for information about the investigation. Unfortunately the information was limited:

Jake had been a student at Western Catholic.

Services were held at St. Ignatius.

He was survived by his parents, James and Caroline, one grandmother, Maxine Baylor, and three siblings, Bella, Naomi, and Luke.

Students, chaperones, and faculty attending the dance had been questioned, as had family and friends and acquaintances of Jake Marcott.

The murder weapon, a crossbow, had been discovered in the maze at St. Elizabeth's and was found to have belonged to a bow hunter who had reported it missing sometime in December. The bow hunter had a strong alibi and was dismissed as a suspect.

There was information about Jake, including the fact that he played football and baseball and had been in an accident during the Christmas break in which another Western student, Ian Powers, had died.

The police were asking the public's help in solving the crime.

The lead investigator for the "Cupid Killer," Detective Mac Alsace, was looking into "new leads every day," but the case had eventually gone cold and references to Jake Marcott's death had disappeared.

Kristen printed out a few of the articles, turned off the viewer, put the microfiche away, and rubbed the kinks from her neck. She was stiff from sitting in one position and hadn't learned much more than she already knew.

That night, she dealt with Lissa, who said in no uncertain terms that she'd never spend another night at Ross's condo.

Real good father-daughter relationship, Kristen thought, keeping mum on her feelings.

To her surprise and Lissa's disgust, Ross came over that evening, bringing with him five white boxes of take-out Chinese. Lissa, who had rolled her eyes upon his arrival, hadn't been able to resist the tantalizing aromas of cashew chicken, sesame beef, and peanut sauce. They ate on the floor in the den, watching some inane music awards show on television, and Ross didn't even remark when Lissa, after receiving a call on her cell, took her plate and phone to her room.

When she didn't immediately return and Ross looked ready to go get her, Kristen pointed a chopstick at his chest. "Don't," she warned.

"But we were having dinner. Can't she give up her calls for half an hour?"

"For God's sake, Ross, how hypocritical can you get? How many times did your dinner get cold while you talked on the phone with some subcontractor?"

"That's different. It was business. Important."

"This is important to her."

"Then we need to set some rules." She raised an eyebrow, daring him to continue, and Ross didn't disappoint. "No phone calls at dinner. Not for any of us."

Kristen frowned as she chewed on a piece of tangy shrimp. "Wait a minute. So you think that we"—she rotated the chopstick in a circular motion to include Ross, herself, and the empty cushion recently vacated by their daughter—"we'll be doing this often?"

"I'm just saying whenever we have a family dinner, some rules should be observed."

"A little late for that, isn't it?"

"It's never too late." He was serious and she caught his meaning, felt the atmosphere in the room shift a bit.

"Wait a minute. We're talking about dinner together as a family, right? Nothing more."

"What more do you want?"

She felt her damned cheeks flame. "Don't do this, Ross, okay? Don't start that talking-in-circles thing you do. Let's just play it straight. If you're talking about you and me getting back together, if you think that we shouldn't go through with the divorce, then you're wrong."

"You haven't filed yet."

"I know." She stared at the fire, while on the television in the background some girl of about seventeen, dressed in next to nothing, was belting out a song as if her life depended upon it. "It's a big step." She sighed and shook her head. "I want you to know that when I took my wedding vows, I . . . I meant them."

"So did I."

Kristen felt overwhelmed. She should never have started wading into this river. The current was too damned dangerous and was bound to pull her under.

Her cell phone rang and she immediately started to get up.

Quick as lightning, Ross's hand clasped over her wrist. She nearly dropped her plate. "Let it ring," he insisted, gray eyes holding hers.

"But—" His hands were warm, fingertips pressed into the flesh inside her arm. How many times had he rubbed his hands up her arms as he'd kissed her? How many times had they tumbled so easily into bed? Her pulse beat unsteadily.

"New rule, remember?"

"I didn't agree to any rule. You know how I hate them." Would he please release her? The feel of his skin against hers was way too distracting.

The phone blasted again.

"It could be important. My mom—"

"Feeble excuse, Kris. Your mom is healthy as a horse."

"How would you know?" She tried to pull her arm away, but he held on tight.

"She called me a couple of weeks ago. Is interested in the condos on the river. Is hoping I'll give her a deal."

"Oh, God . . ."

"You know Paula."

Kristen inwardly groaned. Ever since selling the bakery, Paula Daniels had fancied herself an investor. Ross was right, she was always trying to finagle a good deal.

The phone rang again and Kris gave up, flopping back against the couch. "Okay," she said in surrender and Ross loosened his grip. "You win. Again." She ignored the warm spot where his fingers had touched her pulse, refused to stare into his seductive gray eyes another second. Damn, what was she thinking? Of kissing him? Of making love to him? Now *that* would be a mistake she couldn't dare risk. Ross Delmonico had always had a way of turning her inside out when it came to sex.

Using a key she'd had made two decades earlier, Jake's killer unlocked the door at the bottom of the outside stairwell and moved inside. It was dark and smelled of dust, dirt, and mold. As she closed the door behind her and slid the lock into place, she heard the steady drip of rainwater that had seeped through the cracks of the old school and the scratch of tiny claws against concrete, no doubt rats and mice who had found homes in this little-used storage space that held old, forgotten relics of St. Elizabeth's.

A shame they were planning to tear the old place down.

The wrecking ball was scheduled for sometime next year and by that time, all of her work would be done.

And work it was.

Silently and familiarly, using the tiny beam of a small penlight, she dodged broken benches and desks, lab tables and outdated, now rusted, physical education equipment to reach a long-forgotten closet with an old combination lock she'd installed herself—just to be on the safe side. She held the lock in her palm, turned it over, saw the initials scratched on the back, and smiled to herself.

J.M.

Big as life.

A bell tolled and she froze, then smiled as the peals echoed through the campus, just as they did at each hour of the day. She rotated the dial to the combination. The lock sprang and she was inside her own little chamber, her private place in the universe.

Once the door was closed behind her, she flicked her lighter to the wick of an old kerosene lantern. As the lamp began to glow and her eyes adjusted, she saw the fruition of her years of labor, the perfect room for what she'd planned for so long.

She'd done her work over the years, gathering items at garage sales, estate sales, the local thrift shop run by the parish, St. Vincent De Paul stores, and, when all else failed, resorting to stealing the most valued items. Then she'd lucked into an unexpected bonanza. A few years after Jake's death, the interior of St. Elizabeth's had been remodeled and old desks, equipment, lockers, tables, and the like had been sold at an auction.

Which had been perfect.

She'd bought several lockers, the numbers burned into her brain forever, lockers that had once belonged to that unique circle of friends who were linked by one boy: Jake Marcott.

Under the cover of darkness, she'd brought them here . . . back home to a hidden room beneath the auditorium of the old school. Each of their graduation pictures had been duplicated, laminated, and affixed to the lockers with their corresponding numbers: Rachel Alsace, locker 102; Kristen Daniels, locker 118; Lindsay Farrell, locker 123 . . . and there were others, of course, all of the girls in that certain special clique.

She smiled.

Licked her lips.

Oh, how long she had waited.

Now, it seemed, she was about to be rewarded.

She sent up a prayer of thanks, made a hasty sign of the cross, then opened the locker that had once belonged to Kristen Daniels, now Delmonico. Inside were several artifacts: Kristen's final report card, the one that had sealed her place as valedictorian over the next two in line, Bella Marcott and Mandy Kim; Kristen's list of awards and achievements printed in the yearbook, including scholarship offers, writing commendations, and her duties as editor of St. Lizzy's newspaper and captain of the debate team; her French III textbook, the one she'd thought she'd lost on a trip to visit the University of Washington campus.

And finally, and best yet, Kristen's diary, the little leather-bound book with its ridiculous key, the secret tiny volume of written notes, dreams, and wishes that had disappeared from under her mattress. Kristen had been sick with mortification, worried that her mother had found and discarded the diary—or worse yet, that some of the boys from Western, known for their pranks, might have somehow gotten into her room and found it, only to reveal its contents. She'd been in a panic for weeks when she'd noticed it missing.

The killer smiled when she remembered Kristen's distress.

It had been the beginning.

Now, in the flickering light of the lantern, she opened the diary to one of the last entries, one of her personal favorites:

> *I can't believe it! Jake said yes! I invited him to the dance and he agreed! Lindsay will be upset when she finds out and Rachel already thinks I'm out of my mind, but I'm in heaven. Jake Marcott is going to the Valentine's Dance with me!*
> *Me!*
> *I just know it's going to be a night I'll never forget.*

And so it had been, the killer thought . . . so it had been.

Chapter 7

During the next three weeks, nothing out of the ordinary happened, unless it was that Ross had been sticking around a lot more and that Kristen was beginning to feel safe again. But now, driving home from work, Kristen didn't know whether to be irritated, suspicious, or just accept the situation and see what developed. She'd still not filed the divorce papers and wondered about that. Why the hesitation? She'd made the decision, hadn't she? Just because Ross was suddenly showing some interest in his family wasn't enough of a reason to stop the inevitable—or was it? So far, she'd adopted a "wait and see" attitude; she could always tell her attorneys to continue.

The rest of her life was routine. Her position and responsibilities at the *Clarion* hadn't changed and she was still wondering if she should try and change jobs, look for a new perspective. She'd heard *Willamette Week* was interviewing for an editor but, for the moment, she'd decided against making any more major alterations in her life. She was already on the horns of a dilemma about her divorce, and Lissa seemed even more distant and rebellious. Sometimes, with her daughter, Kristen felt as if she were tiptoeing through a minefield, never certain when the next emotional explosion would occur.

Changing lanes, she squinted against a lowering sun as she headed west. For the first time in months, she scrounged in the console for her sunglasses and plopped them onto her nose before realizing they were dusty and covered with fingerprints.

Tonight was the next meeting of the reunion committee and she wasn't looking forward to it. Though she didn't have the same trepidation as she'd had a month earlier, she still wasn't red-hot on the idea of running the show.

Aurora had reported in twice since the last time they'd met, and everyone was doing her assigned task. Kristen had talked to Sister Clarice, who had spoken with the powers that be at the convent, and a date for the event had been chosen, the venue of the old school approved. Sister Clarice had reluctantly agreed to be interviewed, along with a few of her peers, for a series of articles the *Clarion* would run. According to Aurora, the Western Catholic graduating class was "on board," so at least a portion of the festivities would include their alumni. A caterer had been secured, decorations planned and the official invitations were about ready to be sent.

It looked like the whole damned thing was coming together— and no further warnings had occurred. Kristen had never told any of the reunion committee what had happened at St. Elizabeth's campus the night of the first meeting, nor had she mentioned that she'd been there. She figured if Aurora or any of the others had experienced something similar, they would have said so. So up till now Kristen had decided to bide her time, but tonight she planned to show everyone on the committee what she'd found.

In the interim she'd also tried to track down the photographer who had taken the picture at the dance, just on the off chance that the photo left in her car wasn't the original. Maybe her copy was simply missing . . . maybe . . .

Lost in thought, behind a slow-moving cement truck on Canyon Drive, she nearly jumped from her skin when her cell phone jangled. She found it in the pocket of her purse and, after changing lanes and exiting off the main road, she answered just before voicemail picked up. "Hello?"

"Kris!" Her mother was always delighted to catch her.

"Hi, Mom. How are ya?" Kristen felt a little jab of guilt. She and her mother usually met once a week for lunch or dinner, but lately they'd been playing phone tag, which had been as much Paula's fault as her own. Though Paula Daniels was an AARP card–carrying senior citizen, she hadn't slowed down an iota. "I've been trying to get in touch with you."

"I got your messages and meant to call earlier, but I've been busier than ever, if you can believe that. I've been elected president of our little women's group at the golf course and I've got that bridge group with Henry and, believe it or not, the woman who bought the bakery is wanting me to come in and work a few days a week."

"Are you?"

"I'm thinking it over. Depends on if I move."

"Ross said you asked him about his condos on the river."

"Wouldn't that be fun! And no more mowing the damned grass . . . if the price was right, I'd jump on it like a flea on a dog! And Henry's interested too."

Henry was, as her mother called him, "her main squeeze." Kristen had never asked exactly what that meant and figured she was better off not knowing.

"I hear you're seeing Ross again, that the divorce is on hold."

"Where'd you hear that?" Kristen demanded, slowing for a corner, then nearly standing on the brakes as a squirrel darted across the road.

"Well, is it, or isn't it? You know, I've always liked Ross and he is Melissa's father, and well, I do believe that no matter what your troubles are, you can fix them. No marriage is a picnic, believe me, but there are those vows about sickness and health, good times and bad and . . ."

"We were married by a justice of the peace," Kristen reminded her as she sped up for the final rise to her house. Why was she having this conversation with her mother, *why?*

"You should have had Father McIntyre—"

"But we didn't, okay? That's water under the bridge." She turned into her driveway one-handed and hit the brakes again. Once the car had rolled to a stop, she let the engine idle and pressed the garage door opener with her free hand.

"I didn't call to get into a fight. I thought you and I and Melissa could get tickets to *Dirty Rotten Scoundrels*, it's coming to town, to Keller Auditorium, in July and has had fabulous reviews."

"Sounds good." Keller Auditorium was one of the largest and most upscale theaters in Portland and the venue for a lot of the touring Broadway shows.

"I'll order them . . . if I can get a Saturday night. Should I get one for Ross, too?"

"No!" Kristen scaled back her tone with an effort. "Let's just make it a girls' night out, okay? You, me, and Lissa."

"Henry will be disappointed, and I know Melissa has a boyfriend." Paula was using that wheedling tone that Kristen had always found irritating.

The thought of sitting for hours in an upscale theater with Zeke was too much. He'd probably wear a stocking cap over his ears and be plugged into his iPod, or be trying to make out with Lissa.

"Come on, Mom. Let's make this a women thing."

Paula sighed loudly and Kristen knew she hadn't heard the end of this particular discussion. "I'll let you know when I get them. I think there are some bargains on-line."

"Good seats, though, Mom, okay? Nothing under the balcony. And make sure they're all together this time. I'll pay the extra cost."

"Mmm-hmm . . . I'll get the best I can finagle. Oh, gotta run. Got another call coming in . . . it's Henry . . . and I don't know how to put you on hold."

"Don't worry. We'll talk later."

Kristen hung up as she entered the kitchen through the garage side door. She figured she was doomed. Her mother wasn't one to change her mind easily. For some reason she wanted a group date with the men involved. "Save me," Kristen murmured.

She checked on Lissa, who was seated at her desk, actually working on homework, even though the buds for her iPod were plugged into her ears.

"I'm going out tonight, remember?" Kristen said and when her daughter didn't respond, shouted, "Lissa!" so loudly that Marmalade, who had been seated on the windowsill, scrambled from her perch, hissed at Kristen showing fierce, needle-sharp teeth and an incredible pink tongue, then scurried beneath the skirt of Lissa's bed. She peered out balefully, as if Kristen were suddenly the enemy. "Ingrate," Kristen muttered at the cat.

Lissa pulled out one of her earbuds. "What?" she asked in a bored tone.

"I'm going to a meeting tonight. The reunion again. I shouldn't be gone long. There're some Lean Cuisines in the freezer."

Lissa rolled her eyes.

"Or pizza."

"Big deal. Dad's coming over." Another exaggerated roll of her expressive gray, and overly made-up, eyes. "Didn't he tell you?"

"I must have missed that memo." Of course Ross hadn't said anything. Lately, he didn't seem to understand that she needed some warning before he strolled into the kitchen. Ever since the night of the first reunion meeting, Ross had been making a point of inserting himself into their lives again. It bugged her, but worse yet, Kristen found herself kind of enjoying the attention a bit, too.

Now she gritted her teeth. For whatever reasons, Ross was playing the part of interested, concerned father, and for that Kristen was on board. She wasn't as certain she liked his renewed attentions to her . . . it was as if some switch had flipped back on. Suddenly he was smart, witty, and attentive—more so than he'd been in years. But what did it mean? How long would it last?

Bottom line: she didn't trust him.

And she didn't trust herself when it came to him.

It was just too easy to fall into that trap again.

"He said he was going to bring dinner again. Oh, wow," Lissa said, curling her lip, "another Dad date."

"Could be worse," Kristen pointed out.

"How?"

"Could be taking you to his condo."

Lissa looked stricken. The thought of being stranded in Ross's Portland high-rise was enough to give her apoplexy. Forget the fact that she'd go there with her cell phone and iPod and have e-mail access through his computer; in Lissa's opinion spending a night in the condo was a jail sentence.

"I'll be back before ten, I think," Kristen said, but her daughter was already plugged in again, her nose pointed toward her open algebra book, while on the computer screen someone named ZeeMan was instant-messaging her.

No doubt Zeke.

Kristen bit her tongue and walked the few steps to her room, where she showered, changed, slapped on some lipstick and mascara, then ran her fingers through her hair and called it good. She had just picked up her laptop and notes when Ross, pocketing his keys, walked in.

She tried not to notice how good he looked, but her female antennae picked up everything in a flash. His black hair was unkempt, aviator sunglasses covered his eyes. He was wearing khaki slacks and a white shirt with sleeves rolled to the elbows to show off tanned, sinewy forearms. His tie hung from a loosened collar, which added to the image of hardworking businessman ready for a little R&R. "Hi," he said, tossing his keys and wallet onto the table.

"I didn't know you were coming over."

Taking off the sunglasses, he added them to the pile of his personal things. "Time got away from me. Meetings with those jackasses at the bank, a financing snafu that could hold up the entire Macadam project, and then more problems with a plumbing subcontractor. I didn't have a second to breathe, let alone call and—" He stopped himself, shoved his hair from his eyes, and offered her a rueful smile. "I'm sorry. I should have phoned."

"Amen."

He held up his hands as if in surrender. "Won't happen again."

She didn't believe him for a second, and it must've shown in her expression because his grin widened and he made an exaggerated cross over his chest. "Cross my heart and hope to die."

"Yeah, right. Okay, okay, I forgive you. *This* time, but I gotta go. Already late for the meeting." She grabbed her purse and tried to brush by him.

"Wait."

She looked up into his teasing eyes, so damned seductive with their tiny striations of blue in the gray irises.

"I have to apologize for one more thing."

"And what is that?" Her blood pressure was already elevating.

"This." He pulled on her arm, yanked her to him, and suddenly kissed her. A deep, hot kiss. Surprised, Kristen gasped, and he took advantage of her open mouth, his lips molding to hers, his tongue touching and exploring.

She reacted instinctively, her stupid, wayward body beginning to melt, her bloodstream surging, her heart pounding a staccato rhythm. *You don't want this, you don't,* her mind was screaming at her, but her body, so long without a man's touch, so anxious for the feel, taste, and smell of him, responded eagerly. Heat skittered up her spine, spreading across the back of her neck. Her knees threatened to buckle. She dropped her purse on the floor. It landed with a soft clunk.

"Oh, no!"

Lissa's disgusted voice pierced through the haze of desire, and Kristen pulled back from Ross as if she'd been yanked by an invisible wire. Glancing past him, she spied her daughter, nose wrinkled as if she'd smelled something rotten, staring at her.

Lissa turned and swept down the hallway and quickly into her room. The door banged shut.

Kristen felt her cheeks flushing. She took one step after Lissa, then stopped. "You handle this," she said tightly.

Ross, damn him, was grinning like a Cheshire cat. "I will."

"Good."

"It was just a kiss, Kris. A nice one. A *very* nice one. But just a kiss." He slid his eyes toward the hallway where Lissa had disappeared. "We are grown up and married."

Kristen groaned, more at herself than anything else.

"It's not like we were 'doing it' here on the kitchen floor." Unfortunately Kristen's mind recalled a time when they *had* done it on the kitchen floor. Ross seemed to pick up on her thoughts, because he laughed and his eyes twinkled in the way that really got to her. "You're just mad 'cuz you liked it."

She made a strangled sound but couldn't deny it. "Yeah, all right, I liked it. I didn't want it, but okay, it was . . . nice." She picked up her purse again and grabbed her laptop. "Doesn't mean it'll ever happen again."

"Keep telling yourself that," he said as she walked out the door and pulled it shut harder than she'd planned. What was it about that man that made her so crazy?

She decided she didn't have time to think about it. Not right now. Not when she was on her way to Ricardo's. Tucked inside one pocket of her computer case was the mutilated picture of Jake and her at the dance. In another compartment was the tape. Though she had a small cassette recorder with her, the one she used while interviewing, she didn't intend to play the tape unless she had to.

Ross rapped softly on his daughter's bedroom door, but before Lissa could shout out "Leave me alone," he pushed it open and stepped inside the chaos that was Lissa's room. Not quite a pigsty, it was still messy as hell. She was flopped on her bed, cell phone to her ear.

"I don't want to talk to you," she said, placing a hand over the receiver.

"Tough."

"Dad. No. Not now."

"Yep, Lissa, now. Hang up."

She shook her head and he heard a voice, a male voice, saying something.

"Either you hang it up or I will."

"Oh, puh-leez."

"I'm serious." He took a step forward.

"I'll call you back," she said quickly. "In a few minutes." Then she hung up. Turning rebellious eyes up at him she said, "Satisfied?"

"Nope."

"Oh . . . shit. You don't even live here anymore."

"I'm working on that. Clean up your language."

"It's just words, Dad." She looked about to let fly with a blue streak of four-letter words, then caught his expression and changed her mind. "And don't 'work on it' to move back in. Mom and me, we don't need you."

"Really?" He folded his arms over his chest. "Tell me about it."

"I don't need to tell you anything. You just want to come back here so you can go to bed with Mom." She made an "ick" face as if the picture of her parents sleeping together was the most revolting image she could imagine.

"Your mother's my wife," he said, crossing the room, grabbing her desk chair, flipping it around, and sitting on it backward.

"Not for long."

"You think?" He smiled. "We'll see."

She shook her head. "Don't you get it? Mom doesn't love you anymore."

That statement stung, but he ignored it. "Let's turn this around, okay? I didn't have time to pick up anything on the way, so let's go out for a burger. You can tell me all about *your* life then."

She looked at him as if he'd suggested she eat banana slugs.

"Come on, Lissa. It won't be so bad."

"I'm . . . I'm a vegetarian."

"Since when?"

She made a face and shrugged. "A while."

"Great. I know a place where they make veggie burgers out of tofu or something." He picked up her flip-flops and tossed them onto the bed. "Let's go."

Chapter 8

Kristen tried to ignore her case of nerves, but as she drove to the restaurant she couldn't forget the night of the last reunion meeting and the fact that someone had followed her to St. Elizabeth's afterward. Had it been one of the women on the committee? Or someone who had waited in the parking lot, then followed her Honda as she'd left? Was it the person who had stolen the picture of Jake and her from the attic where it had been hidden for years, or someone else?

Who?

And why?

The same old questions hounded her and she couldn't help but check her rearview mirror and the surrounding traffic as she drove through the congested streets of Beaverton. Twice she thought she noticed a vehicle lagging back, visible in her sideview mirror, but the first time it was a truck with an older man in a baseball cap who had pulled into a convenience store, and the second time it was a dark SUV that passed her, the driver, a soccer-mom type, not giving her a second glance.

"You're paranoid," she told herself as she pulled into Ricardo's lot. She spied Aurora's Subaru wagon in a parking space near the front door and noted several other vehicles that could be reunion committee members' cars. She didn't see Haylie Swanson's BMW.

Grabbing her computer and purse, Kristen locked the car and headed inside. Once again, the tangy garlic-laden scents emanating from the hidden kitchen made Kristen's stomach growl. Somehow, she'd missed lunch and hadn't noticed how hungry she was until this minute.

The restaurant was quieter than it had been the previous time they'd met. There were plenty of people seated at the tables, but the decibel level was lower due to the fact there was no preteen basketball party in progress.

Kristen waved a hello to Aurora. Most, if not all, of the other usual suspects from St. Lizzy's had shown up. Only Haylie appeared to be missing, replaced by another woman Kristen recognized as Laura Triant, the girl who had married Chad Belmont from Western Catholic. Kristen was relieved. She didn't want a replay of the last meeting's scene. Hopefully Laura was a lot more stable than Haylie.

Three tables had been pushed together in a corner close to the bar. Once again notes, yearbooks, pictures, and printouts were scattered among bottles of wine and frosty mugs of beer or cola. Mandy, DeLynn, Bella, Aurora, and Martina were seated around one end of the working surface, leaving Laura Triant Belmont and April on the opposite side.

"Welcome, *El Presidente*," Aurora greeted her.

"Sorry I'm late."

"Nah . . . the rest of us are early."

"Sure." A lie. To make her feel better. She slid into an empty chair next to DeLynn and across from April. "Are we all here, or are we waiting for Haylie?"

"She's not coming. I called," Aurora said. "Left a couple of voice messages. She never called back."

"Which is just as well, considering last time," Bella pointed out. "For as long as she lives, she's going to blame Jake for Ian's death." She shook her head, her hair as dark as her brother's had been. In high school, she'd looked enough like Jake that people had thought they were twins, especially those who hadn't realized Bella had skipped a grade in elementary school.

"She can find us, she has all our numbers," Martina added, her dark eyes sober. "I'm with Bella. Haylie's more trouble than she's worth."

"That's not exactly what I meant." Bella, slightly irritated, picked up her glass of wine.

"Sure it is. It's what we're all thinking . . . Oh, well, doesn't matter. Let's get on with it," Martina said. "Kristen, you remember Laura? I told you she's married to Chad Belmont?"

"Hi, and welcome to the committee."

"Glad to be here," Laura said. "We were just discussing the boys from Western. Martina and I see a lot of them."

The conversation took off from there as they discussed some of the Western grads. Laura had brought a yearbook that caused lots of chuckles, sly glances, and comments like, "I so had a crush on him!" or "He was a friend of my brother. I couldn't wait for him to come over and play basketball." Or "Geez, he was always a nerd in high school, always hitting on me. I heard he made a fortune with some dot-com company."

For twenty minutes they discussed the "boys" from Western.

Just as they had about every waking moment twenty years earlier.

"Chad's all over this reunion," Laura said, sipping from a mug of beer. "One hundred percent!" She was still as freckled as ever, but a few streaks of gray had infiltrated her once-vibrant red hair. "He and some of his friends, including Craig," she added, mentioning Martina's husband, "are already starting to contact classmates."

Martina nodded as she sipped what appeared to be a Diet Coke. "Craig's already put out the word on the Internet. I think they've got over forty guys signed up already."

"I say bring 'em on." April's eyes were full of interest at the prospect of being with "the guys." She'd been married twice before and made no bones about the fact that she was "lookin' for number three."

Aurora pointed to the wine and beer on the table. "Help yourself. It's light beer. And Merlot. That pizza's cheese and pepperoni, and this one"—she indicated the large tray in front of Martina—"is veggie delight. If you want something from the salad bar or a soda, you're on your own."

"A beer sounds like heaven," Kristen said as she reached for the half-full pitcher and an empty mug. "Bring me up to speed."

They did. Laughing, talking, eating, and drinking, they laid out how the event would take place. Bella had great ideas for decorations and was proceeding on ordering them, and DeLynn had managed to get most of the classmates' addresses and was working on the final three.

"Does anyone have any idea about Leslie Bonaventure, or Karleen Signatore, or Bette Lablonsky?" DeLynn checked the spreadsheet she'd printed out. "I'm missing about twenty-six alumnae, but I have leads on all but those three. Here's the list." She passed copies around the table.

"I think I heard Bette's family moved to Chicago," Bella said around a bite of pepperoni, "but don't quote me on that."

"Karleen has an aunt in Oregon City, or did," Martina put in. "I'll see if I have that address."

DeLynn made notes on her spreadsheet. "I also got in contact with Darla Campbell's parents. She died last year in a boating accident, and I don't think Selma Ortega will come. Not only was her husband killed last year in the war, she's battling ovarian cancer. She has to wait and see how she feels."

There were murmurs of shock and concern from the rest of the committee. It was sad and oddly strange to learn of their classmates' troubles and deaths.

DeLynn tapped her pencil on the table. "Selma has two kids and Darla a son. I think the committee should set up some kind of donation fund or something, y'know, as well as acknowledging them at the event."

Everyone agreed with the idea.

"Well, on that somber note," April said, "I think we should move on. Here's the menu and bid from the caterer. It's pretty expensive, but the best I could come up with. You'll see that I got a bid with and without dessert." She passed her sheets around. "I was hoping Kristen's mom might be able to help in that area. It could save us some money if we got a deal on the pastry."

"From my mom?" Kristen snorted as she picked up a piece of vegetarian pizza. "She was never big on giving special price breaks, and she sold Sweet Nothings a few years ago."

"But she still has connections in the industry."

"I can ask," Kristen said dubiously. "But don't count on it."

"Okay," Aurora said. "What about the advertising? Can you run ads for the reunion at the paper and on the Internet? Maybe we can find those last missing souls."

"Will do."

They talked a while more, organizing, and eventually Aurora handed Kristen a stack of nearly a hundred invitations. "These are ready to go. They're already stuffed with registration forms, return envelopes, and questionnaires. All you have to do is add a personal note-slash-invitation as head of the committee and maybe include DeLynn's list of the people we can't find, so that if anyone knows where a missing alum is, they can contact us."

"I think you should write the letter," Kristen teased, though she took the boxes of invitations. "Honestly, Aurora, you've done the work on this."

Aurora waved a dismissive hand. "Give me some credit in the letter and maybe in the little pamphlet that we hand out at the reunion. Just don't make me the person everyone turns to if there's a problem. That'd be you, Kristen."

Kristen didn't want to think about what those problems could possibly be. It was time she told them about what had already happened to her, but she hardly knew how to broach the subject.

Then DeLynn checked her watch and sighed. "Got to go. The baby-sitter can only stay until nine-thirty."

Drawing a breath, Kristen plunged in. "There's something else I wanted to talk about." The committee members turned interested faces her way. "Something I want all of you to see." Unsnapping her briefcase, Kristen reluctantly pulled out the marred photograph.

Everyone at the table stared at the faded, red-marked photo.

"What is this?" DeLynn asked.

"Someone left it in my car, the night after the last reunion meeting."

"What?" Aurora was stunned. "They left it here?"

"No." As succinctly as possible, Kristen relayed her story.

"Why did you go to the school? The *maze*?" Bella asked, her eyes trained on the photograph of her brother.

"I don't know. It was stupid."

"This is beyond creepy," Laura said.

DeLynn agreed. "Who would do this?"

"I think someone followed me," Kristen admitted. "No one knew I would be there. I didn't plan to go. I can't even explain why I felt compelled to drive to the school and walk through the maze."

"You should have your head examined," Martina muttered as she looked away from the photograph. "Where did this picture come from?"

"It might have been stolen from my house," Kristen said with a grimace. "I checked my attic. It's missing. Just the paper folder that it came in was left."

"You think someone was in your house?" DeLynn whispered. She'd forgotten all about her baby-sitter.

"How else would they get the picture?"

"From the photographer?" Aurora asked.

"He's out of business. I checked."

"We have a picture like that," Bella said and swallowed hard. "Or at least we did." She bit her lip. "I, um, I haven't seen it in a while. But Jake paid for the picture and it was sent to our house, you know, several weeks after . . . after he died. My mom fell into a million pieces all over again." She looked up at Kristen. "I'll check with my folks. See if they still have it."

"I don't like this," April murmured, rubbing her arms as if suddenly chilled.

"Whoever left the picture also left me an audio tape . . . it's from the dance." Kristen glanced at Bella. "Look, I'm sorry, this is painful for us all, but I thought you should know. The tape has people's conversations and then . . . well, it ends with a horrible scream. I think Lindsay's."

"Okay, this is sick!" Aurora rubbed her temples and stared at the picture lying between the half-drunk mugs of beer. "Someone's turned complete psycho. Have you . . . did you talk to the police?"

"Not yet."

"Why the hell not?" DeLynn demanded.

"Because I thought it might just be a prank."

"A prank." Her condemning tone conveyed her disbelief. "Kristen, this is malicious, cold, and potentially dangerous." She glanced at her watch and muttered, "Damn. I've really got to go." She pointed a finger at the picture. "Take that and the tape and call the damned police. That's what they're for." Scooping up her purse, she was out the door.

"She's right," Laura said. "You have to take this to the police. Maybe they can pull fingerprints off the cassette or listen to it and piece together different voices . . . a time line. Some of us might remember who was around when those conversations were taped."

"It's been twenty years."

"My guess?" April said. "Haylie's behind it. She had that meltdown. Still blames Jake for Ian Powers's death. And she didn't show up tonight. I'll bet she's guilty as sin."

Aurora shuddered. "Let's not start pointing fingers, but De-Lynn's right, Kris. You have to talk to the police."

The killer watched as cars rolled out of the parking lot. As each woman left the meeting, she looked over her shoulder, then peered inside her car to make sure it was empty. They were all paranoid the bogeyman was hiding inside, and after a cursory search they drove off with cell phones pressed to their ears, doors locked, tires chirping as they hit the gas.

Just you wait, she thought, watching from deep within her vehicle, a dark SUV with tinted windows. She smiled. It was almost delicious.

She was parked near a stand of pines that rimmed the lot, and no one noticed her vehicle wedged between a pickup and a sedan. They were too busy getting away.

Because they were scared.

Because Kristen Daniels had told them about the picture and the tape.

They'd all been shocked, and she'd been able to witness their horrified expressions.

Everyone was edgy.

Nerves strung tight.

Good.

Humming "Dancing in the Dark," the old Bruce Springsteen song that was playing the night Jake was killed, she smiled and put her Blazer into gear.

Things were about to get worse. A whole lot worse.

Chapter 9

No one followed her. She watched, checking her rearview mirror, her hands gripped tight on the steering wheel, but the drive was uneventful until she pulled into her driveway and found Ross's truck parked on the street.

Her heart did a stupid little jump and she looked in the mirror one more time to check her appearance. "Oh, get over yourself," she muttered. "It's Ross. *Ross*. The man you're divorcing. Remember?"

But the woman in the mirror didn't seem convinced.

She walked through the garage to the kitchen and found Ross sprawled on the leather couch in the family room, his shoes kicked off, a fire lit, the television tuned to a sports update show. The cat was curled on the back of the couch, her tail wrapped around her tawny body.

Ross twisted his head as she walked in and flashed that incredible, roguish grin of his again. "Hi, honey, you're home!" he teased, and her heart lurched again.

Don't fall for it. This is just an act.

"Comfy?" she asked, dropping her bag and laptop onto the table as the cat opened her eyes, yawned, then settled back to sleep.

He patted the cushion next to him. "I could be better." His voice was deep. Sexy. Oh, she'd heard it a thousand times in the first five or six years of their marriage—the happy years. "Come on over and take a load off."

She was tempted. "Nah. Too much to do."

He cocked an eyebrow and she noticed that not only the collar

MOST LIKELY TO DIE   97

button but a few more had come undone. His sleeves were rolled
over forearms that were impossibly tanned considering the time
of year. "I believe that was my line. At least you accused me of it,
oh, about a dozen times a day."

"Was I really such a nag?" she asked, walking toward him.
Marmalade, disturbed by all the commotion, hopped off the couch
and sought solace under the kitchen table with an accusatory meow.

"Worse."

"You are so not making points with me," she said. Reluctantly,
knowing inside she wanted to far too much, she took a seat on the
ottoman, facing him.

His eyes assessed her, causing a little frisson of awareness to
slide down her spine. "How 'bout I get you a drink. Gin and tonic?
Glass of Chardonnay?"

"How can you be so damned sure of yourself?"

"Years of practice." Again he thumped the spot beside him in
invitation. "Come on, Kris. What've you got to lose?"

"Lissa's home."

"And my guess is she knows all about us. It won't hurt if she
walks out of her room and finds us together."

Kristen arched a dubious brow.

Ross continued in a conversational tone. "We are her parents
and we own this house. Together. I think she understands the facts
of life. And just in case she doesn't, I told her about them tonight
over tofu burgers and French fries that had been guaranteed not to
be fried in anything resembling animal fat."

"Oh, that's right . . . she's a vegetarian."

"Nope. I think she upped her commitment to the cause. Now
she's a vegan."

"She was last year, too. It lasted a couple of weeks."

He snorted in amusement. Kristen smiled back and quit fighting him. Gave up the battle with herself. Sliding onto the couch,
she tried not to melt against him when his arm pulled her close and
her head nestled so naturally into the crook of his neck. "So, how
was it? Are you hot on the trail of those long-lost classmates?"

His arm felt right around her and the whiff of his cologne reminded her of how easily she could respond to him. "I suppose."

"Don't they know they can't escape? That you're like a blood-
hound when you're tracking something?"

"Actually, DeLynn Vaughn, er, Simms, is in charge of locating everyone, and she's a lot better at it than I am."

"If you say so."

"Mmm." She frowned and decided to tell him about the rest of the meeting. In for a penny . . . "I showed everyone at the meeting the picture that was left on my car and told them about the tape."

She felt him tense a bit, the muscles surrounding her tightening. "And?"

"And everyone agrees with you, that I should call the police."

"Good. And have you?"

"First thing in the morning. I promise."

He lifted her chin with one finger and forced her to look him straight in the eyes. "I'm going to hold you to it, Kris. This is important. You don't know what kind of a nutcase you've got running around. A prankster who's getting his rocks off by scaring the crap out of you or a real psycho, like the person who killed Jake Marcott."

Kristen grimaced. Ross had always accused her of never being able to get over Jake's death, of feeling guilty that the boy she'd loved had died, of never letting go of him. He'd also blamed Kristen's unrequited dreams and fantasies about a boy who had become a ghost for ruining their marriage.

Part of his accusations were true. No doubt about it.

She tried to pull away from him, but he held her fast. "I'm serious. This isn't a random act, and we both know it. Whoever decided to mess with your car planned it. Stole the picture. Either audiotaped the murder years before or stole the tape from someone who did, someone who never mentioned it or gave the tape to the police." Eyebrows drawn in concentration, he added, "It's no coincidence that this is happening now, when you're planning the reunion. Someone's been waiting for just this moment."

"You don't know that."

Ross slowly released her, but his tone was demanding. "You think it was random? That whoever did this was just up at the school, waiting for you to walk into that damned maze?"

"Of course not," she admitted.

"I don't like it," Ross said, frowning into the fire.

"Neither do I."

"I think it would be best if I stuck around."

Her gaze, which had drifted toward Marmalade, flew to his face. "What do you mean? Like . . . stay here? Overnight?"

The fire hissed and crackled as he asked, "Would that be so bad?"

"We're supposed to be separated . . . you can't just . . . move back in." She shook her head though a part of her wanted it badly enough to scare her inside. She shot to her feet. "Look, Ross, nothing's really changed."

"Like hell. *I've* changed. *You've* changed."

"Don't . . ." She struggled to keep a grip on things even though with each passing day she'd begun to believe that he'd never cheated on her. That she'd imagined that part because he'd lost interest in her. In their family. That was the stone-cold truth. "It didn't work before. I don't think it'll work now."

"So kick me out."

"I am."

"And I'm not budging."

She couldn't believe his gall. "We had an agreement."

"An arrangement. I didn't really agree to anything. I was just giving you the space to figure things out. But I'm through with that." To emphasize his point, he pulled the quilt from the back of the couch and tossed it over his legs. Gray eyes dared her to argue.

Kristen glanced at the door to Lissa's room and lowered her voice. "Really, Ross, you can't stay here."

"Sure I can. Just watch."

"You son of a bitch," she said on a note of wonder. He was really pushing this.

"Now, there's the woman I love. I wondered when she'd surface."

"What're you planning to tell Lissa?"

"How about 'Daddy's home'?"

"Fine. If you want to camp out in the family room and make some kind of macho statement, have at it. You can explain it to Lissa tomorrow."

"Sweet dreams," he called after her as she strode into their bedroom and slammed the door.

It was all Ross could do not to chase after her, kiss her for all she was worth, toss her onto the bed, and tumble after her. He knew their lovemaking would be searing. Intense. Erotic.

It always had been.

Even when they'd made light of it and laughed or teased, the physical wanting and desire had always been white hot.

Lying on the couch, watching the fire die, hearing a sportscaster drone on and on about the NBA, he let his mind wander back to the time when they hadn't been able to get enough of each other; when a simple brushing of the elbows, or naughty little glance, or upturned corner of a mouth had started a sensual fore-play process that might have lasted fifteen minutes or more likely hours, touching, kissing, caressing.

They had experimented with positions and places; in fact—he glanced around the house—there hadn't been a room they hadn't christened in one way or another before they'd moved here per-manently. Closing his eyes, he remembered the feel of her tongue sliding down the cords of his neck and lower, over his shoulders and down his abdomen. She would often place her teeth and tongue around one of his nipples before moving slowly, with sweet agony, downward.

His blood heated and even now, alone, thinking of her, his groin tightened and his damned cock grew hard.

He tried to shift his thoughts from her, but it was too late.

They hadn't been able to get enough of each other and if there had been any problems, they had seemed small at the time. True, he'd known from the get-go that she hadn't resolved her feelings for the boy who had died, but Ross had thought with the passage of time, Jake Marcott's ghost would be laid to rest, that eventually Kristen would come to terms with what had happened that night.

He'd been proved wrong.

Jake had always been there.

Standing between them, and in Ross's mind's eye, the dark-haired boy had been laughing at Ross's naïvete. He'd even shown up in some of Ross's dreams, this high-school kid he'd never even met! And always, without fail, Jake was the one walking out of the damned maze with Kristen, and Ross was left shackled to the tree, the greenery closing in on him, Kristen's voice fading in the distance.

He'd always been stark naked in the nightmare, while Jake was in a black tux and Kristen in a differing array of clothing; sometimes in a long, sexy black gown, other times in nothing more than a red teddy and high heels.

He'd always woken up hot, horny, and thankful that Kristen was beside him, sleeping soundly.

So why had he let it slip away? Why let the nightmares of Jake Marcott push him further from her? When had his work, his god-damned work, become more important than his wife and daughter?

Never.

They had just slowly grown apart and they'd let it go too far until questions, doubts, and fears had overtaken love and trust.

But no more.

Whether Kristen liked it or not, he was back. And horny as hell.

So the husband is there.

That was an unexpected wrinkle.

The killer, having parked two streets over, had carefully slunk through the shadows of the tall firs that partially covered the hillsides of this sparsely occupied neighborhood. With houses on partial acres, hidden away, and the few houses close to the road built on steep, forested hillsides, traffic had been light, nearly nonexistent, as she'd neared the Delmonico home at the end of the dead-end street. She'd had to hide only twice when a car had passed.

Now, across the street as she viewed Kristen's home, the killer stared at the big black pickup belonging to Ross Delmonico. She didn't like the fact that Delmonico was in the picture again. He could screw up her plans. Big time. And she had waited so long. So damned long.

Don't panic.

Stay the course.

You've come too far to let this little snag affect you.

She let out her breath, the warm air from her lungs expelling in a streaming fog as it hit the cold night.

Staring at the house, she reached into her pocket, her fingers closing over the key deep inside, a key she'd made from the one Kristen had hidden on a nail tucked under the eaves of the porch, the one she left for the kid who was always forgetting hers.

They'd never known it was missing. The killer had located it one morning after everyone had left for the day and put it back it before anyone had returned. Easy deal. She'd done the same with all the houses she'd needed to enter. Most people weren't that clever when hiding their spare.

Slowly, caressingly, she rubbed her thumb and index finger over the cold metal, pressing hard over the unique, sharp little teeth that were fashioned and cut to ensure the locks on Kristen Daniels's doors would open.

But the husband was a problem.

As was the kid.

Not insurmountable. You can handle them. You just have to be careful and wait for the precise moment to strike. You can do it. You won't fail.

Through the slats of the blinds, she saw a fire glowing, warm and bright, flickering flames reflecting on the windows, smoke curling into the thick, dark night. Every once in a while she'd catch a glimpse of a silhouette moving in front of the window and her gut would tighten.

Don't let anyone see you, she reminded herself.

What the hell was the husband doing there?

The light in Kristen's bedroom snapped on, and though the killer could not see through the closed shutters, she imagined what was happening in that room. With the husband. She imagined the mating, that big man mounting Kristen in the missionary position, or maybe from behind. He would be grunting in pleasure, she gasping, maybe holding on to the rails of her headboard, and there would be the slap, slap, slap of flesh meeting flesh, hotter and faster as the smell of sweat and sex overcame the scents of candles and fire.

Her lower abdomen tightened.

And need started to pulse through her. Did she dare peek through the blinds to watch their rutting? Spy Kristen in the throes of passion, knowing she would be pretending the man thrusting himself into her, making her pant and her blood run like lava, wasn't Ross Delmonico at all, but Jake Marcott?

"Whore," the killer whispered. They were all whores. For Jake.

Her jaw was so tight it hurt.

Tears burned behind her eyes.

Bile rose up her throat.

She clasped the key so hard it cut through her skin, and she might not have noticed the pain except a dog started barking, breaking into her obsessive fantasy.

A big dog, from the sounds of it.

Not a little yapper.

And not penned.

Wrenching her gaze from the house, she narrowed her eyes into the frigid darkness and focused down the hill toward the corner where the main road split and this offshoot continued up the hill. There was only one streetlight between Kristen's house and that fork.

She saw the bobbing beam of a flashlight.

Shit!

Her heart nearly stopped.

Someone was walking their damned dog!

Blocking her way out.

Her ears strained and she heard the pound of footsteps.

She racewalked in the other direction, toward the dead end, where no house could be built as the lot was essentially little more than a sheer cliff.

She had to get away before she was seen!

Slap! Slap! Slap! Slap! A brisk tempo of running shoes hitting pavement.

Oh, hell, the guy wasn't *walking* his dog. He was running. Even though it was almost midnight. The runner and dog reached the lamp post with its eerie pool of bluish light. The man wasn't all that big, but the beast—some kind of Doberman/Rottweiler mix—was huge. Massive. Drooling.

Shit!

The killer took one final glance at Kristen's house and froze.

There, staring straight at her, peering through the damned bedroom window, was Kristen Daniels Delmonico.

The bitch.

Chapter 10

Kristen's hand stopped in midair. The blind she had been adjusting was partially open as she squinted through the window past the shrubbery of her yard, and at the far side of the street she saw movement. A blur.

She sucked in her breath.

What was it?

Was it her imagination, or was someone standing beneath the drooping boughs of the ancient Douglas fir trees that stood like giant sentinels in the vacant lot?

You're seeing things, she told herself, but her heart was jackhammering, her breath caught in her lungs. *Don't do this, Kristen. Don't let your imagination run away with you. It's probably just a deer—or shadows.*

Another movement outside. A dark figure starting to make tracks.

"Oh, God." She switched off the bedside lamp, causing the room to go dark, cutting the reflection and allowing her eyes to adjust so she could see more clearly.

There it was again, that murky blur.

Someone running or walking quickly toward the dead end.

Without thinking, Kristen flew out of the bedroom, down the hallway to the kitchen.

Ross was lying on the couch.

"Someone's outside," she said, searching in the drawer for her flashlight. "Across the street. Watching the place. They took off toward the end of the street when they saw me looking outside."

"What?" He was instantly up, reaching for his shoes. "What do you mean? Who?"

"I don't know. Just that someone's out there. Someone who shouldn't be," she said, and couldn't keep the undercurrent of panic from her voice.

"Then stay inside. I'll check it out." He was halfway to the kitchen.

"I'll come with you."

"No way." His voice was firm. "It's probably nothing, but on the off chance it's trouble, you stay with Lissa. I'll yell if I need you to call 911."

"No, Ross, I've got to show you where I saw—"

He grabbed her by the arms. "Stop it! I'm going out there. You're staying here. With our daughter. End of story!" He scooped the kitchen phone's handset from its cradle and slapped it into her hand. "If I need help, I'll yell. Lock the door behind me." He was outside, letting in a wave of wintry air before she could say another word. She twisted the dead bolt and stared through the kitchen window toward the street, but Ross had already disappeared into the shadows.

Lissa's door opened and she stepped into the hallway. "What's going on? You were shouting. Is . . . is Dad still here?" Wearing faded jeans and a short T-shirt, she looked about five years younger than her age. Kristen couldn't resist hugging her close, startling her.

"Yes, Lissa, your father's here, and he's going to stay overnight." Her daughter opened her mouth as if to protest, but Kristen cut her off. "It's okay. In fact, it's a good thing, so please do not, I mean, do *not* give me one second's grief about it."

"Geez," Lissa said, but she didn't argue further as she scanned the kitchen and family room. "So, what's going on? Where's Dad now?"

"Outside. I thought I saw someone across the street and . . . well, Dad's checking it out."

"You saw someone doing what?"

"I don't know. Lurking."

"Oh." Lissa hesitated, ran a hand through her hair, then admitted, "It was probably Zeke."

"Zeke?"

Gnawing on a corner of her lip, Lissa shook her head as if silently arguing with herself.

"Melissa?"

"I, um, sorta told him to come over."

"But . . . it's after midnight. And why wouldn't he just come in the door and—" The light in her mind suddenly dawned, with a painful, intense brilliance she'd tried to ignore. "You were going to sneak him into the house?"

Lissa lifted a shoulder. As if it were no big deal. "Just for a little while. We were just going to hang out."

"Melissa Renee Delmonico, that is the absolute worst idea I've ever heard of! You can't sneak Zeke or *any* boy, or anyone for that matter, into the house. You know that."

For once Lissa didn't roll her eyes, just stared at the door as Ross returned. Alone. He snapped off the flashlight. His face was set and hard, the lines near the sides of his mouth more pronounced.

"Zeke's not with you?" Kristen asked.

"No . . . why would he be? The only person outside was a guy jogging with his dog. No one else."

"A jogger?" No way!

"With a flashlight and dog. A big dog."

Kristen shook her head. "The person I saw didn't have a flashlight. I'm telling you"—she slid a glance at her daughter, and though she didn't want to frighten Lissa, she figured everyone in the family needed to know what they were dealing with—"someone was lurking outside, across the street. Not moving until they saw me looking through the blinds. This wasn't a jogger or someone walking his dog."

Ross's eyes were dark, his expression even more severe. He set his flashlight on the kitchen counter, leaned a hip against the top of the cupboards, and folded his arms over his chest. His gaze was riveted on his daughter. "Why did you think it might be Zeke?"

Lissa blinked hard, then started to turn as if heading for her room.

"Hold it right there. Answer me. What's going on?" Ross demanded.

Lissa's shoulders stiffened. She sniffed loudly, then finally turned. Her lower lip began to quiver, though she fought breaking down completely. "Nothing. Nothing's going on, Dad, and it's all *your* fault. Zeke . . . Zeke doesn't like it that you're hanging out and . . . and I told him to come over. Yeah, that's right, I know what time it is," she added when Ross glanced at his watch. "Anyway, he was going to come in through my window and—"

"Wait! What?"

"I was going to sneak him in, but it doesn't matter anyway because I guess he stood me up. Again." She swiped the back of her hand under her nose and added acrimoniously, "Happy now?"

Before Ross could respond, Kristen said, "Don't bother with the lecture. Melissa and I have just had it. She knows that she made a mistake, but"—she switched her attention to her daughter—"if this is the way he treats you—"

"Save it, Mom." Lissa glared at her parents.

Ross said, "Call him."

"What?"

The set of his jaw brooked no argument. "Find out if Zeke was here. Maybe your mom and I scared him off."

"I don't want to—"

"Call that little creep right now, or I will."

"Damn it, Dad, don't do this!"

"*Now*," he ordered, though his voice wasn't quite so harsh.

She hesitated, then whipped her phone from a pocket of her jeans. Turning her back to her parents, she hit speed dial, and standing in the hallway, had a quick call in hushed, mumbled tones. Her small shoulders were slumped, her head cocked, one shoulder braced on the wall.

"No one was out there, Kris," Ross said as Lissa finished her short conversation and snapped her phone shut. When she turned to face them again, she was fighting tears. "It wasn't him, okay?" She swiped at her red eyes and sniffed loudly.

"You're sure?"

She nodded, her jaw sliding to one side. Hesitating, she then cleared her throat and squared her shoulders. "I don't think he'd bring someone else over here. He's with Tara O'Riley. I heard her laughing."

"Oh, honey." Kristen's heart cracked for her daughter.

"It's okay," Lissa said. "He's a jerk."

Ross stepped right into it. "You could do better anyway."

"Then why's he with Tara?" she spat, bristling as she threw her hands into the air. "What do you care, anyway?"

"Lissa," Kristen warned, but her daughter's volatile emotions erupted.

All her anger and shame had shifted to her father. "Mom says you're moving back in. What's up with that?"

"I said he was spending the night. That's different from moving back," Kristen reaffirmed.

"So this is just temporary?" Lissa asked, a trace of sarcasm still evident in her voice. "You move in, you move out, you move in again. Just like some kind of yo-yo dad. So who are you to give me any kind of advice?"

Kristen expected Ross to come unglued. To argue. To point out the difficulties of an adult relationship, to explain why both he and she had needed their space to sort things through. Instead his jaw worked, he glanced down at the floor for a second, rammed his hands deep into the pockets of his slacks, then nodded to himself before looking up and meeting his daughter's angry, red, accusing gaze. His voice, when he spoke, was softer. More thoughtful. "I can't give you advice. You're right, Lissa."

There was a beat of uncertain, uncomfortable silence when only the slow sizzle of the fire and quiet rumble of the refrigerator could be heard.

"But I am moving back in," he said, holding Kristen's gaze. "For good."

Chapter 11

Over the next few days Kristen learned how serious Ross had been. She hadn't argued with him when he'd made his proclamation, because a part of her was thrilled to have him back. She wanted to give their marriage one more chance.

But she'd laid down some rules. Ross used the guest bedroom as his office and sleeping quarters for now. They chose a family counselor who would work with them as a couple, as well as with Lissa, to help them repair the rifts in their shattered little family. They both agreed to the changes, though Lissa dragged her heels to the first counseling session and thought the whole idea was "beyond lame."

But it was a step forward . . . a step in the right direction.

As for the reunion for St. Elizabeth's, Kristen did call the police about the tape and photo and a detective came by the office and took her statement, along with the "evidence." Considering the more deadly, higher-profile crimes that were occurring in the city, Kristen didn't hold out much hope that anything momentous would come of the investigation.

She managed to write a letter to the alumnae and stuff and seal all of the envelopes. Then, unfortunately, because of deadlines at work and her own complicated family situation, she forgot to take the damned things to the post office. They sat ready to be mailed on the kitchen table for two days before she finally remembered to haul them to the post office a week after the reunion meeting. Only when Ross had remarked about them and actually offered to take them himself did she realize they weren't already in the post.

Ross was being on his best "family-comes-first" behavior, and though Kristen wanted to trust him, she was holding back. Everything was much too fragile. She thanked him for his offer but she dropped off the envelopes on her way to work the following morning, then caught up with Sabrina, who had decided, against her better judgment, to help her husband Gerard and Chad Belmont with the Western Catholic reunion that was the same weekend and dovetailing into the St. Elizabeth's festivities.

"So I heard about the weird tape you got and that creepy picture," Sabrina said, shuddering as she blew across the top of her caramel/mocha-nonfat-decaf-with-light-whipped cream latte she was sipping. She and Kristen were taking a break at the local coffee shop, seated inside the windows, watching clouds roll over the sky and pedestrians scurry past as the first few drops of rain began to splatter against the sidewalk. With a great rumble, a TriMet bus pulled out of the bus stop and eased into traffic heading east, toward the gray waters of the Willamette River and the Hawthorne Bridge.

"Did you talk to the police?"

"Mmm, but so far, they haven't found anything."

"It would be a great story for the *Clarion*. You could bring up Jake Marcott's murder and then tell what happened to you. Get a little press and a nice byline." She was only half kidding.

"No, thanks. The publicity just might be what whoever did this wants. It could make him frantic for more and more, and he could up the ante."

"Or she."

"Or she," Kristen agreed as they carried the rest of their drinks back to the office. Kristen finished a piece on school funding or lack of it, and near five, she made a phone call to Alabama—one she'd been putting off—where it was almost eight in the evening.

A woman picked up on the third ring. "Hello?"

"Rachel?" Kristen asked. "This is Kristen. Kristen Delmonico, but it was Daniels. From St. Elizabeth's."

"Kris? Daniels?" Rachel replied, clearly surprised. "Hi. It's been years . . . Oh, I get it, you're in charge of the reunion, aren't you?" She laughed, and it was a sound that Kristen remembered well, one that caused a pang of regret to cut through her. How had she let so many years pass without trying to connect with her old friend? "Listen, if you're trying to get me involved, forget it. *You* got drafted for the job, not this girl." Again the soft laughter.

"I did call about the reunion," Kristen admitted, "but I really wanted to talk to you. To catch up. Got a minute?"

"Absolutely."

They talked for nearly half an hour, filling in the gaps and laughing. Kristen told Rachel about her job at the *Clarion,* her husband and daughter, and Rachel revealed that she was divorced and working as a cop.

"I heard that much," Kristen admitted. "That's really one of the reasons I decided to call you today. I know your father worked on the Jake Marcott murder case."

On the other end of the phone, Rachel sighed. "Oh, God, yes. Swear to God, the fact that Dad couldn't solve that one drove him to an early grave."

"I'm sorry."

"So am I. For a lot of things," Rachel admitted. "The Jake thing . . . horrible. For all of us."

"You're right, and it hasn't gone away."

"It never will," Rachel thought aloud. "It really ticks me off that someone got away with murder."

"Me, too, and I'm afraid whoever did it might be back."

"What?" Rachel asked, a little more loudly.

"Either the murderer has returned or . . . someone's getting off on messing with me, probably because of the reunion." She explained everything that had happened, from the moment she felt someone might have been inside her house to the reunion committee, to feeling she was being watched. As Rachel listened, Kristen told her about driving to St. Elizabeth's campus, walking through the maze, and receiving the "gift" of the picture and tape. She finished with, "The photographer is out of business and my picture, the one of Jake and me at the dance, is missing, though I don't know for how long. It's been years since I looked in that box in the attic."

"What about the other people on the committee? Anyone else been harassed?"

"Not that I know of."

"Then you were singled out because you're in charge of the reunion, or because you went to the campus, or both," Rachel surmised. "And you went to the police?"

"They weren't all that interested. They took the tape and the photograph, but . . . really, they've got bigger fish to fry."

"Not if this is really tied to Jake's homicide," Rachel said, and Kristen heard a rhythmic sound, as if Rachel were tapping the end of her pencil on something . . . just like she used to do when she was really thinking hard in Sister Clarice's religion class twenty

years earlier. Religion was one of the few classes Rachel, Lindsay, and Kristen had shared their senior year. "You know, Dad's
partner, Charlie Young, is still with the force, at least I think so.
I'll give him a call and find out what's what."

"I'd appreciate it," Kristen said with feeling. "Well, we all
would. Some of the girls—I mean women, we're bona fide
women now—would, too. They were a little freaked at the last
committee meeting."

"I'll bet," Rachel said. "I'll get back to you."

"Thanks." Kristen hung up feeling slightly better. At least
someone in law enforcement was interested, even if that interest
came from nearly twenty-five hundred miles away.

Two days later, Kristen parked her car in the garage, then
walked out to the mailbox to pick up the usual assortment of junk
mail and bills. There, between an offer for a low-interest rate
credit card and her Visa statement, was the invitation to the reunion. She was surprised because she hadn't bothered to mail one
to herself; she'd kept the prototype in her laptop and figured why
waste the stamp. But there it was, big as life, addressed to Kristen
Daniels Delmonico.

"What the devil?" she asked, as she walked into the house . . .
the quiet house. "Lissa? Ross? I'm home," she called as she
headed down the hallway.

Odd . . . no one save for Marmalade was inside.

"What's up with that?" she asked, and then remembered that
her cell phone's battery had run out after her long conversation
with Rachel and she'd forgotten her charger. Now she fished the
phone from her purse, snapped it into the charger on her desk, and
as the phone went through its machinations of coming to life in a
series of tinkling sounds, she found the letter opener in her desk
drawer.

"You have seven new messages," the computer voice informed her after she entered her password.

"Seven?" she repeated, holding the phone between her shoulder and ear to free up both hands so she could slice open the reunion packet. Marmalade hopped onto the desk and sat squarely in
the pile of mail. "See how popular I am?"

The cat ignored her and began cleaning herself.

"Yeah, yeah. A lot you care."

"First message," the computer voice stated.

"Mom, it's Lissa. I'm going over to Brandy's house to work

on a project for German. Either she'll bring me home or I'll call for a ride."

Click.

That sounded safe enough. Kristen sincerely hoped that her daughter was where she said she'd be.

The machine announced, "Next message."

"Hi, Kris. Hey, I'm running a little late, okay? But I'll be home by seven. If you want, I can pick up something for dinner. Or we could go out, or whatever. Love you."

Ross's voice enveloped her. The words, uttered so quickly, touched her heart. *Don't go there, not yet,* she warned herself as she pulled the thick, folded papers from the envelope.

"Next message."

"Is this your idea of some kind of joke?" Aurora demanded, her voice shaking. "I just got my invitation and surprise, surprise. What the hell were you thinking, Kris? Call me!"

Kristen stared at the phone, then opened the folded pages of her own invitation. Everything was as it should be except there was no letter of explanation signed by her, and her picture, the one she'd copied and cut from the yearbook to be used as part of her name tag at the reunion, had been altered. A harsh red line streaked across her face.

Her lips parted in shock. The threat was clear: someone intended to do her harm.

"Next message."

The phone beeped. A hang-up. Kristen dropped the invitation as if burned.

"Next message."

Oh, no.

"Hi, Kristen, this is Bella. I got my invitation today and . . . well, it's really, really weird. Some of the other girls on the committee got identical ones and I just don't understand. Call me back."

"Next message."

Kristen was shaking.

Aurora said coolly, "Okay, Kris, I talked to other people on the committee. It seems I'm not the only one who got the marked-up invitation. Bella and Mandy got one, too. But the rest of the committee, as far as I know, didn't. What the hell's going on? Call me!"

The next two calls were hang-ups, but caller ID indicated that Aurora had been dialing her every fifteen minutes.

Staring down at her own scratched senior photo, Kristen thought she might be sick. Who had done this and when? She thought of the invitations that had been left on her table for three days. Had they been tampered with?

Had someone been inside her house?

She nearly fell into the desk chair, her mouth dry, her heart pounding. She picked up the phone to dial Aurora when she stopped and listened.

Was she alone?

She thought hard, adrenaline kicking in. She didn't have a weapon in the house. Neither she nor Ross owned any kind of gun. Quietly, she walked to the kitchen, reached for the butcher knife, but it was missing. Probably in the dishwasher. She didn't have time to search and settled for a serrated, long-bladed knife from the drawer, then saw her reflection in the window—a pale ghostlike image of herself with a huge knife, just like one of those idiotic girls in a teen slasher movie.

Too bad. She needed something to protect herself. Moving softly, she walked from room to room, looking in closets, under beds, in any corner where someone could possibly hide. Her heartbeat thrummed in her ears as she searched every inch of the house. She'd nearly satisfied herself that she was alone when she remembered the attic.

Though the temperature was cool, sweat broke out on her back. *Don't be a fool,* she told herself, but walked to the cord hanging from the ceiling anyway, pulling hard. The stairs unfolded into the hallway. The only other access to the attic was through a small window in a gable of the house, so Kristen told herself it was unlikely anyone would be inside. Still, her heart was thundering as she mounted the narrow steps, her muscles stretched tight.

She poked her head up slowly, only to eye level.

Thump!

Kristen gasped and nearly fell off the ladder when she heard the telltale scratch of little claws scraping across the floor. A damned mouse. That was all.

Slowly she stepped upward and flipped on the lights. No one was hiding in the dusty shadows. No dark figure cowered in a corner. No deranged psycho was crouched behind the antique chest of drawers she'd never gotten around to refinishing.

No . . . everything was fine.

She was about to snap off the lights when her gaze swept over the stack of boxes of old textbooks and high-school paraphernalia she'd searched through.

One box was missing.

No. That couldn't be right.

Again her heart began pounding crazily and a lightning chill raced down her spine. She gazed around wildly, her eyes searching one corner to the next. Surely she'd misplaced the damned thing . . . That was it. She'd tucked it somewhere else.

Frantically she scoured the room, not wanting to believe that someone had actually violated her privacy and sneaked into her home.

But the box that had contained all her memorabilia from St. Elizabeth's was gone. She could still see the square shape in the dust where it had sat for so many years.

Sweet—Mother—Mary.

Who was this sicko? What did he want? What if he became violent? Images of Jake Marcott's white-faced body flashed through her mind. She remembered his blood-soaked tux. Lindsay's ruined dress. The pool of red oozing around the base of the oak tree and statue.

Backing toward the stairs, she could almost hear Lindsay's ear-splitting, terrorized scream echoing through the rafters. She thought of the mutilated picture of Jake and her at the dance, the bloodcurdling scream on the tape, and now the marred invitations to the reunion.

Some sick pervert had been in *her* house.

Without breaking a window or knocking down a door.

Someone had a key, and now no one was safe.

Oh, God, *Lissa!* Was she really studying at a friend's house, or had she been coerced into calling? Had she been kidnapped? *No, no, no!*

Fear storming through her, Kristen flew down the stairs.

Carrying the heavy box, the killer slipped into her private lair, deep in the locked, forgotten basement at St. Elizabeth's. It had been a long, hard, but oh so rewarding day. Everything had gone perfectly. As planned.

She set the box on a desk, then, once the door was shut behind her, lit the kerosene lantern. In the flickering illumination she searched through the items in their cardboard container. Little trinkets, photos, even Kristen's essays and diploma were in the box. She thrilled at the personal things, playing with the tassel from the mortarboard of the graduation cap and pulling out the long gold honor cords that Kristen, as a member of the Honor Society, had worn at graduation.

Then there were the pictures . . . in an album or left loose, photographs of the three best friends: Rachel, Lindsay, and Kristen, and, of course, all the snapshots of Jake Marcott.

She fingered those pictures and sighed.

What fools they all were. All of them. Even Kristen Daniels. Despite her soaring GPA and stratospheric SAT scores, she was an idiot.

They all were.

But they would soon learn.

Satisfied, she walked the few steps to the wall and worked the combination to locker number 118. Kristen's locker. A click, then a groan as the metal door opened to reveal the few items already tucked inside. Now along with the French III textbook, awards, final report card, and her diary, she could display the pictures and little mementos that Kristen had treasured enough to keep all these long years.

A thrill ran down through her as she draped the faded honor cords over the jacket hook. They hung like a woman's thinning blond braids.

What a joke.

"Fool, fool, fool," she whispered happily to herself. Carefully she stacked, pasted, and glued items inside the locker. When she was finished, she admired her work, then took out the final item from the box:

The butcher knife she'd stolen from Kristen's kitchen.

A serious stroke of genius, she thought, staring at the blade and seeing her own distorted reflection in the shiny steel.

"Tomorrow," she told herself, shivering with anticipation as she imagined the moment when one of St. Elizabeth's graduates would give up her miserable, useless, whoring life.

She pricked her thumb with the tip of the blade and saw a drop of red blood gather in the small cut.

Oh, yes, she thought, smiling coldly. Oh, yes.

Chapter 12

Kristen picked up her cell and speed dialed Lissa, only to be connected to her daughter's voicemail. *No, honey, oh, no, no, no.* She left a message for Melissa to call home immediately. Frantic, she punched in the number again only to be directed to the voicemail box once more. With an effort she forced her shaking fingers to text a simple message: *Call home. URGENT!*

For the first time in history Kristen hoped her daughter's cell phone was off or that Lissa was screening her calls. She didn't waste a single moment as she located the high-school directory of students and began flipping through the pages for Brandy's number. Brandy . . . Brandy . . . Parker . . . no, Brandy Peters . . . no, oh, what the hell was that girl's name? She found the page with the *P*s, ran her finger down the page until she saw *Brandy Porter*. That was it. She was dialing the number frantically when she saw Ross's truck roll into the driveway.

Thank God!

"Hello?" a girl's voice answered on the other end of the line.

"Is this Brandy?" Kristen asked in a rush, then didn't let the girl respond. "I'm looking for Lissa, er, Melissa Delmonico. I'm her mother."

"Oh . . . she, uh, left."

"What? How?"

"Her boyfriend picked her up?"

"Her boyfriend? What boyfriend?" Kristen demanded, in a full-blown panic. "Zeke?"

"Yeah?"

"When did they leave?"

"Uh . . . I dunno . . . maybe fifteen minutes ago?"

Ross walked through the back door and Kristen sent him a look that warned him not to say a word. He had two sacks of groceries that he set on the table.

"Were they coming straight home?" Kristen asked, the girl's vagueness making her want to tear out her hair.

"I think . . . so?"

"Okay, thanks." She hung up, scared and frustrated.

"Lissa's with Zeke again?" Ross's voice was steel.

Kristen nodded, her mind racing.

He swore roundly. "How do you knock some sense into that kid?"

"Ross, there's something else going on here. I think someone broke into the house. Someone who had a key."

Quickly, she outlined what had happened since she'd returned from work. Ross's expression turned grim, the veins in his neck stood out, and a small tic started at his temple as she handed him the doctored invitation that someone had sent her. She also told him about Aurora's and Bella's calls. "I haven't called either one back yet, but I can't concentrate on that when Lissa is . . . Oh, God, is that her?" She ran from the den to the kitchen where, through the window, she saw the high beams of an SUV splash against the rear of Ross's truck.

Relief flooded through her as she spied Lissa climbing out of the passenger side, shouting something Kristen couldn't hear, then slamming the door of the SUV. Lissa turned and stormed in through the garage, and the vehicle took off with a roar.

"Prick!" Lissa said as she stepped through the door. "Lying, cheating, useless prick!" She caught sight of her mother as she slammed the door and her face reddened. "Sorry. I was talking about Zeke."

"You were supposed to call me," Kristen said, so grateful to see her daughter alive and safe that she really didn't care if Satan himself had given Lissa a ride home. "Let's not argue about it now."

"Did you ever give Zeke a key to this house?" Ross asked.

"What? No." She was shaking her head as she walked to the refrigerator and opened the door.

"Anyone else?"

"Uh-uh. There's *nothing* to eat." She grabbed a bottle of water and cracked it open. "Are we gonna have dinner?"

"Soon," Kristen said. "Now, Lissa, I think someone might have been in the house and taken some things."

"Really? What?"

"A box from the attic."

She looked from one parent to the other. "This is a joke, right? Who would come in here and steal some of that junk?"

"I don't know," Kristen said. "But someone. Dad's going to bring you up to speed while the two of you cook dinner."

Kristen ignored the you've-got-to-be-kidding look on Melissa's face. "I've got some work to do, so you guys whip up something spectacular and then we'll discuss what we're going to do."

"What we're going to do?" Lissa repeated suspiciously. "What does that mean?"

"We'll probably call the police."

"Really?"

"Really," Ross said as he began unloading a couple of grocery bags. "Tell you what, since you and I are on for dinner, I'll dial the phone and you order the pizza."

Kristen left them to argue the merits of pepperoni versus vegetarian and headed to the den. Her cell phone had died on her again, so she replugged it into the charger and sat at her desk. Bracing herself, she punched out Aurora's number on the landline. Aurora answered on the second ring.

"Hi. It's Kris. I got your messages."

"What the hell is—"

"Enough already. I got a doctored invitation, too, and I didn't send it. I wasn't going to bother sending one to myself but it came, just the same."

"You call that slash mark 'doctored'? It wasn't just a little mark, Kris, it was like someone pressed *hard* with a red pen, intent on making a scar. It was drawn to look like a goddamned knife wound."

"I know, but I didn't do it."

"If you didn't send them, who did?"

"That's the point. I don't *know*. I took the invitations to the post office, but I just grabbed the stack that I'd left on the table and dumped them in the mail slot. I never double-checked them. I think someone was in my house, long enough to take out information from the packets and put them into new envelopes." She thought hard, her mind clicking ahead. "If so, the labels probably don't match the others unless the person who did this has the database for our mailing list."

"You think it's someone from the committee?" Aurora was rattled.

"I don't know who it is." She then went on to tell Aurora everything that had happened. Aurora listened without interruption as Kristen explained about her house probably being broken into, the box of her school paraphernalia missing from the attic, and how she suspected someone was stalking her.

"Mary, Jesus, and Joseph," Aurora murmured at the end, and Kristen imagined her making the sign of the cross over her fairly large bosom.

"I'm scared to death for my family. I'm calling the police in the morning, after I figure out who else got the mutilated invitations. You said in your phone call that it isn't everyone on the committee who received one?"

"So far, it's only a few of us. For example, I got one, but De-Lynn didn't. Nor did Martina, but Bella got one and so did Mandy."

"What about Laura?"

"No. Same with April. They got the real deal. No tampering. Their pictures weren't slashed with a red marker."

"Probably the same marker used on the picture of Jake and me that was left on my car."

Aurora sucked in a quick breath. "Oh, shit, you're right. This is going from beyond weird to downright scary."

Kristen couldn't have agreed more. Just talking about it made her blood run cold. She thought of the person she'd seen lurking on the other side of the street. A person staring at her house. Casing the place. Because he wanted to break in and steal junk from her high school days?

Shivering, she wrapped one arm around her abdomen. "What about people who aren't on the reunion committee? Graduates who didn't volunteer?"

"No way of knowing unless they call one of us—you, probably, as your name is listed on the invitation. The girls who moved farther away wouldn't have received theirs yet," Aurora said. "Geez, Kristen, I was just talking to Lindsay, right before I got the mail. It was fun, reconnecting, y'know? Then I hung up and went to the mail and there it was. Freaked me out."

"I know. I just don't get what this is about. Are they mad because we're finally getting it together and putting on the reunion?"

"You mean, you think someone's trying to stop it from happening?"

"Maybe . . . or maybe . . . this is about Jake?"

Aurora sucked in a breath. "You think his *killer's* involved?"

"No . . . I don't know . . . But this reunion's stirred someone up, that's for sure. He or she has been waiting a long time. Twenty years. Now here's his chance, his venue to make whatever psychotic statement he wants to."

"Who would do that?"

"Someone with serious psychoses."

"But why?"

"I've been asking myself that since the night I found the tape and picture in my car." She heard a click in the receiver, indicating someone was calling in. Caller ID flashed a message that *Swanson H* was trying to get through. "Hey, Aurora, I've got to go. Haylie's on the other line."

"You think she received one of the bad ones?"

"I don't know. But when I find out, I'll call you back."

"Do."

Haylie Swanson was about the last person Kristen wanted to speak with, but considering the circumstances, she knew she needed to talk to all of her classmates. Bracing herself, she clicked over to the second line. "Hello?"

"Jesus H. Christ, Kristen, why don't you ever call me back?" Haylie demanded, her voice rising with a harsh, unrestrained fury. "I left three goddamned messages!"

"Haylie . . . I didn't get them. Really."

"Oh, sure! Your machine picked up," she said, nearly accusing Kristen of lying.

"Oh . . . I haven't heard those messages. I usually use my cell."

"It's your home number listed in the damned invitations, Kris," she pointed out, so angry her voice trembled. She was breathless, as if she'd been running, and Kristen imagined her, a bundle of raw nerves, pacing on the other end of the line. "So what's with the reunion picture? The one with my face marked up?" Haylie demanded, then Kristen heard the click of what sounded like a cigarette lighter.

"You got one, too," Kristen said, almost whispering.

"What's that supposed to mean?"

"Several people got the marred invitations, we're not really sure who, but Aurora, Mandy, Bella, me, and now you . . . ."

"Oh . . . so people connected to Jake Marcott," she said, as if the answer were obvious.

Kristen nearly fell off the chair. "Connected to Jake?"

Haylie snorted. "Well, you were dating him at the time he was killed, and Bella is his sister. I'm connected through Ian."

"That's kind of far-fetched, Haylie." Maybe the woman really was having a nervous breakdown. Or maybe she was behind it all.

"Jake and Ian were friends," Haylie explained with extreme impatience. "And whether you want to believe it or not, Jake was at the wheel the night of the accident. Jake killed Ian! I was in love with Ian, and I was once friends with Jake." She inhaled on her cigarette. "We're all connected to him."

"You think the people who knew Jake are . . . targets?" Kristen asked, her nerves stretching as she thought about it.

"I studied everything there was to study about Jake. I made it my mission, Kris."

"What about Mandy and Aurora?" Kristen argued. "Neither one of them dated him that I know of."

"But they wanted to! Everyone had a thing for him, and I don't get it. I never got it. He was bad, Kristen, really, really bad. There was a black spot in his heart, I'm telling you."

"So anyone who ever wanted to date him is also getting marked-up invitations? That doesn't make any sense."

"It's all about people connected to him!" Haylie insisted. "Mandy Kim was one of the girls who helped Jake with his homework, got him through some of his tough classes, and he and Aurora worked together for a while at the pet store . . . you know the one, it used to be in kind of the Burlingame area, at the corner above Riverside Abbey."

Kristen knew the area, south of the freeway, near the Terwilliger Curves. Crosby's Critters. The place had changed hands half a dozen times, if Kristen remembered correctly. It had gone from pet store to athletic equipment sales, then became an insurance company and a Thai restaurant, and even a few other things that Kristen couldn't recall. Now it was a coffee shop.

"You don't believe me," Haylie accused.

"I don't want to believe it," Kris said honestly. "I don't like it."

"I didn't like getting that invitation."

"Haylie, if you're right, other people could be singled out. All Jake's friends at Western Catholic and Washington."

"No . . . no . . . They didn't get invitations, though. Not to the St. Elizabeth's reunion. Those went out only to the girls who graduated from the school."

Kristen's mind tried to follow Haylie's twisted thought process. "Then there should be others."

"Only a few more. Rachel Alsace was supposedly his best

friend, as far as the girls at school went, and Lindsay Farrell, well, everyone knows she was the love of his life."

Kristen heard the truth in that even though she'd always hoped Jake had loved her. It seemed silly now, and she peeked down the hallway, spying Ross at the kitchen table with Melissa. As if he'd felt her gaze, he looked up, and as his eyes found hers she felt a warmth spread through her. Why had she ever mistrusted him? How had she nearly let him slip through her fingers?

"Because I'm an idiot," she whispered.

"What?" Haylie demanded.

"Nothing." She smiled at her husband, then looked away, concentrating on the conversation. "If you're right, then Rachel and Lindsay and anyone else who isn't in the Portland area haven't gotten their invitations yet."

"They will," Haylie predicted.

A cold chill ran through Kristen's body. "How do you know?"

"Whoever is doing this has a reason. A big reason. They didn't wait twenty years for nothing. Look, I gotta go. Think about it. We'll talk later."

She hung up abruptly and Kristen replaced the receiver just as the pizza arrived. Ross paid the pimply-faced kid who delivered it, then opened the box on the kitchen table. The hot aromas of garlic, tomato sauce, and cheese permeated the room. "You can eat this, right?" he said in mock seriousness to his daughter. "At least the cheese side . . . that's okay?"

"Yeah. I'm not really into being a strict vegan."

"Good." His smothered grin told her he thought her fling with avoiding meat and animal products wasn't serious. She made a face back at him but didn't argue.

"So?" he said as Kristen reached for two beers in the refrigerator.

"It's not getting better." She noticed there were eight calls on the answering machine and, placing the long-necked bottles and an opener on the table, punched the Play button. "Lissa, figure out what you want to drink. There's soda and water . . ."

As Kristen had expected, three of the phone messages were from an ever-more-frantic Haylie, one was from Aurora, another from Mandy Kim, and the last was Bella, all with basically the same question: Why had they been sent the mutilated invitations? There was also one telemarketer and a hang-up.

With each message that played, Ross and Lissa, who had been

talking about the merits of vegan versus vegetarian, became increasingly quiet. When the last message ended Ross said, "As soon as we finish dinner we're talking to the police, then we're outta here until we change the locks." He was putting paper plates on the table while Lissa searched through a drawer. "We'll stay at my place."

"The condo?" Lissa closed the drawer and looked in the dishwasher. "No way."

"It'll just be for a night or two." Ross opened his beer, touched the neck of his to Kristen's in the same silent toast they'd observed since college, then took a long sip. Kristen did the same. "It'll be fun."

"Whatever," Lissa said with a disgusted sigh, then added, "Anyone know where the big knife is? The one we use to cut the pizza?"

"The butcher knife?" Kristen asked. "Isn't it in the dishwasher?"

"Nope."

"You're sure?" As if Lissa couldn't see for herself, Kristen peered into the dishwasher, then pulled out the drawer where all the knives were kept. "That's strange."

"Everything's strange tonight," Lissa said and settled for a steak knife.

Kristen glanced over at Ross and their eyes met. They didn't have to say a word. In a heartbeat, Ross had drained most of his beer and was boxing up the pizza. "That's it. We're leaving. Now. Each of you pack a bag and I'll get the cat."

"You can't be serious," Lissa whined. "I don't want to go anywhere. And I'm hungry."

"You're outvoted." Kristen was already down the hallway and in her bedroom. "Eat a slice of pizza before we go." She hated to leave, but they couldn't stay. Couldn't. Who knew what the psycho who'd been in their house might do.

"Dad, this is ridiculous," Lissa was stomping her way to her bedroom while Ross found Marmalade and placed the hissing, unhappy feline in her carrying cage.

Ten minutes later, they were out the door: Lissa, Ross, and the pizza in his pickup; Kristen and a yowling Marmalade in the Honda. "Looks like I pulled the short straw," Kristen told the cat, who only howled more loudly.

Ross backed down the street and waited as Kristen pulled out. Then he followed her down the hill.

No one noticed the figure hidden in the shadows across the street. No one knew that they'd barely escaped with their lives.

The killer watched the vehicles drive away. She was wearing a bulky sweatshirt, and in the wide front pocket she fingered the butcher knife she'd stolen earlier.

Fury rose inside her like bubbling lava. She'd planned to wait another night before she struck, to savor the moments of anticipation another twenty-four hours, but her excitement had gotten the better of her and she'd decided she couldn't stand it one more minute. It had been too long already; much too long.

She'd hoped to catch the bitch at home alone, but the damned husband and kid had shown up. Hadn't she known they'd be a problem?

And now, it was too late! They were leaving!

No doubt Kristen had realized that someone had been in her house, had used a key . . .

Her fist clenched around the hilt of the butcher knife. She'd wanted Kristen first. And she'd envisioned slicing Kristen Daniels's throat just at the moment the bitch recognized her killer.

She knew how it would go down:

Kristen would be in the house, probably at her desk, maybe yakking on the phone. The killer would wait until the conversation was over, the phone hung up, Kristen still lost in thought.

Then she would spring! Attack! Call out Kristen's name, witness the whore turn! There would be a look of bewilderment as she realized who was in her home, then a second when she'd relax and call out the killer's name in mild confusion.

"What are you doing here?" she would ask . . . then she would notice the knife. Her own kitchen knife. Panic would set in. Her eyes would round and she'd start to scream or run. But it would be too late.

The killer would plunge the knife straight into the bitch's useless heart.

Oh God.

She was shaking.

Standing in the darkness, she felt a thrill like no other. She was furious that her mission had gone awry. Shaking with repressed need.

Get a grip.

Don't lose it.

Not now . . . not after you've waited so damned long.

Slowly, without speaking, she counted to ten. Slowly she calmed her raging heartbeat. Slowly she got herself under control.

Maybe this would work out to her advantage.

Maybe she could save the best for last.

There were others. She'd thought about taking the others first, one by one, of course. That had been her original plan, but after being in Kristen's house, finding the slut's diary and all her ridiculous pictures of Jake Marcott, the killer had changed her mind. Her bloodlust had been so overpowering that she'd made a dangerous misstep.

One that she could correct.

Tonight.

Stay the course. Don't veer off track. There's another who needs to die.

Letting out a breath in the cold night air, the killer realized that sometime during her reverie it had begun to rain. A thin, fine mist caressed her skin and caused ringlets to form around her face. She tilted up her head, letting the filmy drops touch her eyes, her cheeks, her throat.

Calmer now, she fingered the cold blade once more.

Get it together. There is still time.

You know what you have to do.

You know who is next.

She licked her lips. Envisioned another victim. This one with surly blue eyes, full lips, and a face framed by long blond hair.

Go now.

She's waiting.

Chapter 13

They talked to the police. For several hours. In Ross's condominium. With the panoramic view of the city lights reflecting off the Willamette River, Ross, Lissa, and Kristen all gave statements about the events of the evening, but the cops were skeptical. The only crimes were a supposed break-in and the stealing of a butcher knife and box of ancient schoolgirl memorabilia. The two cops took down the information and agreed that the special invitations were weird, someone's sick idea of a joke. Same with the tape and letter left in Kristen's car.

Before they left they promised to have someone go over to the house in the daylight and take a look around. They advised Kristen to get an alarm system and a big dog. Forget the wimpy-looking orange cat. Clearly, though they were doing their duty, they felt the perpetrator's actions were more pranklike than a serious threat.

But Kristen was beginning to put more stock in Haylie's theories and hadn't forgotten that someone had killed Jake Marcott, someone who had escaped justice.

Kristen checked the time. It was late. She wanted to call Lindsay and Rachel but decided to wait to learn if they, too, had received tampered-with invitations. If they had, then Haylie's twisted hypothesis might be proven true.

Kristen walked down the short hallway to the second bedroom, where Lissa was asleep on the daybed, the television still flickering blue, the sound hushed. How peaceful their daughter appeared, Kristen thought as she leaned a shoulder on the doorjamb. As if Lissa didn't have a care in the world. Kristen couldn't help but wonder how much of her daughter's teenage rebellion was the normal part of being a kid stretching her wings and how much was because of the deterioration of her parents' marriage.

Guilt dug at her heart, but she pushed it aside. The past was over. It was time to move on.

She didn't hear Ross approach but felt his arm slip around her waist. Pressing warm lips to her ear, he said, "She's fine. I think it's time you and I called it a day."

She felt a secret stirring in her blood as he pulled the door shut, took her hand, and led her farther down the hall to the master suite. A king-sized bed took up one wall and faced the windows. He closed the door, then pulled her through the spacious room to the master bath, where an oversized tub was filling with hot water. Steam rose toward the ceiling, fogging windows that also faced the city lights.

He'd lit half a dozen fragrant candles, and the tiny flames were the only illumination in the room.

She eyed the rapidly filling tub and clucked her tongue. "Looks like you're trying to seduce me."

"Nuh-uh." He let go of her hand to place both of his on her waist. "You got that backward, lady."

"Oh." She laughed. "I'm seducing you?"

He smiled and his eyes glinted devilishly. "How about a fresh start? You and me."

"I thought that's what we were doing."

"No, we agreed to try. Let's forget the trying part and just do it."

"What do you mean?"

"I'm asking you to marry me. Right now. Right here. I want a commitment, Kris, not just a maybe. And don't tell me that we're still married. I know." His deep gaze caught hers. "You know what I mean."

She thought about it a second and looked at his earnest face, his intense gray eyes, the dark hair that was forever falling over his forehead, the face of the man she loved.

Ross said softly, "No more accusations, no more putting work before time together, no more Jake Marcott."

She nodded and felt a rush of stupid tears. Dear God, what kind of moron was she? This was her husband and they'd been married a long, long time. This wasn't a new, untried head rush of first dates.

"Just please don't make me go through another ceremony."

"All I want is for you to say yes."

"Okay. Yes!" She stood on her tiptoes and brushed her lips over his. "Yes, yes, yes!"

He laughed, and shook his head at her enthusiasm.

"Satisfied?"

"Not yet." He reached for the top button of her blouse and grinned wickedly. "But I have a feeling I will be."

The killer cut the engine and parked not far from Westmoreland Park, only a few blocks away from her target's home. She'd been here before, scoped out the place and knew, if she was patient, that she would get her first real opportunity. There was a window that was always cracked and, to ensure that it stayed that way, the killer had slipped inside one day while the bitch was at work and tinkered with the latch so that it would never stick tight again.

Now it was just a matter of raising it, crawling into the house, creeping down a short hallway, and opening the bedroom door, which conveniently had no lock.

Dressed in black, she jogged, as if on an early-morning workout. She was wearing a blond wig and colored contacts, along with a fine set of fake boobs, and beneath the jogging suit, a little extra padding over her ass and waist—a chunky girl trying to shed some extra pounds.

The knife was hidden.

But she encountered no one on this dark morning.

And the house was just ahead.

She ducked into the back alley and caught her breath, but her blood was pumping, as much as from anticipation as the short run.

Finally.

Counting slowly to ten, calming the excitement surging through her veins, she moved through the shadows.

Haylie couldn't sleep.

Probably because of the damned reunion and the closing of the school and the image of Ian that had started creeping into her dreams again. She'd thought she was over him, that she'd put all those painful thoughts about his death behind her.

It's not as if she'd pined for him for twenty years, she thought, sitting up and staring at the clock near her bed. She'd tried to move on. She really had.

She made a sound of disgust. Four-damned-thirty in the morning. An indecent time to be awake. She thought she heard a noise outside but dismissed it. Probably the cat. Or raccoons scavenging in the backyard, trying to get at the Japanese goldfish she kept in a small pond near the patio.

Pulling her pack of cigarettes from the bedside table, she then walked outside to her private back patio where, standing in the old T-shirt she used as a nightgown and her fuzzy bunny slippers, she lit up. No raccoons. The pond was undisturbed, water lilies lying softly on the surface, the fish safe for the night.

Good.

One less problem in a world filled with them.

A cool mist was falling, shrouding the night, and for an inexplicable reason, goose bumps rose on the back of her arms. She was jittery, had been for weeks or months or maybe even years. She lived in a small bungalow in Sellwood, a community in the southeast part of Portland. The house, small to begin with, had been divided into two tiny apartments. Recently the neighbors had moved, leaving the cat she'd reluctantly adopted and a For Rent sign out front.

The cat, a black longhair named Bo, was skulking through the garden now, slinking among the barren pots where petunias and impatiens had thrived in the summer. He'd never shown any interest in the fish, thank God.

"Come here, Bo," she said. "Kitty, kitty, kitty."

The cat turned and looked at her, standing beneath the porch light, his green eyes growing round, but he didn't budge. He was an outside cat and maybe she was lucky that he didn't want to be an inside one. This way she never had to mess with a litter box.

Closing her eyes for a second, she dragged deep on her cigarette, feeling the warm smoke curl and fill her lungs as the nicotine worked its way through her bloodstream.

She should give up the habit, but it wasn't as if she hadn't tried. She'd used the patch, the gum, and even hypnosis. Nothing had worked. Like it or not, she'd have to quit cold turkey.

Before her fortieth birthday.

In the meantime she enjoyed smoking and refused to feel like a criminal just because she liked the buzz. And now, with the reunion looming ahead, with meeting all those people she'd known in high school, with all the talk of Jake Marcott, Ian's face had again crept into her dreams. No way was she going to give up her pack-a-day habit yet!

Ian . . . she thought sadly. She wished she could get over him, give it up, but it was such a damned injustice. Jake Marcott had killed him, pure and simple. Why the cops and everyone who had graduated with her couldn't see it, she didn't understand. But Jake Marcott was not the saint everyone pretended he was. No way. He'd been a sinner in life. It was unfair that he'd become a martyr.

A soft footfall sounded.

Haylie twisted her head.

At this hour?

She looked at the fenced yard, but there was no one there, no one lurking in the shadows where the lamplight didn't touch. The traffic on the street was nonexistent at this hour, and it was even too early for those type-A joggers and bicyclers who were rabid in their need for exercise.

Probably nothing.

She took another drag and looked for the cat again, but he'd disappeared. "Bo?" She didn't want him to go anywhere near the street, though he did seem to have some brains when it came to avoiding cars and roads. "Kitty?"

Nothing.

Not even a sough of wind in the branches of the single pine tree in the yard.

"Fine, stay outside."

Another quiet scrape.

The hairs on the back of Haylie's neck lifted. "Bo?" she said anxiously, turning to go inside. What was it about this night that had her so anxious?

Hisssss!

The cat was at her feet, staring into the night, and Haylie's heart nearly stopped.

Damn it all to hell. She hadn't counted on the cat. Quickly, still hidden in the shadows, blond wig and extra padding left beneath the branches of a rhododendron, the killer slid her knife from its sheath. She didn't have any more time. She was lucky Haylie had stepped outside, unlucky that the cat had sensed her.

She crept forward as stealthily and quickly as the stupid feline who'd betrayed her.

"What is it?" Haylie asked nervously, taking one step toward the back door.

Too late.

Quick as lightning, a dark figure stepped from around the corner of the garage and sprang. A woman. Armed with a butcher knife.

Oh, shit! Haylie, dropping her cigarette, leaped toward the open door. She wasn't fast enough. The killer was on her in an instant.

*   *   *

"No way, bitch!"

Fear screamed through Haylie's body. "No! Don't!"

The knife gleamed in the pale light.

"Wait! Wait!" Haylie cried. The blade swung in an arc. Cutting downward, flashing in the lamp glow. Slicing through her skin.

Haylie tripped over her own feet. Tried to scream. It was cut off with another searing slice. Her own blood sprayed. She stumbled backward.

Oh, God, was this really happening?

The blade struck again, tearing into her flesh.

Pain exploded in her abdomen.

The killer stabbed again and all the rage, all the pent-up fury of twenty long years, screamed through her brain. *Die, you miserable, spoiled brat. Die! Die! Die!*

The blade came out of Haylie with a hideous sucking noise. The killer didn't wait. She plunged the knife into the crumpling body. Again and again, feeling the warm, wet spray of blood and the cold satisfaction that justice, at last, was served. At her hand.

But Haylie was only the first.

She felt the body shudder and let it fall onto the pavement.

Near-lifeless eyes looked up at her.

She stared down into the eyes of her victim.

Haylie was near death, but her lips formed an unspoken *"You?"*

And then the light in her eyes faded.

Haylie, the first, was dead.

Exhilaration sizzled through the killer's body as she worked quickly, unzipping and stripping out of her jogging suit. She stuffed it, along with her extra padding, wig, and knife, into the athletic bag. Now she was in skintight neoprene, which she covered with an oversized hiking parka that reached her knees. Her hair, still wound onto her head, was quickly disguised by a Mariners baseball cap. There was still some blood on her black running shoes, but she couldn't help that. She'd wash them at St. Elizabeth's in the gym and trash the clothes in an incinerator that was still used occasionally at the school. First things first. She had to make this look like a robbery gone bad.

She saw the cat hiding beneath an azalea and then she left, stomping out the still-smoldering cigarette and knowing that she'd sent Haylie Swanson's soul straight to hell.

Part Two

LINDSAY
by
Wendy Corsi Staub

Chapter 14

New York City, May 2006

"Mommy?"

Lindsay Farrell bolted from her bed, heart pounding wildly from the shrill middle-of-the-night ringing that had just startled her from a sound sleep. She gripped the phone tightly against her ear.

"Mommy . . . why did you do it?"

"Who is this?" she demanded, her heart pounding wildly. She strode blindly across the darkened bedroom, stubbing her toe painfully against the footboard of her queen-sized bed, barely noticing.

"It's me, Mommy." The voice was strange, high-pitched. It could belong to a child . . .

But he wouldn't be a child anymore, she reminded herself.

No, her son would be nineteen now—twenty this coming summer.

He was born right here in New York City, the week before she started her first semester at Fordham University in the Bronx. She'd attended her first day of classes with engorged breasts that throbbed painfully, and a heart that ached even worse.

"Why did you give me away, Mommy?"

"Stop calling me!"

Lindsay disconnected the call and tossed the cordless phone across the room. She heard it fall to the carpet with a dull thud.

It wouldn't be broken, though.

She'd thrown it even harder last night, against the wall, and she was certain it wouldn't work when she found it this morning.

She hoped it wouldn't . . . not that she honestly believed a broken telephone receiver would put an end to the eerie wee-hour phone calls. According to her Caller ID box, they were coming from a Private Name, Private Number. Pressing star-sixty-nine on the dial after the calls got her nowhere. Somehow, the number was completely blocked.

Meanwhile, she'd gotten a call just about every other night for the past week or so—always the same voice, always saying the same thing.

Why did you give me away, Mommy?

So somebody knew her secret.

Was it really that surprising?

Of course, she trusted the kindly nuns at Blessed Sacrament, the Queens home for unwed mothers, where she'd arrived that June just after high-school graduation and stayed until she had the baby.

And she trusted Sister Neva, the aging Reverend Mother at St. Elizabeth's, who'd arranged her referral to the home.

She'd confided her secret to no one else—even to this day.

Did she really believe she'd kept it that well hidden?

At the time, yes.

But in her muddled, distraught state—first because of the pregnancy, then because of Jake's shocking murder—she really couldn't be sure of anything.

Looking back, she recalled that she'd bought at least seven home-pregnancy-test kits when she first realized, just before that ill-fated Valentine's Day dance, that her period was late. She'd bought them at various drugstores and supermarkets, thinking that was wiser than returning to the same place over and over again. And she'd always attempted to camouflage her telltale purchase with several other items. Had she really thought the cashier wouldn't even notice a pregnancy test nestled among the packs of gum, magazines, panty hose?

Maybe. She was such a wreck back then, even before the tests confirmed her worst suspicion.

Afterward, she remembered trying to conceal her thickening waistline and swelling breasts beneath her ugly, ill-fitting school uniform in those last four months of school. She had always been slender; a few people—especially her mother—commented that she seemed to be "filling out." Aurora Zephyr even jokingly told her she'd better watch out that she didn't add the notorious "freshman fifteen" pounds when she got to college.

Had her friends been whispering about her escalating

weight—and speculating about the possible cause for the gain—behind her back?

Maybe. Probably. Her group of friends, always tight knit, seemed to splinter after Jake's death. Even Kristen and Rachel, her closest confidantes, became distant.

If that hadn't happened—if Jake hadn't been killed—Lindsay might have confided in them. She might even have told her parents, who would have been disappointed but probably would have stood by her and helped her hide her condition—if only to protect the family name.

But she didn't share her secret with her parents or her friends.

Instead, she miserably battled round-the-clock morning sickness on her own, hoping no one would overhear her daily vomiting sessions in the school bathroom.

When somebody eventually did, it was the last person with whom she would have expected to share such a scandalous confidence.

Perpetually patrolling the corridors in her black habit, leaning heavily on her wooden cane, the Reverend Mother was an intimidating figure. Never more so than the day Lindsay emerged from a bathroom stall to find Sister Neva standing there, expressionless, obviously having heard every last gag and retch.

"Are you sick, child?" she asked, fixing Lindsay with a level stare.

Lindsay started to stutter, then burst into tears.

To her shock, Sister Neva folded her into a firm embrace—more bolstering than affectionate, but it was what Lindsay needed in that moment.

She found herself being led to the inner sanctum: the Reverend Mother's office, furnished only with an austere desk, guest chair, file cabinet, and of course the ubiquitous crucifix on the wall.

There, Lindsay confessed her greatest sin—and was met not with disapproval, but stoic support.

With resignation, the aging nun agreed not to tell Lindsay's parents, on the condition that Lindsay allow her to make arrangements for the baby to be delivered—and adopted—on the East Coast.

There was no question, ever, that she was going to have the baby. She was a devout Catholic.

But Sister Neva stepped in and took all-encompassing control of the situation as if it were her own personal mission to ensure that there would be no other option. She was determined to propel

Lindsay through the pregnancy until the baby was safely delivered to deserving Catholic parents.

Until she arrived on the scene, Lindsay hadn't given much thought to what would happen after she gave birth.

Which seemed hard to believe now, from an adult perspective. As a high-powered Manhattan event planner, her entire career was based on intricate short- and long-term calendar organization.

But back then, she was more concerned with the immediate future—her own—than the long-range repercussions of her condition on herself or anyone else. Even the baby.

So it was a relief to defer that monumental decision to somebody with infinitely more wisdom and connections. The nun cleverly arranged for her to take a summer class at Fordham University so that her parents wouldn't question her early departure for college. Not that they would have anyway, after all she had been through.

They tiptoed around her for months after Jake died, attributing her withdrawn behavior entirely to the fact that her longtime boyfriend had been brutally slain and she had found his body.

They seemed relieved when Lindsay announced she was leaving two months early for college, and they didn't bat an eye when she said the campus dorms were unavailable until the fall semester. No, they never suspected that her temporary summer address was a diocesan-run home for unwed mothers.

Lindsay left the details in Sister Neva's capable hands without a second thought . . . until it came time to hand over her son to the waiting adoption official.

That was her first moment of regret—and far from her last.

But by then, it was too late.

In a matter of seconds, the baby was gone, whisked from her life and into another, presumably with a pair of loving parents, a stable home, and a brighter future than an unwed, unemployed college freshman could provide.

She went on to get her undergraduate degree at Fordham and her MBA at Columbia.

In the two decades that followed, not a day had gone by without Lindsay wondering about her lost son. Wondering what he was doing, where he was, who he was. Every time she passed a boy about his age on the street, she did a double take—especially if the boy happened to have dark hair and eyes like her own . . . and like the father's.

The father.

She had long since taken to thinking of him that way, ever since the nuns in the home first questioned her about him that summer.

"Have you told the father, child?"

"No. He . . . died before I could tell him."

It was easier that way, she told herself and God, asking forgiveness for the lie.

She alone signed the adoption papers. She alone suffered the barren consequences that lingered for years, lingered even now.

Especially now.

Thanks to those unsettling phone calls.

Obviously, somebody had stumbled onto the truth and wanted to torment her now, just when her life felt settled at last.

But who would do such a thing?

Chuckling softly to herself, she hung up the telephone, pleased with Lindsay Farrell's frightened reaction to her taunts.

I bet you thought nobody knew what you did, she silently told her former classmate, picturing her, alone and scared, in her far-off East Coast apartment. *You tried so hard to hide your tracks.*

Or so Lindsay Farrell must have believed.

She'd had no way of knowing that her every move was being watched. That someone had stealthily followed her up and down the aisles of the drugstore, watching her furtively pluck a pregnancy test from the shelf. Her forced nonchalance was laughable. She did everything but roll her eyes skyward and whistle tunelessly as the cashier rang up her purchases.

Of course, I couldn't follow her into her bathroom back at home and watch her take the test . . .

No, but it didn't take a genius to figure out the results. Not when she proceeded to buy test after test in the days that followed, as if hoping to convince herself that the first one was wrong.

So. Lindsay Farrell was pregnant with Jake Marcott's baby.

Whether Jake carried that news to his grave or was oblivious to it was unclear.

What was clear was that to this day, Lindsay remained troubled by what she did.

I can hear it in her voice.

I just wish I could see it in her eyes, too.

But it wouldn't be long now.

The reunion was less than two months away.

Lindsay would be winging her way back to Portland, unaware that her first trip home in twenty years would be her last.

Unless . . .

What if she isn't planning to attend the reunion at all?

That would be a shame.

No, it would be more than just a shame. It would be disastrous.

I'll just have to give her a good reason to come home.

Phone still in hand, she quickly dialed general nationwide directory assistance.

"Yes, I'd like the number for United Airlines, please."

Settling her head against the pillows once more, Lindsay inhaled, held her breath for as long as she could, then exhaled, the way she did when she was stretching and winding down from her strenuous Saturday morning spinning class.

Right now, though, her pulse was racing faster than it ever had at the gym.

Maybe I should call the police, she speculated . . . and quickly discarded the thought.

The NYPD had far bigger concerns. Terrorism, gridlock, a masked rapist who had been attacking women on the Upper East Side. They'd probably laugh at her if she approached them about a couple of prank phone calls.

It wasn't as though she'd been harmed.

Not physically, anyway.

Emotionally . . .

Well, that was a different story. But she'd survive. She always did.

She did better than survive, actually.

Look at me now, Nana, she would think every time she achieved another milestone. Her undergrad degree, her master's, her first entry-level job, her first promotion, the launch of her own business . . .

Look at me now.

Her grandmother would have been proud of her. She owned a spacious—for Manhattan, anyway—one-bedroom co-op on the East Side, with a terrace. She had furnished the apartment with a mix of custom-made pieces and antiques handed down from Nana herself. She had even recently enrolled in a cooking class so that she could become proficient in the kitchen; her own family had always relied on their personal chef.

Plus, she was single-handedly running Lindsay Farrell Events as efficiently as her widowed grandmother used to run Farrell Timber.

Of course, Nana had help from Lindsay's father, Craig, and his brother, Andrew. If you could call it that. The brothers never got along. They couldn't even agree where their mother should be buried when she passed away, back when Lindsay was in high school.

Grandpa had been cremated, his ashes scattered over the timber farm. Nana didn't want that. She was a devout Catholic; she wanted to be buried beneath a granite cross on sacred ground. But the cemetery that adjoined Saint Michael's, her home parish well east of Portland, was too close to the Columbia River. There were old wives' tales of caskets being lowered into watery graves. Dad was vehemently opposed to that.

Uncle Andrew was just as opposed to Nana being buried right in the West Hills, at St. Elizabeth's cemetery. He reasoned that Nana's ties to that church were too recent; she'd only started attending when she moved in with Lindsay and her family, too infirm to care for herself any longer.

In the end, Dad, the elder sibling, won out. He usually did.

Lindsay was pleased. She'd visited her grandmother's grave often—until she left St. Elizabeth's, and Portland, for good.

Now, her mother had told her the last time they talked, the old school and church were about to be razed. The news was unsettling.

"What's going to happen to Nana's grave?"

"I imagine the cemetery will stay intact," her mother said vaguely and changed the subject to yet another investment property she and Lindsay's father were purchasing in Nevada, where they'd moved after retirement.

Lindsay hung up troubled by the thought of the familiar old red-brick school—her alma mater—being destroyed.

Ironic, since her lingering memories of the place were less than positive.

It was there, in the garden labyrinth that lay between the school and the cemetery, that she had discovered Jake Marcott's body, pinned to a tree by a crossbow.

The macabre sight had haunted her ever since . . .

Among other grim memories.

I should be glad that St. Elizabeth's will be closed down, she told herself now. *Maybe that will bring some closure.*

For Jake's horrific death, and for her own persistent maternal ache.

Except . . .

Somebody knew her secret.

Probably somebody from her past who had resurfaced to taunt her in the middle of the night.

It was just a cruel prank.

Now, remembering that Jake's murder had never been solved, she couldn't help but hope, with a shudder, that that was all there was to it.

The arrangements had been made. She was going to New York the day after tomorrow, staying in a hotel on the East Side. Not fancy, but you'd have to be a multimillionaire to afford a fancy hotel in Manhattan for as long as she'd need to be there.

The best part: she had cleverly selected one of those all-suite hotels that catered to business executives who needed to stick around New York for more than a couple of nights. Nobody would question her ongoing presence—a single woman alone in a big city. They'd just think she was there on business.

And I will be.

Important business.

She smiled to herself.

And she kept picking her way through the basement of St. Elizabeth's school, guided by her lighter's flickering beam to the secret supply closet.

After twirling the lock, she slipped inside and closed the door after her—as though it were necessary. As though anyone in their right mind would want to be down here . . .

Anyone other than me.

Then again, some people might think *she* wasn't in her right mind. But they didn't know what Jake—yes, Jake, and the others—had put her through. Nobody knew.

That was why nobody would ever suspect her when this was over and her mission was accomplished.

She lit the lantern's wick and surveyed her handiwork: the reconstructed row of lockers that had once lined the wide corridor a few stories above.

Tonight, she bypassed Kristen's and paused only briefly at Haylie's, with its newest relic added just the other night: that ridiculous black armband she used to wear in ongoing mourning over Ian's death.

What an unexpected bonus it had been to find it tucked into

her jewelry box right on her dresser. She'd discovered it while ransacking the apartment, trying to make it seem as though the murder had been triggered by an interrupted burglary. She took her wallet, some jewelry, and a couple of stock certificates.

Passing Louie Blake, a nefarious local junkie, slumbering on the sidewalk not far from Haylie's apartment, she was struck by inspiration. She tucked the wallet, jewelry, and stock certificates in among his belongings heaped in a shopping cart.

The armband, she kept, of course—and spirited it right over to its place of honor in Haylie's old locker.

Haylie really was a sicko to have saved it for all these years.

But now it belongs to me.

Along with everything else assembled here.

She opened locker 123—Lindsay Farrell's.

The contents were meager, so far. Taped to the door, in an attempt to reconstruct its senior-year state, were dozens of pictures of Jake, surrounded by shiny red paper hearts. There were also a couple of textbooks on the shelves.

On a hook, however, was a prized item: the sleeveless ice blue dress Lindsay had worn to the Valentine's Day dance that night. Lindsay's mother went through the family's closets every season and donated a whole load of clothes to a secondhand shop run by a charitable organization.

The spring after Jake's murder, the ice blue dress was among them, as she had prayed it might be.

What a thrill it was to spot it hanging there on a rack amid designer dresses worn once, if at all, by Portland's elite, then cast off without a backward glance.

It had obviously been cleaned after that night. Yet if she looked closely, she could still see the faintest remnants of a stain in the satiny folds of the skirt.

A bloodstain.

It made her giddy just to look at it, to remember Lindsay covered in blood.

Somebody else's blood, that night.

But soon enough, it would be her own.

The dress was a find, and a steal . . .

And I didn't even have to steal it.

She would have, though. Just as she had stolen—and would continue to steal—all those mementos from the others.

This shrine was a work in progress. She planned to have it

completed before the wrecking ball swung into the brick wall of the old school this summer.

It seemed fitting that these forgotten relics be buried deep in the underground rubble . . .

Just as their owners would, by then, also be buried.

Dead and buried.

But forgotten?

She doubted it. But she sure as hell was going to try to forget all that could never be forgiven.

Chapter 15

"Lindsay Farrell," she said into the phone, her eyes still on the report in her hand.

"Lindsay?"

"Yes?" Then she recognized the voice and set the report aside, surprised to hear from him.

"It's Isaac."

"Isaac! How've you been?" she asked her ex-boyfriend—the man she had honestly thought, if only fleetingly, might be The One.

Yes, he had baggage . . . who didn't?

Yes, he was a couple of years younger than she was . . . who cared?

Not Lindsay. Not at first, anyway.

Isaac Halpern's dark, brooding good looks blinded her to the fact that he wasn't ready for a serious relationship.

Or maybe it was more that his dark, brooding good looks reminded her of someone else.

Someone she still wasn't over, even after all these years.

Someone who'd never even known that she was truly in love with him . . .

Because she'd never realized it herself.

Not back then. Not until it was too late. For them. For a lot of things.

But that was ancient history.

Isaac was more recent—but history nonetheless.

"I miss you," he said simply.

She hesitated. "I miss you, too."

It was true.

She did miss him. But nowhere near as much as she missed his predecessor, who showed her that phrases like *weak in the knees* and *butterflies in the stomach* were rooted not just in the romantic novels she liked to read, but in reality.

Weak knees, butterflies, a pounding heart, a light head . . . those were all things she experienced when she was with *him*.

But she never felt those things with Isaac.

Not with anyone else, ever.

Still, she couldn't help hoping that maybe someone would eventually come along to make her forget *him*. Yes, maybe someday she'd fall in love again, get married, have a baby . . .

Another baby.

One she'd get to keep, raise, love.

But I loved you, too, she silently told the son she hadn't seen since the day he was born. *It sounds crazy, but I really did love you. No, I really do love you. Still. You, and your father.*

The father.

"I thought maybe we could meet for a drink some night after work," Isaac was saying in her ear.

"Why?" It came out more sharply than she intended. "I mean, you know nothing can come of it, right?"

"Right. I know." He hesitated. "I'm with somebody else now, Lindsay."

Her breath caught in her throat. For a moment, she couldn't find her voice. When she did, she couldn't complete a coherent sentence anyway.

"It isn't . . . she isn't . . . you didn't find . . ."

"No. It isn't Rachel. Her name is Kylah."

"Does she know?"

"About Rachel?"

"Yes."

Rachel. The woman who haunted Isaac Halpern the way her baby's father haunted Lindsay. If anyone could understand how that felt, it was Lindsay.

That was why she'd left him. Because she understood. Because she didn't want to settle for second place in his heart . . . even though she was willing to give him second place in her own.

"No," Isaac said heavily. "She doesn't know about Rachel."

"You should tell her."

"Why? So that she can leave me, like you did?"

"Isaac—"

"Look, I don't blame you, Lindsay. Nobody wants to compete with my long-lost first love."

And that, Lindsay thought, was precisely the reason she herself might never meet someone and get married after all. Because she couldn't let go of her long-lost first love. She didn't *want* to let go.

"Sorry," Isaac said, shifting gears, "this was a bad idea. I just thought maybe we could still be friends, like you said."

That's right, she had. Wasn't it what you said when you broke up with someone?

Let's still be friends.

Along with those other old standbys, *There's nobody else* and *It's not you, it's me.*

She'd used all of those lines, many times, with different men, in her adult life.

But she'd never had a chance to say those lines to *him,* twenty years ago—even if she had been so inclined.

To *him,* she'd said nothing at all.

She'd just pretended it never happened, and so had he.

And nobody ever knew there had been something between them that rainy long-ago New Year's Eve, or that Lindsay had borne his child the following summer.

Mommy . . . why did you give me away?

No. She was wrong.

Somebody knew about the baby.

That meant they might know about him, as well.

Maybe it was time for her to revisit the past after all, before her closet doors opened wide and all her skeletons came tumbling out.

"Lindsay?" Isaac said, startling her back to the present. "I'll let you go. I'm sorry I bothered you at work. I just wanted to touch base."

"I'm glad you did. And . . . I'd love to have a drink some night after work. You know, just to catch up. Okay?"

"Okay." He sounded surprised. "How about, um, next Tuesday?"

"I can't . . . I have a cooking class Tuesday nights."

"Cooking?"

She could hear the smile in his voice. He knew she was useless in the kitchen.

"I thought I should learn."

"Good for you. How are you doing so far?"

"Great." She felt obligated to add, "Then again, we're still on prep work—you know, easy stuff like chopping and dicing. But I'm an ace with a Bermuda onion, let me tell you."

He laughed. "Your Nana would be proud. All right, then . . . if you can't do Tuesday, how about a week from this Thursday?"

She faltered. She really didn't want to put something on the calendar.

Then again, she was free that night, and Isaac always could smell an excuse from a mile away.

"Sure," she told him reluctantly, and entered it into her on-line calendar before hanging up the phone.

She could certainly use all the friends she could get these days. Jillian, her longtime across-the-hall neighbor, had relocated to an uptown co-op. Terri and Amanda, her former happy-hour pals, had both married and moved to the suburbs, like most of the other friends she had known along the way.

New York was becoming a lonely place for Lindsay. Sometimes, she found it hard to believe she'd lived here longer now than she had ever lived in Portland.

For some reason, that still seemed like home.

And she suspected that perhaps this never would.

If it was this challenging to get into Lindsay's office suite, it was going to be even more challenging to get into her apartment.

Challenging . . . but not impossible. And she had always liked a challenge.

She knew that New Yorkers couldn't be counted on to hide keys outside their doors. They were much too savvy for that.

But I have a good plan. Not foolproof, but so far it's working, she congratulated herself now, nearing the end of phase one.

Lindsay's assistant was easily distracted by a muscular bike messenger who kept her flirtatiously occupied at the front desk. He had his price, of course—everyone did—and it was a steep one. But he didn't ask questions.

That was the great thing about New York City, as opposed to Portland. People here might not hide their keys in plain sight, but they definitely paid less attention to others. They tended to mind their own business. Yes, they were wary about the usual urban threats—muggers, speeding cabs—but they never really looked strangers in the eye. That went with the territory.

Busy with the messenger, Kara never even noticed the intruder slipping past the front desk, making her way down the short corridor beyond.

There were three offices in the suite. In one, a young man tapped away at a computer keyboard, oblivious to anyone passing by. The next was empty. There was a light on in the third and largest office, and Lindsay's name was on the door.

There was an office machine alcove across from it. The overhead light wasn't on and the machines were off, as if they were rarely used.

Perfect. She ducked behind a copier and waited for Lindsay to leave her desk.

Twenty minutes later, her patience paid off.

Lindsay didn't have her purse in hand when she walked quickly down the hall toward the ladies' room.

Turned out she left it on a hook behind the door of her office.

I was counting on that.

She was also counting on Lindsay's keys being inside. She reached in and felt around for them . . .

Bingo.

It took her less than ten minutes to slip back out of the suite, have copies made at the hardware store down the avenue, and return.

By then, the messenger was gone.

Kara looked up from the desk when she appeared.

"Hi—I just found this by the elevator on this floor," she said, handing over the silver Tiffany key ring, which was, fortuitously, engraved. "Someone must have dropped these. The initials are LF. Are they yours?"

"No, but they're my boss's. Those must be hers. Thanks so much. I'll give them to her."

That was it. Easy-breezy.

From there, she headed over to Lindsay's East Fifty-Fourth Street high-rise building, where she was hoping the doorman would be willing to look the other way, for a price.

Of course, he would have to be used to it. She had done her homework and was aware that the building happened to be home to J. T. Maguire, the former lead singer of a boy band, now hugely famous as a solo artist.

Groupies and paparazzi frequently staked out the place, hoping for a glimpse.

She approached the doorman, a bored-looking young man with a thin black mustache.

When she furtively told him what she wanted, he didn't even seem suspicious that a thirtysomething woman was interested in J. T. Maguire.

Why would he be? She'd read that white-haired old ladies dropped off their panties for the twenty-year-old heartthrob.

The doorman pocketed her wad of bills and motioned her to go ahead into the deserted lobby.

"Thanks," she called belatedly over her shoulder.

"No problem."

Not for you, she thought gleefully. *And not for J. T. Maguire, either.*

But Lindsay Farrell? She was about to have a big, big problem on her hands . . .

Returning from a twenty-minute conference in her assistant Ray's office next door, Lindsay stopped short in the doorway of her office.

That was strange—there were her keys, sitting right in the open on her desk.

How had they gotten there? She could have sworn she had put them back into her purse, same as always, when she unlocked her office door earlier . . .

But then, she'd been a little bleary-eyed this morning, thanks to yet another wee-hour phone call last night. It was the same high-pitched childlike voice that didn't belong to a child. It kept calling her Mommy, asking her why she'd given him away.

She'd finally slammed down the phone in tears, and she hadn't slept another wink.

"Lindsay?"

"Yes?"

She looked up to see Kara, her recent hire, standing in the doorway of her office.

Slender and attractive, she had so far proven herself to be less interested in her entry-level administrative duties than she was in taking long lunch breaks and flirting with the newlywed Ray, with the computer-repair technician, and even, just this morning, with a bike messenger.

Oh, well. It was May. A whole new crop of college grads would be sending out resumes. It shouldn't be hard to find another entry-level assistant when Kara inevitably was fired or quit.

"The mail just came."

"Thanks, Kara." Lindsay accepted the stack and flipped

through it briefly: several bills on top in white legal envelopes, a couple of trade publications and promo catalogs tucked beneath them, and a large manila envelope on the bottom. "Did you remember to book the Gramercy Room at the Peninsula for the banquet in October?"

Kara slapped a hand against her red-lipsticked mouth. "I knew I forgot something. I'll do it right away. It was for the ninth, right?"

"The twelfth."

"Oh, right. The twelfth. Gotcha."

Lindsay sank into her chair and sighed as her assistant scurried from the office. She swiveled away from the desk, the stack of mail in her lap.

The plate-glass window was spattered with raindrops, and the sky beyond it, above a monochromatic skyline, was a milky shade of gray. This kind of weather never failed to remind her of home.

Home being the Pacific Northwest, where rainy, overcast days were as prevalent as honking yellow taxicabs were here. Not just in midspring, but much of the year.

I have to stop dwelling on Portland today, she scolded herself. It only reminded her of things she should be trying to forget.

Seeking a distraction, she flipped through the mail again, coming to rest on the large manila envelope on the bottom.

So much for a distraction.

The return address was in Portland, and the name above it was a familiar one.

Kristen Delmonico.

Formerly known as Kristen Daniels.

Formerly known as Lindsay's *BFF*, as they used to call each other, along with Rachel Alsace.

Best Friends Forever.

Other than Christmas cards that arrived every December with all the regularity—and scintillating detail—of her exterminator's yearly retainer bill, Lindsay never heard from Kristen.

So why now?

With slightly trembling fingers, Lindsay reached for a letter opener and slit the envelope open.

Inside was a thick packet of folded papers.

Oh.

The class reunion.

Twenty years.

Aurora had already contacted her about it, leaving a message asking if she wanted to be involved in the planning. Of course, she'd said no—via a return message, glad she didn't actually get Aurora on the phone, knowing how persuasive she always could be.

Lindsay verbally blamed her lack of involvement on the fact that she was a continent away. But truly, she simply wasn't interested in revisiting the past. There were too many painful things about it.

Now, however, scanning the invitation and the accompanying forms, including a chatty letter from Kristen, Lindsay found herself smiling.

All right, so there were a few good memories, too.

Hmm.

She was almost feeling tempted to consider making a reservation . . . despite serious doubts. It might be nice, after all, to see all those girls again. To catch up, to say good-bye to the old school building, to lay the past to rest at last.

Yes, maybe she should go.

She scanned the reservation form and the update questionnaire. There was also a brochure from a new Marriott Residence Inn that had gone up not far from their alma mater, apparently on the site of the strip mall where she and her friends used to shop before getting pizza at Ricardo's nearby.

So the old neighborhood was changing. She wondered if the old pizzeria was still there, with its red plastic booths where they had all hung out. Maybe it was gone, like the strip mall, and some new hotel or chain restaurant had been built in its place.

Who knew what would stand, a few years from now, on the site of St. Elizabeth's school?

This is your last chance to go back, she told herself.

Maybe she really would . . .

Then she flipped back to the invitation and saw that the reunion wasn't just for St. Elizabeth's alumnae. The Western Catholic grads would be there, too.

Jake had gone to Western Catholic. If he were alive, he'd be at the reunion.

She ran down a mental list of his friends, wondering if they'd show. Dean McMichaels, Nick Monticello, Craig Taylor, Chad Belmont . . .

It would be a kick to see those guys again . . . some of them, anyway.

Maybe you should go, then.

People would expect her to be there.

Once upon a time, she'd had a hand in everything that went on at St. Elizabeth's. Once upon a time, she'd been voted the girl most likely to succeed. It was a narrow contest, between her and Kristen.

Lindsay won that one.

Kristen, however, was valedictorian. And that was more important than any silly senior superlative contest.

Lindsay found herself wondering what her old friend was doing these days. She'd heard sketchy details over the years—Kristen was working as a reporter at the *Portland Clarion*, had married her college sweetheart, had a child. She always signed her Christmas cards—generic, store-bought ones—*Love, Kristen, Ross, and Lissa.* She never even bothered to write a note.

Lindsay always tried to do that, at least. And it was a time-consuming process. She ordered her elegant holiday greetings by the hundreds, imprinted with her name, and sent them to all her family, clients, and old friends.

Yet other than once a year, she had been lousy at keeping in touch with Kristen and the others, despite their tearful promises made at graduation.

Maybe it's time to go back, Lindsay told herself, flipping through the papers again, looking for contact information for someone on the reunion committee.

Then she saw it.

The photograph was a familiar one.

A copy of it still sat, in an eight-by-ten frame, on the bookshelf in her parents' Nevada condo.

This version was smaller, and glossy instead of an elegant matte finish, but there she was: carefree seventeen-year-old Lindsay Farrell, beaming at the camera, blissfully unaware that just months after the photographer snapped his shot, her life would turn upside down.

But this reproduction of her senior portrait now seemed to bear chillingly symbolic testimony to troubles yet to come: her face was marked, from her right temple to the dimple on her lower left cheek, with an angry red slash.

Chapter 16

"How do you think you did?"

"Hmm?" Leo Cellamino looked up to see an attractive green-eyed redhead smiling at him. Her name was Sarah Ann, or Sarah Rose—something like that. She'd been sitting in front of him in biology lab all semester, smiling shyly in his direction every once in a while.

Now she'd fallen into step with him on the way out of the lecture hall where they'd just completed their final exam.

Ordinarily, Leo would welcome the attention from a pretty girl, but today, his mind was far away from this Queens college campus. All he wanted to do was get back home to his computer and take another look at that e-mail he'd received late last night.

What if it was no longer saved in his in-box? What if it had somehow evaporated into cyberspace overnight?

I should have printed it out, he thought, frustrated. But at the time, shaken by what he had just read—and seen—he didn't dare.

He was afraid his kid brother, Mario, would somehow get his hands on it. Most of Leo's stuff wound up in his brother's clutches at some point. That was what you got when you shared a room with a nosy twelve-year-old.

But Leo couldn't afford to move out of their mother's house. Not if he wanted to complete his college education and make a decent life for himself someday. Anyway, Ma needed him around; he was the man of the house now that Pop had taken off for good.

"Leo . . . ? It's Leo, isn't it?"

Startled, he looked up and realized that the girl—*Sarah Rose, that's it*—was still walking along beside him.

"Oh . . . right, it's Leo." He flashed her a brief smile, ever the gentleman, as his mother had taught him.

"How'd you do on the exam?" she asked again.

"All right, I guess. How about you?"

"I don't know . . . I'm not very good at science. And all that genetics stuff was confusing, don't you think? Dominant genes, recessive genes . . ." She shook her head.

Confusing? Ha.

Leo could tell her a thing or two about confusing genetics, if he wanted to.

But he didn't.

It was none of her business that he had grown up the dark-haired, dark-eyed son of blue-eyed, sandy-haired parents of Sicilian decent. That they let him believe he was their biological child until he encountered his first Punnett square in high-school science.

It wasn't until then that he stumbled across a startling scientific fact: two blue-eyed people couldn't possibly have a dark-eyed child.

When he confronted his parents with his puzzling find, he half expected them to say that Mr. Davidson, his biology teacher, was wrong. Heck, he expected them to confirm that Gregor Mendel, the father of human genetics, was wrong.

Instead, they told him that he, Leonardo Anthony Cellamino of Queens Boulevard, wasn't who he thought he was.

He had been adopted as an infant, his mother—not really his mother—told him tearfully, rosary beads tightly clenched in her hand for strength to get through the conversation.

"The doctors had told us we couldn't have children," she sobbed. "We were heartbroken."

"What about Mario, then? How'd you have him?" Leo knew his brother wasn't adopted; he remembered his mother's pregnancy, remembered comforting her through her labor pains while his aunt Nita tried to track down his father, who was MIA as usual.

"We never expected Mario to come along. It was some kind of fluke."

"*Fluke*?" Leo's father—not really his father—bellowed. "You call our son a fluke?"

Our son.

In that moment, Leo realized it wasn't just his imagination that his father always favored his kid brother. That was because Mario was his biological son. Leo was not.

"He was a miracle," Betty Cellamino amended. "Not a fluke. We thought God sent us another baby to save our marriage."

That was pretty funny, in retrospect.

His parents—not really his parents—were divorced not long after Leo graduated from high school. He turned eighteen just in time to become the man of the house, and his father took off for Miami or Fort Lauderdale—somewhere down on Florida's southern Atlantic coast. Leo didn't know exactly where Anthony Cellamino was now and he didn't care; he had no intention of ever seeing him again.

But Ma still cried and prayed every night for his return.

And Mario still called him on the sly—mostly asking for money, Leo supposed. Sometimes Pop sent some cash in an envelope addressed to Mario alone.

Leo tried not to let that bother him. Just like he had tried, for the past few years, not to let the truth about his birth bother him.

But it often nagged at him, like an itchy, aging scab that was still firmly rooted on one edge, and that if touched, would rip open and bleed all over again.

So Leo tried to leave it alone.

That had worked, for the most part . . . until last night.

The e-mail, with the provocative subject line *birth parents*, came from an AOL screen name he didn't recognize: *cupid21486*.

Leo opened it after a moment's hesitation, thinking it was probably spam and wondering why he was bothering.

> *I have information about your birth parents. If you're interested in finding them, please reply to this e-mail.*

He'd still have thought it was some kind of hoax, except for one thing: a jpeg file was attached. He worried just briefly that it might contain a virus. Then temptation outweighed common sense and he opened it anyway.

He found himself looking at a photograph.

It was a professionally snapped portrait of a beautiful dark-haired girl who appeared to be about Leo's age now, maybe a little younger. He could tell by her dated clothing and hairstyle that the photo had been taken years ago.

With her coloring, her delicate bone structure, and that distinct dimple in her lower left cheek, she bore such a striking resemblance to Leo himself that she could only be a blood relative.

My mother?
He had replied to the e-mail, of course.

Thank you for sending the picture. I'm very interested in finding my biological mother and father and I would appreciate any information you might have.

That was late last night.
As of this morning before he left for campus, there had been no reply. But he quickened his pace instinctively now, eager to get back home to his computer.
Sarah Rose kept up with him. "Are you done for the day?"
"With exams, you mean? Yeah."
"Do you want to grab a cup of coffee or something, then?"
"I can't."
He said it hastily, harshly, almost—and instantly regretted it when he saw the hurt expression on her face.
"I have to be somewhere," he explained, softening his tone. "Maybe some other time."
"Really?"
"Sure. Give me your number. I'll call you."
She did give it to him . . . but her expression told him that she doubted he'd dial it.
He doubted it, too.
Then again . . . he did give her his number when she asked for it.
After all, he and his high-school girlfriend, Elisa, had been broken up for months now—ever since she came home from St. Bonaventure over Christmas break and told him she wanted to see other people.
Which meant she was already seeing other people. More specifically, one other person, Leo suspected.
Turned out he was right.
Oh, well. He and Elisa were mostly a comfortable old habit by that time, anyway. Moving on was the right thing to do.
As for pretty, red-haired, green-eyed Sarah Rose . . .
Maybe he'd call. Maybe he wouldn't.
Right now, the only woman on his mind had dark hair and eyes and a dimple to match his own.
"See you," he told Sarah Rose and hurried toward the subway, unaware that he was being watched from the shadows beside a campus bus shelter.

*   *   *

"Kristen?"

"No . . . this is her daughter."

"Oh. May I please speak to Kristen?" Lindsay held her breath, hoping her old friend was at home. It was around noon in Portland. She had tried the work number first, at the newspaper, only to get her voicemail. She hung up. She couldn't just leave a message after twenty years.

You did when you called Aurora back, she reminded herself.

But that was different. She couldn't leave a message about something like this.

"Who's calling, please?" asked the teenaged voice on the other end of the line, sounding polite, efficient, and bubbly—very much like her mother had twenty years ago.

"It's an old friend . . . about the reunion."

"Okay, hang on," the voice said politely. There was a clatter, then a bluntly bellowed, "Mom! Phone!"

Lindsay would have smiled if she weren't still so shaken by the doctored photograph in her hand.

"Hello?" The voice that came on the line was a decidedly grown-up version of the one that had just left it.

"Kristen?"

"Yes . . . ?"

"It's Lindsay."

There was a gasp on the other end. "Oh my God. I was going to call you later."

Yeah, sure you were, Lindsay found herself thinking reflexively. She'd heard that before, senior year, when they were both trying halfheartedly to cling to a doomed friendship, pretending they still cared about each other, that they were still making an effort.

Then she reminded herself that this wasn't high school anymore. Kristen was no longer holding a grudge against her over Jake . . . she couldn't be.

Really? Then why did she disfigure your picture?

Lindsay told herself, yet again, that it had to be some kind of accident. Kristen couldn't possibly be that immature even if she hadn't gotten over Jake.

Maybe somebody had spilled some red nail polish on Lindsay's photo, or . . .

Something.

That was why Lindsay had decided to call her old—perhaps

former—friend. To find out what was up. To reassure herself that there was nothing sinister behind the red slash.

"Listen," she began, "I just got the reunion invitation, and for some reason my picture was—"

"You heard about Haylie, right?" Kristen asked simultaneously.

"What?" they both said, after a brief, startled pause.

"Lindsay . . . your picture was . . . what were you about to tell me?"

"There was a red mark slashed through it."

"Across the face, right? I didn't do it," Kristen said in a rush.

"The envelope had your name on the return address."

"I know, I put the packets together, but the picture didn't come from me. Somebody tampered with the envelopes and put them in. We all got them."

"All . . . who?"

"Me, you, Rachel, Bella, Aurora, Mandy . . . and Haylie."

All our old friends, Lindsay thought incredulously. What was going on?

When she asked Kristen, she said, "We think Haylie sent them. She had just lashed out at all of us at the last reunion meeting."

"Why?"

"Same old thing. Ian. Jake."

"Still?"

"Some things never change, apparently. She was still a real nutcase."

"Did you guys confront her and ask her if she sent those pictures, then?"

"We would have if she hadn't—"

"What?" Lindsay prodded when Kristen cut herself off.

There was a pause. "So you don't know?"

"Know what?"

"Haylie's dead, Lindsay."

She gasped.

Somehow, even now, with years and miles separating her from her old life, her old friends, she was sickened, shocked, at the untimely demise of the girl she once knew. "How . . . when did it happen?"

"I don't know exactly when, but the police think it's been a couple of days at least. She, uh, lived alone, except for a bunch of cats, so nobody found her right away. One of the neighbors noticed a smell . . ."

"Oh my God."

"I know. It's horrible. Lindsay, I'm scared."

"You're . . . scared? Because Haylie died?"

"She didn't just *die*. She was murdered—"

"*What?*"

"—and the police don't know who did it."

Murdered. Just like Jake. Lindsay's thoughts whirled madly as Kristen's shocking words sunk in. *Somebody killed Haylie? And got away with it?*

And now somebody is calling me in the middle of the night, and sending me pictures with my face crossed out . . .

"They think it might have been a random thing." Kristen's voice broke through her frantic thoughts. "It wasn't the greatest neighborhood, and her apartment had been burglarized . . ."

"But you don't think so?"

"I . . . I don't know."

Lindsay pondered that.

"Listen," Kristen said briskly, "you're not home, are you?"

"No, I'm in New York," she replied, before she realized that New York was supposed to be home.

But Kristen was talking about Portland, as if she sensed how Lindsay felt about it even now, after all these years. Home. Portland was home.

"Good. You still live there, right?" When Lindsay murmured an affirmative, Kristen said, "You should stay put, then, Lindsay. Just in case you were thinking of coming back for any reason."

"I was going to come to the reunion."

"It's not until July. Hopefully by then the police will have figured out what's going on with Haylie's death. But if I were you, I'd stay as far away from Portland as possible until they find out who did it. I'm not even living at home right now. I'm too scared someone will come after me next."

"Then . . . what are you doing there now?"

"We just happened to be here packing up some more stuff because there's no telling how long we'll have to be away."

"Where are you staying?"

"I'm at—" Kristen broke off suddenly.

Then she said, her voice laced with trepidation, "I'm afraid to say over the phone. It might be tapped or something."

"You're not serious . . . are you?"

"Yes, I'm serious. Listen, somebody broke into my house and my car, stole some of my old stuff, and tampered with those reunion invitations . . ."

"I thought you said it was Haylie."

"I'm pretty positive it must have been. But . . . well, what if it wasn't?"

Lindsay shuddered with renewed consternation about those wee-hour phone calls she'd been getting.

"I guess with Haylie gone, we might never know for sure who sent the pictures," she said slowly.

But she did know that the phone calls couldn't have come from her. Not if she had been dead for several days.

"I should go. Somebody's at the door. But listen, Lindsay, if you need to reach me, just try me at work or use the e-mail address on the reunion invitation."

"But . . . what should I do about the picture? Do you think I should call the police here in New York?"

"I don't think so. I mean, what would they do about it? They'd just think it was some stupid, childish prank. Which it probably was. And Haylie probably did it . . ."

Lindsay could hear the rumble of a male voice in the background, and Kristen said, "Wait, Linds, hang on a second."

Linds.

She found herself swept by nostalgia at the sound of the familiar nickname. What she wouldn't give, in this moment, to go back to those innocent high-school days—before everything fell apart. Before Jake's murder, and New Year's Eve, and Valentine's Day, and the baby . . .

But there was no going back. Especially now.

Jake was dead, and now Haylie was dead, too. *Murdered.*

"Lindsay?" Kristen was abruptly back on the line, her friend's formal name back on her lips. "Ross said a couple of detectives just got here and they want to talk to me about Haylie. I've got to go."

"Why do they want to talk to *you*?"

"I don't know . . . because of the picture? Because we were friends years ago? Because I just saw her?"

"Oh, right. You said she came to the reunion committee planning meeting. So she was still spouting off about Ian and Jake?"

"Still. After all these years."

Lindsay considered that. "You don't think her death has anything to do with—"

"I don't know what to think, Lindsay. All I know is that I'm going to be really careful until the police figure out who did this. And you should be, too. I know you probably feel safe in New York, but you never know, even there."

"Right," Lindsay agreed absently, thinking about the phone calls, wishing she could tell Kristen—tell *someone*—about them.

But that would mean revealing that she'd had the baby.

Maybe I should . . . especially now. Maybe the calls are connected to Haylie's death. Or Jake's. Or both. Maybe everything is connected. Maybe I'm not dealing with just a crank caller, but a killer.

"Kristen," she heard herself say impetuously.

"Yeah?" Kristen sounded impatient; Lindsay heard someone talking in the background on her end again.

The moment, the impulse, were lost.

"Never mind. I'll let you go. Just be careful, okay?"

"You, too. And listen, quickly, Aurora is supposed to be in New York City sometime this month for a mother-daughter weekend with her oldest—that's her wedding present."

"Aurora got married again?"

That probably shouldn't have been surprising, considering that she'd wed her high-school sweetheart not long after they'd graduated. Those marriages rarely lasted—but Lindsay assumed that if anyone could make it work, it would be Aurora and Eddie.

"Are you kidding? Aurora's marriage is still going strong," Kristen said with a snort. "But their daughter just got married and now she's expecting a baby. Aurora's wedding gift to her was a girls' weekend in New York, which they were going to do this fall. But now she wants to do it before her daughter is too pregnant to get around."

Aurora . . . a grandmother.

"Wow," Lindsay murmured. "That's hard to believe."

"A lot of things that have happened are hard to believe. So . . . should I tell Aurora to look you up when she's there?"

"Yes . . . make sure that you do." It would be good to see her, Lindsay thought, suddenly longing for her old friend's zany sense of humor.

"Just watch your step, Lindsay," Kristen advised her again. "Whatever you do, wherever you go . . . watch your step."

With that final warning, the call was disconnected and Lindsay's pathway to the past was severed once again.

Close up, in person, the boy looked just like his mother . . . but not much like his father at all, she noted in mild surprise, stealing a furtive glance over the top of the open *New York Post* in her hands.

They were on the eastbound number seven train that ran on elevated tracks above Queens Boulevard. At this time of the afternoon, it wasn't very crowded. Rush hour wouldn't begin for another hour.

There were plenty of seats, and she had chosen one diagonally across from his, facing him. She wanted to get a good look at the son of Lindsay Farrell and Jake Marcott.

Yes, he looked very much like Lindsay, with hair and eyes more black than brown, and features that were almost too delicate for a man. All except his jawline. His was squared off and rugged where Lindsay's was gently rounded.

But Jake's jaw hadn't been that pronounced, and there was a deep cleft in the boy's chin. Jake had had none. Jake's hair had been a lighter shade of brown. And he had been broad where this boy, his son, was lean and lanky. Yes, they were both tall—but Jake had towered at six-four in his socks. This boy was, by her estimation, about six-one.

So? He didn't have to look like his father, or have his father's height and build.

But she was expecting to be reminded of her late nemesis when she came face-to-face with his son, and that hadn't happened.

No, instead, she was reminded solely of that bitch Lindsay.

The train jerked to a stop. The conductor announced the station: Eighty-Second Street in Jackson Heights. An elderly Asian woman, who had been dozing beside Leo, jumped to her feet and headed for the door rustling several white plastic shopping bags.

Something—an apple—dropped from one and rolled across the floor.

Leo jumped up, snatched it, and handed it to her with a fleeting smile before she darted from the train with a muttered thanks.

That smile . . .

There and gone in a flash, it had revealed a familiar dimple, she realized, pretending to be engrossed in her newspaper as he settled back into his seat and the train rumbled on.

Lindsay's dimple.

And there was something else . . . something familiar about Leo's smile.

Yes, in the unique way that he tilted his head, curved his sensitive lips, and bared a row of even white teeth for a mere instant before resuming his straight face . . .

Leo reminded her of someone from the past.

Someone other than Lindsay.

And it wasn't Jake.

She just couldn't put her finger on who it was . . .

Oh, well. It would probably come to her eventually, she thought.

For now, she'd just keep an eye on him . . . and on his mother. It was almost Lindsay's turn . . .

But not yet.

Not until I've had my fill.

It was still too much fun to taunt Lindsay Farrell, to imagine the nightmares those late-night phone calls must inspire, to imagine her growing trepidation as she comprehended that somebody was in on her deep, dark secret.

Did she realize yet that somebody wanted to watch her suffer, see her die?

She'd definitely become aware of that in time. But not yet.

The train jolted around a curve in the track and the power shorted out.

Under the unexpected cover of darkness, she took the luxury of smiling to herself, thinking of Lindsay's impending demise. She relished the knowledge that she alone was aware of Lindsay's fate. She alone was in control of it.

Oh, yes. This was more fun than she'd had in years.

Or ever.

When the lights flickered back on a moment later, her face was carefully masked in neutrality once again.

Chapter 17

"Why did you leave me? You have to pay for what you did."

Terror pulsed through Lindsay's veins as she faced the shad-owy stranger who held a loaded gun in two outstretched hands, pointed right at her.

"Please . . . please don't hurt me."

"Sorry, but you have to pay, Mommy."

The stranger stepped into the pool of light and she saw that he was an adult-sized, squinty-eyed, red-faced newborn with tufts of black hair.

"No! Please!"

There was a shrill ringing sound then, and her creepy tormen-tor abruptly evaporated.

A dream. It was only a dream, Lindsay realized, sitting up.

Yes, and it was morning. Sunlight streamed through the sheer curtains that covered her window, an eastern exposure high on the thirty-fourth floor.

She reached for her alarm clock before realizing that the ring-ing was coming from the telephone.

Her stomach roiled as she picked up the receiver. It wasn't the middle of the night, but it wasn't a reasonable hour yet, either.

Was she in for another eerie prank phone call? A couple of days had passed now since she'd had one, but it was taking her a long time to fall asleep every night. She kept tossing and turning, her body tensed, as if waiting for the inevitable call.

Now, as she pressed the Talk button and said a tentative hello, she braced herself all over again.

She could hear only heavy breathing on the other end of the line.

"Stop calling me," she said tightly, clenching the phone.

"*What?*"

The voice was masculine. Not an unearthly falsetto.

"I'm sorry . . . who is this?" she asked quickly, glancing at the clock again as she stood up. It was just past seven. Who would call at this hour?

A client might . . . but none of them had her home number, thank God.

So who was on the line?

She lowered the receiver to check the Caller ID window.

"You don't know me," the voice was saying when she raised the phone to her ear again, "but my name is Leo Cellamino, and I live in Queens . . ."

Her gaze automatically shifted to the window. From it, she could see the East River and the sprawling rooftops of the outer borough beyond. The caller lived there, in Queens.

You don't know me . . .

So who was he?

Oh.

Oh my God.

Somehow, she knew. Before he even said it, she knew.

It was partially because of the voice—the voice was vaguely familiar.

But it wasn't just that.

Maybe it was some long-suppressed maternal instinct as well. Some connection that had been forged twenty years ago, and never fully detached.

In any case, she knew, before he said it, that she was talking to her son.

She sank down onto the edge of the bed again as his next words confirmed her suspicion.

"I think you might be my birth mother."

Leo heard her gasp on the other end of the line.

He shouldn't have called.

He should have just gone over there in person. He had her address.

But when he'd Googled it, he had seen that it was a fancy high-rise near Sutton Place. There was undoubtedly a doorman. It wasn't as though Leo could walk right up to her door, knock, and introduce himself. And explaining the situation to a uniformed sentry in an effort to see her in person seemed much too awkward.

So he opted to call.

From a pay phone, because he didn't want his mother to overhear him talking to her from home, and because his mother paid his cell phone bill and he didn't want her questioning any unfamiliar Manhattan phone numbers.

And now here he was, with his biological mother on the line, trying to figure out what to say next.

She relieved him of that duty, sounding dazed as she asked, "How did you find me?"

"Someone e-mailed me the information. About you, and my father."

"Your . . . father?"

"I know he died," Leo assured her swiftly. "I saw the articles."

"Articles?"

He hesitated, struck by a terrible thought. What if she didn't know? About Jake Marcott? And the murder?

"From the Portland papers," he said gently. "I got some links in that e-mail, and I read them all. You knew . . . right?"

"About the e-mail? No, I have no idea what you're—"

"About Jake Marcott. You know . . . that he's . . ."

"Dead. I knew. I was the one who found him," she said, and he could hear the stark pain in her voice, could imagine it on her face.

A face that looked so like his own, even now.

He knew that because along with her contact information and the links to the newspaper archives, he had received another jpeg attachment. It was a digital photo, a little fuzzy and snapped from some distance. It showed a woman who was easily recognizable as the girl he'd seen in the other picture. She had the same dark hair, the same delicate beauty, the same slender build.

She was walking down a Manhattan street—he knew it was Manhattan because he could see the subway entrance disappearing into the sidewalk in the background, though he couldn't make out the sign above it.

She wasn't looking at the camera, which suggested she had no idea her photo was being taken . . .

Which gave him the creeps, really.

He was fascinated by the shot, though. He'd studied it for days, memorizing every detail, trying to work up the nerve to get in touch.

He finally had, and here she was, Lindsay Farrell—*my mother?*—on the other end of the line.

"I didn't know you were the one who found Jake's body," he said, trying to remember the details from the articles. *Jake's body.* It sounded so impersonal. And it was . . . except that the stranger in question, Jake, was his father.

"I just knew it had been a friend of his," Leo rambled on, "but it didn't say who."

"The paper couldn't print my name. I was underage then. Seventeen."

"You were eighteen by the time you had me in August, though. Right?"

No response.

Not at first.

Then, so softly he had to strain to hear it, she said, "Right."

Thud. His heart seemed to split in two and land in the soles of his feet.

So she really was his mother, and his father really was dead. As badly as he wanted to find his mother, to think that Lindsay Farrell was her, he hadn't wanted to believe the other part. About Jake.

There went his fantasy of playing catch with a man who wouldn't check his watch impatiently and say he had to go after the first couple of tosses.

There went his ideal father, someone with patience and attention and a heart full of love for his son.

There went another dad, gone, poof! Just like that. Just like Anthony Cellamino.

It wasn't fair.

"Leo . . . did you say that was your name?"

It wasn't fair, but *she* was still there. Lindsay. Sounding tentative. Vulnerable.

As tentative and vulnerable as Leo himself was feeling.

"Yes," he replied somewhat hoarsely, "that's my name."

"Are you happy?"

That was a strange question. He didn't know how to answer it.

"Happy?" he echoed stupidly. "What do you mean?"

"Just . . . are you happy?"

"You mean right now?"

"I mean in general. Your life. Has it been happy?"

He thought back to the time before his father left. And even about some times after he was gone.

"Mostly," he admitted. "It's been mostly happy. But there's been sad stuff, too."

"Everyone's life is like that. But it wasn't bad, right? Nobody beat you up, or starved you, or anything like that, right?"

"Right."

She sighed. "I just want to know that I did the right thing. I want to know that you were raised by someone who loved you with all their heart."

"My mother did. *Does*," he amended, before he remembered that Betty Cellamino wasn't really his mother.

No, but she loved him with all her heart. That wasn't in dispute here, and never would be.

"What about your father?"

Leo's thoughts darkened at the question. "He's gone."

"Gone? You mean he died?"

"No." *Worse.* "He left."

Silence.

Then, "I'm sorry."

"I always thought—I mean, since I found out I was adopted a few years ago—I thought that maybe . . ." Leo trailed off.

"What?"

"Forget it. It's stupid."

"No, tell me. What were you thinking?"

"I had this fantasy of finding my dad . . . you know, my birth dad. And he would be this great guy. And he would be in my life. For good, you know? But that's not going to happen now, so . . . it's stupid."

No reply.

"I mean, he's dead," Leo continued, unable to keep the bitterness from his voice. "And my other father is as good as dead. So there go all my options. I guess I'm on my own, where dads are concerned."

Again, silence.

Until she said, so faintly that he could barely hear her, "Maybe not."

Lindsay hung up the phone with a trembling hand and a wildly beating heart.

Why did I say it?

Why to him, of all people?

Why now, of all times?

But the answer was clear, really.

Because he, of all people, deserved to know the truth.

And because now, of all times, he was reaching out to her.

That was either a monumental coincidence or a monumental sign that somebody was manipulating fate.

Leo said he didn't know who sent the e-mail that led him to her.

But when he mentioned the screen name, it made her blood run cold.

Cupid21486.

Jake had been felled by an arrow through the heart, on Valentine's Day. 2-14-86.

That screen name couldn't be a coincidence.

Nor could the timing of the e-mails sent to Leo.

The only saving grace, as far as Lindsay was concerned, was that the mysterious person behind them believed Jake was the father of her child.

Still, whoever it was had found out, somehow, about the pregnancy. It might be only a matter of time before they also found out the truth about the father and contacted him as well.

I'd rather he heard it directly from me. He deserves that.

He deserved a lot of things she hadn't given him.

Because I couldn't.

Not back then.

Who knew where he was now? Probably married, with a family.

Or maybe not.

Probably not.

He never did seem like he'd turn out to be the marrying type, she thought, remembering his rakish grin . . . his rakish ways.

Kind of like Jake—only Jake was darker beneath the surface. Much.

But he hid it well. People thought Jake Marcott was this great guy beneath that devil-may-care attitude.

I even convinced myself of that, for the longest time. But I knew, deep down, there was more to that bad-boy demeanor than just image . . .

Just as she knew that there was more—much more—to the *other* bad boy in her past—the one who stole her heart on that long-ago New Year's Eve, then vanished from her life.

Whose fault was that? an inner voice demanded.

Both of ours, she told it stubbornly.

Then she amended, *maybe it was mostly mine.*

She just couldn't handle what she'd done. She wasn't the kind of girl who had a one-night stand with a guy she barely knew. And she had no excuse, other than the fact that she was feeling down that night, still trying to get over Jake, knowing he'd be there, probably with somebody else.

It was just a rebound thing. At least, that was what she'd told herself then. That was her excuse.

Yet she still remembered every detail about that night. She remembered looking up, and there he was. They talked, and she was wildly attracted to him . . . and she sensed that it was mutual. And she left the party with him.

For once in her life, she allowed herself to do exactly what she wanted to do.

Then guilt—good old-fashioned Catholic guilt—took over.

She couldn't deal, so she walked away.

Of course, the next time she spotted him, he was with another girl. That wasn't surprising. He was a ladies' man. Everyone knew that.

For all she knew, he still was.

Or maybe happily married with a bunch of kids.

But after all these years of wondering about him, she was going to find him. She was going to drag him back into her life.

She had no choice.

The tide had turned. Another classmate had been murdered.

Maybe it was random—it probably was—but maybe it wasn't.

Maybe the phone calls were just a prank—but maybe they weren't.

Lindsay was no longer frightened just for herself and for her friends back home. She was frightened for her child.

It made no difference that she hadn't seen him since the day he was born, that he was somebody else's responsibility.

Leo's adoptive mother didn't know what she knew.

Leo's adoptive mother didn't know that her child might be in danger.

Only I know that.

The time had come at last for Lindsay to unburden herself of the weighty secret she had carried for twenty years.

Of course, she hadn't told Leo the whole truth on the phone just now. She'd only revealed that Jake Marcott hadn't been his father.

"Who was he, then?" Leo asked breathlessly.

"I can't tell you . . . not yet. Not until I tell him."

"He doesn't know about me?"

"No," she admitted around a lump in her throat. "He doesn't. I'm sorry."

"What do you think he'll say?"

"I have no idea."

Now, with a trembling finger, she pushed three numbers on the telephone pad. 4-1-1.

But I'm about to find out.

"Telephone." Allison held out the receiver in a manicured hand.

"For me?"

"For you." She smiled briefly, coldly, then returned to the bedroom where, presumably, she was packing the last of her things. She had been up at five a.m. to get it done.

She was moving from his four-bedroom Colonial in a gated shore community to a small garden apartment in Stamford. The complex had a pool and a gym, she had told him, as if she were trying to convince him—and herself—that she couldn't wait to get there.

He didn't believe that for a minute.

He just wished he believed she was as disappointed to be leaving their failed relationship behind as she was to be leaving his house, which had a beautifully landscaped private pool off the back terrace and a home gym on the third floor.

He had been trying to stay out of Allison's way, puttering around his well-equipped gourmet kitchen throwing together a spinach and goat cheese omelet, pretending—to himself, and to her—that he was sorry she was moving out.

But he wasn't.

The day she'd moved in with him in January, he'd known it was a mistake.

Maybe if it had been a different day—any other day of the year, really—he wouldn't have felt that way.

But it was January 1. Like some cosmic coincidence.

Oh, come on . . . people always moved on the first, didn't they? It was the first day of the month, when new leases kicked in. Besides, January 1 was the beginning of the year. Traditionally the day to make a fresh start.

How ironic, then, that twenty years ago, January 1 marked the end of something that held so much promise for him.

The end?

It had barely begun.

He and Lindsay Farrell had merely spent a couple of hours together, ducking out of that New Year's Eve party long before midnight.

Nobody saw them leave.

And nobody would have guessed they'd left together, heading out into the icy rain hand in hand.

He, the womanizing bad boy, and Lindsay, the beautiful heiress whose heart had belonged to Jake Marcott for as long as anyone could remember.

The two of them had broken up just before Christmas. He had assumed she was still licking her wounds, that his private fantasies about her could never become a reality.

But their eyes met that night, and for the first time ever, she seemed to really see him—and not just that. She seemed to see beyond what everyone else saw.

And something just . . . clicked between them. Across a crowded basement rec room. It was like something out of an old John Hughes movie.

They didn't even spend all that much time talking before he asked her if she wanted to get out of there.

He never expected her to say yes.

He never expected her to agree to go to his house, where his parents were out, of course. Not just because it was New Year's Eve, but because they went out all the time. He was usually alone when he was home. For once, he was glad of it.

When he took Lindsay in his arms, he never expected her to kiss him back. He'd imagined it, of course—so many times that the sensation of her lips beneath his almost seemed familiar.

There she was, just like he had dreamed: running her hands over his bare shoulders beneath his T-shirt, wantonly pressing her soft flesh against his hard angles, throwing her head back when he kissed her neck, kissed her collarbone, found his way to her bare breast.

At first he thought she might have forgotten that it was him, and not Jake.

But he looked up to find her gazing at him, staring tenderly into his eyes, and that was all the encouragement he needed. He dared to keep going, further and further, lost in the familiar, overwhelming throes of teenaged passion.

But that night, in his boyhood bedroom, he found himself venturing into uncharted territory.

Lindsay Farrell was different from the other girls he'd had. She made him feel different. She made him *feel*, period.

It wasn't his first time. Far from it.

But it was his first time with emotion—real emotion, as powerful as physical sensation, and then some.

When his body joined with hers, their eyes locked, he nearly cried at the intensity of it.

But of course, he held back.

Boys didn't cry. His father had reminded him of that fact often enough through the years.

You have to toughen up, his father used to say when he was very young, at the mercy of Shane and Devin, his two bullying older brothers. *Toughen up, son, or the world will eat you alive.*

Boys didn't cry.

Men didn't cry, either.

Looking back at that New Year's Eve, he always knew that was the night he became a man. The night he first fell in love.

January 1 was the day he realized that some things weren't meant to be.

She left in the wee hours of the new year, whispering that she had to get home. She didn't look at him when she said it.

In fact . . .

She never looked at him again.

It was as though she was ashamed of what had happened between them. As though she had remembered he wasn't good enough for someone like her.

He never got the chance to tell her that he had been infatuated with her from afar for a long time, from the first time he spotted her at a Western Catholic dance—on Jake Marcott's arm, of course.

Yes, he had been infatuated, but now he really loved her. Only her.

It didn't matter. He was who he was, he couldn't change his reputation or his financial and social status. Not then, anyway.

He and Lindsay Farrell weren't meant to be. She left, and he wanted to cry, but he didn't.

He soon heard, through the grapevine, that she was still in love with Jake, that Jake was still in love with her. That Jake, in fact, was dating one of her best friends, Kristen Daniels, just to make her jealous—and it was working.

That alone was enough to make him back off. He didn't compete for girls. They had always been drawn to him, drawn to his dark hair and eyes, his lean, lanky build, his quick grin.

Ironically, one of the girls who popped up on his radar in Lindsay's wake had been Bella Marcott, Jake's sister. He'd told himself he'd have been attracted to her even if she didn't go to St. Elizabeth's. Even if she weren't a good friend of Lindsay's. She was cute and quick-witted—the kind of girl who always had a sharp comeback. He liked that. He liked her—but of course, he didn't love her.

He loved Lindsay.

And when he was with Bella, Lindsay was usually in the vicinity. He could sneak glances at her when she wasn't looking. Bella caught him a few times, though. She seemed to shrug it off. Most girls did.

Everyone knew he wasn't the steady boyfriend type; there were plenty of girls in his life back then. Always had been.

Still were.

And now another one bites the dust, he thought, watching Allison disappear into the bedroom without a backward glance.

Easy come, easy go.

Yeah, and his life had become a series of bad cliches.

Become? It always was.

With a sigh, he tossed aside the knife he'd been using to chop the onions for the omelet and lifted the phone to his ear.

"Yeah, hello?"

Stunned, he listened to the response—and heard the voice he'd been longing to hear for twenty years.

Her voice. Uttering his name.

"Is this Wyatt Goddard?"

Wyatt Goddard?

She frowned in surprise at what she had just overheard. Why on earth would Lindsay Farrell be contacting him after all these years?

After all these years?

Come on. Why would she contact him *ever*?

It was hard to imagine that someone like her had ever crossed paths with someone like him.

He wasn't from the wrong side of the tracks, exactly . . . but pretty darned close.

He had been kicked out of two Catholic schools—once for smoking, and once for truancy—and his parents were both alcoholics. Not that those things made him an instant loser.

Far from it, actually. Wyatt Goddard was popular well beyond the boundaries of Washington High. He always had more girlfriends than Oregon had bridges . . . and Lindsay Farrell always had a boyfriend.

Well, she did until a few months before Jake died, anyway.

As for Wyatt, yes, he was popular—but a little scary, too, as far as the girls of St. Elizabeth's were concerned.

There was something intriguing, enigmatic, even, about him—a series of contradictions.

He was athletic, a track star—as well as a pack-a-day smoker.

He had a reputation as a loner—still, there he was at every party, with girls hanging all over him.

He had been kicked out of two Catholic schools, but he got decent grades—and he continued to dutifully attend Sunday Mass, usually solo.

His family was lower middle class, if anything—yet he drove a BMW convertible.

He always wore the same clothes: well-worn blue jeans, plain T-shirts, and low-heeled boots . . . even though his mother was a clerk in the young men's department at Nordstrom and his father worked at Nike. Sunglasses, too, most of the time—even on cloudy days.

He occasionally revealed a sharply honed sense of humor, but he rarely smiled. When he did, it was there and gone, like a flash of summer lightning that came out of nowhere and left you wondering if it was ever there at all . . .

The smile . . .

That's it!

She *knew* it seemed familiar.

Leo Cellamino—who looked nothing like his supposed father, Jake Marcott—happened to have precisely the same smile as Wyatt Goddard.

She hadn't been able to put her finger on who he reminded her of at the time, but now she knew.

Hmm.

Meanwhile, here was the esteemed Lindsay Farrell, placing a call to Wyatt out of the blue, never stopping to consider that her telephone might be tapped . . . even after Kristen's warning.

Hmm.

This, she realized, listening intently for whatever was to come, *should be interesting.*

An unexpected bonus, if her hunch was correct.

"It's Lindsay," she managed to say, sounding deceptively levelheaded when her brain felt as though it were about to explode.

"Lindsay Farrell. From Portland. St. Elizabeth's," she prodded when the man on the other end of the line didn't react.

"I know." She heard him exhale loudly, as though he were puffing the air through his cheeks. "I know who you are."

No, you don't, she found herself thinking. *You know who I was . . . not who I am now.*

And I never knew you at all.

"You're in Connecticut now, huh?" she asked, still marveling at the coincidence that Wyatt was living right here on the East Coast, in Fairfield County, less than fifty miles away.

Coincidence? There were over twenty million people in this metropolitan area. That they had both ended up here wasn't nearly as coincidental as it would be if they both lived on some remote island.

Still . . .

"Yeah," he said. "I've lived all over the place, but I've been on the East Coast a few years now."

"What . . . what do you do?"

"I'm self-employed," he said briefly, as if that explained everything—or anything at all. "You?"

"Same thing."

"In New York." It wasn't a question.

"Yes . . . how did you know?" she asked, wishing her stomach wouldn't flutter at the prospect that he'd kept track of her.

"Caller ID," he said simply. "I just checked it and recognized the 212 area code."

"Oh."

So much for his keeping track of her. She was lucky he even remembered her name.

Lindsay struggled to pull herself together, to remember what it was, exactly, she had just rehearsed saying to him, before she actually dialed.

Wyatt, you should know that I got pregnant the night we were together and I gave birth to your son. I came to New York and had him, then gave him up for adoption because I thought he could have a better life that way. And now he's found me . . . and he wants to find you.

Yes, that was what she was going to say. It had seemed best to go the straightforward route.

Before this moment, anyway.

Now she found herself acutely aware that she couldn't go

around dropping bombshells like that over the telephone. Not when she was less than an hour away from the person whose life would be forever altered by her news.

She had to deliver a bombshell like that in person.

"I need to see you," she hastily told Wyatt Goddard, trying not to wonder if the woman who had answered the phone was his wife. It didn't matter. This wasn't about him. About the two of them. It was about their son.

"Did you say you want to see me?" he echoed, sounding surprised . . . and intrigued.

"No. I said I *need* to see you. As soon as possible, actually."

She expected him to argue.

He didn't.

He said, "I'll come to New York."

"When?"

"Now."

Chapter 18

Driving down I-95 along Long Island Sound in morning rush-hour traffic, Wyatt Goddard was careful not to let the Pagani Zonda's speedometer rise past eighty. He didn't want to get another ticket and wind up in traffic school again.

Sure, he always drove fast—speed was as much a fact of Wyatt's life as his good looks and fat bank account were.

Today, however, he was tempted to raise the velocity not as much out of habit as out of anticipation.

But a traffic stop would only delay the payoff.

The payoff: after two decades, he was going to see Lindsay Farrell again.

He had dressed carefully, formally for the occasion. Sure, he still favored jeans and T-shirts in his everyday life. But he now had a closet full of well-cut designer suits, custom-made shirts, Italian silk ties, shiny leather shoes, and sunglasses that cost almost as much as his first car did.

It had taken no time at all this morning to go from the boxer shorts he'd slept in to the elegant attire he now wore. His dark hair, still damp from his shower, was cut much shorter than it had been back in high school, but he still had a full head of it. Luckily for him, receding hairlines didn't run in the family. Even his father had aged well, despite his years of hard living.

And so had Wyatt. Nobody he met ever realized he was closing in on forty. He forgot, most of the time, himself. The only hint of his age, whenever he looked in the mirror, were the faint beginnings of crinkly lines around the corners of his eyes.

At the moment, they were concealed behind a pair of black designer sunglasses.

No, the sun wasn't shining brightly today—not yet, anyway. But he had donned the glasses despite the overcast sky, the way he used to back in high school. Back then, he used them as an impenetrable fort that could keep the world at bay.

Not anymore. He didn't have to hide anymore.

And he wasn't hiding from Lindsay—not really. But the glasses would give him an advantage. He wouldn't have to look her in the eye until he'd had a chance to get used to the fact that he was with her again. Until he figured out how he felt about that— and had a chance to look at her and maybe figure out how she felt about him, and why she had called him so abruptly.

He supposed she was going to tell him. She'd said she had to talk to him about something. What could it be?

Whatever.

That she had crashed into his world out of the blue for the second time in his life seemed fitting. He only hoped that this time, she wouldn't blow right on out of it again.

Maybe she won't. We're both adults now.

Right. They had that in common, if nothing else, he reminded himself wryly. That and, oh yeah, irony of ironies: money.

During their brief conversation, she had acted clueless about his life now—and he had pretended to be just as clueless about hers.

Of course he knew she was an event planner in Manhattan—a successful one, judging by her address and her client list.

Keeping track of her was simple, despite the fact that Wyatt's parents were long deceased, his brothers had relocated, and he'd lost touch with his other hometown connections when he left.

Google was a handy invention. Plug in someone's name and poof! There they were: name, location, occupation . . .

He only wished there had been a photo of Lindsay on the Web, but there never was when he checked.

And he checked often.

Well, now you don't need a photo. Now you'll get to see her for yourself.

His right foot pressed down on the accelerator before he remembered to lighten up.

This wasn't a race. After twenty years, he could wait another half hour to see her.

Yeah, sure you can.

He forced himself to steer his way into the right lane, allowing the luxury sports car to languish behind a relatively slow-moving double semi.

Why did she call him? What did she want? And in person, no less.

Maybe she was interested in him now that she'd found out that he could now buy and sell her old man—and Farrell Timber—from here to the West Coast and back.

She wouldn't be the first opportunist from his past to resurface.

Then again, Lindsay had never struck him as a gold-digger.

Come on . . . she didn't have to be.

She had her own money, plenty of it. Everybody in Portland knew that money grew on the Farrell family tree.

Anyway, information about Wyatt wasn't readily available on the Internet. He was a silent partner in the business, importing exotic luxury cars for high-profile clients.

Cars had always been his thing, even back in high school.

That was how he first noticed Lindsay, in fact. He'd turned his head to admire a sleek black Porsche that had pulled up in front of church one Sunday morning before Mass. Then she'd emerged from the backseat, and he was instantly more captivated by her than the car. Which was saying a lot.

In those days he worked his ass off, holding three part-time jobs to save enough for his used BMW. There were plenty of days when he got home at three a.m. after washing dishes at a local restaurant, too exhausted to wake up for school the next morning. You miss one too many days, and you're expelled.

And once you've been expelled from one school, the next one has a zero-tolerance policy. Get caught having a cigarette on school grounds, and you're out. No excuses accepted, no questions asked.

Of course college was beyond his reach anyway, so he didn't worry much about his academic record. After graduating from Washington High, he found his way into automobile sales—first in Portland, then Indianapolis, then Daytona. Race cars.

From there, he got into luxury imports, found his way up the East Coast through a series of stepping stones, and here he was. Still working his ass off.

But the reward now was much greater. He was wealthy, living among blue bloods who made Lindsay's privileged family look like paupers.

It wasn't about money, though. Not for Wyatt.

And it wasn't about Lindsay rejecting him all those years ago because he wasn't good enough.

It wasn't even about his parents, who never believed in him, or his brothers, who didn't either—until he sent them each a Jaguar for Christmas a few years back. Of course Shane promptly sold his to keep his L.A. townhouse from going into foreclosure, and Devin totaled his during an icy Montana rain that spring.

Oh, well. Let bygones be bygones, Wyatt figured. No need to hold grudges.

If Wyatt Goddard ever had anything to prove, it was to himself.

He should have been satisfied now, a bon vivant living life on his own terms.

He wasn't.

Not entirely.

But he figured he was as close to satisfied as he was ever going to get on his own.

Sure, something was missing. Something he couldn't even put his finger on, most days.

Today, however, he could.

Maybe because Allison had moved out.

More likely because Lindsay had contacted him.

No, *she* wasn't the thing that was missing, per se . . .

It was just that hearing from her reminded him—far more than Allison's departure had—that he was alone.

Alone again, alone always . . .

Alone.

There were plenty of people in his life, but he held them at arm's length, the way he always had. It was his nature. In his relationships with women, with family, with friends and colleagues.

If he didn't let them in, he didn't have to push them out—or worse, let them out when they wanted to leave.

He didn't have to take Psych 101 to know that it was a defense mechanism, honed by years of being a latchkey kid with parents who were absent even when they were physically there. He had long ago forgiven both of them, quite some time before he found himself at their consecutive deathbeds, keeping vigil, holding it together while his older brothers fell apart and stayed away. His father went first: cirrhosis of the liver. No surprise. His mother followed within a year: emphysema. No surprise there, either.

Wyatt had long since quit smoking, and he never touched a drop of liquor. Never did drugs, either, not even pot. Not even when he ran around with that crowd back in school.

No, he was an expert at always remaining in control . . .

Even at high speed.

He checked the rearview mirror, glanced over his shoulder, then flicked on his turn signal and swerved left.

Then he allowed his foot to sink onto the accelerator, gunning the sports car down the highway toward New York, and Lindsay.

This was going to be tricky.

She couldn't help but wish Lindsay and Wyatt were going to meet at Lindsay's apartment so that she could easily eavesdrop in the comfort of her Lexington Avenue hotel room a few blocks away.

But when Wyatt said he was coming to New York right away, Lindsay immediately suggested meeting in a public place.

She didn't say it that way, of course.

When he asked, "Where do you live?" she replied immediately, and nervously, "Oh, I'll just meet you somewhere. I was going out to run some errands on the way to work, so . . ."

Errands? On the way to work?

No, you weren't, Lindsay. You made that up—why? So that you wouldn't have to meet Wyatt Goddard in your apartment?

She could think of just two reasons a woman wouldn't want to be alone with a man. One, because she was afraid he might hurt her.

Two, because she was afraid he might make a move on her.

With Wyatt Goddard, either scenario was a possibility.

Not that he had ever hurt someone, to her knowledge. But there always was an air of danger about him.

In fact, to her own private amusement, his name came up a few times in the wake of Jake's murder—as a suspect.

Not officially, though the police did question him. But they questioned everyone who had been at the dance that night. Methodically. Taking more time with some kids—like Lindsay, who had found him, and Kristen, who had been his date—than with others.

Wyatt was never an official suspect, but there was plenty of talk, particularly among Jake's friends, that he could have done it. Mostly because he was an outsider, never one of them. And because he had been there that night, with Jake's sister.

Of course, she kept her distance from him after that.

Pretty much everyone did.

Then again, they all kept their distance from each other, too, their close-knit group hopelessly frayed as graduation loomed.

By that July, everyone had gone their separate ways.

This July, they were planning to come together again at last before the old school was destroyed.

But some of them wouldn't live to see that day.

And those who did would be forever haunted by all that had gone before.

Lindsay Farrell would be part of the former group.

She hadn't yet decided where Wyatt Goddard was going to wind up now that he was back on the scene.

She'd just have to wait and see what happened between him and Lindsay.

They were meeting just down this next block, in a large, popular coffee shop Lindsay had suggested. It would probably be crowded at this hour of the morning.

Crowded enough that no one would give a second glance to a frumpy, heavyset blonde dining solo.

But too crowded, she saw in dismay as she arrived in the doorway, for her to possibly land a seat anywhere near Lindsay and Wyatt.

There they were, greeting each other right now at a small booth near the back, surrounded by other booths and tables, all of them occupied.

Lindsay she had already glimpsed many times these last few days, having kept her under close surveillance. She had been seated when Wyatt arrived, her back to the door.

Now, after they had exchanged a brief, awkward grasp of each other's arms—which wasn't a hug, but wasn't anything else, either—Wyatt sat down facing the door, and she did a double take.

She hadn't seen him in twenty years.

If she weren't looking for him, expecting to see him there, it would have taken her a while to recognize him.

He was still tall, dark, and handsome. More so than ever, in fact.

But there was a sophistication about him that had never been there before. He wore a dark suit, white shirt, and tie—obviously expensive, even from here.

Even if she were able to sidle into the vicinity—confident they wouldn't recognize her between the wig, the padding, and the glasses—she wouldn't be able to hear what they were saying. It was much too loud in here: chattering voices, clattering silverware and plates, jaunty Greek music playing in the background.

Disappointed, she turned and left the coffee shop, realizing she'd just have to piece it all together later.

* * *

There he was.

Right in front of her.

Looking at her, presumably, from behind the dark glasses that shielded his eyes.

Touching her—his hands on her lower arms in a brief grasp— but that was all.

And that's good, Lindsay told herself, trying not to be disappointed that he didn't initiate a hug or kiss. That would have been too awkward. It wasn't as though they were officially long-lost friends—or long-lost anything.

Not officially.

"You look really good, Wyatt."

Why did I say that? she wondered on the heels of her impromptu comment as they both settled into the booth—she for the second time.

I said it because it's true, for one thing. He does look really good.

Great, in fact.

She never in a million years expected Wyatt Goddard to show up dressed like a successful businessman, clean-shaven below his sunglasses, his black hair attractively cut with a bristly top that seemed to beg her fingers to spike it further.

Was he a successful businessman?

He must be successful at something, living where he does. The Fairfield County shore towns weren't affordable otherwise.

"You look pretty good yourself, Lindsay."

Dammit, she could feel her cheeks growing hot at the innocuous compliment.

Or maybe it wasn't so innocuous.

She looked up to see that he had removed his black shades and was looking at her as though . . .

Well, as though he hadn't forgotten what had happened between them that New Year's Eve.

She hadn't, either. Not for a second.

But not, apparently, for the same reason as him.

Oh, she definitely remembered what it had been like—Wyatt Goddard making love to her.

You don't forget your first time.

But she had a feeling she wouldn't have forgotten Wyatt even if he had been her hundredth lover, or her thousandth.

How ironic that after going out with Jake for so long—two

years—she never could bring herself to sleep with him. Everyone assumed that they were. And he assumed that they would.

Right, and he pressured her from the start. Jake Marcott was used to getting what he wanted—including sex. He couldn't believe his girlfriend wasn't willing to provide it. Back then, Lindsay marveled that he stuck around anyway.

Now, having learned infinitely more about human psychology, she had a feeling that if she had given in, he wouldn't have stayed with her for as long as he did.

You always want what you can't have.

And, if you were Jake Marcott, you were hell bent on getting it.

That was what kept him around.

And it was why he finally got fed up and dumped her.

She wasn't quite sure why she never gave in to Jake back then, she only knew that it wouldn't be right. She loved him, yes—but there was something about him that she just didn't trust.

How strange, then, that she instinctively trusted Wyatt Goddard from the moment they first connected. Really connected—at that New Year's Eve party.

She knew who he was before that, of course. He was always around, on her peripheral radar, but she was with Jake. And even if she hadn't been, Wyatt wasn't her type. He had too much of an edge . . . or so she believed.

Maybe that was because she'd never gotten a good look at him. At his eyes. Not until that night.

Unless you were a rock star, you could hardly show up at an indoor party, in the evening, in the dead of winter, wearing sunglasses. So there he was, without his ever-present shades—looking at her. She could feel his stare long before she allowed herself to meet it. And when she did . . .

Well, it might just as well have been midnight. Fireworks and confetti seemed to erupt with fanfare somewhere inside her, heralding the beginning of something new and promising.

She was drawn to Wyatt Goddard as she had never been drawn to anyone before.

At the party—and afterward. When they were alone together.

Even now, twenty years later, she knew that if she closed her eyes, she'd see the look in Wyatt's that night as he lay intimately above her, propped on his elbows, her face cupped in his hands . . .

So Lindsay didn't dare close her eyes.

She didn't want to remember that. Especially not now.

She didn't want to remember the unexpected tenderness that lay beneath his rough exterior . . .

No, because she'd feel even guiltier for not telling him about the baby.

Back then, in the months that followed their brief connection, she had managed to convince herself that she was doing him a favor not revealing her pregnancy. That a guy like Wyatt Goddard wouldn't have any interest in a child, not even his own.

It was only when it was too late, when Wyatt—and the baby—were long gone from her life, that the fog lifted. It had comforted her in that year—the numbing haze that had enveloped her like a protective cloak, shielding her from the icy reality of her pregnancy and the harsher one of Jake's murder.

But when her head began to clear, the memories came back. She was forced to acknowledge, if only to herself, that there might have been more to Wyatt Goddard than met the eye. More than she was able to see before they got together, more than she was willing to recall after she left him.

I cheated him, she told herself now—not for the first time. Not by far.

But sitting here across from him, looking into his eyes, the knowledge hit her harder than ever before.

"Coffee?" a waitress asked briskly, appearing with a steaming glass pot and a couple of laminated menus.

Wyatt nodded and turned over the cup before him in its saucer.

Lindsay did the same, though she was sure that if she tried to take a sip of anything right now, she'd gag.

In fact, she might gag anyway. She might throw up right here and now, in front of Wyatt and the waitress and everyone else.

To distract herself from the wave of nausea washing over her, she focused on returning the waitress's brief, efficient smile as she poured their coffee.

Good. That's better. She focused on the middle-aged woman's faded gray eyes that matched her faded gray hair. Her plastic name tag said Marissa. That was interesting. She didn't look like a Marissa. She looked more like a Bea or a Madge.

"Are you okay, honey?" she asked, peering at Lindsay with motherly concern. "You look a little green."

"I'm fine . . . just a little . . ." She trailed off, conscious of Wyatt's eyes still on her.

"Green," the woman supplied, and chuckled.

"Right."

"I'm right there with ya. I'm still in my first trimester—this is my fifth kid—and I've got morning sickness every day."

Morning sickness? She can't be much older than me, then, Lindsay realized with a start. She had her pegged for at least a decade beyond.

Well, Marissa was a coffee-shop waitress in New York with four kids to support and another on the way. She'd probably led a difficult life, and her struggles had taken a physical toll.

Which would indicate, in turn, that Wyatt must have led a relatively easy one. He didn't look a day over thirty.

"I've been scarfing down saltines all morning," the waitress continued conversationally, lifting the small stainless steel creamer from their table and making sure it wasn't empty. Nope. She set it back down. "Every damned time I get pregnant, pardon my French, I tell myself it's going to be different. I tell myself I'm not going to throw up every morning for the first couple of months. And every damned time—pardon again—it happens worse than ever."

Lindsay murmured something appropriately sympathetic, because the woman seemed to be mainly addressing her.

"Oh, I'll be okay in the end. The reward is worth it. I just love my babies."

Lindsay offered her a taut, queasy smile.

"How about you? Do you have children, hon?"

Talk about a loaded question.

It certainly wasn't one she wanted to answer in front of Wyatt Goddard.

She merely shook her head.

The waitress looked from her to Wyatt and back again. As if she'd been assuming they were a couple—and now realized her mistake—her smile lost some of its cheer.

"I'll be right back to take your order."

With that, she was gone.

Wyatt picked up one of the menus and wordlessly handed it to Lindsay.

She glanced at it blindly, her thoughts rushing along like a swollen mountain stream in April.

I have to tell him.

Right now.

Just get it out there, in the open.

Just get it over with, for God's sake.

But somehow, the words refused to come.

"Do you know what you want?"

Yes. I want to tell you that you have a son.

But I can't seem to do it.

She glanced up to find him looking over his own menu.

"I'm just having toast," she said, because she felt as though she'd have to order something.

"I'm having it, too." He snapped his menu closed. "With eggs, bacon, and a side of sausage."

She couldn't help but grin. "Hungry?"

"Always. There are just some things I can't resist."

He's talking about food, she reminded herself, even as she noted the provocative quirk in his brow.

For some reason, she found it necessary to say, "Like cholesterol?"

"Among other things."

Okay, so he's not talking about food.

But you should. Just to keep things straightforward and make it clear that nothing is going on here, under the surface.

"Do you, um, eat a huge breakfast every morning?" She could hear the nervousness in her voice.

"When I'm home, I do. I like to cook. In fact, I've always known my way around the kitchen, ever since I was a kid."

"Really?"

"You sound surprised."

"I am."

"A lot of things about me might surprise you, Lindsay."

He set his menu aside, leaned back in the booth, steepled his hands, and looked at her.

"So," he said, "what's up?"

And away we go.

Except . . . she still wasn't ready.

So she hedged. "It's been a long time, hasn't it?"

"Twenty years last New Year's."

Whoa. Nothing like throwing it right out there, she thought, ducking her head to gaze at her menu again so that she wouldn't have to look at him.

Wait a minute.

This was ridiculous. She wasn't a teenaged girl anymore. She didn't have to skirt around the fact that she'd had a, a—*thing*—with him. Wasn't that essentially why they were here?

Forcing herself to meet his gaze again, she saw a glint of amusement there and actually found herself relaxing. Just a tad.

"I wasn't talking about that, specifically," she allowed herself to say, referring to their one night together.

"No, but you were thinking about it . . . right?"

He leaned forward abruptly, and she found herself with a close-up view of the face—the eyes—she had tried so hard to forget.

No wonder she couldn't.

She was mesmerized all over again.

"I've thought about it a couple of times, too," he told her.

"You mean . . . about that New Year's Eve?"

"Yeah. Come on, you didn't forget . . . did you?"

You have no idea.

She shrugged.

"You couldn't have," he said simply, leaning back again, folding his arms. "Otherwise we wouldn't be here now. Right?"

"What do you mean?"

"You looked me up. It must have something to do with the past . . . unless you're looking for a Lamborghini."

"What?"

He frowned slightly. "Cars," he said inexplicably.

"You lost me."

"That's what I do. Exotic luxury cars."

"Oh!" She hesitated, wondering if she should let him think she had invited him here on business.

What? Have you lost it?

What are you going to do, buy a Porsche from him to throw him off the scent?

"I didn't know that was what you did," she said, buying time.

He shrugged. "That's what I do. You?"

"I'm an event planner."

He nodded as if he already knew that.

Had she told him?

She doubted it—but she seriously couldn't remember.

Right now, under the heat of his gaze, she seriously couldn't remember much of anything at all.

Oh, yes she could.

She remembered his lips . . . his mouth . . . his hands . . . his skin against hers; his weight, pressing the hard length of his body against hers, into hers . . .

He remembered, too. She could see it. He was remembering right now.

Her breath caught in her throat.

Dammit. Why was there always this . . . thing, this connection, between them?

Always?

Talk about an exaggeration.

There was no *always* where Wyatt Goddard was concerned. It was more like . . .

Never.

"Did we decide?" the waitress asked breezily, materializing beside their booth again, shattering the moment.

Thank you, Marissa.

Lindsay ordered toast.

"White, wheat, rye, whole grain, pumpernickel . . . ?"

"Whole grain."

"Butter, margarine . . . ?"

"Butter."

"On it, or on the side?"

Oh, for God's sake, it's just toast! she wanted to scream, the distraction she had just welcomed now irritating the hell out of her. She wanted to be left alone with Wyatt again.

Truly alone, though.

Not here, in a public coffee shop.

Alone.

She ordered the butter on the side.

Wyatt ordered eggs, toast, bacon, a side of sausage.

"How do you want your eggs?" Marissa began. "Scrambled, over, up, poached—"

"Surprise me," he cut in, and thrust the menus at her. "On all of it."

The waitress sent him an amused, knowing smile and left them alone again.

"You might get hard-boiled eggs and pumpernickel toast with margarine," Lindsay informed him with a grin.

"Sounds good." He shook his head, reached across the table unexpectedly, and grabbed Lindsay's hands.

There went her heart again, a ricocheting hockey puck skittering around in her rib cage.

"It's good to see you again," he said. "Really, really good."

He was a flirt. She knew that; had always known.

This was part of his charming routine, she told herself sternly. Once a womanizer, always a womanizer.

"I haven't seen anyone from back home in years."

"Actually, neither have I," she admitted. "Except my parents. But they don't even live in Oregon anymore."

"Where are they?"

"Retired. Near Las Vegas. How about yours?"

"They passed away."

"I'm sorry."

A shadow slid over his face. "So am I." He squeezed her hands, let go. "But people die, and you move on. That's life, right?"

He's trying to be cavalier, she thought, *and it isn't working. Not at all.*

"Are you married?" she asked, realizing she didn't even know, grateful he had let go of her hands. Just in case he was.

Not that anything could possibly come of this if he wasn't. But still . . .

"No."

Her hopes soared ridiculously.

"Divorced?" she asked.

"Nope. You?"

"Nope."

"So you're . . . Are you married?"

She shook her head quickly, trying not to smile. But she felt so damned giddy, realizing he was interested in her status.

"I'm surprised," he said, and poured a generous amount of creamer into his coffee. "I always pictured you married to a great guy, with a couple of kids."

Kids.

About to sip her own coffee, she set the cup down again hard, the untouched black liquid sloshing over the edge.

"No," she said tersely. "Not married to a great guy with a couple of kids."

"Any particular reason why not?"

She shrugged.

"Let me guess. You're still waiting for Mr. Right to come along. Right?"

She forced herself to look at him. "Isn't everyone?"

It was his turn to shrug.

You have to tell him.

Now.

She couldn't just sit here shooting the breeze with him, flirting, letting him think this might be some kind of casual reunion for old times' sake.

Or worse, the deliberate sparking of an old flame.

He deserved to know the truth before this went any further.

I just wish I didn't want so badly for it to go further.

Wyatt insisted on picking up the check Marissa had dropped on the table. Lindsay argued, but she let him.

She didn't argue, however, when he suggested that they take a walk through the park. He had a feeling that wasn't just because she wanted to delay getting to the office or because it was a beautiful May morning.

Something was weighing on her mind.

Something she hadn't been able to articulate back in the coffee shop.

A couple of times, he got the feeling that she was about to say something significant.

Other times, he sensed that she was tempted to bolt.

He was glad she hadn't.

Seeing her again, he felt almost as if there had been a real and enduring relationship between them in the past, something more than a one-night stand.

Of course, there hadn't been.

Yet somehow, they had reconnected the way a former boyfriend and girlfriend might, distinctly aware of rekindled chemistry, deliberately keeping the conversation light and rooted in the present.

As they ate—or rather, he ate, and she toyed with her toast— he told her about the various places he had lived and about his business. He deliberately downplayed the scope of his success, having realized that she didn't know, after all. She had called him for a specific reason—that much was obvious from her preoccupied air—but as far as he could tell, his newfound wealth had nothing to do with it.

They made their way from the bustling, pedestrian-and-traffic-clogged corner of Fifty-Ninth Street and Fifth Avenue into the comparative solitude of Central Park.

The warm, brilliant morning sunlight gave way to cooler dappled shade, and he shoved his sunglasses high over his forehead. No real reason to wear them here.

And no real reason to hide. Not anymore.

Birds chirped from leafy overhead branches, bikers and joggers whizzed past, and strangers strolled in their midst . . . yet essentially, they found themselves alone together.

It was time for Wyatt to find out why Lindsay had reached out to him today.

He looked over his shoulder. There was no one remotely in earshot other than a plump woman pushing an expensive-looking baby carriage along, maybe a hundred feet behind on the path.

She was probably a nanny, he found himself noting idly. The sleek buggy was stereotypical for an Upper East Side family, but the woman pushing it was not your average upscale Manhattan mom. She was too overweight, sloppy looking, unsophisticated.

And you're stalling, speculating about random strangers instead of focusing on why you're here with Lindsay.

Breaking the silence that had settled between them, he turned to her at last and said, "So . . . tell me."

Her head jerked toward him and he saw that she was startled—and dismayed.

"Tell you what?" she asked slowly.

"Why you called. You don't want a car from me, I'm assuming . . . So what is it that you *do* want?"

She didn't answer.

Their footsteps crunched on the gravel.

Behind them, he could hear the nanny strolling along, her footsteps padding along the path, the cushy rubber tires of the baby's buggy almost soundless.

In the distance was the faint sound of street traffic, along with the distinct clopping of a horse's hoofs and the rumble of the carriage it was pulling, undoubtedly occupied by romantic tourists.

Wyatt found himself picturing himself riding in one with Lindsay snuggled beside him. In his fantasy it was night, and winter, and they were a couple.

Then Lindsay spoke, shattering the image—a good thing, because he wasn't back in high school, daydreaming about a girl he couldn't have. He was a grown man, for God's sake . . .

Right. Daydreaming about a woman you can't have.

Or could he?

When he heard what she was saying, hope came to life within him.

"It's something I should have told you years ago. I should have said it as soon as I knew, but . . . I couldn't."

As soon as she knew? Knew what?

Oh.

Whoa.

All at once, he realized what she was going to say.

She was about to tell him that the feeling he had assumed was one-sided twenty years ago was, in fact, mutual. That she had figured out after they slept together that she was falling in love, just as he had. But she, like he, chose not to reveal her feelings.

His pulse quickened in anticipation.

Say it, Lindsay. Just say it.

But she was in no hurry to play her hand.

He did his best to coax her along. "It's okay that you couldn't say it back then. I mean, you can still say it now."

He tried to catch her eye, but she refused to look at him. She stared straight ahead, inhaled deeply, exhaled audibly, her nerves palpable.

He waited, fighting the urge to touch her fingers, take her hand, guide her along.

"It's not easy." She sounded almost . . . distraught.

"I know. Would it help if I told you I felt the same way?"

"What . . . ?"

"I should have told you, too. But I didn't."

"What are you talking about?"

"I felt the same way, Lindsay. My God, I mean . . . I never expected that to happen that night. And when you took off afterward, I figured you weren't interested in someone like me. So I kept it all to myself."

"What?" she asked again, turning to look at him at last.

That was when he saw the utter confusion in her eyes, and his heart sank.

"Wyatt . . . I don't think we're talking about the same thing here."

"I guess we're not." He shook his head. *Fool!*

"Oh my God," she whispered.

She knows. She knows what I was talking about, even if I have no idea what she was talking about.

Terrific.

He had gone and let his guard down for an instant, spilled his guts, and all for nothing.

"For a second there," she said slowly, "I thought you might have known all along . . . and that would have made this so much easier."

"Made what so much easier? What the hell are you talking about, Lindsay?" he demanded, his patience fraying fast.

"That night—the night we—Wyatt, I got pregnant," she blurted.

Her words swept through him like a tsunami.

Above the roar that consumed him, body and soul, he heard the rest. "I had a baby. The baby. Your baby."

Keeping a careful distance, she watched Wyatt Goddard abruptly stop walking and rake a hand through his hair.

The motion knocked his sunglasses to the ground. He appeared not to notice.

Her hands tightened on the handle of the empty baby carriage she had just stolen from its vulnerable sidewalk parking spot outside a deli on a nearby side street.

She slowed her footsteps, not wanting to overtake them.

A breeze rustled the branches overhead, so that it was impossible for her to hear.

Lindsay faltered, touched Wyatt's shoulder, then leapt back as if she had been burned when he appeared to brush her off with a brusque comment.

Lindsay seemed to be pulling herself together for a moment, then she said something else to him.

The breeze stopped and a snatch of conversation reached her ears.

She stopped pushing the buggy altogether and bent over it as if adjusting the nonexistent baby's blanket.

". . . so sorry, I just didn't know what to . . ."

That came from Lindsay.

So, louder and more clearly, did, "Please, Wyatt, don't—"

The wind gusted again, dammit.

Wyatt was talking, she saw, sneaking a glance in her direction as she fussed over the imaginary occupant of the buggy.

Then a couple of phrases reached her ears even though the leaves overhead were still stirring. They were separated by unintelligible comments, or protests, from Lindsay.

"How could you?"

"Dammit, Lindsay, I had a right to know."

And finally, "So he's in Queens?"

I was right, she thought triumphantly.

Wyatt Goddard had fathered Lindsay Farrell's baby.

She only wished Jake Marcott were alive to know about his girlfriend's shocking betrayal.

Ex-girlfriend, she amended.

Still, even when it was over between Jake and Lindsay that December of their senior year, people assumed it wasn't over. You didn't forget a longtime relationship just like that. Unfinished business still seemed to linger between them. Jake still loved Lindsay; Lindsay still loved Jake. Everyone figured that was the case, including Kristen Daniels, who dated Jake next— and last.

The rumor was that Jake dumped Lindsay because she wouldn't sleep with him.

She had heard it many times during the two years they were dating.

When she realized Lindsay was pregnant, she assumed the rumor was obviously false.

Now, all at once, it was viable again.

Lindsay might not have been sleeping with Jake, but she was sleeping with Wyatt Goddard behind his back. How scandalous of her. How daring. And how cunning.

In fact . . .

It almost makes me admire Lindsay, she realized with an ironic smile, watching her watch Wyatt Goddard striding away.

But that doesn't change what I have to do to her.

If anything, it would make it even sweeter, knowing that perhaps Lindsay Farrell's true love hadn't been buried after all in the Marcott family plot on that bitter February day.

No, it appeared that her true love was alive and well.

Look at Lindsay, bereft, standing there alone on the path as Wyatt disappears. Potent yearning practically radiated off of her.

Despite the obvious turmoil between them, she was probably still hoping they had a second chance.

Maybe she was thinking that together, they could meet the son they'd given up. That the three of them could walk off into the sunset and live happily ever after, a family at last.

Sorry, but that's not going to happen, Lindsay.

You're not going to live happily ever after.

You're not going to live at all.

Oblivious to her chilling fate and the figure watching her from a distance, Lindsay gazed at Wyatt walking away.

Storming away, really, and she watched him go until he disappeared around a bend in the path.

Then the ache took hold, a longing so fierce that she actually doubled over, just briefly, hugging herself. When she straightened and looked around, she saw a heavyset woman with a baby buggy, poised behind her in the path.

She was looking up, at Lindsay, but she quickly looked down again, at the baby in the carriage.

Typical New Yorker. She probably thought Lindsay was in some kind of physical trouble, and didn't want to get involved.

Whatever.

Lindsay didn't need help. She was fine.

Just fine.

She took a deep, trembling breath, steeled her nerves, and walked on in the direction Wyatt had taken.

She wasn't going after him, though; she knew better than that.

He needed time to absorb what she had told him. Time to cool off.

Maybe he never would.

But at least she had done the right thing at last.

That was what mattered here. All that mattered.

Lindsay had no business longing for something more with Wyatt.

Maybe not, but you are.

All right.

So she wanted more. She couldn't help it. She wanted to see him again, she wanted him in her life.

Absorbed in wistful, futile fantasies, she never looked back.

She never saw the plump blond nanny abandon the baby buggy in the path.

She never saw her reach over to pick up the sunglasses Wyatt had dropped, tucking them into her pocket with a thoughtful smile.

Chapter 19

Leo Cellamino's cell phone rang just as he was walking past a group of old men playing checkers in the Thursday evening twilight outside a prewar apartment building off Queens Boulevard.

His first thought was that the caller would have to leave a message; he was carrying a large, flat white box that was already fifteen minutes late. How well he knew, after three years delivering pizzas for his Uncle Joe's pizzeria, that hungry customers had low blood sugar; low blood sugar made a person irritable and impatient; and irritable, impatient people didn't tip well, if at all.

Anyway, it was probably Sarah Rose. She had called his home number looking for him, and his mother said she'd given her his cell number, too.

Then Leo remembered that he had given Lindsay Farrell his cell phone number, too, the other morning when they spoke.

He immediately looked around for somewhere to set the pizza box.

Spotting no convenient resting places, he set it carefully on the ground at his feet and pulled his ringing cell phone from the pocket of his shirt.

The Caller ID window showed an unfamiliar Manhattan number.

"Hello?" he said eagerly, ignoring the disapproving stares from the old men.

"Leo, this is Lindsay Farrell."

His mother.

"Hi." His voice came out sounding strangled.

"I'm sorry it's taken me so long to get back to you. There were just a few things I needed to do."

Right. Like inform my father that I exist.

Truth be told, he hadn't expected her to get back in touch this soon, if at all.

"That's okay," he told her, and took a step away from the glaring old men.

His foot nearly landed square in the middle of the pizza box on the ground; it was all he could do to keep it airborne and maintain his balance.

Good save. At least I didn't squash the merchandise, he told himself, turning his back to the old guys and carefully straddling the box on the ground.

"Leo, I was wondering if you were going to be around this weekend at all. We'd . . . like to meet you. If that's what you want."

"We? You mean . . . ?"

She cleared her throat. "Your, ah, father. And me."

"Are you kidding? I would love that."

He heard her exhale as if she'd been holding her breath.

It was only then that he realized, for the first time, that he wasn't the only one who had a lot at stake.

Lindsay Farrell did as well.

And so did his father . . . whoever he was.

Heck, it didn't even matter who he was.

What mattered was that he knew about Leo now . . . and he wanted to meet him.

"Wyatt, it's Lindsay. I, um, got your message and I went ahead and set something up for this weekend in Connecticut, like you said. Saturday afternoon at your place, right? I hope that still works for you. I told him you were sending a car to pick him up . . . but really, you don't have to send one for me. I'll get myself up there, so don't worry about—"

A second beep cut off her final word.

. . . me.

Oh, well. She doubted he was worried about her.

It wasn't as if he had touched base with her these past few days, after she'd made her big revelation that morning in the park.

His reaction was pretty much what she expected.

He was shocked, angry, upset.

He'd made it obvious that he wasn't interested in excuses, so she didn't offer any. She offered nothing other than a heartfelt apology, several of them, all of which he brushed off.

Can you really blame him?

They had gone their separate ways, and she had at first thought she might never hear from him.

She supposed she probably deserved that, in the grand scheme of things . . . and she could accept it. She really could.

But where would that leave Leo?

Perhaps no better off, or worse off, than he'd been before.

After all, you can't miss something you never had.

That's bullshit, and you know it better than anyone, she told herself, hanging up the phone and heading into the bathroom.

There, she splashed some water on her face and looked at herself in the mirror.

She hadn't realize how much she had missed Wyatt until she saw him again.

Until he left her there, in the park.

Somehow, Lindsay pulled herself together and went to her office. Somehow, she made it through that workday, and then another, and another.

She even made it through the long nights, untainted by further prank phone calls.

With the news of Haylie's murder almost a week old by then, and the memory of the prank caller's eerie voice fading as well, she was no longer as fearful about her own safety, or Leo's.

In fact, she'd almost convinced herself when she woke up this morning that she should just let go of everything connected to the past: the reunion, Haylie, Jake, Leo . . . and yes, Wyatt, too. Especially Wyatt.

Then, tonight, she came home from work and found her message light blinking.

"Lindsay, it's Wyatt . . ."

His voice—even a recorded version—stole her breath away.

"Listen, I've thought about it and I think we should meet him, if that's what he wants. I'm assuming it is. I mean, that's why people track down their birth parents, right?"

He made a sound, a bitter laugh, it sounded like.

He went on to instruct her to set up a meeting for Saturday at his house. It had to be Saturday, he said, because he was flying out first thing Sunday on business and wouldn't be back for a week. He'd send separate town cars for her and for Leo at two o'clock, to transport them up to Connecticut, and he'd arrange for the cars to take them back later.

His instructions were businesslike, his tone void of emotion.

She recognized the air of detached efficiency; she herself adopted it whenever she was working, making arrangements for upcoming events.

But this wasn't just an event, she told herself as she rummaged in a drawer for a tube of lipstick.

Saturday's meeting loomed as a life-altering milestone.

You'd think he'd have exhibited a little more awareness of that.

Leo certainly had, when she'd called him minutes ago to spring it on him.

His voice had radiated enthusiasm, especially when she told him that his father was sending a car for him.

"Is he rich, then?" he asked.

"I'm not sure," she lied.

She had discerned from Wyatt's appearance, from what he told her about his business, and from what she knew about where he lived, that he was rich.

There—she plucked a soft pink lipstick from the drawer, bypassing the red one Isaac had once complimented her on when she wore it.

She was meeting him for a drink tonight, but she wasn't trying to impress him. Not these days.

Wyatt was a different story, though. She'd taken great care with her appearance the morning they met. She wondered if he had done the same or if he always dressed so elegantly.

Maybe he did. He had to travel in fancy circles these days.

The money had changed Wyatt outwardly, but she could tell, even from the brief time they'd spent together, that it hadn't changed him inwardly.

He hadn't lost his sensitive core that had captivated her twenty years ago, would captivate her still, if he'd let her in.

He was going to . . .

She could tell. Before she dropped the news on him, his walls were coming down. He was making her laugh, trying to put her at ease . . .

Then I went and ruined everything.

Not that she'd had a choice. She had to tell him; that was why she'd contacted him. He wasn't going to pretend they were merely catching up; he knew there was something on her mind.

Right, but he thought it was something else.

Would it help if I told you I felt the same way? he had asked.

I never expected that to happen that night. And when you took off afterward, I figured you weren't interested in someone like me. So I kept it all to myself . . .

Kept all what to himself? His feelings? He had feelings for her?

She couldn't help wondering, in the moments before everything fell apart between them, whether there was actually a glimmer of hope.

Was there some way she and Wyatt could—

The ringing of the telephone shattered that thought.

She swiftly finished outlining her lips, set aside her lipstick, and hurried to answer it, checking her watch on the way. Lost in her reverie about Wyatt, she had taken too long to get ready. Now she was late—only by a couple of minutes, but it was probably Isaac on the phone, wondering if she'd forgotten.

"Hey, stranger," a female voice greeted her.

"Who—oh my God! Aurora?"

"Hey, very good! But would you have known it was me if Kristen hadn't told you I was going to be calling?"

Truth be told, she had forgotten all about that.

"Are you in New York, Aurora?" she asked, remembering what Kristen had said about their friend's travel plans. That conversation seemed so long ago.

"Yup, we just got here. Gosh, it's huge. I've wanted to see it all my life, and now here I am. I just wish Eddie could have come, too."

"Why didn't he?"

Aurora launched into a brief description of her husband's duties back home, holding down the fort and shuttling their other kids to their activities.

"He complains, but he's a great daddy. He's loved every minute of it. He cried harder than anyone at Tina's wedding."

"I'll bet." Lindsay found herself thinking of Wyatt again.

She'd never even given him a chance to be a great daddy. And he might very well have been.

But it was too late now.

Their son was grown.

Wyatt had been robbed.

"So when can we get together?" Aurora asked. "Are you busy tonight?"

"Actually, I'm supposed to be somewhere right now."

"Hmm . . . tomorrow, then? Or Saturday? We wanted to see a Broadway show, but we don't have tickets yet. Everything we want to see is sold out."

"This is a busy time of year," Lindsay told her. "But what did you want to see? Maybe I can pull some strings."

"Are you serious?"

Lindsay grinned, noting that Aurora sounded like her old animated self. "Sure. Just tell me which shows you're interested in, and I'll try to get a pair of tickets. They might not be the greatest seats, but—"

"Are you kidding, Linds? Any seats would be great. You're such a doll to do this."

Linds.

There it was again—the affectionate old nickname that was such a stark reminder of the girl she used to be.

Nobody called her that now. Strange, because shortening somebody's name was a natural thing to do when you were close to someone.

Then again, nobody was as close to her as those girls—her high-school friends—had once been. You didn't bond that intensely with others as a grown woman; there wasn't enough time in the day as it was. And anyway, you weren't in a phase of your life where you were insecure and dependent on other people.

But you still needed friends.

And Lindsay was more conscious now than ever of the loneliness in her life.

Maybe it's not just about longing for friends.

Maybe what you need is a different kind of companionship. Something more lasting. More . . .

Passionate.

Again, Wyatt Goddard popped into her head.

No, he had never really left. Thoughts of him were always there now, lurking just beyond her consciousness, ready to intrude at any given moment.

Hmm . . . it was really turning out to be quite a week for Lindsay Farrell when it came to catching up with old friends, the killer thought.

First Kristen, then Wyatt, and now Lindsay had just agreed to a Friday night dinner date with Aurora.

She'd even sounded enthusiastic when she agreed with Aurora's request that they dine at Sardi's, one of the most touristy restaurants in town, over in the theater district.

But then, she always was a fake and a liar, so what do you expect?

She checked her watch, wondering where Lindsay was off to now. She'd said she was meeting an old friend.

It couldn't be Wyatt, could it?

No. She'd had Lindsay's phone tapped all week, and as far as she knew, the only contact she'd had with him had been in messages. They weren't supposed to see each other until Saturday, when they had their little family reunion up in Connecticut.

A plan was already forming in her mind for that special occasion.

A daring plan, and one that deviated pretty drastically from her vow not to harm anyone other than the targets on her original list.

But now that the idea had sparked, it was pretty hard to ignore.

It was the perfect way to get to Lindsay, to make her suffer what people—some people, anyway—considered to be "a fate worse than death."

That had been Caroline Marcott's pathetically wailed phrasing at her son's wake on that long-ago February day.

Was losing a child really a fate worse than death?

She wouldn't know.

Maybe she'd soon find out, though. Through Lindsay.

Yes, she'd see that Lindsay suffered that so-called fate worse then death—and then she would suffer death itself.

And then we'll decide which was worse, she thought.

Oh, wait a minute, Lindsay . . . you won't be around for that part.

I guess I'll just have to decide on my own, won't I?

Her lips curved into a wicked smile as she hurried out of the hotel room and onto the street, hoping to get to Lindsay's building in time to tail her to wherever she was going.

"You don't seem like yourself tonight," Isaac observed, setting down his margarita glass and studying Lindsay from across the small table, which held an untouched basket of chips and a bowl of salsa.

Lindsay blinked. "I don't?"

"No. Normally, you would scarf down those chips in a hurry and ask for more. I'd assume it was because you had eaten dinner before you came, if you weren't so quiet."

"Sorry," she said, and made an effort to smile at him. "I guess I'm just thinking about work."

"No, you aren't." Isaac's gaze was intent. "Who is he?"

She frowned. "What makes you think there's a *he*?"

He raised an eyebrow. "Is it a she?"

"No."

He swung his arm and snapped his fingers in feigned disappointment. "I was convinced for a second there that the only reason you dumped me was because you played for the other team."

She winced even as she grinned. "I didn't dump you, Isaac. It was mutual."

"I'd have kept it going if you wanted to."

Maybe that was true. Maybe it wasn't.

It didn't matter now.

He had moved on to Kylah . . . but not, by the sounds of it, past Rachel.

Oh, well.

That was somebody else's problem now.

And you have enough of your own, she reminded herself, her mind clouding over again at the thought of Wyatt. And Leo.

She was almost tempted to confide in Isaac. He, after all, was far removed from the world she'd left behind twenty years ago. There was no danger that he'd spill her secret.

But you don't have to worry about that anymore, anyway. Wyatt knows.

Yes, and he was the reason she had kept it so carefully hidden all these years. Because she didn't want it to get back to him.

Now that he knew what she had done . . .

Well, there really wasn't a compelling reason to protect her past so adamantly.

Sure, her parents would be disappointed. But they had mellowed through the years, and anyway, their approval didn't carry the weight it had when she was living under their roof, dependent on their bank account.

Her old friends would be shocked.

Jake would have been, too.

But his imagined reaction was moot. He had been dead for two decades. And even if he had lived, she wouldn't possibly still be trying to shield him from the evidence of her fling with somebody else, would she?

Not unless they were married or something . . .

And she and Jake Marcott never in a million years would have gotten married.

She knew that now.

Jake didn't have the qualities she'd want in a husband.

Jake didn't even have the qualities she wanted in a boyfriend.

But she never let on about that—about what kind of person he had really turned out to be. You didn't speak ill of the dead.

"So who is he?" Isaac asked again, thoughtfully nibbling the curved triangular edge of a tortilla chip.

"He's just someone I used to know, back in Portland," she heard herself admit.

Must be the tequila.

"Old boyfriend?"

"Not really."

"Did he get back in touch with you?"

"I did, actually."

"Have you seen him, or just talked to him?"

"Seen him."

"And you wish you hadn't, right? Because things have fizzled?"

"No, that's not it at all."

"I didn't think so." Isaac nodded. "There was still something there, right? And it scared the hell out of you?"

"There's more to it than that."

"There always is. Is he married?"

"No!"

"In prison?"

"No!" She shifted her weight uncomfortably. "I don't really want to talk about it."

"I can tell. Let me just say one thing, and then I swear I'll change the subject. You haven't seen this person in years, and he was someone you once cared about. You're not married, he's not married . . . or in jail. An added bonus."

She barely cracked a smile at his weak joke.

"All I'm saying is that I can see how someone like you would get scared off and walk away. And you shouldn't do it. Take it from me, Lindsay. You don't want to have regrets. If I ever had another chance with Rachel—"

"It isn't like that at all," she cut in.

"In some ways, it is. We all lose people we love, Lindsay. Not all of us are lucky enough to find them again. If we do, we shouldn't let go that easily."

"You're talking about you and Rachel, not me and—"

"You're right," he said, his dark features having taken on the potent expression he always wore when Rachel's name came up. "I'm sorry. I guess I'm just—"

"Obsessed?"

She meant it lightly, but his scowl told her this wasn't a joking matter. Not to him.

Not any more than Wyatt was to her, but for far different reasons.

"Let's just drop it," she said. "Okay?"

"Definitely."

And they tried to talk about other things. Her job, his work as a computer-software engineer, his new girlfriend, the Yankees, the weather.

But none of it banished the ghosts of the past that swirled around their table, and Lindsay was grateful to call it a night.

Isaac offered to walk her home, but she declined. She lived only a few blocks east of here, and it was hardly on his way; he had to go west to take the subway downtown.

They parted with a promise to get together again soon, but she wasn't entirely sure that they would.

As she made her way along the narrow block leading east from Lexington Avenue, a vaguely uneasy feeling crept over her.

The street wasn't deserted; not in this neighborhood at this hour on a beautiful night in May. The block was lined with luxury apartment high-rises and a smattering of older brick buildings, some with security-gated storefronts on the ground floor. Colorful annuals tumbled from stray planters and the occasional window-box, and every so often the sidewalk blocks were broken by a carefully tended young tree.

A few people were out and about: an elderly man leaning heavily on a cane, a young couple strolling holding hands, a stout middle-aged woman walking a pair of impossibly small dogs joined by a single leash.

Lindsay snuck a glance over her shoulder and glimpsed a dark figure about a third of the way down the block behind her. It seemed to dart into a doorway abruptly . . .

Almost as if the person didn't want me to see him.

But it was probably just her imagination.

Whoever it was must have happened to arrive at his destination just as she looked back. Paranoia made her think he was trying to hide from her.

She turned her head forward again and walked on, much more quickly, looking over her shoulder all the way home.

That was a close call.

The killer crouched in the shadows beside a tall yellow brick apartment building, trying not to breathe in too deeply. A foul-smelling garbage can was just a few feet away.

What if she had seen you?

Relax. Even if she did, she wouldn't recognize me.

The wig, the thick glasses, the padding . . .

It was an apt disguise. Such an apt disguise that she didn't even recognize herself whenever she caught a glimpse of her reflection in a plate-glass window as she passed.

That was a strange feeling—being invisible right in plain sight.

But it shouldn't have been.

Not for her.

Wasn't that the reason all this had started in the first place?

Yes. And now it was almost time to bring it full circle.

What goes around comes around . . .

Hearing the voice echoing in her head, bringing with it a vague memory of something painful, she tried to remember who it was who'd said that to her.

One of her teachers?

Sister Neva?

Oh.

It was Jake, she realized. Well, wasn't that a coincidence.

"What goes around comes around," he'd said, laughing at her as she'd cried.

Now, looking back, she couldn't remember what she was crying about—only that he'd hurt her, in return for some perceived injury she'd supposedly inflicted on him.

Trembling, hiding in the building's shadows beside the smelly garbage can, she closed her eyes and saw Jake Marcott's smirking face.

What goes around comes around.

Yes, it sure does, Jake, she told him now, remembering the satisfying whiz and thwack of the arrow as it slammed into him, pinning him against the tree. Remembering the look of shock on his face as he glanced in horror at the slowly spreading red stain on the front of his shirt, then up at her.

He asked why, in a voice that was almost too weak to discern.

Why, indeed.

She didn't bother to answer his pathetic question.

There wasn't time; she had to get away, back to the others. She had to prepare herself to react to the shocking, so-called tragedy that was about to strike them all.

And anyway, there was no reason to explain it to Jake. He should have known why.

It was his own fault. His, and theirs—the girls whose lives had, in some way or other, been intertwined with Jake's, and, fatefully, with her own.

Jake had paid the price for his sins.

Haylie had, too.

And one by one, the others would join them, forever becoming part of the legend of St. Elizabeth's school.

Oh, yes, what goes around comes around, she thought gleefully, brazenly stepping out of the shadows after all, into the pool of light from a street lamp.

She gazed down the block, hoping to see Lindsay scuttling off like a frightened child.

She was already gone.

Oh, well. It was enough, for now, to know that she was poised at the perimeter of Lindsay Farrell's charmed life.

Poised like the wrecking ball that would soon claim the old school where it had all begun.

And when it came time for release, she would swing in with all her might, destroying everything in her path.

Chapter 20

Lindsay would have known Aurora Zephyr anywhere.

Spotting her old friend perusing the wall of famous carica-tures just inside the entrance at Sardi's on Forty-fourth Street just off Broadway, she stopped short and took in the sight of her.

She had the same dark curly hair, the same crinkly hazel eyes that widened in delight when she turned and saw Lindsay.

"Oh my God! Look at you!" she squealed, hurrying over to embrace her. "You're so sophisticated!"

"I am?" Lindsay looked down at the trim black suit she still wore from a long day at the office. There had been no time to run home and change.

"God, yes! Especially standing next to me!" Aurora had a point, but Lindsay would never admit it to her.

Slightly overweight in a bright colored dress, sheer tan panty hose, and a pair of low-heeled white pumps that were at least a few years old, her friend fit right in with the hordes of tourists crowding the lobby area of the famous restaurant.

"You look terrific, Aurora," Lindsay told her. Maybe not so-phisticated, but who cared about that? Her old friend truly was a breath of fresh air, and Lord knew she needed one tonight.

"Oh, come on, I'm an old frump. I'm going to be a grand-mother before the year is out, you know. I never thought I'd live to see the day, but here it comes."

"I know—congratulations! Where's Tina?" Lindsay looked around for Aurora's daughter. "I can't wait to meet her."

"She couldn't come at the last minute. Poor thing. She was ab-solutely wiped out after all the shopping we did today. Neither of us are used to so much walking, but it really did Tina in. When you're pregnant, you're pretty much exhausted through the whole first trimester," she added unnecessarily.

How well Lindsay knew that.

She remembered how hard it was to get out of bed for school when her alarm went off on weekday mornings as their senior year dragged on, and the numbing fatigue that often nearly caused her to fall asleep in class.

But of course, Aurora didn't know about any of that.

And she appeared to feel sorry for poor, childless Lindsay now, as they waited for their table. She sounded almost apologetic as she chatted about her impending grandchild.

They were seated more quickly than Lindsay expected, thanks to changing their existing reservation from three people to two. She had been prepared to slip a big tip to someone if necessary to secure a good table, but they landed one anyway.

"Look at this place!" Aurora marveled, spreading her napkin in her lap and gazing at the portraits that lined the walls of the large main-floor dining room. "I've always wanted to eat here. Is the food good?"

"I'm not sure," admitted Lindsay, who favored out-of-the-way restaurants in the Village and Tribeca.

"You must eat out all the time, though," Aurora said a little wistfully, "living here in Manhattan, being in your business."

"I do eat out a lot," she said just as wistfully, imagining Aurora presiding over cozy family dinners in a suburban kitchen back in Oregon.

She wondered what it would be like to be married to someone you had loved for all those years, to have a family and grow old with him . . .

Could there be anything more precious in the whole wide world?

No, there couldn't.

Lindsay just hoped Aurora knew how lucky she was.

Grimly, she cast aside the thought of Wyatt and Leo. Again.

They'd been haunting her all day, but she had already decided she wasn't going to let tomorrow's looming confrontation intrude upon her evening with Aurora.

They ordered white wine, chatted amiably, and studied their menus.

"What do you think prix fixe is?" Aurora asked, pronouncing the French phrase as if it rhymed.

When Lindsay gently corrected her, hoping she wouldn't be embarrassed, Aurora burst out laughing at herself.

"Do you think anybody overheard me?" she asked, sneaking a peek at the diners occupying adjacent tables.

Lindsay took a quick look around. "Nah." They were mostly older couples and families of tourists, all engrossed in conversations of their own. A large blond woman was dining solo at the next table over and had her back to them, but who cared if she, or anyone else, had been privy to Aurora's gaffe?

"God, I'm such a bumpkin. I don't know how you managed to move here and fit in so well, Lindsay."

"I've been here twenty years, and you are not a bumpkin. You're a sweetheart who happens not to speak French."

Aurora grinned. "Or who tries, and ends up talking about pricks in a fancy restaurant."

Yes, she really was a breath of fresh air, Lindsay thought, glad she had made time to meet her old friend. As she nibbled her smoked salmon appetizer, she found that she didn't even have to do much talking, as was always the case in Aurora's company.

Aurora munched and chatted her way through her tomato-basil-mozzarella salad, talking animatedly about her family. Then, as they sipped their Merlot, waiting for the entrees to arrive, she changed the subject to the upcoming reunion—and Haylie's death.

"I heard about it from Kristen," Lindsay said, twirling the stem of her glass back and forth in her fingers. "I can't believe it."

"Nobody can. Eddie told me when I called home this morning that they arrested someone last night," Aurora said unexpectedly.

Lindsay lowered her goblet. "Who was it?"

"Do you remember Louie Blake?"

She shook her head. "Should I? Did he go to school with us?"

"No!" Aurora wrinkled her nose. "Please, he's got to be in his late forties, at least. He's a bum, basically. He's been hanging around the streets for years, getting into trouble. I guess you must have been gone by the time he showed up, though."

"He killed Haylie?" Lindsay asked, relieved not just that they had someone in custody but that it was no one connected to high school, or Jake.

"They think so. He was caught trying to use one of her credit cards at a liquor store, and they found out that he had a bunch of stuff he must have stolen from her apartment."

"Poor Haylie."

"I know . . . I feel guilty that I didn't go after her with Kristen the night she freaked out and ran out of the reunion meeting. Not that Kristen managed to catch up with her and calm her down anyway. Did she tell you what happened?"

"Kristen? She just said that Haylie was still really upset over Ian and Jake after all these years."

"Right. She made a big scene, accusing us all of ridiculous things, and took off. It was awful. And I feel so sorry for her, really. I mean, *felt*."

They were both silent as they realized, again, that they could only refer to Haylie in past tense from now on.

Aurora added, "She never got over what happened to Ian."

"I know. Poor Haylie."

"What about you, Lindsay?"

"What about me?"

"Did you ever get over what happened to Jake?"

About to sip her wine, Lindsay found herself taking a gulp instead. She looked around, wishing the waiter would show up with their meals.

"I don't like to talk about that, really, Aurora," she said. "It was so traumatic."

"Of course it was. God, I'm so sorry I even brought it up. I guess I just wanted to know that you were okay. You know, that you had moved on. Because you moved away right after and you never really came back, and I figured that was why."

Right. That was probably what everyone thought, that she had left for New York because she was distraught over Jake's murder. And who would blame her?

They were broken up, but she was still widely regarded as the bereaved girlfriend, much to Kristen's dismay—and barely concealed resentment.

"It was hard to get over what happened," she told Aurora now. "But you move on, you know? You have to get on with your life."

"I know." Aurora reached over and squeezed her hand. "I didn't mean to drag all that out tonight, Linds. Let's talk about something more upbeat."

Lindsay forced a smile. "Good idea. And I have just the topic. I got those *Jersey Boys* tickets you and Tina wanted. A matinee tomorrow afternoon."

"Ooh!" Aurora hugged her across the table. "You're the best, Lindsay. How can I ever repay you?"

"You don't have to. What are friends for?"

* * *

"This is Lindsay. I'm not in; please leave a message and I'll get back to you as soon as I can."

Wyatt disconnected the call in the midst of the answering machine's beep.

A message?

What was he supposed to say?

If you don't know, then why did you call her?

That was a good question.

He didn't know the answer. He had simply found himself walking restlessly around the house with his cell phone in hand; her number was programmed into it.

He still didn't even know why he had done that. Why not just keep it jotted on a slip of paper tucked into the kitchen drawer where he kept stray business cards and receipts and order numbers? That was what he did with most women's phone numbers. Very few were eventually programmed into his phone. And those he did program in were always eventually removed.

Allison's was the most recent.

He hadn't heard from her since she'd moved out; he didn't expect to.

As for Lindsay . . .

After tomorrow, he wouldn't be in touch with her again. There would be no reason to.

In fact, if he had any way of meeting his son without her present, he would have arranged to do so.

Oh, come on, Wyatt, who are you kidding?

You don't need her here tomorrow. You could have just gotten the kid's contact info from her and met him on your own.

So why didn't he?

Why had he gone ahead and arranged this little family reunion?

Anyone would be furious with Lindsay for what she'd done.

And he was. Absolutely.

But there was a part of him, deep down, that was also, maybe, just a little . . .

Grateful.

If she had come to him, pregnant, twenty years ago, what would he have done?

He knew exactly what he'd have done.

He'd have convinced her to have the baby and marry him.

He was in love with her; knowing she was carrying his child would have put him over the moon.

And she would have either walked away from him—again— had the baby, and given it up just as she wound up doing . . .

Or she would have married him, and they would have tried to raise their son together.

Tried.

There wasn't a doubt in Wyatt's mind that if they had married and become parents at eighteen, they couldn't have made it work. The odds would have been stacked tremendously against them. Yes, he'd loved Lindsay back then, but was he really equipped to be a husband and father?

Not in the least.

So, being Catholic, they would have ended up either bitterly married, merely sticking it out, as his parents had . . .

Or divorced, and riddled with guilt—Catholic and otherwise. And their son would have come from a broken home—*which he does anyway*, Wyatt reminded himself. But still, that wasn't Wyatt's fault. It was some other man who had walked out on his wife and kid.

My kid.

Every single time he thought of it—the miraculous fact that he had a son—his stomach was consumed by a flurry of Christmas-morning butterflies.

Yes, Lindsay's decision had denied him the option of being a part of his son's life until now . . .

But she had also denied him the chance to screw it up. And he would have.

Back then, he was ill equipped, emotionally and financially, for the responsibility.

Now?

Bring it on.

He was more than ready. He was going to wholeheartedly support his son emotionally and financially, give him whatever he needed—hell, whatever he *wanted*. He was going to spoil the kid rotten if he felt like it, and there was no reason not to.

What about Lindsay, though? a nagging voice intruded. *What are you going to do about her?*

He was going to try to forgive her for what she had done, knowing, intellectually, that it was probably the wisest, most self-less decision she could have made in her situation.

That was the mature and logical thing to do.

Then he was going to maturely and logically move on. Try to forget her.

Right. Just like he had before.

And look how well that turned out.

All she had to do was call and you went running to her, no questions asked. All she had to do was look at you and twenty years fell away, and you were like a teenaged boy with a one-track mind again.

Yes, and now you're calling her number and hanging up. Perfect.

With a scowl, Wyatt tossed his cell phone onto the granite countertop and headed up to his gym to work out—and thus, work her out of his system—so that he could get a good night's sleep in preparation for what lay ahead tomorrow.

Forty-Fourth Street was bright with neon lights and packed with people when Lindsay and Aurora emerged from Sardi's after a long, leisurely meal. They'd had dessert at the table followed by after-dinner drinks in the upstairs bar. The time flew by, and the conversation flowed.

Now it was getting late, and the post-theater crowd packed the sidewalks.

"Uh-oh—it's going to be hard for me to get a cab back to the hotel, isn't it?" Aurora observed, gazing at the street clogged with honking taxis, town cars, and limousines. They were forced to creep along far more slowly than the pedestrians who moved along the sidewalks.

"It won't be hard to get a cab. It will be impossible," Lindsay replied. "But you're staying right at the Grand Hyatt next to Grand Central Station, aren't you? It's an easy walk from here. Just a few blocks."

"Ha, that's what the doorman said when he told me I could walk here. I didn't know he meant a few of those really long, long crosstown blocks," Aurora said ruefully. "I thought he meant the short uptown-downtown kind. I can't make it back."

"Sure you can. It won't be so bad. Come on, I'll walk you there."

"Is it on your way home?"

"More or less," Lindsay told her.

Aurora seemed to consider her offer, but only for a minute.

"No, thanks, my feet are killing me. I did way too much walking today. I can take the subway instead."

"The subway?" Lindsay asked dubiously, wondering if her friend could possibly negotiate the complicated network of train lines that ran beneath the city streets.

Then again, if she got on right here at Times Square, she'd only have to take the crosstown shuttle two stops to Grand Central and walk right upstairs to her hotel. Or she could take the number seven train, which traveled the same route before heading beneath the East River out to Queens.

Queens.

That made Lindsay think of Leo. And Wyatt. Again.

This time, she couldn't seem to push them back out of her head.

"I've always wanted to ride the subway," Aurora said cheerfully as they made their way across Broadway toward the station. "I've seen it in so many movies and TV shows. I can't believe I actually get to ride it."

Lindsay grinned at her friend's giddy enthusiasm. She remembered feeling the same way when she first moved to New York. Not right away, though. She didn't get out into the city until after the baby had been born and she had gone on to college, getting on with her life.

"Where do I get my token?" Aurora asked as they descended from the noisy neon glare of the street to the dank depths of the station below.

"We don't use those anymore. We use Metrocards," Lindsay told her. "I'll help you get one before I go."

"You're not taking the subway home too?"

"No, I'm going to walk," she said, anxious to be alone with her thoughts now that the evening with Aurora was drawing to a close.

Yes, it was time to try to prepare herself for what she faced tomorrow.

Standing beneath a large wall map, pretending to be studying the network of subway lines, she watched Lindsay remove a fare card from the automated machine and hand it to Aurora.

Then Lindsay pointed at the row of turnstiles, obviously explaining how to get through them, then find her way down the stairs to the right track.

The place was a zoo even at this hour of the night. And she herself was intimidated. There were so many different numbered and lettered lines coming through this station that she couldn't imagine how people figured out where they were going. She wondered how Aurora was ever going to find her way back to the hotel.

Lindsay was obviously not planning on accompanying her. Otherwise, she wouldn't be giving such a detailed explanation. She kept emphatically indicating the overhead sign, as if trying to make sure Aurora understood exactly where she was supposed to go.

Finally, they both seemed satisfied, and they exchanged a long, tight hug.

She found herself feeling resentful, watching them.

They looked as though they cared so much about each other, even after all these years.

They never cared about me that way. They pretended to, like everyone else did, but they didn't really care.

Nobody did. Not even Jake.

And toward the end, he didn't even bother to pretend anymore.

Fury bubbled up inside her, and it took her a moment to realize that Lindsay had disappeared.

She looked around, trying to spot her in the crowd. No sign of her.

There, though, was Aurora, about to go through the turnstile, poking her fare card into the slot.

Ah, the turnstile failed to open.

Momentarily amused, she forgot to look for Lindsay. Instead, she watched Aurora bang on the turnstile, then kick it.

Still it didn't open.

Aurora whirled around abruptly, as if hoping to find Lindsay still standing there.

Oh my God . . .

Shocked, she found herself locking eyes with Aurora despite the throng of people that bustled between them.

She sees me!

Relax, you're wearing your disguise.

Yes, she was . . . but it didn't seem to matter. There was no mistaking the flicker of recognition, then shock, in Aurora's gaze.

Then a uniformed MTA officer materialized at Aurora's side to check the turnstile, and she seized the opportunity to duck behind a nearby signpost.

Oh my God.

She definitely saw me.

Now what?

Peering out from behind the sign, she watched as the officer leaned in and did something to the turnstile. It immediately opened.

Aurora faltered, glancing over her shoulder.

She's looking for me.

The officer was gesturing impatiently for Aurora to hurry up and go through the turnstile, and several impatient locals waited behind her for their turns.

Helplessly, Aurora slipped through the turnstile with one last backward glance.

She still doesn't see me . . .

No, but she did. She definitely did.

And you know exactly what you need to do about that.

What on earth was she *doing here, in New York, of all places?* Aurora wondered uneasily as she waited on the packed, cavernous platform for the next subway train to pull into the station.

Still unsettled by the unexpectedly familiar—yet unfamiliar— person she'd glimpsed upstairs, she tried somewhat unsuccessfully to ignore the hordes of strangers surrounding her down here.

She had never been entirely comfortable in crowds, and this was extreme. So many people, some passing so close they were practically touching her, some with terrible body odor, others speaking in various languages. There were crying babies and panhandlers shaking cups of change and someone, somewhere, was playing Van Morrison's "Moondance" on a clarinet.

Maybe that wasn't her upstairs, Aurora tried to convince herself, yet again.

But that didn't work for more than a hopeful second or two.

It was her. Definitely.

She was wearing some kind of bizarre disguise. Her body was much heavier, and she had on a blond wig.

But her face was unmistakable.

And the look in her eyes . . .

God, that was scary.

Never before had Aurora seen her look that way. Darkly serious, almost . . .

Sinister.

That was why she kept trying to convince herself that it had been somebody else, standing there, watching.

Because it didn't make sense for a friend to be looking at Aurora that way—much less be here in New York City at all, in fact.

Aurora stared blindly into the train tracks, wondering what she should do about what she had seen.

I'll call Eddie the second I get back to my room and run it by him, she decided.

She always shared troubling developments with him first. Shared everything with him, really. Bad, good, exciting, scary.

Suddenly, she was fiercely homesick for her husband. For her house. For Portland.

Especially when she spotted movement amid the litter strewn over the rails just below the platform and realized it was a rat.

A real live rat.

Oh, God. This was too much. Aurora wanted nothing more than to go home.

Nothing was reassuringly familiar here, not with Tina so uncharacteristically wan, with Lindsay no longer at her side—and with *her*, up there in the station, looking eerily like a stranger.

Except a stranger wouldn't have returned Aurora's gaze so intently.

She shivered at the thought of that strange stare.

No, there was nothing familiar about New York on this night at all; she felt as though she had been dropped into an exotic foreign land—a war zone or something, because she had a vague, inexplicable sense of impending peril.

That's just because you're alone in a big city. Thirty-eight years old and you feel like you desperately need to hold somebody's hand.

It was kind of pathetic, really.

I really am a bumpkin. That's all it is. A bumpkin, and a baby.

Below, on the track, the rat scurried away abruptly and she felt, then heard, a distant rumble. It scared her for a moment—was it an earthquake? A terrorist attack?

Oh my God. Eddie . . . I'm so scared, Eddie.

Her heart pounded as the rumble grew steadily louder.

Dear God in heaven, Blessed Mother, please, please help me.

She looked up to see the proverbial light at the end of the tunnel.

The train.

Oh.

That was all it was.

The subway train was roaring into the station.

Aurora instinctively stepped back from the edge of the platform as it approached—rather, she tried to.

Somebody was right behind her, of course—it was crowded. She felt herself being jostled. The person behind her was pressing up against her. Hard.

No.

Not pressing.

Pushing.

Panic worked its way into her throat as she realized she was too close to the edge.

She was losing her balance, and the train was coming, and she was falling, *dear God, please, no*, she was falling, and—

The last thing that went through Aurora Zephyr's mind was that she wasn't going to live to be a grandmother after all.

Chapter 21

Saturday morning, Lindsay went to the gym first thing for her usual one-hour spinning class. Whenever she was stressed, she could count on finding relief there, mindlessly riding the stationary bike over imaginary mountain roads in the dark, music blasting.

But the exercise didn't relieve her physical tension today, and it wasn't mindless.

She kept seeing Wyatt's face, and Leo's.

Rather, seeing Leo's as a younger version of Wyatt's. In Lindsay's mind's eye, her son had morphed into the Wyatt she had known back in Oregon, tall and lean with a shock of black hair, flashing black eyes, and a smile like a sunburst.

The grown-up Wyatt still had that same smile, the same dark hair and eyes. But he was more muscular now; she had been able to see the masculine changes in his body even beneath the sleeves of his suit coat.

She hated that she still, even now, days later, found herself fantasizing about his biceps, pecs, and abs—about seeing him shirtless, or in nothing at all.

Let's face it, she told herself as she stepped from the steamy shower in the gym's locker room and reached for a towel, *you're hopelessly overdue for some physical . . . release. And not the kind you get in a spinning class.*

It had been months since she and Isaac broke up; there had been no one since him. A few dates here and there, nobody she wanted to see more than once.

But it wasn't just about Lindsay needing some kind of physical release.

It was about her needing Wyatt himself.

Why? Because he had been her first? Did you always long to repeat that experience, right down to the man with whom you had shared it?

Or was it something more?

Who are you kidding? she asked herself, wrapping the towel around her waist and padding back into the main locker room. Of course it was something more.

And it wasn't just physical.

But none of that mattered—or was supposed to, anyway. As relationships went, she and Wyatt Goddard barely shared a past, and certainly not a future.

"Hey, Lindsay, how've you been?"

She looked up to see Amy, a casual friend from spinning class.

"Great," she lied, "how about you?"

As she made small talk with Amy and got into her clothes, she couldn't help but compare this slightly stilted conversation to the effortless one she'd had with Aurora last night.

They had picked up right where they'd left off, finding so many things to talk about that she was reluctant when the evening came to an end and she had to say good-bye.

The last thing she'd told Aurora, before she sent her off on the subway, was that she would plan on going to the reunion in July.

"Oh, Lindsay, really? That would be great. Everyone would absolutely love to see you."

"I'd absolutely love to see them, too."

She and Aurora had shared a big hug, one that left Lindsay overcome with unexpected emotion. She found herself with tears in her eyes and, embarrassed, hurried away quickly. She didn't want Aurora to go home and tell everyone that she was a sentimental wreck.

That, however, was exactly what she was. Last night, and today.

But today wasn't about her old girlfriends or stepping into a familiar, nostalgic past.

It was about stepping into a role she had both willingly and reluctantly abandoned—and a decision she had both regretted and celebrated.

No wonder she was tense.

"Did you hear that we're supposed to get a big storm later?" Amy asked conversationally as, fully dressed, they both slung their duffel bags over their shoulders and headed for the door.

"I'm so bummed. I was supposed to go boating on the Hudson this afternoon with this guy I've been seeing."

"Well, hopefully it won't happen and you'll have smooth sailing."

"I doubt it. It's supposed to be really bad, wind, rain, maybe even hail."

Lindsay found that hard to believe as she stepped out into the surprisingly hot May sunshine and walked the three blocks back to her apartment.

The first thing she did was book her plane reservations back to Portland for the reunion, and a room at the new Marriott not far from the school. She arranged to be there a week early, thinking she might be able to help the committee with some last-minute details. Event planning, after all, was what she did.

At least, that was her official excuse for arranging to spend so much time in her hometown. Really, she was anxious to indulge this wave of nostalgia.

All right, that was set.

Now what? She had a few hours still to kill before Wyatt's car arrived.

It was too early to start getting ready yet, so she wandered around the apartment, watering plants, throwing away newspapers and junk mail, emptying the dishwasher.

She realized she was famished. She opened the fridge and reached past the carton of eggs for a container of yogurt.

Then it occurred to her that she could actually cook something. That would occupy her for a while.

In class this week, they had progressed from chopping and dicing to making simple omelets.

Lindsay didn't have on hand many ingredients they had used, but she did have onions and tomatoes.

She washed and placed them on the counter, pulled out a cutting board, and hunted through her drawer for a suitable knife.

If you're going to take this cooking stuff seriously, you're really going to need to be better equipped, she told herself, at last locating a knife that looked closest to the one she'd used in class.

She began dicing the onion, trying to remember to use the technique she'd learned, but it wasn't easy with this knife. The blade was much duller.

Not entirely dull, though. She found that out the hard way when it sliced into her forefinger.

"Ow!" She grabbed a dish towel and wrapped it to stanch the blood that poured from the painful wound, but it took a while. Every time she lifted the towel to check her finger, she saw that it was still bleeding profusely.

Finally, the flow subsided, and she winced as she cleaned the cut in the bathroom. She wondered if she might need stitches . . . but it was a Saturday. She'd have to go to the emergency room, and that, she knew from the notorious experiences of others, could take hours.

Which would mean postponing today's meeting.

No. No way.

Better to let the wound heal and hope for the best.

Her finger bandaged, she returned to the kitchen, where she tossed partially chopped onion into the garbage and put away the eggs, tomatoes, and butter.

Then she opened a container of yogurt, flopped on the couch, and turned on the television.

It was tuned to the twenty-four-hour local news channel— pretty much the only thing she ever watched when she did bother to turn on the TV at night.

Whoa, Amy was right. Severe thunderstorms were expected late in the day.

Lindsay hoped it wasn't an omen that this afternoon wouldn't be smooth sailing for her meeting with Wyatt and Leo.

Come on . . . Do you really expect it to go off without a hitch?

There were too many emotions involved all around. Leo might be her own flesh and blood, but he was a stranger.

Wyatt might as well be a stranger, too.

She sighed, spooned some yogurt into her mouth glumly, and stared at the television. Above the news anchor's left shoulder, an ominous graphic showed the black outline of a human figure and a train, with a red splotch between the two.

"A tragic accident last night—"

She'd had more than her fill of bloody injuries for one morning. She reached for the remote, deciding to find something a little more uplifting to watch before she got ready to go to Wyatt's.

Maybe there was an old sitcom or a cooking show or something. Anything to take her mind off the day ahead.

"—beneath the streets of Manhattan as an unidentified woman was struck and killed by a—"

Lindsay aimed the remote and curtailed the anchor's grim report, then channel-surfed until she came across a Steve Martin movie that was a few years old. She'd seen it and knew it had a happy ending.

Good. At least something would today.

She surveyed the array of items spread before her on the hotel desk.

A wallet filled with old pictures, some of family, but others of her friends. A small bottle of Aurora's favorite perfume. A date book filled with notes pertaining to the upcoming reunion. Vanilla-flavored lip balm—not lipstick—the kind she had used back in high school. A brush that held strands of curly black hair.

She couldn't wait to get it all back to Aurora's locker beneath St. Elizabeth's; what a wonderful and unexpected treasure trove to add to the collection.

There had been considerable cash in the wallet, which would come in handy today. She had, as usual, found someone who was willing to accommodate her request and keep his mouth shut about it. But he wanted a hell of a lot of money for his compliance.

So much money that she thought it would almost be easier to just steal a damned town car—or hire one and ask the driver to take her to a remote spot, then catch him off guard and get him out of the way.

Easier, perhaps, but far riskier.

She stashed Aurora's cash in her purse. She had more than enough to pay the driver for the use of his car. She just hated to keep spending it this way. Life would be easier when she was back home, back in her element, not having to rely on strange people in a strange city.

Using a pair of nail scissors, she carefully snipped Aurora's Oregon driver's license, credit cards, and plastic hotel key into tiny pieces. She tucked those into a small plastic bag and put that in her purse, too. She would have to remember to toss it into a garbage can on the street when she left the hotel.

Those identifying items were the reason she'd grabbed Aurora's purse from her shoulder as she fell. The longer it took to identify her, the more time she would buy for all that needed to be accomplished.

Shoving Aurora in front of an oncoming train wasn't nearly as satisfying as it had been hacking into Haylie's body, but it achieved a far more important goal.

Aurora had seen her, recognized her. She had to be stopped before she told someone—and the perfect opportunity had presented itself, which was a sign from God that this was meant to be.

The platform had been so jammed that it took a few seconds for anyone to realize someone had fallen in front of the train.

By the time she heard the inevitable commotion, she was halfway up the stairs. From there, it was easy to get out, lost in the crowd. She heard sirens wailing in the distance and saw uniformed transit authorities rushing for the track, but by that time, she was halfway to the street.

This morning on the news, she had seen coverage of the incident.

In a city like New York, it was eclipsed by other stories: the masked rapist who had been terrorizing women on the East Side, the mayor's latest ribbon-cutting ceremony in Harlem, even the weather forecast.

Little airtime was devoted to the report about an unidentified woman who had fallen from a crowded subway platform at the Times Square station. Witnesses said it had been crowded down there, as always; Times Square was, after all, "the crossroads of the world," as the reporter pointed out.

Nobody seemed to have seen anything suspicious; it was assumed that the poor woman, whoever she was, had simply lost her balance.

Perfect. Everything was just humming along, nobody piecing anything together yet. That would buy her some time.

She wondered how long it would take before Aurora's daughter, who must have reported her mother missing by now, heard about the subway accident. How long before the police connected the missing tourist with the dead woman?

With any luck, it would be at least another day or two.

Just long enough to let me do what I have to do and get back home to Portland.

Of course, her work was cut out for her there as well.

Hopefully, there wouldn't be further complications.

Wearily—she hadn't slept well last night—she reached for the sunglasses she had picked up in Central Park the other day.

She put them on and studied her reflection in the mirror above the desk.

They were meant for a man; they masked most of her face.

Perfect, she thought again.

*　　*　　*

Looking out the fourth-story master bedroom window above Queens Boulevard, Leo reminded himself that he still had twenty minutes before the car was supposed to arrive.

He couldn't help it, though; he was anxious to get moving.

He had been ready for over an hour, pacing the small apartment wearing his best suit—his only suit, purchased when he was a pallbearer for his grandmother's funeral last year. The pants were too short now; about an inch of black sock was visible above his scuffed dress shoes. He had tried to polish those with little success; he had donned them to go to Saint Luke's School every day of his senior year, then again for Grandma's funeral—they were all but worn out. Tight, too, at a size twelve and a half.

Were your feet supposed to keep growing as you headed into your twenties?

He wondered if his father had big feet. His real father.

He'd be able to ask him today.

Come on, move, he thought, glancing at the hands of the clock on the bedside table. They seemed to be glued down.

It was an old-fashioned wind-up alarm clock he had won at a street fair a few years ago. It used to be beside his own bed, but he gave it to his mother for the master bedroom when his father—his *adoptive* father—moved out and took the digital one.

He found himself wishing that his father knew what he was doing today . . . and glad his mother did not.

She had taken his brother, Mario, into the city to visit Aunt Rose and Uncle Paul. She wanted Leo to go, too, but he told her he had to work.

He felt guilty about that—and even guiltier knowing she wouldn't check up on him. Uncle Joe, who owned the pizzeria, was her ex-husband's brother. She didn't talk to that side of the family anymore.

But she didn't stop Leo from working there. He needed the job, the money. And anyway, Uncle Joe was good to him. Better to him than his father had been.

He paced across the bedroom, then back again, coming to a halt before the window air-conditioning unit. He probably should turn it on, actually. It was pretty hot out today. Ma would appreciate coming home later to a nice, cool bedroom.

As he reached out to adjust the knob, he glanced down to the street again.

Hey, what do you know!

A sleek black town car had just pulled up to the curb.

Those were a rare sight in this neighborhood, especially on a Saturday.

And the car was early. But there was no reason not to head right out now, since it was here.

Leo had forgotten all about the air-conditioning and about his mother—his adopted one, anyway.

He hurried to the door, scarcely able to believe it was time to meet his birth parents at last.

He wondered, as he bolted down three flights of stairs, if they were going to live up to his expectations—and, more importantly, whether he would live up to theirs.

Unlike him, they'd had twenty years to imagine what he was like.

What if they don't love me?

Love you? an inner voice scoffed. *They don't even know you. And they don't even love each other.*

If they did, they'd be together now.

So much for that fantasy family you always dreamed of, he thought dismally as he hurried out onto the boulevard and the waiting car.

To his surprise, the driver was a woman.

He didn't know why that caught him off guard; it shouldn't have. But somehow, he had pictured an elegant male chauffeur, not a dumpy-looking lady in a black suit, cap, and almost ridiculously oversized sunglasses.

"How are you today?" she asked pleasantly, opening the back door for him.

"Good," he said briefly, and slid into the backseat, trying to act as though he did this sort of thing every day.

As they headed north toward the Triborough Bridge, Leo didn't give the driver, or the route she was taking, another thought.

He had no way of knowing that later, he would regret it.

Wyatt heard the crunch of car tires on the driveway and looked up from the *New York Times* he had been reading—rather, trying to read—in his recliner.

Through the tall window overlooking the manicured front lawn with its towering shade trees, he could see a shiny black town car pulling toward the house.

Lindsay should be first to arrive. He'd told her driver to get to her house a bit early and had scheduled the other driver to get to Queens a little later than expected.

He didn't want to spend a lot of time alone with Lindsay before Leo arrived, but he did think it would only be right for them to face their son for the first time as a united front.

And, perhaps, to discuss just what it was that they hoped to get out of this meeting today.

He set the paper aside, rose from the door, and walked to the front entry hall. He caught sight of his reflection in a long mirror as he passed and was glad he had opted for casual clothing today.

He was wearing loafers, jeans, and a polo shirt. He looked comfortable and unintimidating, like any other suburban dad.

Funny, because that wasn't what he was at all.

It's just what I wish I could be.

But maybe . . .

No. No expectations. Whatever is meant to be will be.

Steeling himself, he opened the door and stepped out onto the covered porch. For a fleeting moment, he wondered what he would do if his son had somehow arrived first.

But it was Lindsay who emerged from the backseat of the town car.

Unaware that he was there watching her, she smoothed imaginary wrinkles from her pale green sleeveless dress and patted her dark hair, which was worn pulled back in a simple ponytail.

She's nervous, he realized.

Somehow, that fact helped to put him more at ease.

She thanked the driver, turned toward the house, and stopped short, spotting Wyatt.

"Hi," he said, wishing he had sunglasses on. He tried not to look her up and down, but there went those teenaged-boy hormones again.

"Hi." She walked hesitantly toward him as the town car pulled away, and he remembered that he was the host.

"How was the drive up?" he asked cordially, as though he were greeting a new client.

"Fine. Was that your, um, driver?"

"No," he said with a laugh. "That was a car service I hire sometimes, though. For clients, or when I have to go to the airport or something."

"Oh." She glanced up at the three-story white Colonial, with its black shutters and majestic pillars. "I thought maybe you ride around in a limo all the time."

"Nope. I do my own driving." He wasn't about to tell her that his four-car garage held four luxury cars that, along with the others he kept in storage near his winter place near Daytona, were worth almost as much as he'd paid for this house.

He could see that she was impressed as it was by his surroundings—not because she wasn't accustomed to such things, but more likely because she was. This was her world, and now he was a part of it.

But not in the ways that count, he thought as he held the door open and ushered her inside.

She looked around the entryway, with its sweeping staircase, framed artwork, and hardwood floors. "This is nice."

"We can wait for him in the living room."

"So he's not here yet, then?" She looked relieved.

"No. But he should be soon."

He . . . him . . .

So neither of them could bring themselves to say their son's name.

Or even just the word *son.*

He felt an unexpected bond with Lindsay as they sat down, somewhat stiffly, on the couch.

They both took care to keep a physical distance between them, but they were unmistakably in this together, whether they liked it or not.

"Thanks—what happened to your hand?" he asked, breaking a near silence punctuated by the ticking grandfather clock in the hall.

"Oh, this?" She lifted her bandaged finger. "I sliced into it with a dull knife this morning, trying to dice an onion."

He winced. "Ouch. Why were you using a dull knife?"

"It was the only one I could find. I just started taking these cooking classes, and I thought I would give it a whirl at home, but I'm not exactly stocked up on the latest gourmet cutlery."

"What kind of cooking classes are you taking?"

"Just the very basics. That's right—you said you cook."

"I do. Do you want anything to eat?" he remembered to ask belatedly.

"No, I'm good, thanks."

"How about something to drink? Iced tea? Coffee? A shot of tequila?"

She looked up at him, startled, and he grinned. "Just kidding. Sorry. I couldn't help it."

She smiled back, to his surprise. "Too bad. I was going to take you up on it."

"Really?"

"No . . . but it was tempting for a second there. I guess I'm a nervous wreck. How about you?"

"Me, too," he admitted. "How are we going to handle this?"

We.

The forbidden pronoun had popped out of him with surprising ease.

Which was interesting, because in all the time Allison had lived here—and in all the relationships that had preceded her— he'd had a hard time referring to himself as one half of a *we*.

"I don't know," Lindsay said slowly, and he couldn't tell whether she was fazed by the *we* or the question itself.

"Have you talked to his mother? I mean, his adoptive mother."

"I knew what you meant," she said wryly. "No. I didn't think it was my place. He's over eighteen. And anyway, he asked me not to."

"When?"

"When I called him back to set up today's meeting."

"Oh." For a moment there, he had thought she might have already met Leo on her own, without him.

But he knew instinctively that she wouldn't do a thing like that. He trusted her.

Which was ironic, considering what she had already gone and done behind his back, then kept from him all these years.

Wyatt was surprised to realize that he held no deep well of resentment about that. What he had felt had faded considerably these last few days.

That was because he not only trusted her, he ultimately understood her motives.

She had believed she was making the right choice, the unselfish choice, for their baby. In doing so, she had shown more strength than he had known she had.

More strength—more selflessness—than he would have had himself.

Admiration was slipping in to replace his anger, and he didn't know how he felt about that.

Anger made it easier to keep her at arm's length.

Now that she was, quite literally, at arm's length, it was all he could do not to turn to her and pull her closer, if only in a comforting hug.

Instead, he said, "We should decide what we're going to say when he gets here. You know . . . what each of us wants to come out of this."

The *each of us* was meant to defuse the *we*. To show her that he didn't expect them to be a *we* after today; that they would meet their son, then go their separate ways as they forged their own relationships with him. Not with each other.

"I don't really know what I want," Lindsay told him quietly. "Do you?"

"I guess it isn't about what we want or need," he replied. "It's more about what he wants and needs. Right?"

"Absolutely."

"In that case, I guess all we can do is wait until he gets here."

She nodded and settled back stiffly, arms folded.

So did Wyatt.

In the backseat of the town car, Leo was increasingly apprehensive.

According to the clock on the dash, it was almost three-thirty. They should have been there by now . . . shouldn't they?

Maybe not. He didn't know, after all, exactly where his father lived. But he was pretty sure it was supposed to be in Connecticut, and he didn't think Connecticut was supposed to be in the middle of nowhere.

Which was pretty much where they were now.

They had gone from the interstate to a series of two-lane highways to what seemed like rutted back roads to him. He had expected fancy suburbs, not dumpy little towns that were increasingly few and far between, with mostly rural countryside separating them.

Now the driver made another turn and the rutted back road gave way to a wooded dirt road.

"Is this it?" Leo asked her, leaning forward over the seat.

"This is it," she replied, and he found himself trying to catch a glimpse of her face in the rearview mirror.

He couldn't see her eyes behind those big dark glasses, but her jaw seemed to be set resolutely.

He leaned back uneasily in the seat and glanced out the window.

Nothing but trees.

This couldn't be right.

Could it?

He looked again at the driver, who appeared to be searching for something. Maybe she thought they were lost, too.

He watched her turn her head again, and that was when he saw it.

The wisp of hair at her temple.

It was darker than the rest of her blond hair . . .

Oddly so.

Fixated on it, he realized, in the moment before she turned her head toward the windshield again, that the rest of her hair wasn't hers at all.

She was wearing a wig.

Heart pounding, he stared at the blond waves beneath the back of her cap, noting that they were, indeed, synthetic. Now he recognized the unnatural uniformity of the strands; his aunt Rose had worn a wig when she was going through chemo a few months ago.

But Aunt Rose had been bald beneath her wig. She had a good reason to wear it.

This person wasn't bald. Her own hair was right there, sticking out.

What reason would a woman have to hide her own hair? It wasn't as though she were all dressed up for a fancy party, or Halloween, or something.

Leo realized the car was slowing.

"Where are we?" he asked, and he heard the panic that was beginning to edge into his own voice.

This time, she didn't answer.

That was ominous.

So was the fact that the car had come to a stop in a desolate spot, with nothing in sight but deep forest on either side of the road.

"Shouldn't he have been here by now?" Lindsay asked—again.

Wyatt looked at his watch. "Definitely." He didn't sound—or look—as reassuring as he had the last time she had asked.

In between wondering about Leo's arrival, they had been talking with almost surprising ease about where their lives had taken them since high school. They'd covered everything but their romantic relationships—assuming he must have had at least a few.

But he had said he wasn't married now and had never been divorced. She wondered why he was still single after all these years but didn't dare ask.

She was afraid of the answer.

She wouldn't be surprised if it was because he was still the ladies' man he'd been back in the old days.

"What time is it?" she asked him, her thoughts still on Leo.

"About three-forty."

"He should have been here almost an hour ago, shouldn't he?"

"Yes."

"You don't think . . . I mean, what if there was an accident or something?"

"Right, maybe there was. That happens all the time on 95. Especially in bad weather."

They both looked toward the window. A steady rain was now falling, and the sky hung low and gray.

"Maybe they just got stuck in some kind of rubbernecking traffic behind an accident," Wyatt said.

Or maybe, Lindsay thought uneasily, they were actually *in* the accident, if there was one.

Was Leo okay?

Had he been hurt?

So this was what it felt like to be a mother.

Now she knew what the expression *worried sick* meant.

No, you don't, she corrected herself. *You've dealt with this for only an hour. His adoptive mother is the one who's borne the brunt of the maternal worry.*

She felt a twinge of guilt. She shouldn't have agreed to keep this a secret from Leo's mother. She deserved to know what her son was doing, even if he was almost a grown man.

That's the first thing I'm going to tell him when he shows up, Lindsay decided. *I'm going to insist that he let her know he's made contact with us.*

"I'll go call the car service and see what's going on," Wyatt said, grim faced, going to the next room.

She nodded, walking to the window and staring bleakly at the falling rain, wishing thc car would appear in the driveway.

But it didn't.

And Wyatt was back, wearing a troubled expression.

"What is it?" she asked.

"They said he was waiting right out front of the building when the driver got there a little after two. They got almost all the way here, and then he suddenly jumped out of the car at an intersection and took off."

"Took off?" she echoed incredulously. "What do you mean, took off?"

"The driver said he just ran away. He waited for a while and he drove around looking for him, but he couldn't find him."

"What?" Lindsay shook her head. "Why would he do that?"

"I guess he just chickened out," Wyatt told her with a shrug. "It was probably too much for him."

"I guess we can't blame him."

"No. I guess we can't. He's just a kid, really."

They stared at each other.

Lindsay wondered if he was thinking the same thing she was. What now?

"Dammit! Where are you, you brat?"

As if the kid was going to answer her.

He was probably a mile from here already. It had been fifteen minutes, at least, since Leo had jumped out of the car just as she was about to get out and deal with him.

It was almost as if he knew . . .

She could tell he was getting suspicious back there. She should have thought this through better, the way she had thought through the rest of the plan. She'd even had the foresight to hire that neighborhood kid to get into the other town car—the one Wyatt Goddard was sending—and pass himself off as Leo.

That way, nobody would realize right away that he was missing.

She'd told the kid to ride up to Connecticut, then get out of the car before he got to Goddard's house. She'd given him two hundred bucks.

"But how am I supposed to get back home again?" he'd whined.

"I don't know. Isn't there a train you can take from there?"

"How am I supposed to get to the train?"

She'd given him another hundred, told him to take a cab, and crossed her fingers that he wouldn't screw it up.

No, but Leo Cellamino sure had.

He had disappeared into the underbrush in a flash.

He must have realized he was in trouble.

Okay, so he was smart.

But not smarter than I am.

Chapter 22

"Here you go." Wyatt handed Lindsay a goblet of Pinot Grigio and settled on the couch beside her again with his Pepsi.

"Thanks, Wyatt."

Had he ever heard her say his name before? He must have.

But not like this. Not in casual conversation, as though they did this all the time.

Intrigued, he snuck a peek at her and saw her take a cautious sip of her wine.

"I have other bottles," he offered, "if you don't like that one."

"Oh, it's fine. I'm not a wine connoisseur." She motioned at the glass in his hand. "Why aren't you having any?"

"I don't drink."

"Ever?"

He shook his head. "My parents did," he said, as if that explained everything.

For him, in fact, it did.

"Oh, right. I knew that," Lindsay said sympathetically—then looked as though she wished she hadn't.

"It's okay. I knew people talked about them back then. About me, my family . . ."

"They talked about me and mine, too." She shrugged. "It might as well have been a small town in some ways, you know?"

"Yeah." He paused, reflecting on the past. And on the present. "The funny thing is, this *is* a small town, and I know nothing at all about the people who live here."

"That's how it is in the city. It's kind of . . . lonely sometimes, don't you think?"

Her candid question surprised him.

He met it with one of his own. "You're lonely?"

She shrugged. "Sometimes. Usually I'm too busy to be, but . . . well, sometimes."

"What about . . . I mean . . . don't you have anyone in your life?"

"I've got friends, and I visit my parents out west a few times a year, so . . ."

"No," he said, "that's not what I meant."

"You mean am I involved with anyone?" She refused to meet his eye. "No. Not really."

"Not really? What does that mean?"

"I should have just said no." She took a deep breath, let it out. "No, I'm not involved with anyone. What about you?"

"No. I'm not involved with anyone, either." He slid a little closer on the couch, wondering what the hell he was doing.

Still, she refused to look at him.

Why was he trying so hard to make her?

That wasn't all he wanted—eye contact. He wanted to touch her.

Outside, in the distance, thunder rumbled.

It seemed to startle her. She looked up at the window, then, at last, at him.

The look in her eyes told him everything he needed to know—for now, anyway.

She was feeling it, too.

He dared to reach out a hand and let it rest on her forearm. Her skin was soft, cool to his touch.

He heard her breath catch in her throat.

"Don't," she said, but she didn't flinch or pull away.

"Why not?"

"It's not a good idea."

"You're right," he said, "but you and I were never known for common sense when we were together."

A faint smile touched her lips. "You make it sound like we were *together*, together."

"I know. That's because somehow I keep forgetting that we weren't."

"You know what? I keep feeling like that, too. Do you think it's because of . . . you know, him?"

Our son.

She still couldn't bring herself to say it.

"No," he said, "because I felt that way even before I knew he existed. He's not the only connection we have. You do realize that, don't you?"

"Yeah," she said softly. "I think I do."

He kissed her, then . . .

Later, looking back, he would wonder where he found the nerve.

But he didn't think about it, couldn't think at all as his mouth brushed hers lightly, then boldly, then claimed it with a hunger too long denied.

Yes, she was smart.

Smart enough to know better than to waste too much time trying to hunt the kid down in this weather.

It was raining like hell, thundering, lightning. It wasn't safe to be out there, poking around in the woods, looking for Lindsay and Wyatt's son.

Anyway, he was really just a little detour from the main journey. An added means of making Lindsay Farrell suffer.

She didn't really believe losing a child was a fate worse than death.

What could be worse than death?

Particularly the death she had in store for Lindsay Farrell.

It had taken her well over ninety minutes to get back to the city. Traffic was horrendous, accidents everywhere, flooding, trees down in a few places, too.

She could only hope that if Lindsay had left Wyatt's place when Leo failed to show up, she hadn't yet made it home.

I have to stay a few steps ahead of her. That's the key. A few steps ahead, and everything will work out just fine.

For the second time in her life, Lindsay Farrell found herself lying naked in Wyatt Goddard's arms.

This time, though, the sheets that entangled them were soft, imported white cotton rather than worn, nubby blue polyester. The mattress was a luxurious king-sized pillow-top, not a lumpy twin bunk.

Only the rain that steadily pelted the roof overhead was the same.

The setting didn't matter, though. Nothing mattered but how he made her feel when he made love to her.

And afterward.

Even now, when she should be utterly spent, lingering ripples of pleasure refused to ebb entirely.

Propped on his elbow, the naked length of his body stretched alongside her own, he ran a fingertip down her bare rib cage.

"Stop," she said, not meaning it.

"Why?"

"Because when you touch me like that, you get my hopes up all over again."

"Really." He did it again, and his hand came to rest on her hip.

"Really. And you can't possibly follow through . . . again."

He grinned wickedly. "You don't think so?"

She shook her head, and he took her into his arms and kissed her again. And again.

This time, his lovemaking was languid, as opposed to the last, when they had fervently found their way up here, pent-up passion erupting like a volcano.

Now, she felt as though she were filled with molten lava as he trailed a lazy tongue across the taut slope of her belly. She moaned when it dipped lower, lower still, clutching his hair and gasping his name as he brought her to the brink, then beyond.

"You don't have to get home tonight, do you?" he asked with a grin.

"No," she said, still panting. "I definitely don't."

"Leo? Is that you?"

"Yeah, Ma," he said, and shoved the soggy tissue into the pocket of the jeans he'd changed into when he arrived home. He grabbed the latest issue of *Sports Illustrated* from the floor and hurriedly opened it. "It's me."

He heard footsteps, then she poked her head into his bedroom and saw him lying there on his bed. "You're done working early tonight."

"Yeah." He tried to remember where he'd stashed his sodden suit when he stripped it off. On the floor by the closet? At the foot of the bed?

"How come?"

"Slow night." He forced himself to look at her. Her graying hair looked damp from the rain, and her round face was accentuated with make-up. She was wearing a pair of dress slacks and the comfortable shoes she liked to wear when she went to Manhattan. It was an eight-block walk from the subway to Aunt Rose's apartment. "How was your day, Ma?"

"Good. Aunt Rose is feeling great. She looks great. She's putting everything behind her and she and Uncle Paul are planning a trip to Myrtle Beach next month."

Leo did his best to muster some enthusiasm. "That's good. Where's Mario?"

"He ran into Jose downstairs and went over there to play PlayStation." Betty Cellamino fixed her older son with a worried gaze. "Are you okay, Leo?"

"Yeah, just tired."

"Did you eat? Aunt Rose sent some manicotti for you."

"I'll have it later."

His mother hesitated in the doorway, then shrugged and went to her own room.

Alone again, Leo tossed the magazine aside and rolled morosely onto his back again, wondering what to do.

He couldn't tell his mother what had happened—that was for sure.

Nor could he tell the police, because they would tell Ma, and she would be devastated.

Why hadn't he stopped to think about that before he agreed to meet his birth parents?

Because he was carried away by the fantasy, that was why.

Because he believed that he was actually going to meet them.

How could he have been so stupid? How could he have fallen for such an obvious Internet hoax? You read about stuff like that all the time—on-line predators who preyed on teenagers.

He'd never thought it could happen to him, at his age. He'd never thought he could be so recklessly idiotic.

But how did she know about me? About the adoption?

You moron. How do you think?

People could find out anything on the Internet.

But that hadn't occurred to him then. No, he had actually thought he was talking to his biological mother—not some fraud who had conned him with a picture of some woman who happened to look a lot like him.

What was she going to do to him when she drove him up to the boondocks on the pretense of taking him to meet his birth parents?

Rob him? Rape him?

What would have happened if he hadn't gotten away? There he was, soaked to the skin in his good suit, pathetic, hitchhiking his way back to the Bronx, where he managed to get the subway home.

The whole time, he fought back tears, telling himself that he was a man, and men didn't cry.

But once he got home, the floodgates opened. He couldn't help it.

It was sick.

Sick, sick, sick, and he had fallen for it like a gullible little kid being offered a lollipop by some pervert.

No, he couldn't tell the police. He couldn't tell a soul.

He just wanted to forget that any of it had ever happened.

"Are you hungry?"

"Hmm?" Lindsay lifted her head from Wyatt's chest. She had been on the verge of dozing again, more relaxed than she had been in days.

She felt as though she could lie here indefinitely in his arms, her head pressed against his chest so that she could hear the steady beating of his heart, seemingly in rhythm with the rain that dripped from the eaves outside the window.

"I can make us something," he said, stroking her hair. "I'm starved."

"So am I."

"Come on, then."

He pulled on a pair of shorts and gave her one of his T-shirts to wear. As she pulled it over her head, she was enveloped in the scent of him, and it was all she could do not to bury her nose in the fabric.

In the hall outside his bedroom, he flipped a wall switch.

Nothing happened. The hallway remained dark.

"A power line must be down somewhere," he said. "That happens a lot when it storms like this."

He took her hand and led her through the darkened house to the kitchen, where he lit several candles.

In the flickering light, he rummaged through the fridge and cupboards.

"I've got steaks, potatoes, and stuff for a salad," he told her.

"You don't have to make a big meal."

"We've got to eat the stuff. It'll go bad, and anyway, I'm leaving tomorrow for a week."

She watched him assemble the ingredients on the counter, along with a large wooden cutting board and a couple of knives he removed from their special sleeves.

"I'll chop the stuff for the salad," she volunteered.

"Are you sure?"

"Positive. That's about all I know how to do."

"What about your finger?"

"You know what they say. You've got to get right back up on the bike if you fall off."

"I thought it was the horse."

She grinned. "Whatever."

They worked companionably in the candlelit kitchen, Wyatt seasoning the steaks and getting them under the gas broiler as she sliced and diced the vegetables.

"I can't believe what a difference a great knife makes," she commented. "I've got to get a couple of these. Where did you buy them?"

"In France," he said. "They're actually hard to find here."

"I'll make a note to pick some up the next time I go to Paris, then," she said wryly, and he laughed.

"That's not where you're going on this trip tomorrow morning," she asked, "is it?"

"No. Italy this time."

"Do you travel to Europe a lot?"

He nodded and checked the steaks. "Have you ever been?"

"No," she said. "I'd love to go, though, someday."

"Maybe you can come with me."

She clenched the knife handle, hoping he didn't think she was hinting around.

"What do you think?" he asked, his back to her as he shook some kind of seasoning over the steaks.

"Maybe," she said noncommittally, when what she really longed to do was give him a fervent yes.

There was no guarantee, really, that they were going to see each other after tonight.

And if their son didn't want them to be a part of his life, there was really no logical reason to reconnect.

But there was nothing logical about what Lindsay was feeling right now. Nothing logical at all.

Wyatt watched Lindsay sleep, the room illuminated by the candles he had lit earlier. The power had been back on for some time, but he kept the candles burning downstairs as they ate, and up here in the bedroom, where they returned immediately afterward.

He had worn her out, he supposed, with a voracious appetite

that couldn't be sated by food. She'd been sleeping for a while now, her breath whisper soft, stirring the hair on his forearm as he held her.

He never wanted to let go, but he was going to have to. For a while, at least. It was past three a.m., and he had to pack for his business trip to Italy. A car was picking him up here in a little over an hour to take him down to JFK Airport.

If he could have canceled the trip, he would have, but he was handling a car for a new client who happened to be one of the most well-connected financiers in the world. He could probably retire on the eventual word of mouth this was going to generate.

He took one long, last look, relishing the sight of Lindsay, eyes closed, lips slightly parted. He kissed them gently, then gingerly slipped his arm out from under her.

She stirred, opened her eyes.

"Sorry," he said. "I didn't want to wake you."

She blinked.

She doesn't know where she is, he realized. She was looking at him as though she was wondering what he was doing there.

He smiled. "Remember me?"

"Definitely." She stretched. "What time is it?"

"It's the middle of the night. You don't have to get up, but I do. I've got to leave for the airport. You can stay here and sleep, and I'll arrange for you to be driven home in the morning . . . or whenever you want. You can stay here, use the pool . . ."

Wait for me to come home next week . . .

Please stay, Lindsay. Don't ever leave.

She shook her head and sat up, running her fingers through her passion-tousled hair. "No, thanks—I mean, that's so sweet of you, but I've got to go home."

"*Now?*"

"When you leave."

"If you want, my driver can drop you on the way to the airport."

"That would be good—if it's not a problem."

"It's not." And that way, he would have another hour to spend with her. It wasn't much, but it would have to be enough to last him until next weekend.

You're assuming you're going to see her again.

What if she doesn't want to?

What if this is it?

"Lindsay," he said, glancing at the clock, hating that he had to worry about the time, "we need to talk when I get back."

"About Leo?"

She had actually said it.

Hearing their son's name on her lips was bittersweet now.

"About Leo," he echoed, "of course. And about . . . us."

Us, like *we*, was a foreign word on Wyatt's tongue. Yet it, as *we* had earlier, now managed to roll off with ease.

He held his breath, waiting for Lindsay to dispute it.

To tell him that there was no *us*.

She merely smiled.

It was a smile that spoke volumes, so that she didn't have to.

"I'll be here when you get back," she told him simply.

And for the first time in his life, Wyatt found himself wholeheartedly looking forward to the rest of it.

Whore.

That's what you are, Lindsay. You're a whore.

She paced across the now-familiar living room like a caged panther, then back again, and looked at her watch.

5:21.

A little over sixty seconds had passed since the last time she'd checked.

There was no telling when Lindsay was going to show up. She had obviously rekindled her old flame with Wyatt Goddard.

For all I know, she'll spend the rest of the weekend with him.

She couldn't stay here waiting for her indefinitely. She had already arranged to check out on Sunday, and she was scheduled to fly back to Oregon in about twelve hours.

I can't leave New York without taking care of Lindsay.

No, but she couldn't take care of Lindsay until she resurfaced.

She yawned deeply and realized she was on the verge of exhaustion. Her shoulders burned with fatigue and her legs ached from standing. She should go back to her hotel room, arrange to stay at least another night, and get some sleep.

She could try again tom—

She froze, hearing a sound at the door.

It was a key in the lock.

Lindsay.

Her gloved hand closed around the handle of the butcher knife she'd stolen from Lindsay's kitchen drawer.

Heart beating in anticipation, she hurried back to the hiding spot she'd chosen hours earlier.

* * *

Lindsay was smiling as she stepped over the threshold into her apartment, her thoughts on the good-bye kiss Wyatt had just given her in the backseat of the limo, along with a sweet, unexpected parting gift.

"I'll call you when I land," he promised as she tucked it into her purse. "And I'll see you the second I get back."

It was a promise, and she met it with one of her own.

"Good. I'll be waiting for you."

Now, at last, exhaustion was beginning to steal in to meld with her dreamy afterglow.

She started to reach for the light switch just inside the door, then changed her mind. The sky beyond the large window above the couch was already pink, and the first light of dawn that seeped into the room was enough for her to see her way through to the bedroom.

All she wanted to do was fall into bed and think about all that had happened in the last twenty-four hours—then sleep.

Yawning, she kicked off her sandals and left them where they landed, under a table by the door. Her purse still over her shoulder, she walked into the bathroom to brush her teeth and wash her face.

Then she thought better of that.

She'd rather fall asleep still tasting Wyatt's last kiss, her skin, slightly raw from his razor stubble, still smelling faintly of his aftershave.

She was about to hang her purse on the knob, strip off her dress, and put on the nightie that hung on the back of the door . . .

Then she was struck by something odd.

The bathroom was dark.

There was no familiar glow from the night-light she kept plugged into an outlet above the sink and never turned off.

She had changed the bulb just the other day.

It couldn't have burned out again so soon.

Frowning, she reached for the switch and flicked it.

The light turned on.

Huh.

That was strange.

Had she flipped it off without thinking yesterday?

She doubted it; she had never done that before.

She looked at herself in the mirror, noticing the apprehension in her own expression.

Okay, don't get carried away. You're just being paranoid. Maybe the power went out because of the storm. And maybe that tripped something in the outlet, and the light turned itself off.

A reach, but she was willing to believe it, because what else could possibly have—

Lindsay froze.

Behind her, in the mirror, she could swear she had just seen a human shadow pass along the wall beyond the bathroom door.

Leo waited until dawn, when he heard his mother moving around in the kitchen.

Then, after an entirely sleepless night, he quietly sat up and swung his legs over the edge of the bed.

Ma always got up early on Sunday mornings.

By the time Leo and his brother woke up to the scent of frying eggs and bacon, she would have drunk her coffee, read the paper, walked to seven o'clock Mass and back, and mixed the meatballs for the homemade spaghetti sauce they'd have for dinner.

Never, until this particular Sunday morning, had Leo appreciated the comforting ritual. Nor had he fully appreciated his mother.

A wave of sentiment swept through him when he spotted her from the kitchen doorway, standing at the sink in her faded pink terry cloth housecoat, filling the old coffee percolator with cold water.

He had to force his voice past a lump in his throat to say, "Ma?"

She gasped and jumped, spinning around. "Leo! You scared me!"

"Sorry, Ma."

"What are you doing up? Are you sick?" she asked worriedly. "No."

He hesitated. He had lain awake all night, shaken to the core and riddled with guilt. Now, he wondered if he had made the right decision.

But his mother wore an expectant look, and it was too late to change his mind now.

Anyway, he felt like a frightened little boy who needed his mommy.

Thank God she's here for me. Right here, where she's been all along.

He took a deep breath and plunged in. "There's something I need to tell you."

Her back flattened to the wall, her hand gripping the handle of the knife, she sent up a silent prayer.

Now there was nothing to do but wait, barely breathing, for her prey to step across the threshold.

And when you do, you won't have a chance, she promised, knowing she had the element of surprise in her favor.

She waited for what seemed like endless hours, holding her breath.

Then, at last, she poised the knife as she heard movement from the other side of the wall.

Out of the corner of her eye, she saw a figure move stealthily into view.

In that instant, she leapt into action, attacking with a vengeance, and blindly. She could feel the knife sinking into flesh, heard the high-pitched cry of pain.

She saw that the blade had caught her in the side just below her rib cage; blood was pouring from the wound.

Yet suddenly, shockingly, she somehow found herself on the defensive, fending off a violent retaliatory assault. Her enemy was a force to be reckoned with—now her only thought was getting the hell out of here, hoping she was going to escape with her life.

They wrestled on the bathroom floor and she struggled to hang on to the knife, to reposition it so that she could use it again. She was enraged now, hell-bent on doing whatever she had to do to survive.

I can't die now. Not when everything is coming together for me at last. Please, God . . .

They rolled over on the hard tile, rolled over again and she found herself on top. She seized her chance, knowing that if she didn't, she wouldn't get another.

With a primal grunt and a mighty arc of her arm, she shoved the blade as hard as she could.

Again, it found its target, and she could feel it sink sickeningly into flesh and bone, until it hit something more unforgiving than either.

Wallboard, she realized . . . she had just pinned a human hand to the wall like that arrow had, twenty years ago, pinned Jake Marcott to the tree.

Her ears rang with the terrible howl of agony that erupted, echoing through the tiled bathroom.

For a moment she was frozen in sheer horror at what had just happened—at what she had just inflicted upon another human being.

Then she bolted from the apartment, spattered with blood, leaving her assailant pinned to the wall with Wyatt's Parisian chef's knife, bestowed upon her as a parting gift.

"Take it," he'd said with a smile. "I don't want to come home next weekend to find that you've chopped off a finger with your dull one."

She had thanked him, never knowing, as she tucked it into her purse, that it was about to save her life.

There was no traffic on the FDR Drive at this hour on a Sunday morning. Wyatt would be at JFK Airport with plenty of time to spare before his flight. Too much time.

Wyatt was wistful as he gazed out the window at a barge on the East River, realizing that he could have lingered at least another fifteen, twenty minutes, with Lindsay.

Yeah, but so? What's fifteen minutes? he asked himself, feeling vaguely foolish.

It's damned significant, he answered his own question. Particularly when you hadn't seen someone in twenty years and weren't going to see her again for an entire week.

There were plenty of things he could have told Lindsay in fifteen minutes.

Yeah, and you probably would have regretted all of them the second you left.

Wyatt Goddard was no stranger to morning-after ardor. It had led to his moving in with Allison and making doomed commitments to a couple of other women in the past.

Maybe it was better that their good-bye had been so hurried.

He'd kissed her, at least, and given her that chef's knife she had coveted in his kitchen.

Someday soon, I'll take her to Paris and buy her a whole set, he vowed—then shook his head.

Morning-after ardor again. Making plans, making promises. Good thing they were only to himself this time.

It was a good thing he was going to be an ocean away from Lindsay for the next six days.

That would keep him from saying or doing anything rash, would give him enough space to figure out whether his feelings for Lindsay were rekindled infatuation . . . or something more enduring.

* * *

"Stay back," the burly NYPD officer cautioned Lindsay as he and his partner, guns at the ready, prepared to enter her apartment with the key they'd quickly retrieved from Bob, the building super.

The door had swung shut and locked after her when she bolted. Ten minutes, perhaps fifteen, had passed since the ordeal in her bathroom, but her heart was still racing, every breath painful in a constricted chest.

She had insisted on coming back up here with the cops, needing to face her incapacitated attacker.

I have to get a glimpse of her face.

That it had been a woman had caught her entirely off guard, but there had been no mistaking the feminine pitch of the voice as it screeched in agony.

The sound still echoed chillingly in Lindsay's head.

This wasn't a typical crime. She knew that, even before she had seen the passing expressions of surprise on the officers' faces when she told them.

They asked if she was positive that it hadn't been a man lying in wait for her in the darkened apartment. She knew what they were thinking: that the notorious masked East Side rapist had ventured a dozen or so blocks south, into new territory.

She assured the police that she was a hundred percent certain it had been a woman.

She could tell they weren't convinced, even now.

Weapons poised, they crept into the apartment as Lindsay and Bob hung back a safe distance down the hall.

Lindsay hugged her aching rib cage, still trying to catch her breath, beginning to feel the physical evidence of the struggle. Her head throbbed where it had slammed against the tile floor, her elbows stung where the skin had been scraped away, and she suspected that her face, which felt raw, was covered with scratches. But she'd survived.

Thanks to Wyatt.

From inside the apartment, she heard one of the police officers curse loudly.

They reappeared in the hall moments later.

"What is it?" Lindsay asked, but she already knew. It was obvious from their disheartened expressions.

"There was blood all over the bathroom, and on the wall where you said you left him—I mean, her. But whoever it was got away."

* * *

"Are you upset with me, Mom?"

Betty Cellamino looked up at Leo, startled, as though she had been lost in thought. She had spoken very little as he spilled his story, and her expression had been impossible to read.

"Am I upset with you?" She leaned across the kitchen table and pulled Leo close to her, stroking his head as she held it against the soft terry cloth of her robe. "Oh, honey, no. I just can't believe you didn't tell me what was going on. When I think of what could have happened—"

"I'm fine," he pointed out quickly. "No harm done."

"We should call the police."

"I knew you were going to say that." He shook his head. "No, Ma."

"This woman might go after somebody else—and who knows what's going to happen then? Maybe the next person won't be as lucky."

"Yeah, but I don't know how the police would find her anyway. It's not like I had a license plate for the car or anything. And I didn't even get a good look at her face. Plus she was wearing a disguise."

"What about the phone number you called? And the e-mail? She can be tracked that way."

"No," he said, realizing he had done something stupid. Really stupid. "When I got home yesterday I deleted the number from my phone's incoming calls log, and I deleted her e-mails, too. I was just so . . . disgusted with myself."

"Don't be disgusted with yourself. Be disgusted with her. You didn't do anything wrong."

"I was trying to meet my biological mother behind your back. And father, too."

"I know, but I don't blame you. Maybe we shouldn't have kept you in the dark about all that for as long as we did. Maybe we should have been more open about it."

"It's okay."

"No, it isn't." She took a deep breath, sipped her coffee. Then she said, "Listen, I'm going to help you find your birth parents if that's what you want."

Was it?

He wasn't so sure now.

"Can I think about it?" he asked.

"Sure you can." She looked at the clock. "I've got to go get ready for church."

"Mind if I go with you?" he asked, and she looked at him in surprise. "I owe someone up there a big thank-you," he explained.

His mother grinned, leaned over, and kissed him on the head.

He found himself inhaling her familiar scent: coffee and talcum powder and . . .

Her.

That was what it was.

Just her. His mom.

She might not have given birth to him, but she had been there for everything else. Everything that mattered most.

"I'm making extra sauce tonight," she said, patting his arm, "if you wanted to invite anyone over for dinner."

"Why would I do that?"

"Did you see the message I left for you the other day? From someone named Sarah Rose?"

He had seen it—and ignored it, too caught up in everything else in his life.

Now he grinned.

"Maybe I will invite someone over for dinner. Thanks, Ma."

"And what can I get for you, ma'am?" asked the flight attendant, smiling as she looked right through the passenger in seat 15F.

"I'll have a ginger ale, please."

Her stomach was still roiling from this morning's ordeal, but nausea was the least of it.

Thank God the wound in her side had been superficial, nothing more than an agonizingly deep cut. Another fraction of an inch over, and she'd have been in serious trouble.

The same was true with her hand. The blade had stabbed through the fleshy skin and tendon between her thumb and forefinger, and it hurt like hell. It was all she could do not to pass out on the spot when she pulled out the blade, but she managed to keep her cool.

And she got away.

Bloodied, disheveled, in terrible pain . . .

But she got away.

"Here you go, ma'am." The flight attendant handed over a clear plastic cup filled with ice and soda, still not making eye contact.

She accepted it with her right hand, keeping her wounded left carefully concealed at her side.

"Enjoy the flight."

She smiled. "Oh, I definitely will."

In a little over five hours, she would land in Portland, where she'd be able to get medical attention for the wounds she'd temporarily cleaned and bandaged herself.

There, nobody would connect her to the seemingly random Manhattan attack.

There, she could get on with her plans.

But I haven't forgotten you, she told Lindsay Farrell silently. *Not for a second. And I'll see you in Portland at the reunion.*

Part Three

RACHEL
by
Beverly Barton

Chapter 23

Huntsville, Alabama, May 2006

Her partner lay bleeding to death at her feet. As she radioed for help, she tried to protect him as best she could by dragging him into a protected corner of the alley. Rapid fire from a semiautomatic bombarded her. Dear God, where was the backup she had ordered at least ten minutes ago? With her heartbeat racing and adrenaline rushing through her body at breakneck speed, Sergeant Rachel Alsace realized she was caught in a life-or-death battle with an escaped killer.

Suddenly, without warning, as she got off several quick, well-aimed shots, return fire caught her in the shoulder, the bullet searing through her flesh like a white-hot branding iron. Somehow, she managed to pull the trigger of her Glock two more times. Then reality blurred as agony enveloped her and darkness descended, a smoky gray fog of fear and pain dragging her down, deeper and deeper into unconsciousness.

Sweat coated her body, drenched her oversized cotton T-shirt emblazoned with the words *Roll Tide* and the famous Alabama elephant, and dampened the cotton sheets on her queen-size bed.

Rachel woke with a start. She tossed the light covers aside, jerked straight up into a sitting position, and took several deep, calming breaths. Since coming home from the hospital three days ago, she had been plagued by nightmares of the day her partner had been killed and she had been severely wounded. Twenty-seven-year-old Officer Bobby Joe Poole had left behind a wife and

two young children. For about the hundredth time since that horrific day, Rachel had wondered why a man with so much to live
for had died and why she, a divorced, childless woman just two
years shy of forty, had been spared. Luck of the draw? Fate? Divine providence?

As she turned around and slid off the bed, Rachel felt an overwhelming sense of guilt and an equal measure of relief. Guilt that
she was alive and her partner dead. Relief to still be alive, to have
a second chance to find some sort of personal fulfillment beyond
her job as a police officer on the Huntsville, Alabama, police force.

She looked at the lighted digital bedside clock. Five-ten. Only
twenty minutes earlier than her normal wake-up. At least five-
thirty had been her regular get-up time before she'd been forced to
take an extended leave of absence. Medical leave. She probably
wouldn't be reinstated to active duty for another couple of
months. Recovering from a near-fatal bullet wound, as well as the
battery of psychological tests, would take some time. Not to mention the internal investigation already underway, looking into the
death of the man she had killed—Randy Grimmer—who had
murdered a convenience store clerk and two customers in a bold
daytime robbery before shooting her partner and her.

Rachel padded barefoot into the bathroom, turned on the sink
faucet, and splashed cold water onto her face. After drying off,
she flipped on the light switch that flooded the small room with illumination from three sixty-watt bulbs over the vanity. Momentarily shutting her eyes against the offending brightness, she lifted
her good arm—the right one—and rubbed the back of her neck.
Slowly, cautiously, she opened her eyes and stared at her reflection
in the medicine cabinet mirror. Lord, she looked a sight, her short
blond hair sticking out in every direction. Using her fingers, she
combed through the rats' nest of curls as she made her way out of
the bathroom.

While walking through her bedroom and into the hallway, she
thanked God for air-conditioning. Springtime in the South was
usually warm, but hot weather had arrived early, just in time for
Mother's Day, and seemed intent on sticking around for a while.

Rachel dismissed thoughts of her own mother, missing her
more with each passing year. If not for a few close friends and a
scattering of cousins, she would be all alone in the world. Her father had died years ago, back in his hometown of Portland, Oregon,
and her mother had passed away six years ago. Rachel had buried
her mother alongside her relatives in her hometown cemetery in

Chattanooga, Tennessee. That had been a horrific year. She had suffered a miscarriage, lost her mother to cancer, and finally admitted that her six-year marriage to Hamilton County, Tennessee, sheriff's deputy Allen Turner was over. Three losses in the span of ten months had forced Rachel to reevaluate her life. By year's end, she had moved to Huntsville and joined the police department, after having served eleven years with the Chattanooga P.D.

Since the day her father died, Rachel had devoted herself to one goal—becoming the kind of law enforcement officer he would have been proud of.

After entering the kitchen, she clicked on the lights, then punched the ON button of her coffeemaker. As the coffee began to brew, she disarmed her security system, opened the back door, and stepped onto the sidewalk that led around the house to the driveway. The nearby streetlight radiated through the early-morning darkness, allowing her to locate her newspaper where it lay in the middle of her concrete drive. She liked her friendly neighborhood in the Harvest area, loved her neat three-bedroom brick house and appreciated the variety of nice guys she'd met since moving here. She was actually beginning to enjoy dating again. She wasn't seriously involved with anyone, but she kept hoping the real Mr. Right would come along one of these days. But if he didn't, she'd be okay on her own. She had a pretty good life, hadn't she?

When Rachel went back inside her house, she removed the half-filled coffeepot, poured a mug of the steaming black brew, and carried it, along with the newspaper, over to the kitchen table. After sitting down, she spread the paper apart to the front page and took a sip of coffee. Scanning the headlines, she noted that there had been another Beauty Queen Killer murder—this time in Alabama, in a little town south of Huntsville. Cullman. A former Cotton Queen had been brutally killed, her head chopped off.

Rachel shuddered.

The poor woman.

Zipping through the brief article, Rachel shook her head. She had been in law enforcement over sixteen years, and she still couldn't understand what drove a person to murder. Self-defense, she understood. Cold-blooded, brutal murder, she didn't understand.

She had been keeping tabs on the slew of Beauty Queen Killer murders for the past few years. The perpetrator was a vicious serial killer who had struck throughout the South over and over again. An old friend of hers from their days with the Chattanooga

P.D. was working for a private PI firm that had been hired by a victim's family to independently search for the killer. She and Lin McAllister kept in touch on a semi-regular basis. Mostly e-mails, but a few phone calls once or twice a year.

As Rachel flipped through the newspaper, she finished off her first cup of coffee. The caffeine stimulated her into full consciousness. A second cup should make her even more alert. But alert for what? Another day of crossword puzzles, watching *The View* and *Oprah* and *As the World Turns*? Trying to concentrate on the most recent Sandra Brown novel?

Two cups of coffee later, with her fourth cup in hand, Rachel sat down in front of her laptop computer, which she kept at the built-in workstation in the corner of her kitchen. When she downloaded her e-mails, she deleted several, then paused when she saw a couple from old friends, high-school classmates from St. Elizabeth's. Her index finger hovered over the Delete key, itching to erase the messages without reading them. It wasn't that she had anything against her two old friends—friends she hadn't seen in twenty years—but she knew both e-mails would be about the upcoming reunion. Rachel had no intention of returning to Portland. Not now or ever. Although she had some wonderful memories of her high-school days, those good memories were overshadowed by two tragic losses. A boy she had adored—Jake Marcott—had been murdered at the St. Valentine's Day dance their senior year. A part of her still mourned him, although she had long ago stopped loving him. And less than two years after Jake's unsolved murder, her father—the lead detective on Jake's murder case—had died of a sudden heart attack. Everyone who knew Mac Alsace suspected that being unable to solve Jake's murder had literally worried him to death.

Just read the damn e-mails.

Rachel hesitated. A week ago, she had received her packet of information about the high-school reunion, a combined St. Elizabeth's and Western Catholic High reunion. When another classmate, Aurora Zephyr, had phoned her several months ago, she'd made it clear that she wouldn't be attending. But Kristen Daniels Delmonico had mailed her the packet and the invitation.

And what an invitation it had been! The very special invitation had included her senior picture cut out of their high-school yearbook. A cute idea—with a sinister twist. A vicious red line marred her smiling face. A bloody slash. Somebody's idea of a sick joke? She'd known Kristen well enough, way back when, to know despite the fact the packet came from her, she wasn't the type to do such a despicable thing. She'd never do anything to desecrate Jake Marcott's memory, not when she'd been in love with the guy, just as Lindsay Farrell had been. And only God knew how many other girls, including Rachel herself, had been fools over him.

You weren't in love with Jake. Not really. You were infatuated with him. Dreamed of what it would be like for him to kiss you, make love to you, pay you the kind of attention he paid Lindsay and Kristen.

If not for the fact that he'd been murdered that long-ago February night, he would be little more than a vague memory, along with so many other memories of her high-school years. But because of Jake's death at the hands of a still-unknown assailant, no one who had known him as well as Rachel had would ever be able to forget him.

No more procrastination. Read the e-mails!
Rachel opened Kristen's e-mail first and read it hurriedly. Her stomach muscles knotted painfully.

Hi Rach,
    I hate like the devil to be the bearer of more terrible news. I can hardly believe it myself. It was only last month that I felt compelled to let you and Lindsay know about Haylie Swanson dying and that a homeless man was arrested for her murder. Now, we've just found out that Aurora Zephyr died while on a trip to New York City. She and Lindsay had gotten together while she was there and . . . No one knows for sure what happened, but it looks like she tripped and fell onto the subway tracks. She didn't have any ID on her at the time, so it took a while for the police to identify her.
    I know you are opposed to our having the class reunion, but with two more classmates gone . . .
    Look, Rach, I wouldn't say this to just anybody, but my gut instincts—maybe my reporter instincts—are screaming that there's something just not right about Haylie and Aurora dying within weeks of each other, and both dying violent deaths. I've pointed this out to others on the reunion committee and suggested we consider canceling our plans, but everyone else thinks I'm overreacting. What do you think?
                                                        Kris

The Kristen Daniels that Rachel had once known was not the nervous, hysterical type, and she doubted that the thirty-eight-year-old Kristen Delmonico was either. So, if Kris's gut instincts were warning her that something was off center about the recent deaths of two old classmates, then Rachel believed her.

So, what could she do? She wasn't in Portland or New York City. She hadn't seen either Haylie or Aurora in twenty years. Although she was sorry to hear about their deaths, their dying had no effect on her life.

Or did it?

Get real, she told herself. *Don't buy into some weird theory that Kristen has concocted in her imaginative reporter brain.*

Rachel scrolled down to the e-mail from Lindsay, opened it, and read rapidly through the brief message.

Hello Rachel,

I'm sure by now someone has contacted you with the sad news that Aurora Zephyr died accidentally while visiting here in New York City. I still can't believe she's gone. We had such a nice visit while she was here. Like old times.

Strange, isn't it, that two of our old gang have died recently under such tragic circumstances. I know it's stupid of me to even think it, but I can't shake the idea that somehow their deaths are connected to the reunion Kristen and the others are planning. It's as if fate is trying to warn us not to have a reunion.

What's your take on this? You were always the sensible, levelheaded one. If anyone can sort through this craziness, you can.

XOXOXO . . . Lindsay

Rachel took a deep breath, then released it. The corners of her mouth lifted in a tentative smile as she remembered that the sweet, emotional Lindsay always signed all her notes with *Xs* and *Os.* Hugs and kisses.

Staring at the computer screen, Rachel read part of the last line. *If anyone can sort through this craziness, you can.*

Rachel stood, carried her mug of cool coffee to the sink, and dumped it in; then she poured herself a fresh cup. Glancing at the clock on the microwave, she realized it was nearly six. Her stomach growled. She needed to eat a bite of something before she took her medication. More antibiotics. But no more pain pills. Those damn things made her brain fuzzy. She hated that. Being a bit of a control freak, she didn't like the idea that the drugs influenced her brain.

Pacing in her small kitchen, she thought about the basic facts. From what she'd been told, Haylie Swanson had been slightly unbalanced for the past twenty-plus years, ever since her boyfriend, Ian Powers, had died in a car crash their senior year of high school. It was unfortunate that she hadn't been able to pull her life together, and just as unfortunate that a homeless guy had robbed and killed her. But how could her death have anything to do with Jake's murder or the upcoming reunion? And poor Aurora. Rachel remembered how much the dark, curly-haired girl had longed to be an actress. Instead she'd married young and had a baby. Tragic that she had lost her footing and wound up crushed to death by a subway train. But her death had nothing to do with the reunion or with Jake. Accidents happened every day, every hour.

Yeah, so why are you questioning the facts about how they died? It's more than just your normal policewoman curiosity. Maybe you're letting your imagination run wild because Kristen and Lindsay are.

But why would three intelligent women have the same doubts?

Because of Jake Marcott. Because one horrible night years ago, a boy all three of them had loved was murdered at the school dance, and this reunion was stirring up memories all of them would prefer to forget.

She knew what she should do—e-mail Kristen and Lindsay to tell them how sorry she was to hear about Aurora, then add that she hoped the reunion came off without a hitch but she wouldn't be there.

After all, she had the perfect excuse, hadn't she? She was recuperating from a near-fatal gunshot wound.

Before daylight, while others slept peacefully in their soft beds inside their safe homes, she made yet another pilgrimage to the shrine she was constructing in the basement of St. Elizabeth's, now abandoned and awaiting demolition. This was her secret place, one she had created for her eyes only, not to be shared with anyone else. Except maybe Jake's ghost. Sometimes she felt his presence down here in this dark, dank basement. A whiff of the aftershave he'd worn often scented the musty air. And she would swear that every once in a while, she could hear his laughter. She had both loved and hated Jake's laugh, as she had both loved and hated him.

If only things had been different . . . If only Jake had been different. He had loved her. She knew he had. But he had been cruel to her and had allowed those bitches to be mean to her, to ignore her, to treat her as if she were nobody.

They thought he had loved them—Lindsay and Kristen. Even Rachel thought he'd cared about her. Fools. All of them. She was the only one he'd ever loved.

Shining the flashlight over the row of lockers in the basement, she smiled. One item at a time. Adding one memento here and there, building this monument to Jake, to his death, to the past. And all the while planning the next execution. They had to die. If she could kill all of them before the reunion, fine. If not, she would find a way to end their lives that night.

She ran her hand over her side, recalling the feel of the knife slashing through her clothing and into her side. Thank God, it had been a superficial wound. And although her hand was healing nicely, it had caused her a great deal of pain. Since she was a gourmet cook, it was easy enough to explain that a paring knife had slipped and slit open the fleshy skin and tendon between her thumb and forefinger.

You'll pay for the pain you caused me, Lindsay.

She giggled.

Jake had been hot after Lindsay.

All these years she had believed Lindsay's baby was Jake's. Boy, had she been wrong! She was glad the child hadn't been Jake's. Lindsay was not worthy of being a mother to Jake's child.

If only she had known the truth years ago. The truth could have saved her from such anguish, such torment, thinking Jake had a child out there somewhere. Alive and well.

Her plans to eliminate Lindsay in New York City had failed. But there was more than one way to accomplish a goal. The reunion was less than six weeks away. If she was lucky, Lindsay and Rachel would come home for the big event. And if not?

Just wait and see.

Was there a way to entice both Lindsay and Rachel back to Portland? Think. What would bring them back here early? Everyone had a weak spot, didn't they, an Achilles' heel?

Lindsay's weakness was her son. Wyatt Goddard's bastard.

She giggled again.

Do you hear that, Jake? She asked the question in the stillness of the basement beneath St. Elizabeth's. *He's not your son. He's Wyatt Goddard's. Lindsay was screwing around on you and you didn't even know it. Her son's name is Leo Cellamino. And I came this close to killing him.*

She held up her thumb and index finger to indicate just how close she had been to murdering Lindsay Farrell's child.

Oh, what a fitting punishment that would be for Lindsay, if her son died. But even more so if the child had been yours, Jake.

It wasn't fair that Lindsay's child was alive. Not when her child was dead.

If she could somehow use Lindsay's child to lure Lindsay back to Portland . . . But how? If not her son, then what?

The death of a good friend?

She smiled at the thought of killing another of Jake's women.

What about Rachel Alsace? She was a cop now, in some small city in Alabama. At least that's what Kristen had told them. So what would draw a policewoman back to Portland? Maybe a twenty-year-old unsolved crime.

Giggling as she danced around in the dark, her feet smacking against the concrete surface, she imagined what it would be like to kill them. One by one. Kristen. Lindsay. Rachel.

Lindsay Farrell and Wyatt Goddard sat side by side in the private detective's office. Wyatt reached over and clasped Lindsay's hand, which rested at her side. He gave it a reassuring squeeze.

"What time is it?" she asked.

"A minute since the last time you asked," Wyatt told her.

"He's not coming."

"He'll be here, Ms. Farrell," Gene Lester said. "His mother"— he glanced sympathetically at Lindsay—"his adoptive mother is coming with him."

Wyatt had hired one of New York's top PIs to locate their son. Although Lindsay had wanted him to wait, to give Leo the time he needed to come to them, Wyatt told her that they had been waiting nearly twenty years.

"But after what happened to him, being abducted by some crazy person the way he was and thinking that when he talked to me, he was talking to her . . ." Lindsay swallowed the emotion threatening to choke her. She had tried not to think about how close her son—their son—had come to dying, but the very thought plagued her day and night.

Wyatt squeezed her hand again. "Who knows how such a terrible thing happened, but it could be as Gene suggested and someone found out that Leo was my son, knew I was wealthy, and intended to kidnap Leo."

Before Lindsay could reply, a soft rap sounded on the closed office door. Gene Lester's secretary opened the door and announced, "Mrs. Betty Cellamino and her son Leo are here."

"Show them in," Gene told her.

Lindsay's heart stopped. For one endless millisecond, she didn't breathe. The young man entered the room first, and he was all that Lindsay saw. The sight of her son filled her world.

Leo was tall, lanky, and handsome, very much his father's son in that respect. But his dark hair, his eyes, his nose, the shape of his face were all Farrell. God, he looked so much like her. Except the mouth. His mouth was a replica of Wyatt's.

Her son stared at her, his dark eyes filled with questions. Their gazes met and locked. She released a tight, chest-clutching breath and rose to her feet. Wyatt came up off the sofa and stood beside her as they faced the child their one night of wild teenage passion had created.

"Hello," Leo said.

Wyatt made the first move, taking a step forward and holding out his hand. "I'm Wyatt Goddard. I'm your father, your biological father."

Leo stared at Wyatt's hand for a minute, then took it, and they exchanged a cordial shake. Wyatt reached back and pulled Lindsay forward and to his side, his arm resting around her waist.

"This is Lindsay Farrell, your birth mother," Wyatt said.

Lindsay stood frozen, speechless and unable to move.

Leo nodded, then turned and motioned to the woman still standing in the doorway. "This is my mother, Betty Cellamino."

Betty shook hands with Wyatt and then with Lindsay.

She looked right at Lindsay when she said, "Thank you for Leo. He's been a good son, a true blessing."

Tears gathered in the corners of Lindsay's eyes. *Damn! Don't do this.*

"Thank you." Lindsay cleared her throat. "I prayed that my baby would go to a loving family, that he'd have a good mother."

"Ma is the best," Leo said, as if he needed to defend Mrs. Cellamino.

Lindsay focused solely on her son. "I'm sure she is. It's what I wanted for you when I . . . It wasn't easy for me to sign the papers, to relinquish my rights to you, but I was just a teenager and

my parents didn't know I was pregnant." She looked at Wyatt.
"And neither did your father."

"Look, I know this is awkward for all of us," Wyatt said. "Especially after what happened with the fake limo driver. God, what a nightmare for you, son." Wyatt hazarded a glance at Leo as if questioning his right to call the young man son.

"I thought the entire 'you've found your birth mother' was some crazy hoax that a pervert had played on me," Leo told them. "When Mr. Lester came to see Ma and told her about you two . . . It's a lot to take in."

"We don't want to rush you," Lindsay said. "If you can't find a place in your life for us, we'll understand. But we wanted you to know that we care, that we'd very much like to get to know you, for you to get to know us."

"Not necessarily as your parents," Wyatt interjected as he glanced at Betty Cellamino. "If you'll give us a chance, we'd like to be your friends. But it's up to you."

"I—I think I'd like to get to know both of you." Leo stared directly at Lindsay. "But nobody will ever take Ma's place. She'll always be my mother."

Intense pain and unbearable sadness enveloped Lindsay, but she bore it as best she could and even forced a fragile smile when she looked at her son. "Just being given a chance to be a part of your life is more than I'd ever expected." It was all she could do not to reach out and grab him. Her arms ached to hold her child.

Betty Cellamino nudged Leo forward. Reluctantly, he held out his hand to Lindsay. She opened her arms. Leo hesitated. Betty gave him another nudge. He walked into Lindsay's open embrace, his long, lean body stiff as a poker.

Lindsay hugged him. Briefly. But it was enough. For now.

When Leo stepped back, Wyatt wrapped his arm around her shoulders and held her close. When his lips brushed her temple, she sighed. After twenty long years, both the man she had always loved and their child were back in her life.

At eight-thirty West Coast time, Rachel placed a telephone call to her father's old partner on the Portland Police Bureau. Charlie Young was now the chief of police, a man only a few years younger than her father would have been had he lived. The first few years after Rachel had moved to Tennessee with her mother after her father's death, Charlie and his wife, Laraine, had kept in touch on a regular basis. Charlie had wanted to keep tabs on Rachel, his old friend's only child. And despite the fact that her parents had divorced a few years before her father's deadly heart attack, her mother and Laraine Young had remained good friends.

When she heard Charlie's gravelly voice, the sound brought back memories from her teenage years when she had been like a daughter to the childless Youngs.

"Uncle Charlie, it's Rachel."

"Well, hello, girl. How are you?"

"I'm fine. How are you and Aunt Laraine?"

"Older, fatter, and grayer." He chuckled.

"I—I'm thinking about coming to Portland for a visit."

"Hmm . . . Coming back in July for the reunion at St. Elizabeth's."

"Probably, but I may come in before July."

"You'll stay here with us, of course. Laraine wouldn't let you stay anywhere else."

"I'd love to, but do you think you can put up with me for five or six weeks?"

"That long, huh?" He chuckled again. "Are you planning on taking a leave of absence or—"

"I'm on leave already," she told him. "I was wounded in the line of duty a few weeks ago."

"Are you all right?"

"I'm getting there."

"Then hop on the next plane and come on out here."

"Uncle Charlie?"

"Yes?"

"I want to ask a favor."

"Sure thing. What do you need?"

"I would like to take a look at the files from the Jake Marcott murder case."

Charlie Young let out a long, low whistle. "Why do you want to do a thing like that? That case is colder than the polar ice cap."

"Let's just say that all this talk about a high-school reunion has brought back a lot of memories. Besides, I'll need something to occupy my time while I'm there."

"You're not still pining away over that Marcott boy, are you? I'm sure your dad never told you that we found out a few not-so-pleasant things about that kid."

"No, I'm not still pining away over Jake," she assured her dad's old partner. "And when I get to Portland, I want you to tell me all about those not-so-pleasant things you found out about him."

Chapter 24

Portland, Oregon, June 2006

Nearly two weeks after Rachel spoke to Charlie Young, she arrived in Portland, the town where she had grown up. The City of Roses. Originally, she had thought she could just pick up and go, but she'd been wrong. First of all, her doctor had refused to allow her to travel until after her scheduled checkup, and then she'd had to okay leaving the state with her captain at the Huntsville Police Department. Odd how she'd done a complete turnaround about going back to Portland for the St. Lizzy's reunion. When Aurora had called her back in March, she'd been totally uninterested. No way in hell. The past was better left there, along with all the memories, both good and bad.

Now, Aurora was dead.

An accident.

Or was it?

Haylie was dead, too.

A victim of a robbery gone bad.

Or was there more to her death than met the eye?

Those e-mails from Kristen and Lindsay had piqued Rachel's curiosity, her law-enforcement training kicking in and making her ask a hundred and one unanswered questions about the deaths of two old friends. If she'd been smart, she'd have simply accepted both deaths for what they probably were, what the police in Portland and in New York City had accepted. But a niggling doubt in the back of her mind kept bothering her, kept eating away at her until she had known what she had to do. Go back to Portland, under the guise of a St. Lizzy's alumna returning to the city for a long-overdue visit before the twenty-year class reunion.

Adding to the two untimely deaths of old classmates were the not-so-coincidental situations with Lindsay and Kristen. Lindsay had been attacked by an unknown assailant in her own apartment, and Kristen had been—and possibly still was being—stalked by some unknown person.

And what about those marred senior photographs? The dead women had each received one of the ruined invitations.

Rachel could not accept that two deaths, an attack, and a stalking, all of the victims her old friends, all four women connected to Jake Marcott and St. Lizzy's, were mere coincidence. No, it didn't wash. There was something wrong with the scenario, and her gut instincts told her that in some crazy way it had something to do with the reunion, with her group of friends from high school, and with Jake Marcott. He was the common denominator. A boy who had been loved and hated in equal measure. A boy who had been shot through the heart with an arrow—Cupid's arrow—at their senior high Valentine's Day dance.

She had arrived at PDX, Portland International Airport, and picked up her rental car yesterday. Then the twenty-minute drive through town had allowed her to see just how much had changed and yet how so many things remained the same. The Willamette River, which flows northward to the Columbia River, divided the city into east and west sides; the west side waterfront was the business section of town, with Northwest Twenty-third a trendy area with boutiques, shops, and restaurants. Where the Blitz brewery had existed, now the area was referred to as "The Pearl District" with trendy condos and lofts.

Uncle Charlie and Aunt Laraine now lived in a gorgeous new house in a new neighborhood. Uncle Charlie had been at work when she arrived, but Aunt Laraine had welcomed her with open arms and shown her to a guest bedroom and bath on the ground level.

"You'll have your own key, of course," Laraine had said. "And you can come and go as you please. There's a side entrance and a kitchenette, too. We bought this place when Mother moved in with us." Laraine had sighed heavily. "We lost Mother three years ago. But she lived a good life. She was eighty-nine."

Despite how much she had wanted to go directly to Charlie's office and get started with going through the old files on the Jake Marcott case, Rachel had spent the rest of the day with Laraine.

But at dinner that evening—yesterday evening—she had brought up the subject with Charlie.

"Well, if you're that determined, I suppose I don't see what harm it'll do for you to spend some time going through all the old records," Charlie had said. "It's been a cold case for nearly twenty years, so it's not like you're stepping on anybody's toes. Plus it was your dad's case, and you are a police officer."

So, this morning she had awakened early, showered, and dressed in a pair of tan slacks, pale blue silk blouse and light-weight navy blazer, comfortable loafers, and an oversized shoulder bag. After breakfast with Charlie—coffee and an apple Danish—they headed for downtown.

Headquartered at 1111 SW Second Avenue, the Portland Police Bureau was larger than Huntsville's, but the office space had a familiarity that put Rachel at ease. And it helped that several of the older officers had worked with her dad and they remembered her from the old days.

"I'm going to turn you over to one of our detectives in the Cold Case Homicide Unit," Charlie told her. "He'll authorize you to have access to any and all material from the Marcott case. Like you, he had a connection to Jake."

"Oh?" Rachel wondered which one of her former acquaintances had gone into law enforcement as she had. One of the St. Lizzy's girls? Or maybe a Western Catholic or Washington High grad?

Charlie led her to a cubicle in the back where a man sat, his head down as he peered over *The Oregonian*, a statewide newspaper.

Charlie cleared his throat. The man glanced up. Rachel's heart skipped a beat. She stared into a set of golden brown eyes the color of rich, dark honey. He grinned. What a wickedly flirtatious grin.

The man stood to his full six-two height and held out his big hand. "Hello, Rachel. It's been a long time."

She studied his handsome face. Square jaw. Hawkish nose. High cheekbones. And a mane of thick wavy sun-kissed brown hair.

"Dean McMichaels?"

"Yeah. Don't tell me you didn't recognize me."

"No . . . yes, I mean, not at first."

"Well, since no introductions are necessary, I'll turn her over to you, Dean." Charlie put his arm around Rachel's shoulders and gave her a paternal hug. "If you need anything, honey, just let me know." He looked right at Dean. "You treat her right, you hear me?"

"Yes, sir." Dean saluted Charlie, who chuckled, hugged Rachel again, and walked away, leaving her to face the boy who had made her life a living hell when they were kids.

"Have a seat." Dean indicated the swivel chair at his desk.

Rachel sat. He propped his hip against his desk and faced her. "So, why do you want to put yourself through the misery of looking at all those old records about Jake's murder?"

"I don't know," she lied. "I'm on leave from work—" When he raised a speculative eyebrow, she explained, "I was wounded in the line of duty and won't be going back to active duty for another month. As I said, I'm on leave and Kristen and Lindsay wanted me to come to the reunion, and Uncle Charlie and Aunt Laraine insisted I stay—"

"Cut the crap," he said. "This is Dean, remember. You can't lie to me. You couldn't when we were kids and you still can't."

"What I remember when we were kids and teenagers is your tormenting me to death."

He leaned forward, just enough to put them face-to-face, less than a foot separating them. "Ever ask yourself why I picked on you the way I did?"

"Because we couldn't stand each other. You were such a little shit. Pulling my hair, stealing my purse, calling me names, laughing at me, making fun of me for having a crush on Jake."

"You were too good for a guy like Jake," Dean said as he got up off the desk. "Want some coffee before I give you a tour and we find you an empty desk somewhere?"

"Coffee's fine." She followed behind Dean, the act reminiscent of when they'd been preteens and had lived next door to each other. Even then she'd wanted to do everything the boys did and hated being told she couldn't do something because "you're just a girl." How many times had she heard Dean say those fighting words?

He stopped at the coffeemaker, poured the strong dark brew into two disposable cups, and handed one to her. "Black okay?"

She nodded. "What did you mean when you said I was too good for Jake?" As she recalled, Dean and Jake had been buddies.

"There was a lot more to Jake Marcott than you knew. He had a dark side, believe me."

"Didn't anyone ever tell you that you shouldn't speak ill of the dead?"

"You aren't still hung up on Jake, are you?"

Rachel took a sip of coffee. God, it was awful. Way too strong. And bitter. "Jake hasn't been a blip on my radar for most of the past twenty years. Do I remember him? Yes. Do I occasionally think of him? Yes. Do I remember what it felt like to have a major teenage crush on him? Of course I do. But there was never anything more than friendship between Jake and me. And there have been several men in my life since then, including a former husband."

"Divorced?"

"Yeah."

"Me, too."

"Kids?" she asked.

"Nope. But we did fight for custody of Brighton, our cocker spaniel. She won custody."

When he grinned, Rachel's stomach flip-flopped. God, what was wrong with her? Why was she reacting this way? For pity's sake, this was Dean. Dean McMichaels.

"What about you?" he asked. "Got any little rug rats?"

"No children." *I lost a baby four months into my pregnancy. Six years ago.*

"Guess that means we're both footloose and fancy free."

"I guess it does."

"How about dinner tonight?"

"What?" Her eyes widened in absolute shock. Had Dean McMichaels just asked her for a date?

"I'm not a guy who wastes time with subtleties," he told her. "I've been divorced four years, been through two semiserious relationships since then, and have been free as a bird for the past six months. Unless you've got a jealous boyfriend back home in Alabama, I'm putting my hat in the ring."

She stared at him, still in a state of shock, still not quite comprehending that this drop-dead gorgeous police detective who was putting the moves on her was Dean McMichaels. "Dinner, huh? Okay." Why not? He was right—they were both footloose and fancy free. And it wasn't as if she had to worry about the thirty-eight-year-old Dean pulling her hair, teasing her unmercifully, or telling her that she couldn't play with the boys.

"You're staying with the chief and Mrs. Young, right?"

Rachel nodded.

"I'll pick you up at seven this evening."

His grin widened, showing off his perfect white teeth.

"Seven's fine." She swallowed hard, wondering if she'd lost her mind. The last thing she had expected when showing up with

Charlie this morning was finding out Dean McMichaels was now a detective with the Portland Police Bureau. And right up there running a close second of unexpected happenings was agreeing to go out on a date with him. "About the records on the Marcott murder case . . ."

"Are you going to come clean and tell me why you're really going through the records of the Cupid Killer cold case file?"

"Maybe. When we get better acquainted and I know I can trust you."

Kristen Delmonico couldn't shake the feeling that someone was watching her. A few months ago, she would have thought herself paranoid, but not now. Not since someone had invaded her privacy, forcing her to leave her own home and flee into the arms of her almost-ex-husband. A great deal had changed since she and their daughter Lissa had moved in with Ross, the least of which was the impending divorce. After admitting that they still loved each other, she and Ross had agreed to give their marriage a second chance. So far, so good. Ross showered her with attention and had become a diligent father, keeping close tabs on their only offspring. The unseen, unknown stalker who had been plaguing Kristen for a couple of months now had brought out all the protective instincts in Ross, and she had to admit that she didn't mind having a big, strong man around, no matter how independent and self-reliant she had always been.

No one is going to attack you in the middle of the day at a downtown restaurant. It's broad daylight. There are dozens of people surrounding you.

Yeah, well, there had been dozens of people surrounding Aurora when she'd fallen beneath a subway train in New York City. You didn't have to be alone in your home, the way Haylie had been, to become a murder victim.

A homeless man robbed and killed Haylie. Aurora accidentally fell into the path of a subway train.

Kristen hoped that if she told herself often enough, she would eventually begin to believe it. There was no lunatic methodically killing members of their old high-school gang, the bevy of little planets that had circled around the sun god, Jake Marcott.

Then what about the photos slashed with red?

Stop thinking crazy thoughts like that, she told herself. *Unless someone followed you from your office, no one knows where you are or who you're meeting.*

Maybe some guy at the bar was looking at her or maybe someone at a nearby table thought they knew her and was staring at her. Any number of reasonable explanations came to mind as to why she felt she was being watched.

"Kris?" A female voice with just a hint of a Southern accent called her name.

She looked up to see Rachel Alsace walking toward her. She would have recognized Rach anywhere, anytime, and yet she was different. Not just older. There was a confident swagger to Rachel's walk. A chin held high, shoulders back, I-am-a-force-to-be-reckoned-with attitude. Rachel had always been a bit of a tomboy, dressing casually, keeping her blond hair short, not wearing very much make-up or jewelry. This new and improved version still had short hair, but with soft curls that framed her face, and her make-up flattered her fair skin. A pair of small, fat gold hoops shimmered against her earlobes.

"Rachel." Kristen shot up quickly and grabbed her friend's hands. "Girl, you look fabulous." She'd never have dreamed Rachel would turn out to be such a looker.

Rachel hugged Kristen, then the two sat down facing each other at the small table. "You haven't changed a bit, Kris. You're still as pretty as you were twenty years ago."

"Flattery will get you the best meal in this place. The Serrano ham is to die for. I usually get a sampling of several of their specialties. Andina's has scrumptious stuffed yucca. You've got to try it. I went ahead and ordered. I hope that's okay. "

"Yes, of course, that's fine with me." Rachel stared at her. "It really is so good to see you again."

"Yeah. I feel the same way."

Silence.

Their smiles disappeared.

"Are you really going to look into Jake's old files?" Kristen asked.

Rachel nodded. "You'll never guess who's one of the two detectives assigned to the Cold Case Homicide Unit."

"Dean McMichaels."

"You knew and didn't tell me!"

Kristen's smile returned. "I honestly didn't even think about it. I knew Dean was a detective with the Portland Police Bureau, but I really didn't know he was working the Cold Case Homicide Unit."

"He has certainly changed," Rachel said.

"Has he? How?"

"Well, for one thing, the guy is drop-dead gorgeous."

"He always was," Kristen said. "You just didn't notice because all you could see was Jake." She sighed. "Like so many of us. You, me, Lindsay, Mandy, and half our class. Were we idiots or what!"

"Jake didn't love any of us, you know," Rachel said. "Not even Lindsay."

"Yeah, I know." Kristen grimaced. "God, I hate the very thought of opening all those old wounds. I wish Aurora had never talked me into heading up the reunion committee. She told me that because I was valedictorian, it was my duty."

"Now Aurora's dead."

Silence.

The waiter brought the food Kristen had ordered, along with a bottle of wine from the Pearl Wine Shop located on a lower level of the restaurant.

"Kris, if Aurora's death wasn't an accident and if that homeless guy didn't kill Haylie, you do know there's a possibility that someone—maybe whoever killed Jake—has decided to eliminate the girls who formed the inner circle around Jake."

Kristen took a deep breath and exhaled slowly. "The thought has crossed my mind, but the question is why now? Why wait twenty years? And why kill any of us? What is this person's motive?"

"Why now, twenty years later? My guess would be the reunion ignited some kind of spark in this person. All of us getting together again stirred up the past for him or her. Why this person would want to kill us—I don't have a clue." Rachel reached for her wineglass. "Of course, all of this is merely conjecture on my part, but as a cop, I've learned to rely on my gut instincts, and they're screaming like crazy. I think the only way to find out if my assumptions are correct is to look into Jake's murder case and find out just who Jake Marcott really was."

After taking a sip of wine, Kristen nodded. "And it doesn't hurt that you'll be working side by side with to-die-for Dean."

Rachel grinned. "He asked me out."

"Dean asked you for a date?"

Rachel nodded. "Tonight."

"You work fast, my friend. You do know he's one of *the* bachelors in Portland. Ever since his divorce, he's played the field, broken a few hearts, and walked away from two incredible ladies, both wild about him, or so I hear."

"Are you informing me or warning me?"

"A little of both."

"Did you know his wife?"

"No, not really, but I met her once. A perky little blonde. I think she was a cheerleader in high school. She had her own local thirty-minute TV show for a while. She came here from Sacramento, and I heard she went back there after the divorce."

"I despised him, you know," Rachel said as she picked at her plate of edible delights. "When we were kids."

"I know you two fought like cats and dogs, but I always suspected that was because you two were really hot for each other and neither of you had sense enough to admit it."

"You're kidding, right?"

"Are you telling me that you really weren't hot for him back then and that you don't think he was nuts about you?"

"We are talking about the same person, aren't we? Dean McMichaels. Student at Western Catholic. The guy who lived next door to me and pestered the crap out of me almost every day of my life from kindergarten through high school."

"Don't you remember my trying to tell you once that you should forget about Jake and grab Dean before he got away?" Kristen said.

"Yeah, I remember, but at the time I thought you were just trying to steer me away from Jake and cut out some of the competition."

Kristen and Rachel laughed simultaneously, relieving some of the tension that the mere mention of Jake's name created.

"Let's enjoy our meal and forget about everything else for a little while," Kristen said. "And now that you're here in Portland and planning on staying until the reunion, we've got plenty of time to catch up on everything."

"Including trying to figure out who might want to kill you and me and Lindsay."

She sat far enough away from Kristen and Rachel so that they couldn't see her, but by scooting her chair to the edge of her table, she could watch them from a distance.

She couldn't believe her good fortune—Rachel had come to Portland four weeks before the reunion, and word was that Lindsay and Wyatt Goddard might come in early, too, a couple of days before the reunion. Everything was working out even better than she had hoped. She wouldn't have to seek them out, wouldn't have to make another out-of-town trip the way she had when she went to New York City. All her victims were coming to her. How sweet!

Today, she had followed Kristen from her office, keeping a discreet distance so she wouldn't notice the car that was tailing her. She'd had no idea Kristen was meeting Rachel for lunch, although she'd heard that Rachel was planning to spend a month with Chief Young and his wife. If by any chance Rachel and Kristen walked by her on their way out of Andina's today, they wouldn't recognize her, not in her elaborate disguise. She had begun to enjoy trying out different disguises. She now owned three wigs—blond, red, and black. Today she wore the red wig, along with a pair of frog-eyed glasses and a row of ear studs that made it appear that she had pierced both of her ears at least a dozen times. Purple nail polish and lipstick complemented the outlandish orange and purple gossamer robe that swept behind when she walked.

Look at them sitting there laughing, enjoying themselves, reminiscing about the good old days. They were probably talking about Jake, about how handsome he'd been, what a stud he'd been, how his kisses had tasted, what it had felt like to have him ramming into each of them. She didn't know for sure that he'd fucked Kristen and Rachel, but knowing him the way she had, she figured he had fucked them all.

But he never loved any of them. Not even Lindsay.

He loved me. Only me.

And I loved him.

Jake, why did you make me do it? Why did you force me to destroy something so precious?

You deserved to die after what you did.

And they deserve to die. All of them.

Two down and four to go.

One by one, they're each going to join you in hell.

Chapter 25

Mandy Kim Stulz felt uneasy. And not for the first time in recent weeks. *Overactive imagination,* she told herself. No one was watching her, following her, keeping tabs on her comings and goings. At their most recent class reunion meeting, hadn't everyone been on edge? Kristen, DeLynn, Martina, April, and Bella had each admitted that the deaths of fellow classmates Haylie Swanson and Aurora Zephyr unnerved them more than just a little. After all, both women had died violently in the past two months and both had been on the reunion committee.

And both had known Jake Marcott. One had hated him; the other had adored him.

Stop thinking such nonsense. Haylie had been murdered during a home robbery and Aurora's death had been an accident. Neither had anything to do with their being on the reunion committee or with Jake Marcott.

But try as she might, somehow Mandy couldn't shake the notion that the two deaths were more than a horrible coincidence. And she couldn't forget the sick photograph she'd received in her invitation to the reunion.

Kristen hadn't come right out and voiced what they were all thinking, what they all feared—that someone, perhaps Jake's killer, had targeted some or all of the girls who'd played a major role in his life.

A whimpering sound came over the baby monitor sitting on Mandy's home office desk. She listened intently, waiting to see if little Emily was simply whining in her sleep or if she was waking. Mandy held her breath. It had taken her an hour to get her eighteen-month-old daughter to sleep so she could get the class of '86 bio booklet printed, stapled with a back and front cover, and ready to box up for the big night. Although the actual reunion was four weeks away, she hated leaving anything to the last minute.

Silence. No crying. Good. Emily was still asleep.

Mandy and her husband, Jeff, had tried unsuccessfully to have a child for nearly ten years. Nothing had worked. In the end, after two in vitro attempts failed, they had opted for adoption. Emily Amanda Stulz was a godsend, a beautiful doe-eyed little girl they had found through an overseas adoption agency. Emily's biological mother, a biracial Vietnamese prostitute, had sold her baby to the highest bidder. Only through the grace of God had the precious child been saved from a fate worse than death.

Mercy, Mandy! Is every thought in your head these days about death? Weren't you the idiot who voiced loud and clear at the first reunion committee meeting, "Why haven't we had a reunion before now?"

No one who graduated in '86 could ever look back without remembering that cold February night, the St. Valentine's Day dance, and the Cupid Killer. The person who had shot Jake through the heart had never been found. Was he or she still out there and had for some unknown reason resurfaced and started killing again?

The phone rang. Mandy jumped as if she'd been shot.

Her hand actually trembled as she picked up the receiver.

"Is this Mrs. Stulz?" the peculiar voice asked.

Damn, why had she automatically answered without checking the caller ID? This was no doubt a telemarketer.

"Yes, this is Mrs. Stulz, but whatever you're selling, I'm not interested."

Just as she started to hang up, she heard the voice say, "Aren't you interested in staying alive?"

Mandy's hand clutched the receiver with white-knuckled tension. "Who is this?"

"Your worst nightmare."

"If this is some kind of sick joke—"

"No one is laughing about Haylie's death or Aurora's, are they?"

For a millisecond, Mandy couldn't breathe.

Diabolical laughter echoed through the phone line. Mandy gasped for air.

The dial tone hummed in her ears.

Sweet Jesus, who? . . . why? . . .

Mandy slammed the receiver down on the base, then sat there shaking from head to toe. After regaining a little of her composure, she checked the caller ID. A number, but no name. She redialed. It immediately went to voicemail.

"Hi, this is Minnie Mouse," a squeaky, almost inhuman voice said. "Leave a message and Mickey will call you back."

Mandy shook her head. What kind of crazy nonsense was that? What should she do?

She would have to tell the others.

Call Kristen first. She'll know what I should do. Then call Jeff and tell him to come home right away.

As much as she hated to admit it, Mandy was scared out of her mind.

She slipped the prepaid cell phone into her purse and smiled. It was time to shake things up a bit more, to up the ante. She wanted the others running scared, wanted them to spend sleepless nights worrying and wondering, wanted them to keep looking over their shoulders searching for the boogie man. Originally, she had wanted to kill the threesome—Rachel, Kristen, and Lindsay—first, but when it hadn't worked out that way, she had revised her plans. She'd get rid of the others first and leave Kristen, Rachel, and Lindsay for last. She hated them all, but especially Lindsay. If it were possible, she would love to kill each of them at the reunion. What if she somehow managed to lure them, one by one, here into the maze outside St. Elizabeth's? Wouldn't that be just too incredibly wonderful?

She looked up at the dreary gray sky that threatened rain this afternoon and breathed in deeply. Surrounded by the labyrinth of hedges, deep within the quiet sanctuary, she let her gaze travel over the sculpture of the Madonna, white and bleached as bones, then on to the ancient oak tree that towered high above the hedges. The tree was green and lush, brimming with late springtime life, so unlike the way it had looked that night twenty years ago. In February. It had been leafless, barren, the skeletal branches quivering in the cold wind.

As much as she had tried to erase the memories from her mind, she couldn't. Over the years, those memories had haunted her, growing in intensity and vividness with each passing year. She had fought the hatred, the envy, the bitterness she felt for the

others, trying her best to forgive them for what they had done, just
as she had tried to forgive Jake. Jake, whom she had loved.

But he didn't love you as much as you loved him. He used you.
He made you destroy the life growing inside you.

"You can't have my baby," he had told her.

But Lindsay had given birth to his baby. Her son had lived.
No, no, that's all wrong. You just thought the baby belonged to
Jake. But Leo Cellamino isn't Jake's child. He never was.

Maybe Jake wasn't the father of my baby either, and he made
me kill it for no reason.

If she had told Jake that there was someone else, someone
who loved her and was good to her, would he have let her have her
baby? But she couldn't tell Jake that he wasn't the only one. He
would have been furious. He might have . . .

It doesn't matter now. My baby is dead. Jake is dead.
I killed them both.

A warm breeze stirred to life, rustling through the thick hedges
and swaying the top branches of the old oak tree. Narrowing her
gaze, she stared at the tree, at the very spot where Jake had stood
leaning against the trunk, a half-smoked cigarette between his fingers. He'd been so cocky, so sure of himself. Mr. Irresistible.

He had grinned when he saw her peeking at him through the
hedges where she'd hidden in an area of shrubbery that had died
and been trimmed into an alcove shape. And that smile had stayed
in place until the arrow hit him dead center, in the heart. A lucky
shot? Divine providence? What did it matter. Jake Marcott had
paid for his sins with his life.

Tears welled up in her eyes as she remembered the way he had
looked, his body pinned to the tree trunk, blood oozing from the
wound, him gasping, his eyes wide with shock. He hadn't died instantly, but soon enough. And all the while, he had stared right at
her, as if asking for her help.

She had slipped away, leaving him, glad that he was dead.

Dean McMichaels considered himself a good guy. Friendly,
courteous, likable. Ever since junior high, he had attracted the
ladies. Teenage girls back then. But his first conquest had been an
older woman. He fifteen and she seventeen. Teena had been the
cousin of a friend of a friend, a girl all the guys in his circle had
screwed at one time or another. In retrospect, he wasn't all that
proud of the fact that he'd been one of them, but he'd been a

horny kid and she'd been putting out. After Teena, he had become a bit more discriminate, usually going steady with a girl before they had sex. But the one girl he had really wanted—wanted so much that he'd honest-to-God compared every other woman in his life to her—had been hung up on another guy: Jake Marcott. May his black soul rot in hell.

He had known Rachel Alsace since kindergarten when her family had moved back to Portland, her dad's hometown, from where her mom had lived all her life, Chattanooga, Tennessee. From day one he had kidded Rachel about her hillbilly accent. Once he'd even made her cry and had instantly regretted it. She'd been a tomboy, climbing trees, riding her skateboard, racing her bike, playing baseball. A real live wire, full of energy and enthusiasm.

He wasn't sure when he'd stopped thinking of her as just one of the guys and starting seeing her as a girl. About the time she went through puberty and grew a set of perfect knockers. Man, how he'd wanted to see her boobs. Once—just once—he'd kissed her, at Lindsay Farrell's thirteenth birthday party when they were playing some crazy kissing game. Being a good sport, Rachel had allowed the kiss, but when he'd copped a feel, she had slapped him. Their gazes had locked in a heated exchange. He had wanted to kiss her again but knew he'd blown his one chance to become more than just buddies.

By the time Jake Marcott showed up in their lives, when they were sixteen, he had already begun to pester the hell out of Rachel, doing everything he could to make her notice him. Why was it that all the other girls had paid attention to him, but not the one he'd wanted?

After Jake's murder, nothing was ever the same for any of the old gang, least of all for Rachel and her family. She had moved back to Tennessee with her mother after her father's death, and he'd lost track of her. Once in a blue moon, he'd run into Kristen and asked about Rachel, but she hadn't known anything more than her address. Both of his serious girlfriends in college had been cute, petite blondes; when he'd married in his late twenties, his wife, Kellie, had fit the same description. He hadn't been consciously aware of the fact that he had repeatedly tried to find a substitute for the one and only girl he had always wanted.

And here she was back in Portland, back in his life, and walking straight toward him. All he could say was she cleaned up damn good. Just looking at her took his breath away. Nothing flashy, just understated beauty. The kind of clean, wholesome, all-American beauty that turned Dean inside out.

They were both thirty-eight, both divorced and childless, and together again after twenty years. Was fate giving him a second chance with Rachel? Or was he a fool for letting himself believe in second chances?

Dean stared at Rachel, drinking in the sight of her. Her short blond curls framed her heart-shaped face. Her big blue eyes sparkled with mischief and curiosity just as they had when she'd been a kid. She had dressed casually, her outfit suitable for just about any place he might take her in Portland for dinner. White slacks in some gauzy fabric with a matching loose-fitting blouse that billowed out from a row of tiny beading directly under her breasts. Heaven help them both, but she looked good enough to eat.

"You have her home at a decent hour, young man," Charlie Young said jokingly as he patted Dean on the back.

"Is two in the morning a decent hour?" Dean asked.

"I'll be home before midnight," Rachel informed both men.

"You two have a nice evening," Laraine called after them as they left the house.

Once alone together in Dean's white Thunderbird, he started the engine, then turned in his seat and looked directly at Rachel. "You look beautiful."

The corners of her mouth lifted ever so slightly. An almost smile. "I'm not beautiful and I know it, so don't waste your time with flattery because it will not get you laid tonight. Got that?"

Dean laughed. God, she hadn't changed. At least not in the way she reacted to him. Hackles raised. Spitting fire. On the defensive.

"I really do think you're beautiful." *I always have.* "And to set the record straight, I don't put out on a first date. A girl has to woo me a little before I let her have her way with me."

"I can't believe this—you act like you did when we were sixteen." She glowered at him. "I'm cute, vivacious, spunky, and have a really nice rack, but I am not now nor have I ever been beautiful."

He shifted gears, backed his Ford sports car out of the Youngs' driveway, and gunned the engine, shooting the Thunderbird like a rocket down the residential street.

"You'll get a speeding ticket driving so fast," she told him.

He slowed down to just ten miles over the speed limit. "I have friends on the police force who can fix a ticket for me."

Rachel gave him a real smile then, and his stomach knotted.

"Would you be interested in a movie before dinner?" he asked, already having a particular movie in mind.

"I guess so, if there's something good showing."

"Define good."

She glanced his way. "Something that isn't all blood and gore. Something that won't give me nightmares and something where every other word isn't *MF*."

"Well, there goes my idea of seeing a movie."

They both laughed.

That evening after leaving Emily with Mandy's parents, Mandy and Jeff drove over to Ross Delmonico's apartment. Mandy had called earlier and told Kristen they had to talk, that it was urgent. Now, after she'd had the entire afternoon to rationalize the eerie phone call she'd received, Mandy was able to tell Kristen about it without crying or freaking out.

"Is there anyone who might want to frighten you or even hurt you?" Kristen asked. "Someone not connected to St. Lizzy's or the reunion"—she sighed heavily—"or to Jake?"

"No, no one," Mandy said.

"I think Mandy needs to report the call to the police." Jeff glanced from Kristen to her husband Ross.

"I agree," Ross said. "When Kristen sensed she was being stalked—"

"Rachel Alsace is back in Portland," Kristen blurted out. "She's a police officer in Alabama and Chief Young is allowing her to go through the old Cupid Killer files. She's working with Dean McMichaels. You remember Dean, don't you?"

Mandy stared at Kristen, trying to decipher any hidden message in what she'd said, doing her best to read between the lines. "Have you seen Rachel, talked to her?"

"We had lunch today."

"And?"

"She thinks there might be a connection between Haylie's and Aurora's deaths, something the police here in Portland and in New York City weren't aware of that would have made them look beyond the obvious."

"What?" Ross and Jeff voiced the word simultaneously.

"She isn't sure, but she feels certain there's something," Kristen said. "And if Rachel senses something isn't right about their deaths, and we do, too, then we'd be fools to ignore our gut instincts, wouldn't we?"

After deciding not to go to a movie, Dean had driven Rachel around Portland. When she suggested going by St. Elizabeth's he had hesitated.

"Why spoil a perfectly lovely evening?" he had asked.

"We won't get out," she'd told him. "I'd just like to drive by and take a look."

He had driven by, barely slowing down, as if the ghosts from the past were hot on his heels.

"You and Jake were buddies, but sometimes I thought maybe you didn't always like him," Rachel had said.

"He could be a jerk." Once the old red-brick school that had originally been built in 1920 was out of sight, Dean added, "Jake could be a real son of a bitch. He kept his dark side well hidden."

"It's easy enough to defame his character now, when he can't defend himself."

After she had made that really stupid comment, silence hung between her and Dean for quite some time—until they arrived at their original destination. Bar Pastiche was an odd little restaurant on Southeast Hawthorne Boulevard. Odd in that it was a small eatery where the updated-daily menu was written on the wall on butcher paper and where customers threw their paper napkins on the floor as people might do in a true tapas spot in Spain. The ambience was nonexistent, but the food was fabulous. They sat together at the small bar, sipped their drinks, and nibbled on mini-meatball sandwiches and Spanish deviled eggs.

After dinner, as they headed for Dean's Thunderbird, he asked, "It's too early to take you home. Want to go dancing? Pick up some ice cream? Run by my place and let me introduce you to my cat?"

"You have a cat?"

He chuckled. "Nah, not really, but I thought that sounded better than saying 'want to come up and see my king-size bed?' "

She playfully punched him on the arm. "No running by your place for any reason. And no dancing. Not tonight. However, if you're offering to buy me a double scoop of cherry vanilla ice cream—"

Rachel's cell phone chimed. A no-nonsense ring. Not a cute song or music of any kind. She reached inside her white handbag, removed her small phone, and flipped it open.

"Hello?"

"That had better not be another man." Dean winked at her.

"What?" she said into the phone. "Oh, crap! Yes, y'all wait right there." She glanced at Dean and mouthed one word. *Kristen.* He immediately knew she meant Kristen Daniels Delmonico.

When she'd closed her phone and dropped it into her open bag, Dean asked, "What did Kristen want?"

"She wants us to come to her apartment—her husband's apartment. Mandy Kim, who is now Mandy Stulz, and her husband are there with Kristen and Ross. It seems Mandy received a threatening phone call this afternoon, and both she and Kris are convinced that someone is stalking them . . . stalking all of us."

Dean raised a questioning brow. "All of us as in . . . ?"

"The girls who were once closely involved with Jake in some way—Kris, Mandy, Bella, Lindsay, and me. Maybe even some of the others. We're not sure."

"You know how crazy that sounds, don't you?"

"If you want to hear crazy, then listen to this theory: we, as in Kristen, Lindsay, and I, think that Haylie and Aurora may have both been murdered by the same person. Maybe the same person who killed Jake. Several of us received pictures that had been scratched, as if we were being singled out. Maybe warned."

"You think the Cupid Killer is killing again after twenty years?"

"Yes, we do. And that's the real reason I've come back to Portland. I intend to catch Jake Marcott's murderer."

Chapter 26

After Rachel and Dean met with Kristen, Mandy, and their husbands last night, they had all agreed that someone was stalking Kristen and Mandy, but the guys pointed out that they couldn't be certain this had anything to do with the reunion or Jake Marcott's twenty-year-old murder. However, the one thing they all agreed on was that Kristen and Mandy shouldn't take any chances, that someone wanted to, at the very least, scare them. And at the very worst?

That question had become a bone of contention between Rachel and Dean in their discussion of the situation when he drove her home.

"What if the person stalking Kris and Mandy killed Haylie and somehow implicated the homeless guy? What if this person went to New York, killed Aurora, and tried to kill Lindsay?"

"That's a lot of what ifs," Dean had said.

"Well, here's one more for you—what if the two deaths, the attempted murder, and the stalkings are all connected to the reunion and to Jake?"

Dean had played devil's advocate, pointing out the holes in her theory and asking *the* one unanswerable question—what was this unknown person's motive?

Rachel had no reply. Dean was right when he'd asked why Jake's killer would resurface after twenty years.

Today, Rachel had sat in the corner of the squad room at the police bureau headquarters and gone through the Cupid Killer case files. There was far too much information to absorb in one or two days. But after only a few hours yesterday and again today spent sorting through the facts, she had come to one conclusion—

she had never really known Jake Marcott. The flirtatious, fun-loving, handsome boy she remembered had apparently been little more than a figment of her fertile teenage imagination. Just as Dean had told her, there had been a dark side to Jake. Why hadn't she seen it? He had been a troubled boy from a troubled home, but he had hidden it well, as had Bella.

Rachel and Bella had never been buddies, but they had gotten along better than Bella had with most of Jake's friends, especially the girls in his life. Bella had resented the fact that she didn't quite mesh with the in crowd, the St. Elizabeth's and Western Catholic students that her big brother had hung out with. Rachel had always felt sorry for Jake's little sister and had thought there was something strangely sad about her.

Wonder if she's still that quiet, brooding girl she was twenty years ago?

Well, Rachel would find out in a few minutes just what Bella was like now. She rang the doorbell as she waited on the front porch of Mandy and Jeff Stulz's sprawling ranch house, which must have cost them a small fortune. But from what Kristen said, Jeff Stulz's accounting firm had become one of the most prestigious in the Portland area and the guy was raking in the big bucks.

"Mandy worked for him," Kristen had said. "That's how they met. He's probably ten years older than she is, but he doesn't look it, does he?"

When the door opened, Rachel came face-to-face with someone she didn't recognize. Expecting Mandy to greet her, she paused, wondering if she might be at the wrong house.

"Rachel?" the attractive black woman asked.

"Yes, I'm Rachel." She stepped into the two-story foyer. "I'm afraid I don't know—" She stared questioningly at the woman.

"I'm DeLynn Vaughn. Actually, it's DeLynn Simms now." Smiling warmly, she closed the door behind Rachel. "Come on in. Mandy's upstairs with little Emily, putting her to bed for the night. The others are in the great room, having drinks and discussing what's been happening to Kristen and Mandy."

When Kristen had called her first thing that morning, Rachel had agreed to join the members of the reunion committee who were meeting at Mandy's house that evening. But their hen party had been called not to discuss the reunion, but to compare notes and see if only Mandy and Kristen were being stalked.

As Rachel entered the great room, Kristen met her and offered her a glass of white wine, which Rachel accepted.

"Come on in," Kristen said. "You met DeLynn at the door. April and Martina are eager to see you."

By the time Kristen had reintroduced her to Martina Perez Taylor and April Wright, Mandy had joined them. Although Martina had gained at least fifty pounds in the past twenty years, Rachel would have recognized her anywhere. April was another matter. Her once-brown hair was a sun-kissed blond, her teeth were capped and pearly white, and contacts had replaced the thick glasses she had once worn.

Then there was Bella Marcott, who shook hands with Rachel but said nothing. Still quiet and shy? Still a bookish wallflower? With her curly black hair and light blue eyes, Bella should have been strikingly beautiful—as beautiful as Jake had been—but despite the similarity in their features, Bella was simply a pale imitation of her brother's beauty.

"It's good to see you again," Rachel said.

"You've changed," Bella told her. "You're prettier."

"Thank you." *I think.* As in the past, Rachel didn't quite know how to take Bella. She'd always been a rather odd bird, a girl who didn't seem to fit in anywhere. And she didn't really fit in here with the others tonight. Except for the fact that Kristen had said the reunion would include the guys from Western Catholic and even the kids from Washington High, Rachel would have been puzzled by Bella being on the committee.

For the first fifteen minutes, the women chitchatted about children, husbands and ex-husbands, their jobs, and the upcoming annual Rose Festival here in Portland. Then the one person Rachel had never thought would bring up the subject asked the question that had been hanging in the air like a dark cloud.

"So, Rachel, with your background as a police officer, what do you think is going on?" Bella asked. "Has Jake's killer returned? Did the Cupid Killer murder Haylie and Aurora and is he or she stalking the rest of us?"

An unnatural silence fell over the room. Suddenly the only sound was the combined soft breathing of the six women congregated in Mandy's great room.

Rachel focused on Bella. "I think it's possible."

"But why would Jake's killer suddenly start killing again?" Martina asked.

"And why kill Haylie and Aurora?" April inquired.

"We—Kristen and I—think it has something to do with this

reunion y'all are planning," Rachel told them. "For some reason, knowing that the old gang will be reunited has set this person off, but there has to be more to it than that. And I plan to dig as deep as possible into the Cupid Killer files and see if I can come up with something that will warrant the Portland Police Bureau reopening Jake's case."

"Oh." Bella mouthed the one word, an expression of surprise on her pale face.

"I'm sorry, Bella," Rachel said. "I know this has to be painful for you, but—"

"No, no. Really. I understand and I'm all right with whatever you need to do. No one would like to see Jake's killer brought to justice more than I. Even now, after all these years."

Rachel offered Bella a sympathetic half-smile. "Look, there's nothing we can do to help Haylie or Aurora, but we can help ourselves, protect ourselves. Someone is stalking Kristen and Mandy. Anybody else? Do any of you feel as if you're being watched? Followed? Anything missing from your houses? If anything odd has happened to you lately, tell me."

One by one, they shook their heads, then Bella gasped. "It might be nothing, but . . . well, several of my scarves are missing. I thought it odd, but since I have a habit of misplacing things, I just dismissed it as that. You don't suppose someone stole them, do you?"

"Was there any sign of a forced entry into your home?" Rachel asked.

"No, but I usually open the window in my bedroom at night. I like the fresh air. And I have been known to forget to close the window when I leave in the morning."

"But you haven't sensed that someone was following you or watching you?"

Bella shook her head.

"From now on, I want each of you to be alert. Not paranoid, just careful."

"Are you working with the police?" Martina asked. "I mean, is the Portland Police Bureau aware of what's been happening?"

"Actually, Rachel is unofficially working with Dean McMichaels," Kristen said. "Dean is a homicide detective now. He works in the Cold Case Homicide Unit."

"Dreamy Dean?" April sighed. "Is he as gorgeous as ever?"

"Oh, yes, he certainly is," Kristen said.

"I used to have crazy dreams about that guy," DeLynn admitted.
"I think it was his eyes," Martina said. "He's the only person I've ever met with golden eyes."

Feeling just the slightest bit uncomfortable listening to the girls talk about Dean, Rachel cleared her throat. "Ladies, I think we got off the subject, didn't we?"

"Okay, so you're working with Dreamy Dean. I'd say that's a plus since you two were friends from the time you were in diapers, right?" April said. "It shouldn't be any trouble for you to convince him to reopen Jake's case, especially if you really think it is somehow connected to what's happening now." April looked directly at Rachel, her gaze intensely focused. "Do you think we're all in danger? I mean, I wasn't one of Jake's girlfriends or anything. Actually, we weren't even friends."

"I don't know for sure who is in danger and who isn't. We're not even certain the scratched photographs are significant," Rachel admitted. "For now, I'd say everyone working on the reunion committee should be careful and watch for anything unusual happening. At this point, there is no way to know for sure who has been targeted and who hasn't or what criteria this person is using to choose his or her victims."

"But my brother Jake, his murder, is somehow at the core of what's happening," Bella said, her voice a mere whisper. "Poor Aurora. She never did anything bad to anyone. And Haylie . . . well, we all know she was unstable, don't we? Neither of them deserved what happened to them."

"If you need us to sign a petition or whatever to get the police to reopen the Cupid Killer case, just let us know," DeLynn said.

The others piped in with their endorsement of DeLynn's statement.

Half an hour later, Rachel left Mandy's feeling as if she had not only reconnected with old friends, but had also accomplished a great deal toward achieving her goal. She wasn't the only person who wanted to solve the Jake Marcott murder, and in doing so, possibly save the lives of potential victims.

In the dark, dank basement of St. Elizabeth's, she pointed her flashlight at Mandy Kim's locker. Mandy, with her moon-pie face and expensive salon haircut and rich husband. Mandy who was and always had been too smart, too cute, too everything. Jake used to talk about what a living doll Mandy was and how he'd love to get in her pants. She knew he'd told her that because he wanted to make her jealous, wanted to hurt her. The only time he had ever said sweet things to her was when he was softening her up for the kill. That's how she had thought of sex with Jake. Each time he touched her, each time he buried himself inside her, she died a little. By the time she'd murdered Jake, she was totally dead inside, her uterus empty, her emotions frozen, her future destroyed. That's why she'd been able to kill Jake so easily, without any regrets. It had been all his fault. If he hadn't ruined her so completely, she wouldn't have . . .

Killing Mandy would take cunning. And intricate planning. She would be cautious. Waiting. Expecting. Anticipating the worst.

That's all right. Let her be on guard. I simply have to devise a plan that will enable me to take her by surprise, to sneak up on her blind side.

She has a toddler whom she adores. Perhaps I can use little Emily Stulz in some way to lure Mandy into a trap.

A deep rumble of laughter fluttered up from her diaphragm and erupted into deliriously happy giggles. She had them all running scared. Each of them would be looking over her shoulder all the time, waiting for the unknown killer to strike.

Even wiseass policewoman Rachel Alsace had no idea who was marked for death, who the next victim would be.

But you have to know that you're on my list. You, Kristen, and Lindsay. The ones who loved Jake the most.

Rachel had to admit that the following day when she arrived at 1111 SW Second Avenue and went to her desk in the corner of the squad room, she had hoped to see Dean. When she hadn't caught even a glimpse of him by two that afternoon, she had begun to think he was avoiding her. Then when she was absorbed in looking over the photos from the Cupid Killer crime scene, she felt a hand on her shoulder. She jumped and yelped at the same time.

"Sorry," Dean said. "I didn't mean to scare you."

Exhaling a calming, relieved breath, Rachel swivelled around to face him. "Next time, blow a whistle or something." She laid the photos aside.

Dean sat on the edge of her desk and glanced at the glossy prints. He fingered them, separating the top two, one a full shot of Jake from head to toe, his body pinned against the oak tree by a crossbow arrow, the other a photo of the bow, found at the scene.

"Nasty stuff," Dean said.

Rachel nodded. "You know, back then all of us suspected one another. Crazy, huh? We were all a bunch of kids who knew nothing about crossbows. And it's not as if St. Lizzy's or Western or Washington High offered archery classes."

"Yeah, it never entered our minds back then that it would take an expert with a bow to hit a guy dead center in the heart and pin him to a tree."

"Even if the person had been fairly close, they still would have had to know what they were doing. I can't think of anyone in our circle of friends that would qualify." Rachel spread the photos apart, placing them side by side atop her desk. "When I first read over the file, I started wondering if a woman would be strong enough to handle the rigid tension on a crossbow, but then I read where there's some kind of lever on a crossbow that would enable just about anybody to cock it."

"Yeah, but just anybody couldn't hit the target, especially not dead center."

"I've looked at the report on the man who owned the crossbow, but apparently he was a dead end." Rachel searched through the file folder until she found that specific report. "His name was—"

"Patrick Dewey," Dean said.

Rachel stared at him. "You've taken a look at these files, haven't you?"

"Sure. More than once," Dean told her. "There was a time when Jake and I were good friends."

"What actually happened between you two? When did you stop being best buddies?"

"You want to know the truth?"

"Yes."

"When I found out that Jake had been driving the car the night Ian Powers was killed and that Jake laid all the blame on Ian because he was dead and couldn't defend himself. Jake wasn't about to take the rap for vehicular manslaughter."

A tight fist constricted around Rachel's heart and for a brief half second, she couldn't breathe. So, it was true. All the accusations that Haylie had made against Jake had been true!

"How do you know that Jake was driving that night?"

Dean grunted. "Jake told me. A few weeks after Ian's funeral. One night when we'd both had a few too many beers."

"And you never told anyone?"

Dean didn't respond. Instinctively Rachel knew there was

more. The question was, did she really want to know exactly what the "more" was?

"Tell me the rest of it," she said.

"Are you sure?"

She nodded.

"Jake threatened me," Dean said.

"What? Are you saying Jake threatened to kill you?" If Jake had threatened Dean, wouldn't that have given Dean a motive to murder his onetime best friend?

"He didn't threaten to kill me," Dean told her.

"I don't understand, if he didn't—"

"He threatened to harm someone who meant a great deal to me."

Puzzled, Rachel stared at Dean.

"He told me that if I ever breathed a word about what he'd said about driving the car the night Ian died, he would seduce you and then drop you like a hot potato. I knew that if he did that, it would not only break your heart, but it would break your spirit."

Rachel sat there staring at Dean, absorbing what he had just told her, coming to terms with distorted memories and shattered dreams. She'd had a major crush on Jake, had thought he hung the moon, despite the fact that she knew he could be a self-centered jerk. But she had never seen his truly dark side. And Dean, who had been the bane of her existence from kindergarten through high school, had been her hero, her champion. Why had she been so blind?

"Are you okay?" Dean reached out, clasped her hand resting on the desk, and gave it a squeeze.

"Yes, I'm okay. Just stunned. I thought I knew Jake. I was wrong about him." Her gaze met Dean's. "I was wrong about you, too."

"Old news, honey. Jake's history. He's the past. He can't hurt anybody now."

"I'm not so sure about that."

"Look, I can't officially reopen the Cupid Killer case, but in my free time, there's no reason I can't help you sort through the old records, snoop around, and ask some new questions."

"Are you saying you believe us—believe me—about the possibility that Jake's killer murdered Haylie and Aurora and is stalking—"

He tapped his index finger on her lips. "Nah, I'm offering to do this just to make brownie points with you."

It took Rachel a couple of seconds to realize Dean was joking. Or was he? He was looking at her like a hungry man staring at the last bite of food anywhere in sight.

"I'll take you up on your offer," she said. "And earning brownie points with me is dependent upon just how much help you are."

"Fair enough."

"Where do we start and when?"

"No time like the present."

"But you're still on duty."

"I'm on an extended coffee break."

"I wouldn't want to get you in trouble," she said. "Uncle Charlie and Aunt Laraine are having dinner out with friends tonight, so why don't we borrow Uncle Charlie's home office this evening, order in, and plan a strategy?"

"What time? Six?"

"Make it six-thirty."

"It's a date."

She shook her head.

He chuckled. "Think of it as a study date."

Every afternoon, about an hour before she started dinner, Mandy took Emily for a stroll up the street and through a nearby park. Today, she had considered not going. After all, if someone was stalking her . . .

But her neighborhood was one of the safest in the Portland area. And it was broad daylight. Besides that, she had a whistle and Mace, didn't she? And even Jeff had agreed that she couldn't live in terror every second of every day.

Five minutes later and only two blocks away from her house, Mandy was on the verge of a panic attack. She kept seeing shadows, kept sensing dark figures behind every tree, kept hearing odd sounds.

Ridiculous!

It was one of those spectacular days in Portland—bright sunshine flooded over the earth in warm, shimmering glory. The breeze was mild, birds were singing, and butterflies were fluttering all about. She should be enjoying this afternoon stroll with her daughter, not anticipating some sinister character to come out of nowhere and grab her.

By the time she pushed Emily's stroller into the small park a few blocks away, Mandy felt calmer and more assured that all was well. She had passed by Mr. Hensley working in his flower garden, Mrs. Kennedy walking her dog, and the Monroe twins skipping rope on the sidewalk. And in the park, she ran into another stay-at-home mom and neighbor, Erin Minor. They talked for a while, chatting about nothing of any importance and comparing notes about their toddlers.

On her walk home, Mandy actually enjoyed herself, as she usually did, all her anxieties now under control. As she approached the back door that led into the mudroom where she kept the folding stroller stored, she noticed something stuck on the glass storm door.

Sweet Jesus!

Someone had taped an arrow on her door. Her pulse raced. Glancing from side to side as if she thought she might spot the culprit who had left the arrow, Mandy eased around to the front of the stroller and lifted Emily up and into her arms. Resting her daughter on her hip, she walked closer to the door and stared at the arrow. A child's toy arrow, the kind with a rubber tip. But there was something red and wet dripping from that rubber tip. Blood? Surely not!

Mandy clenched her teeth to keep from crying out. Taking several steps backward, behind the stroller, she reached down into the diaper bag inside the back pocket on the stroller and retrieved her cell phone. Under ordinary circumstances, the first person she'd call would be Jeff. But not this time.

She dialed the newest number she had programmed into her phone. Rachel Alsace's phone number.

Chapter 27

During the eight days Rachel had been in Portland, a wave of anxiety and fear had swept over the reunion committee, spreading from Kristen, and Mandy to the others—DeLynn, Martina, Bella, and April. And Rachel. Each one had received at least one weird phone call and a strange, threatening note. And each member of the group had come home on various days to find a child's toy arrow taped to their back door. The rubber tip on each arrow had been dripping red paint. Not blood. Paint. But the message was clear—*Remember how Jake Marcott died.*

Initially, the police handled these incidents as misdemeanors, as nothing more than silly pranks. But because of Rachel's involvement and the fact that one of those arrows had been attached to Chief of Police Charlie Young's back door, an investigation was under way to look into the matter more thoroughly. The arrows and paint were easily traced, both sold at a variety of stores in the Portland area, making it virtually impossible to pinpoint the buyers. The phone calls had all been placed on prepaid cellular phones purchased by Minnie Mouse. The words in each note had been cut from newspapers and magazines and taped to a sheet of plain white paper.

At first, after Mandy had returned from a walk in the park with her child and found the first arrow on her door, Dean had tried to convince Rachel that someone was playing a sick prank. Maybe it was someone who, for his or her own perverted reasons, wanted to resurrect the past, to remind everyone about Jake's brutal murder. But after each committee member found an identical paint-tipped arrow on her back door, Dean had come around to Rachel's way of thinking. Someone was targeting the women who had been a part of Jake's life back in high school. But why? And was the stalker the same person who had killed Jake?

Day by day, Rachel sifted through the Cupid Killer files, with Dean assisting her in his free time. As she worked diligently to put together the pieces of a twenty-year-old murder, she often felt that she was betraying her father's memory. Mac Alsace had been the best detective in the world, bar none. If he hadn't been able to find Jake's killer, what made Rachel think she could?

Time and distance often had a way of clearing the gray areas, of making things more black and white. Sometimes even the best investigator could be too close to the forest to see the trees. As she had studied the photos, read the reports, gone over the facts again and again, a clear picture had emerged. Jake Marcott had not been the boy she'd thought he was, that was for sure. But more important, the likelihood that one of his teenaged peers had killed Jake was slim to none, unless one of them had been a skilled archer and had been able to keep that fact a secret.

Back in the day, the police had released very little information about the case, hoping to keep the killer in the dark. And Rachel's father had never discussed the particulars of the case with her, partly because he was duty-bound to keep certain things private, and partly because he had wanted to protect her from some ugly truths.

Even after all these years, she still missed her dad. As much as she had loved her mother, she'd always been a daddy's girl. His death at age forty-seven had come as a shock. Such a waste. A man in his prime.

Rachel couldn't help wondering how her life might be different now had her dad lived. One thing she knew for certain—her mother wouldn't have moved home to Tennessee as long as Rachel remained in Portland, and Rachel would never have left Portland as long as her dad was alive. And if she had stayed here in Portland? She wouldn't have a slight Southern accent, wouldn't be referring to a group of people as y'all, and she would never have married Allen Turner.

Would she be working alongside her dad now, who would probably be chief of police instead of Uncle Charlie? Would she perhaps be partnered with Dean McMichaels? Would the two of them have hooked up years ago, maybe gotten married and had a couple of kids?

Wow! Where had that thought come from—Dean and she

married? Back then, she hadn't even liked Dean. But back then, she hadn't really known Dean. If she had, she never would have suspected him of killing Jake—and she had! After all, it hadn't exactly been a secret that the two guys, once best buddies, had parted ways, and no one had understood why. Now Rachel did. It had been because Dean had known one of Jake's deep, dark secrets. Because Jake had used Dean's feelings for Rachel to blackmail Dean to keep him quiet.

Dean placed two brown paper bags on Rachel's desk. "Lunchtime," he said as he pulled up a chair and sat beside her.

"You didn't have to bring me lunch." She twisted her swivel chair around so that she faced him. "But it's a sweet gesture. Thanks."

"It's no big deal. I had to eat anyway, so I just picked up something for you, too." He eyed the brown paper bags. "Do you still like Reubens? Kosher dills? Diet Coke?"

Her mouth opened wide in surprise. Why would Dean remember her teenage favorites? "If you've got a Snickers candy bar in there for dessert—"

"If I do, what?" he teased.

"I won't believe it until I see it." She opened one sack, removed two sandwiches, two giant dill pickles, and two single-serving bags of potato chips.

Dean opened the second paper sack and removed a regular and a diet canned Coke and a couple of straws, then he turned the sack upside down and shook it. Out popped two Snickers bars.

Rachel gasped, then giggled. "Dean McMichaels, you have a memory like an elephant."

"Only for the important stuff." He winked at her.

Her heart did a crazy little rat-a-tat-tat. "I imagine that kind of memory has helped you become a top-notch detective."

He unwrapped his roast beef sandwich. "What makes you think I'm a top-notch detective?"

She popped the tabs on both colas, stripped the paper off the straws, and inserted them into the openings of the two cans. "Uncle Charlie told me. You're a highly decorated officer, made lieutenant younger than anyone else on the force, and you're in line for a big promotion."

"I just do my job. That's all."

He seemed genuinely embarrassed by her praise. A modest man. Imagine that. So different from her ex-husband. So different from Jake.

Rachel unwrapped her sandwich, lifted it to her mouth and took a bite, then sighed. After chewing and swallowing, she said, "Delicious."

Dean opened both potato chip bags. "I tracked down the man who owned the bow that was used in Jake's murder."

"You did?"

Dean nodded. "Patrick Dewey moved his family to Salem nineteen years ago. I phoned his home today, right before I went out to pick up our lunch."

"And?"

"I spoke to his wife, Marilyn. She said Patrick died a couple of years ago."

"Hmm . . . too bad, but I don't suppose he could have told us any more than he told the police twenty years ago. He reported the bow stolen a week before Jake was killed."

"Yeah, and the only reason we know it was Dewey's bow is because he registered it with the manufacturer right after he bought it. They keep a record of the serial numbers for the warranty registration."

Rachel nibbled on her potato chips. "I saw a report where my father interviewed several bow hunters who lived in the area, but none of them, including Dewey, knew Jake or his family."

"Yeah, and besides that, they all had alibis for the night Jake was killed."

"You really did go through all these old files, didn't you?" Rachel sipped on her Diet Coke.

"A few years after I joined the force, I asked permission to take a look at the Cupid Killer files," Dean said. "It wasn't that I actually thought I could find anything your dad and his partner missed. I was curious. You know, because the victim was Jake and because of how things happened. I think Jake's murder affected all of us in some way or other."

"Mmm . . ." Rachel washed down the bite of sandwich in her mouth with another sip of cola. "Sometimes, I think the reason I went into law enforcement after college, other than the fact I wanted to follow in Dad's footsteps, is because of what happened to Jake." She looked directly at Dean. "Is that crazy?"

"I don't think so, but I'm the wrong person to ask. I figure the way Jake's murder hit all of us so hard is one of the reasons I joined the Portland Police Bureau."

"It seems you and I have a great deal in common, don't we?"

Dean reached out and brushed a stray curl off Rachel's cheek and moved it behind her ear. Their gazes connected and held for a heart-stopping moment.

"Too bad we didn't realize that years ago," she said.

"Better late than never."

Oh, no. Those pesky butterflies were doing a jitterbug in her belly again. Every time Dean looked at her as if he wanted to kiss her, she felt the kind of rush that comes only with falling in love. But she wasn't falling in love with Dean, was she? Not Dean McMichaels! Of all the men on earth, why him?

It's just good old-fashioned lust, she told herself. *You haven't been with a man in a long time and you're horny. That's all there is to it. You need to have sex.*

Did that mean she should have sex with Dean?

"So, we're on for tonight," Dean said.

"Huh?"

"You haven't been listening, have you? Where did you go just then?"

"Nowhere. Just woolgathering."

"Were you thinking about Jake?" Dean pulled away from her and sat back in his chair.

"What? No, I wasn't thinking about Jake. Actually, I was thinking about—" *Are you out of your mind? You can't tell Dean that you were thinking about having sex with him, to use him to scratch an itch.*

Dean glared at her.

"I was thinking that we should pick up a bottle of wine to take to Kris and Ross's tonight."

Dean gave her a skeptical look. She knew he didn't believe her.

"No problem. We can pick up a bottle on the way there."

Rachel laid her hand over Dean's. "I haven't been carrying a torch for Jake all these years. After I moved to Chattanooga with my mother, I got on with my life and I hardly ever thought about Jake."

"You didn't ever think about me either, did you?"

"As a matter of fact, I did. Every once in a while." She punched him playfully on the arm. "I thought about how you were always giving me a hard time." The minute the words were out of her mouth, she wished she could recall them and rephrase that statement.

Dean grinned. "Interesting choice of words."

She blushed. *Heavenly days!* "Don't read anything into them," she told him. "They were just words."

"If you say so, but you've got to wonder . . ."

"I'm not finishing that sentence for you."

"All right," he said. "I'll finish it. You've got to wonder what it would be like if we hooked up, did the horizontal"—he lowered his voice and added—"had sex."

"Even if I might be curious, that doesn't mean I'm going to jump into bed with you," she whispered. "Believe it or not, there are still some women in this world who do not have casual sex, and I'm one of them."

"If we ever had sex, it wouldn't be casual."

Before she could respond, Officer Ray Middleton approached them, calling out to Dean as he walked toward Rachel's desk.

"Hey, Dean, that eyewitness from the Henderson case showed up early," Officer Middleton said. "He's pretty nervous, so I thought it best to come tell you and not make him wait too long. He might bolt."

"Yeah, thanks," Dean said, then turned to Rachel. "See you later."

He winked at her again.

And her insides quivered.

Kristen crinkled her nose with worry as she spoke to Lindsay Farrell, who had telephoned while she was in the middle of setting the table in Ross's apartment dining room. Their daughter Lissa was at a friend's house studying, so dinner tonight would be a foursome.

"Look, Linds, I'd like nothing better than to cancel the reunion, but Rachel and I are a majority of two," Kristen said. "Even Mandy, who's as nervous as a cat these days, says we can't let some nut job dictate what we should and shouldn't do. The others agree, so the reunion is still on."

"I had planned to come in early," Lindsay said. "And we still might, if—"

"You and Wyatt?"

"Yes, Wyatt and I. Who would ever have thought that we'd wind up as a couple? But then again, who would have believed that we had a one-nighter in high school that resulted in a son who is now nineteen?"

"Why didn't you tell me or tell Rachel? We might have been able to help you."

"What could either of you have done?" Lindsay asked. "You

were both teenagers, too, and would have agreed that my giving my baby away was the only thing I could have done."

"I can't imagine what it's been like for you, knowing he was out there somewhere. Lissa tries my nerves, but the thought of having no choice but to give her up at birth—"

"If Wyatt and I can work things out with Leo—you know, the three of us figure out what kind of relationship we each want—then I'll get a second chance with my son as well as with his father."

"Linds?"

"Huh?"

"Stay safe, will you. Okay?"

"I will. You, too."

"Not knowing where he or she will strike next is the worst part," Kristen said. "Ross is so concerned about me that he'll barely let me out of his sight. And Mandy's husband is talking about hiring a bodyguard for her. And even Rachel, who's a trained professional, carries a gun, and knows karate or one of those martial arts, has Dean looking out for her."

"Are they together now?" Lindsay asked. "Once again, who'd have thought it—Dreamy Dean and our Rach. She was always hung up on Jake."

"Yes, she was, just as you and I were."

"We were fools, weren't we?"

"Yes, we were, but we were just kids who didn't know any better."

"Kris, please keep me posted on what's happening."

After she replaced the phone on the cradle, Kristen finished setting the table, then went into the kitchen to check the roast in the oven.

If she had her way, they would cancel the reunion, but then again maybe the others were right about not giving in to pressure, not allowing their fears to dictate their actions. And who was to say that if they canceled the reunion the threats would stop? If the person who was behind the child's arrow stunt, the notes, phone calls, and break-ins had killed Aurora and Haylie, they could strike again at any time. But without proof that Aurora's death was not an accident and with such damning proof that the homeless bum killed Haylie during a robbery, there was no way to definitely connect either crime to what had happened to Lindsay in New York. Nor could their deaths be connected to what had been happening with her, with the other committee members, and with Rachel.

They were up there now, Kristen and Rachel and Dean McMichaels, with Kristen's rich hubby Ross Delmonico. Just like back in high school, they were having fun, enjoying the good life, while she was on the outside looking in. Damn them. Damn them all. Kristen, so pretty and oh so smart. And never without a boyfriend. Even Jake had turned to her when he'd broken up with Lindsay. And Rachel, the good sport, everybody's friend, even Jake's. It had been unfair twenty years ago that girls like Kristen and Rachel and Lindsay had everything going for them, that they got all the breaks, had all the fun. And it seemed that very little had changed in all this time. Maybe they hadn't been deliberately cruel to her, but ignoring a person was more than simply being unkind. Sometimes she used to feel invisible, as if none them ever saw her. She had longed to be one of them—really one of them—and not just one of those girls hanging around on the periphery.

She stood outside the building, gazing up at the high-rise apartment that belonged to Ross Delmonico. She had followed Rachel and Dean, wanting to see just where they were going, and wasn't the least bit surprised to find that their destination was a visit with an old friend. Probably dinner. She'd noticed that Dean was carrying a bottle of wine.

Have fun tonight. Enjoy dinner. Talk and laugh and discuss old times. The last laugh won't be on me—it'll be on you. On you, Kris. And on you, Rachel. But most definitely on Lindsay. Bitch!

But killing them would have to wait. She knew now that the time and place for their deaths would come soon enough. But for those three, the end should be special. She had jumped the gun with Kris and even more so with Lindsay, because she hated Linds the most.

God, how she hated those cute little nicknames. Kris and Linds and Rach. She especially despised those names when Jake had used them.

"Ma'am, are you all right?" a voice asked.

Astonished by the fact that someone had spoken to her, she gasped loudly. Her gaze connected with a set of dark brown eyes. A young couple, apparently walking their dog, were standing there staring at her as if she had two heads.

"I—I'm fine," she replied, then hurried away, up the street. *Don't panic*, she told herself. They wouldn't remember her. Besides, they hadn't gotten that good a look at her, there in the semi-darkness. And who would be asking them about her anyway?

She all but ran back to her car, which was parked a block away, got in, and started the engine. *Leave Kris and Rach for another day—for the night of the reunion. There is someone else who deserves your immediate attention, someone less important than the exalted three, but someone as guilty as they, someone who deserves to die. And soon.*

Dinner with the Delmonicos had been nice. Dean liked Ross and hoped he and Kristen would continue trying to make their marriage work. And not just because they had a kid together, but because they seemed to genuinely love each other. Maybe when all was said and done in a relationship, love really was all that mattered. Real love. Not lust. Not fleeting passion. Not memories of raging teenage hormones.

Who was he kidding? He didn't know the first thing about real love. As a teenager, he'd bonked just about any girl who'd let him. And later on . . . well, he'd been around the block a few times before he got married. He had loved Kellie and she him, but it hadn't been enough, hadn't been real and true and meant to last a lifetime. His parents had had that. Still had it. They were off traveling across the country in their motor home, loving life and loving each other as much as if not more than ever.

He wanted that kind of relationship. Hell, he wasn't getting any younger. If he was going to remarry and produce a few offspring, he needed to get started pretty soon. After all, he was scaring forty to death. So maybe that was the reason he kept putting Rachel into the scenario, kept thinking about her as a life partner, as the future Mrs. Dean McMichaels. Ever since they were kids, he'd been protective of her, almost like a brother, but somewhere along the line, he'd become possessive, too, and by their senior year in high school, he'd known he loved cute, bubbly Rachel Alsace.

He glanced over at her where she sat looking out the passenger side window in his Thunderbird. "Penny for your thoughts."

She turned to face forward, then glanced at him. "I was just thinking how lucky Kristen is. She and Ross. They have each other and a daughter and . . . And Lindsay just reconnected with Wyatt Goddard. I told you about them and their son and . . ."

"And at our age, being alone isn't all that great, is it?"

"You're right," she said. "And it makes us more vulnerable to getting involved with the wrong person or persuading ourselves that a relationship is more special than it actually is."

Dean harrumphed.

"Was that a laugh or a grunt?" she asked.

"A bit of both," he admitted. "I was actually thinking along the same lines. About us, to be honest."

"Us as in you and me?"

"Yeah. I used to care about you, back when we were kids. My feelings were sort of complicated. I pestered the hell out of you and tried to protect you, sort of like a big brother, but then when we were teenagers, I wanted you . . . you know, *wanted* wanted you."

"I wish you'd told me . . . back then."

"It wouldn't have made any difference. You were too infatuated with Jake."

"If you had just told me how you felt—"

"I'm telling you now. I'd like to take you back to my place and screw you all night long," Dean said. "But if we did that, then we would both be even more confused about our feelings than we are now. Heck, I've halfway convinced myself that I'm in love with you, and I think you're starting to wonder if we might not have a budding relationship in the works. Right?"

"Maybe. Why is that so wrong?"

"For the very reasons we just discussed. We're both nearly forty, unmarried, no kids, and envy old friends who seem to have what we want. I don't want us to make a mistake and wind up hurting each other by jumping into a relationship."

Rachel didn't reply. He glanced at her and noticed she had turned to look out the passenger window again.

"Rachel?"

"Hmm?"

"Did I say something wrong?"

She cleared her throat. "No, no, you didn't say anything wrong."

When he pulled into the Youngs' driveway and parked the car, Rachel opened the door and hopped out, then called, "Don't bother seeing me in. It's late and I don't want to disturb Uncle Charlie and Aunt Laraine." Just before she slammed the door closed, she added, "I'll see you tomorrow."

Dean sat there and watched her practically run to the door and let herself in, not once looking back. He released the tight hold he had on the door handle, then huffed loudly. Women! He'd never understand them.

Don't just sit here, he told himself. *Go home. You messed up big-time with Rachel, and it's not something you can fix tonight.*

Exactly what had he done? He'd been honest with her. Why was that so wrong? He'd thought she felt the same way—that they were in danger of thinking themselves in love, and that before taking their relationship to the next level, they needed to make sure of just where they were headed. Not for his sake, but for hers. He cared too much about Rachel to use her to simply scratch an itch.

Apparently, sometimes honesty wasn't the best policy.

Chapter 28

Rachel spent the next week with two objectives in mind. One: to continue searching for the answer to a twenty-year-old murder case. Two: to spend as little time with Dean McMichaels as possible. The first had been easy enough because it was within her control. The second had proven to be more difficult. Dean acted as if nothing had happened, as if he hadn't all but told her to back off, that he wasn't interested in anything serious happening between them. She had to accept the fact that Dean probably flirted outrageously with every woman he met, that the sexual banter they had exchanged was simply par for the course for him. And all that garbage about him once having feelings for her was probably little more than a ploy to get into her pants. After all, he did have a reputation with the ladies, something she'd found out from others who knew him. Since his divorce, he had dated dozens of women. She figured she was just one more "date" to him.

Apparently he had realized she was beginning to fall in love with him, and that was the last thing he wanted. Okay. Fine with her. It wasn't as if she couldn't live without him. Her feelings for him hadn't deepened that much that fast.

Or had they?

If she wasn't hung up on the guy, why did she feel as if he had slapped her in the face with a major rejection? Why did she get tight knots in her stomach whenever he was around? Why did she catch herself daydreaming about him?

Because you're an idiot!

Rachel's cell phone rang. She picked it up from where she had placed it on her desk here at headquarters, checked caller ID, and hesitated when she didn't recognize the number. Another cell phone coming off a Portland tower.

She flipped open her phone and identified herself immediately. Silence.

"Hello. Is anyone there?"

Breathing. Heavy breathing.

This is ridiculous. "Look, if you have the wrong number, just say so or hang up."

"I have the right number," a disguised voice said. Rachel immediately knew that whoever was on the other end of this conversation was using some type of voice-altering device, just as he or she had done for other calls. Those voice-altering things could be bought just about anywhere for little to nothing or for hundreds of dollars. Trying to trace who might have bought one in the past few months would be time consuming. A fruitless endeavor.

"Who is this and what do you want?" Rachel kept her voice calm and even.

"Someone is going to die."

Every nerve in Rachel's body came to full alert. Reacting as the professional she was, she asked, "Is that right? Are you going to kill them?"

"Yes, I am. Just like I killed Jake."

Rachel's heart lodged in her throat. Was she really speaking to Jake Marcott's killer? "Did you kill Haylie and Aurora?"

Laughter. Harsh, anguished laughter.

"Did you kill them?" Rachel demanded, her voice remaining calm, but with a commanding tone.

"That's for you to find out. You're the smart policewoman, aren't you? Find me, if you can. Stop me, if you can."

"Why are you doing this? Why kill Jake's friends?"

No response. Rachel realized the caller had hung up.

She sat there for a couple of seconds, her phone in her hand, her heart beating at breakneck speed. Hurriedly, she checked her phone for the number of the last call and hit the Recall button. The phone rang repeatedly. No one answered, which didn't surprise Rachel.

"Trying to crush that phone with your bare hands?" Dean asked.

Nearly jumping out of her skin, Rachel gasped, then whirled around and glared at him. "You scared the bejesus out of me."

"Sorry. I seem to make a habit of unnerving you. What's wrong? Unpleasant phone call?"

Rachel flipped the phone closed and laid it on her desk. "I was talking to Jake's killer. Or at least he or she claimed to have killed Jake."

Dean sat on the edge of Rachel's desk. "No wonder you look pale. Did you recognize the voice?"

"Just like with the other calls we've all gotten recently, they used something to disguise their voice."

Dean nodded. "Could you tell if the caller was male or female?"

"Not really. I tend to think it was a woman, but that's merely a guess."

"Working under the premise that it was a woman, exactly what did she say?"

"Not much, just that she had killed Jake and was going to kill someone else."

"I don't suppose she told you who."

"No. And there won't be any way to trace the call or even pinpoint where it came from. My guess is she was using a prepaid cell phone again. My caller ID showed Portland."

"Probably, but we'll run a check and see, just to make sure." He glanced down at her cell phone. "You tried the number, right?"

"Right. And no one answered."

Dean placed a lid-covered paper cup on her desk. "White chocolate latte. It's your favorite, right?"

She eyed the cup as if it were a snake. For the past week, he'd been doing thoughtful little things for her. Peace offerings? Or just business as usual for a notorious flirt?

"Thanks." She opened the lid, lifted the cup, and took a sip.

"If the person who called you is on the level and did kill Jake, then we have a problem on our hands, don't we?"

"Yes, we do. The question is, who has she chosen to be the next victim?" Rachel stated the obvious.

"The first thing we do is contact everyone on the reunion committee and warn them to be even more careful than usual."

"I can do that. There's no need for you to—"

"Look, honey, let's get something straight, I'm involved in this, too. Maybe not officially, but I've bought into your theory— yours and Kristen's and Lindsay's—that whoever killed Jake might have killed Aurora and Haylie and is targeting other girls Jake knew."

Rachel patted the stack of files on her desk. "I've been through these time and time again. I've talked to numerous people who were there at the dance that night and I've gone over everything I personally remember." She heaved a heavy, defeated sigh. "I have to admit that I'm as stumped as my dad was. There is just no evidence pointing to any one person. Jake was loved and hated in equal measure, yet nobody had a strong motive to want to see him dead."

"Other than Haylie, maybe. But she was one of the first suspects cleared twenty years ago, and she was the first new victim."

"Someone else hated Jake enough to kill him and do it in a spectacular way."

"Yeah, and it was someone who wanted to look Jake in the eye when they offed him." Dean glanced at the file folders on Rachel's desk. "The coroner stated that the shot was at fairly close range and that in order to pin Jake to the tree that way, Jake had to have been right up against the tree."

"He was probably leaning against the tree while he smoked."

"I've wondered more than once if Jake realized what was about to happen and simply froze, or if he didn't understand what was about to happen until it was too late."

"Jake had been drinking that evening. And when he drank, he became more cocky and arrogant than usual. I can see him staring at his killer and laughing in his face. He probably thought it was a joke." A fine mist of tears clouded Rachel's vision.

Dean cursed under his breath. "Damn it, don't waste any more tears on that asshole." He shot up off her desk.

She noted that he had balled his hands into tight fists and held them on either side of his thighs. What was his problem anyway?

"Give me a little credit, will you? I'm not crying. I'm just a little misty-eyed, and it's not about Jake."

Dean glared at her. "If you're not all weepy and sentimental about Jake, then what?"

"About everything. The past, the reunion, Haylie and Aurora . . . and if you want to know the truth, I'm uneasy about the threat this person made and concerned about the safety of my old friends and even myself."

The tension in Dean eased. He loosened his clenched fists and relaxed his stiff shoulders. "I'm sorry I jumped to the wrong conclusion."

She nodded.

"Look, I dropped by with the latte hoping we could talk, and for more than two minutes," Dean said. "I've been looking into something and I wanted to run it by you, get your take on it."

She eyed him inquisitively. "Sure. What is it?"

"Call it my cop instincts or just a gut reaction, but ever since I talked to Patrick Dewey's widow, I've had this niggling feeling that something was off with her."

"Did she say something that—"

"No, it wasn't what she said. It was more what she didn't say and the way she answered the few questions I asked her."

"Maybe it was nothing. After all, her husband wasn't involved in Jake's case, except in a roundabout way. His bow was used in the murder, but he had reported it stolen a week earlier."

"That's what's been bothering me ever since I talked to Marilyn Dewey. I asked her to confirm what your dad's old report stated, that the bow that was used to kill Jake was the only item stolen from their home."

"It was," Rachel said. "I distinctly remember reading that report. Nothing else was missing from their home or garage, only Mr. Dewey's bow."

"Why that specific bow?"

"What do you mean?"

"I mean why just that one crossbow? Dewey owned several bows, one newer and more expensive. Why steal none of the other bows or his rifle or shotgun or none of his wife's jewelry?"

The wheels in Rachel's mind spun at lightning speed. "You don't think the bow was stolen, do you?"

Dean shrugged. "It might have been, but let's say it wasn't stolen."

"Then why report it stolen?"

"Why indeed."

"If it wasn't stolen, then Dewey had to have a reason to report it. Insurance money? No, that wouldn't make any sense. The bow was used to kill Jake, and whoever used it left it at the scene of the crime, as if they wanted it to be found."

"Let's say that, for whatever reason, a bow hunter wanted to kill someone and intended to use his bow to do it. What better way to cover his butt than report the bow stolen?"

"A logical scenario," Rachel said. "Except for two things: Patrick Dewey didn't know Jake and therefore had no motive to kill him, and he had an alibi for the night Jake was killed."

"Do you recall who gave him his alibi?"

"Uh . . . yes, I remember now. His wife said he was at home with her." Rachel gasped. "His wife could have lied for him. But why?"

"Before we take this supposition any further, we should talk to Mrs. Dewey. After all these years and with her husband now dead, if she knows something, we might be able to persuade her to tell us."

"Did the Deweys have a son? If so, maybe he knew Jake, maybe they—"

"The Deweys' two sons were five and seven at the time of Jake's murder."

Rachel frowned. "So much for that thought."

"I say we drive down to Salem tomorrow and talk to Mrs. Dewey, face-to-face."

She hesitated momentarily, not sure that she wanted to spend an entire day with Dean, especially not trapped in a car with him for several hours making the trip to and from Salem. "Can you take tomorrow off?"

"I think I can arrange it." He grinned. "I have an in with the chief."

"So you do. Okay then, I'll meet you here at—"

"I'll pick you up at the chief's house around eight-thirty, if that's not too early."

"It's not too early. I've never been one to sleep until noon."

"Eight-thirty it is."

"You realize that this could turn out to be nothing, that your gut instincts could be wrong," she told him. "I mean, what are the odds that the owner of the bow that shot the fatal arrow was actually involved in the crime?"

"I'm not saying he was involved, just that I got odd vibes from his widow."

"Well, it's better than anything I've come up with. And if there's even a one in a hundred chance that Mrs. Dewey knows— Oh my God! What if *she* knew Jake? What if he was fooling around with an older, married woman and her husband found out?"

Dean grinned. "Honey, I like the way you think."

After Rachel's call telling her about the threatening message she had received from someone who claimed to have killed Jake, Mandy thought twice before taking Emily out for her afternoon stroll. But she couldn't stay cooped up in the house, scared to go anywhere without Jeff. Doing that would be handing over control of her life to some lunatic. Besides, what could happen to her in broad daylight, in their neighborhood and in a park filled with other women and children?

As with so many days here in Portland, the sky was overcast

and gray, a hint of rain in the air. But being late June, the breeze
was warm and balmy.

Enjoy this daily ritual with your daughter, she told herself.
Don't allow fear to control your actions. She had heard other
mothers say that their children picked up on their moods and always acted up whenever they sensed something was wrong with
Mom. Emily had been cranky all afternoon. Mandy had taken her
temperature, which had been normal, and had asked her if she felt
bad or hurt anywhere.

Emily had frowned at her and shook her head, then proceeded to knock down a house constructed of colorful building
blocks, a project they had worked on for over an hour after
lunch. And then Emily had refused to go down for her nap,
screaming her head off when Mandy placed her in her crib and
left the room.

But now, outside in her stroller, rolling along the sidewalk,
Little Miss Spoiled Rotten was smiling and waving at everyone
they passed. For Emily's sake if not for her own, Mandy couldn't
allow the fact that someone might be stalking her to bring her life
to a standstill. But try as she might, she couldn't quite get Rachel's
warning phone call off her mind. Was the person who had spoken
to Rachel really Jake Marcott's killer? Had this person killed
Haylie and Aurora? Would they kill again? Or had the call been
some terrible hoax?

"Afternoon, Mandy," elderly Mrs. Johnson said as they met
her at her mailbox. The white-haired woman glanced up at the sky.
"Looks a bit like rain. You brought along an umbrella, didn't you?"

"Yes, I always do." Mandy patted the pouch attached to the
back of her daughter's portable stroller. "We're just going over
to the park, so if it starts raining, we can be back home in no
time."

Clasping her mail in one hand, Mrs. Johnson stared down at
Emily. "She's growing like a weed and getting cuter every day."

"Thank you. We certainly think she's a little beauty." Mandy
waved at her neighbor but kept pushing Emily along. As much as
she loved Mrs. Johnson, once in a conversation with her, you
might be trapped for a good twenty or thirty minutes.

Moving at a steady pace, Mandy reached the neighborhood
park in five minutes. As she strolled along the brick sidewalk
shaded by towering trees and lined with colorful summer flowers,
she remembered how often she had jogged through here in the
past and spotted mothers with their young children. Oh, how she

had envied those women. But now, with the blessing of Emily, she was one of them. A mother.

When they reached the kiddie swings, Mandy removed Emily from the stroller and set her in one of the swings, double-checking the safety harness. Only one other parent and toddler were using the swings. Mandy recognized the divorced dad who had gotten custody of his two-year-old.

"Hi, Tim." Mandy waved at her neighbor, who lived in a two-story Colonial only three houses down from her.

"Afternoon," he replied. "You two might not get to stay long. I think we're going to get some rain. Joey and I are heading out in a few minutes."

Before Tim and Joey left for home, Mandy and Tim chatted about their children, about this year's Rose Festival, and about the Neighborhood Watch. When the wind picked up and the sky grew darker, Mandy considered leaving despite the fact that they had just arrived. But Emily was enjoying herself so much, Mandy decided to give them a few more minutes. After all, windy and gloomy didn't necessarily mean rain. Not in Portland.

Ten minutes later, Mandy realized the park was all but deserted. Time to go. As she released the swing's safety harness, she felt the first drop of rain.

"Drat." She removed Emily from the swing—despite her pouting protest—slipped her into the stroller, and then pulled the umbrella from the pouch. When she tried to open the umbrella, the strong wind blew it inside out. As she struggled with the unruly umbrella, she felt someone approach her from behind. A long-fingered hand reached out and grabbed for the umbrella handle. Mandy cried out, horrible thoughts flashing through her mind. She released the umbrella, whirled around, and grasped the handlebars of the collapsible stroller, intending to run.

"Mandy, it's all right," a familiar voice said. "It's me."

She glanced over her shoulder. With her heartbeat roaring in her ears and her pulse racing like mad, she gasped for air when she recognized the person standing behind her, working diligently to turn Mandy's umbrella right side out.

What is she doing on this side of town, in this park, at this time of day?

"You really shouldn't be out here with a storm brewing." She handed the umbrella to Mandy as small, soft raindrops peppered down from the sky.

"Emily loves our afternoons in the park so much that I hate for her to miss them."

Why is she staring at me that way? Mandy wondered. *There's something odd about her being here and something strange about the way she's acting.*

"Well, you'd better head for home now. As it is, you're going to get drenched."

A streak of cloud-to-ground lightning zigzagged through the sky behind them. Mandy gasped. When the deafening boom of thunder followed, Emily let out a yelp and then started crying.

Clutching the umbrella in one hand and the stroller handle in the other, Mandy glanced back and said, "You're right. We'd better head for home. See you later." Every instinct Mandy had screamed, "Get away. Run. Run for your life."

Don't be ridiculous. You two have known each other since high school. You're on the reunion committee together. She's not the type of person who could kill another.

Or is she? It's not as if you two have stayed close all these years.

Just as she gave the stroller a quick push, intending to flee, Mandy suddenly realized it was already too late. Something came down and around her from behind, circled her throat and jerked her backward. She clawed at the silk scarf tightening around her neck, but the harder she fought, the more powerful her attacker's hold became, strong and fierce enough to subdue her.

How could I have been such a fool? Why didn't I stay home today? Why didn't I try to get the Mace out of the diaper bag? Are you listening, God? Don't let her kill me. Please, I don't want to die! What will happen to Emily if I die?

Rachel stood in the doorway of police headquarters and watched the late-afternoon thunderstorm. She really hated getting out in this mess, but she had promised Aunt Laraine she'd come home early today. They planned to go shopping for Uncle Charlie's birthday present while he attended his Shriners meeting.

"Need to borrow an umbrella?" Dean asked as he walked up beside her.

"No, thanks, I brought one with me."

He skimmed his gaze over her. "Where is it?"

She huffed. "In my car."

He chuckled.

"Why don't I walk you to your car?" He popped open a large black umbrella.

"Hey, McMichaels," the desk sergeant called.

"Yeah, what's up?" Dean replied.

"Call for you." He held up the telephone receiver. "It's the chief. He said to ask you why you aren't answering your cell phone."

Dean patted his belt where he usually kept his cell phone, then groaned when he realized it wasn't there. "Wait for me, okay?" He handed her the umbrella.

Rachel waited. Not because she had promised she would. Not because she wanted Dean to walk her to her car, but because she was curious as to why Uncle Charlie had called Dean.

After closing the umbrella, she walked over to where Dean stood talking quietly to Charlie.

"I must have left the damn thing upstairs on my desk." Dean listened then, frowning at whatever Charlie had told him.

Rachel could tell by the expression on his face that something was wrong. Her gut tightened. Dean groaned as if he were in pain. Whatever had happened, it must be something terrible.

"Yeah, she's still here. I'll tell her." Pause. "No, I can't do that."

Rachel tugged on Dean's arm and when he looked at her, she mouthed the question *What is going on?*

"Yes. I know. I understand," Dean said to Charlie. "So the baby is fine, right?" Pause. "No way we can ignore the implications, not this time."

Dean handed the phone back to the desk sergeant, then turned to face Rachel.

"What? Who?" she asked.

He grasped her shoulders. She sucked in a deep breath, waiting for the news the way a condemned prisoner awaits execution.

"Mandy Kim—Mandy Stulz's body was found in her neighborhood park thirty minutes ago. It appears she was strangled."

At first Rachel couldn't speak, couldn't think. Stunned by the news and yet at the same time not completely surprised, she stared at Dean. Then she started trembling. He ran his hands down her arms and back up again.

"Rachel?"

"Yes. I—I heard you. Why were you asking Uncle Charlie about Emily?"

"Emily?"

"Mandy's baby."

"Oh, the baby. She's fine. Someone found her alone in the park, in her stroller, screaming like a banshee. When this person looked around for the baby's mother, she found Mandy's body behind some bushes."

"It's happened." Rachel's voice sounded odd, even to her own ears. Solemn. Soulful. Sad. "The person who called me has killed again."

"We can't be certain of that. Not until all the facts are in." He squeezed her shoulders.

"I know it." She placed her fist over her belly. "I know it in here. The person who killed Haylie and Aurora and tried to kill Lindsay in New York is the same person who killed Mandy."

Chapter 29

The flashlight's glow traveled along the row of senior lockers, then stopped on Mandy Kim's. Soon this display would be complete. Item by item. Added with loving care. And with Mandy now dead, one more of the girls in Jake's harem had joined him in hell.

She smiled, thinking of Jake burning in an eternal fire, tormented endlessly. The way he had tormented her. A frown replaced her smile as memories crept in around her, like dark shadows with treacherous tentacles reaching out to grab her. She shuddered.

"Go away," she whispered. "Leave me alone. I don't want to remember."

But the frightening shadows grew darker and more sinister, quickly enveloping her, grasping her in their evil clutches.

"No, no, please don't, Jake. It hurts when you do that."

"Hush, baby, hush. We don't want anyone hearing us, do we?"

She felt him push himself inside her, stretching her, hurting her. She whimpered loudly. "No, please. Don't. Stop."

He held his hand over her mouth to quiet her cries as he rammed into her again and again and again.

She couldn't bear it. *Stop! No! Go away! Leave me alone!*

"I love you, baby. I love you best of all," Jake said.

She fought the black shadows of memory, pushing them back, fighting them off as she had once tried to fight off Jake. Slowly, painfully, the shadows released her and settled around her, seemingly satisfied that she was now crying.

Jake used to wipe away her tears.

The tears he had caused.

The tears all the girls in his life had caused.

They thought he cared about them, maybe even loved them. But he hadn't. He had loved only her. But why hadn't he told them how much he loved her? Why hadn't he made them include her in their elite little group? Why had he needed any of them when he'd had her?

Shoving Mandy's small diaper bag under her arm, she swiped the tears from her eyes and her damp cheeks. It wasn't fair that after all these years, he could still make her cry. But not for much longer. Once they were all dead and St. Elizabeth's had been turned into a heap of rubble and buried with Jake and their past, she would be free.

But free for what?

Free from the past? Free from the memories? Free from the bitter hatred she felt?

With Mandy's bag under her arm and the flashlight in one hand, she walked directly to the locker marked with Mandy's name and number, just as it had been back in high school. She undid the snap on the diaper bag and rummaged around inside, searching for any personal items of Mandy's. If she'd had time after strangling Mandy, she would have taken the items and left the bag in the stroller pouch. But with little Emily screaming her lungs out, she'd had to work quickly. She hated leaving the toddler alone in the park in the middle of a storm, but it couldn't be helped. If Mandy hadn't made it so difficult to get inside her house, the deed could have been done there.

She yanked a set of keys out of the bag. The shimmering metallic trophies jangled like bells as she shook them.

She placed the large, heavy-duty flashlight on the concrete floor, adjusting the attached stand so that the beam directly hit Mandy's locker. She opened the door and placed Mandy's keys inside on the upper shelf, then rummaged around in the diaper bag until she found a compact and lipstick. She added those two items to the locker.

So like Mandy to take a compact and lipstick with her on a short afternoon trip to the park with her child. The little bitch had always been preoccupied with her appearance. Every strand of her shiny black hair in place. Her make-up perfect, her perfume expensive, her fingernails and toenails manicured. Even in her St. Elizabeth's uniform, she had managed somehow to look neater and cuter than the average student.

"Mandy's a living doll," Jake had said. "I'm thinking about making her my own little China doll."

"Your China doll is on her way to hell to see you," she said aloud, the sound of her voice echoing in the cavernous basement beneath the old school.

After removing all the personal items from the diaper bag, she tossed it aside. She closed Mandy's locker, then reached down, picked up the flashlight, and shined it up and down the row on the other lockers.

Three down and four to go.

Maybe I should kill at least one of them before the reunion. But which one? Lindsay isn't here in Portland and I don't dare risk another trip to New York, even using the fake ID. And I have other plans for Rachel during the next couple of weeks. A little game of cat and mouse. Perhaps I should find a way to get to Kristen. No, damn it, that husband of hers is practically attached to her side twenty-four-seven.

No matter, I can take them all out the night of the reunion, if it comes to that. One by one. I simply have to devise a foolproof plan. And if I get lucky and the opportunity arises to eliminate any one of them before the reunion, all the better.

But until then, I'm going to make Rachel Alsace's life miserable.

The heavy rainstorm had all but destroyed any possible evidence from the scene of the crime. Rachel stood under the huge black umbrella Dean held and watched as the Oregon State Crime Lab technician team packed up and headed for their vehicles. They had stayed out of the team's way, but during the investigation, Dean had been unable to persuade Rachel to leave. She had tried to make him understand that she couldn't leave, that she needed to do something—anything—even knowing that there was little she could do at this point.

"Come on, Rach," Dean said. "Let me take you home. You need a hot bath and a good night's sleep."

She shook her head. "What I need is to find out who killed Mandy."

"Then let's go somewhere, get a cup of coffee or a stiff drink and talk."

"All right. Coffee sounds fine to me." Her senses numb, her mind focused on a single objective—to find the killer before someone else died—she let Dean lead her to his Thunderbird parked across the street.

Dean opened the car door, held the umbrella over her until she was seated, then closed the umbrella and locked her safety belt. When he got behind the wheel, Rachel turned to him. He ran a hand through his wet hair and flicked raindrops from his fingertips onto the floorboard.

"I don't understand any of this," Rachel said. "Why kill Mandy? I don't think she ever had an enemy in the world. She was always so nice to everyone." Rachel heaved a deep, sorrowful sigh. "Poor little Emily. That sweet child has now lost a second mother. And Jeff . . ."

"I know, honey. I know." Dean reached over and took her hand in his. "This has turned into a nightmare for you . . . for us."

When he squeezed her hand, she squeezed his and held on tightly for a full minute before pulling her hand free, leaning her head back, and closing her eyes.

"The killer warned me that she—or he—was going to strike again. If only I'd had more time to figure out who and why and—"

"You warned each of the reunion committee members and Lindsay, everyone who received a doctored invitation. What more could you have done?"

Dean started the car and pulled out into the late-night traffic. The windshield wipers swished back and forth, fighting the pelting rain. Rachel stared sightlessly out the window, her mind filled with a hundred and one what ifs and if onlys.

The one question foremost in her mind—Who had hated Jake Marcott enough to kill him?—was followed by other questions she couldn't answer. Was the person who killed Mandy and possibly Aurora and Haylie the same person who killed Jake? If so, why wait twenty years to kill again? The whole thing was one giant jigsaw puzzle with several key pieces missing.

Behind every crime was a motive. Sometimes an illogical motive, but a motive all the same. Why would anyone want to kill the members of the reunion committee?

Because they didn't want the class of '86 to come together again? Could it be that simple? No, of course it couldn't. Besides, Lindsay had been attacked and she wasn't on the committee. No, but she had been Jake's girlfriend. So was the killer eliminating committee members or the girls Jake had dated or— no, not the girls Jake dated. He hadn't dated Haylie or Aurora or Mandy. And although she and Jake had been friends, they'd never dated.

Scratch the girls he dated. Scratch committee members only. Each victim had known Jake, but not all had dated him or loved

him. Haylie had hated him. So what was the common denominator? What was the one thing that united them?

Mentally sorting through her knowledge of each victim,
Rachel reached a conclusion rather quickly. Each woman had attended St. Elizabeth's, and they had all been a part of the same
clique.

Did that mean anyone who didn't fall answer to that description was safe from the killer? Maybe. But until Rachel could
prove her theory, it was best to err on the side of caution.

"There's an all-night diner about three blocks from here,"
Dean said. "Want to stop there or—"

"Sure, that's fine."

"It's not your fault."

"What?"

"If you're thinking you could have somehow prevented what
happened to Mandy, stop thinking it. There's no way you could
have saved her."

"If I could just figure out who might hate all of us enough to
want us dead . . . after all these years."

Dean pulled into the small parking lot adjacent to the diner,
killed the motor, and turned to Rachel. "If we have only one
killer—and that's not a definite—then I'd say we have a mental
case on our hands. Pinpoint someone who is mentally unstable
and we just might have a suspect."

"That's it! We'll run a background check on everyone who
graduated in eighty-six from all three high schools and—"

"Wait up, honey. Who is going to do this investigation? As officers of the law, we're limited as to what we can and can't do. Besides, even if we were able to cut through all the red tape, it could
take six months or longer to get the kind of information we need
on that many people."

"Damn. You're right. Okay, then we'll start with the people
who were the closest to Jake, especially those on the reunion committee. That's only four people. I think it's safe to eliminate Kristen and Lindsay, since they've both been targeted by the killer."

"I tend to agree with you, but as an objective investigator, I'd
say check them out, too. Never eliminate someone for personal
reasons."

"You're right, but—"

"If you're eliminating suspects, drop Bella Marcott from the
list. She's Jake's little sister and she adored the guy."

Rachel reached for the door handle. "Come on, let's brainstorm over some hot coffee. Maybe a shot of caffeine will boost our mental powers enough to plot a course of action."

Mandy's autopsy report confirmed what the ME had told the investigators at the scene of the crime—she had been strangled. Ligature strangulation. There had been bruises, abrasions, and contusions found on Mandy's neck due to the use of excessive force during the act. Excessive force was quite common when a killer used either his bare hands or a rope or scarf.

Rachel reread the autopsy report. Using all his official influence, Chief Charlie Young had managed to get a rush job done on Mandy's autopsy—five days. Unheard of as a general rule. And during those five days, Mandy's friends had banded together to help Jeff and Emily, each taking turns staying at the house with them and others bringing food and fielding phone calls.

And on each of the five days, Rachel had received a phone call from the killer. Or at least the disguised voice claimed to be the killer. The caller knew things about the St. Lizzy's students that only someone who had been around in the old days would know. If only she could recognize the voice. If only the caller would say something that would identify him or her. But the messages were succinct, each taunting Rachel, telling her that she was no better at solving murder mysteries than her father had been.

This morning's call had ended with Rachel losing her temper, something she seldom did.

Just as she flipped her cell phone closed and slammed it down on her desk, Dean approached her. She felt his presence before she actually saw him. Whether she recognized the sound of his distinctive walk or had smelled a hint of his light citrus aftershave, she wasn't sure.

She looked up into those now-familiar golden eyes and knew immediately that something was up. Her heart lurched as fear radiated through her. *Please, dear God, don't let it be bad news.*

"Another call from our self-proclaimed killer?" Dean asked.

Rachel huffed. "Yeah." She kept her gaze connected to his. "Whatever it is, just tell me."

"I tried to set up an appointment with Mrs. Dewey, but she refuses to see us."

"What? Why?"

After Mandy's murder, Dean and Rachel had postponed their

trip to Salem to question Patrick Dewey's widow about her husband and the fact that his bow had been used in Jake's murder.
Then yesterday, Dean had suggested they make the trip today.

"The only reason her son gave me for her refusal was that she
had nothing new to add to what she'd told the police twenty years
ago," Dean said.

"Did you tell her son why we—?"

Rachel's cell phone rang again. She tensed instantly.

Dean eyed the phone lying on her desk. "Want me to get it?"

She shook her head. "Our killer calls only once a day." She
lifted the phone, flipped it open, and breathed a sigh of relief
when she recognized the caller ID name and number.

"Hello, Lin," Rachel said. The day after Mandy's murder,
Rachel had called her old friend from their days as cops together
on the Chattanooga P.D. Lin McAllister now worked for Powell's
Private Security and Investigation, one of the most prestigious
firms in the country.

"I've got the information you requested on those six women,"
Lin said. "We did a rush job just for you."

"Thanks. I owe you one."

"You owe me more than one. A job like this took several days
of Powell's brainpower, as well as calling in a few favors and bypassing some laws."

"If I could afford to pay you what this info is worth, I would."

Lin laughed. "Wait until you read the report, then decide what
it's worth. I sent each report as a separate e-mail attachment.
Check your e-mail as soon I hang up."

"Was there anything that stood out, anyone that appeared suspect for any reason?" The last thing Rachel wanted was for one of
her old friends to have a suspicious skeleton in her closet, but if
there was information that might point to them as being capable
of murder . . .

"Just about anybody over the age of thirty-five probably has a
secret or two," Lin said. "Your friends are no different, but nothing that sent up a red flag."

"Thanks."

"Sure thing. Look, take care of yourself. I don't want to hear
that you've become a victim of this resurrected Cupid Killer."

A shiver of foreboding tingled along Rachel's nerve endings.
"I'll be careful."

After she ended the conversation and placed the phone on her
desk, she turned on her laptop computer and waited for it to boot

up. "I need a printer I can connect to," she told Dean. "My old Chattanooga P.D. friend who's now with Powell's Private Security agency got the info I wanted."

"You know, it's just wrong somehow that a private agency can get hold of information the police can't legally obtain, at least not without going through an act of Congress." Dean motioned to Rachel. "You can use the captain's secretary's printer. Tracy won't ask too many questions."

Fifteen minutes later, with six reports in one hand and her closed laptop in the other, Rachel headed to Dean's office cubicle. When she didn't see him at his desk, she looked around, searching for him. He came toward her, a cup of coffee in each hand. She placed her laptop on his desk, set the reports on top of the computer, and pulled up a chair from a nearby empty desk.

Dean handed her a cup.

"Thanks." She accepted the coffee, then sat.

Dean put his cup on his desk, then pulled out his chair and sat beside Rachel.

"How do you want to do this—you take three and I take three or we read each one together?"

"It's your call," he told her.

"You take Lindsay, Kristen, and Bella. I'll take April, De-Lynn, and Martina."

She handed Dean three of the six reports, then pulled up the fourth one and began reading. As she read and then reread portions of each report, she felt as if she were invading the privacy of her old friends. There were things in her life that she would rather keep private.

"Finished?" Dean asked.

"Uh-huh."

"I suggest that we shred these reports," Dean said. "Keep them on your laptop for the time being, but we don't want to share this info with anyone else. Not yet, possibly not ever."

"Agreed." Rachel realized that he felt as she did—that these reports revealed things no one else needed to know. Not unless one of these six women turned out to be a murderer.

He glanced around, checking to make sure their conversation would be private. "I can make this quick," he told her. "Lindsay's as clean as a whistle, except for the illegitimate son she gave away nineteen years ago."

Rachel smiled. "She and Mandy were always the good girls."

"So were you, honey."

Rachel shrugged. "I just didn't have the guts to do anything bad."

"No, that wasn't it. You were just too smart to do anything really stupid."

"I had a crush on Jake. That was pretty stupid."

"That was youthful foolishness."

She cleared her throat. "DeLynn had a nervous breakdown right after college and attempted suicide. She spent two years in therapy. And April Wright had an abortion our senior year of high school, then in college she got hooked on drugs, but she turned her life around a few years later and has been clean and sober ever since."

"Kristen did some drinking and used marijuana in college. That's it for her, except for one police report about a minor road rage incident five years ago."

"Martina went through a court-appointed anger management course," Rachel said. "It seems she had a problem with a neighbor and wound up painting red polka dots on his chartreuse green house. That was eight years ago."

"There seems to have been an epidemic of teenage pregnancies," Dean said. "Bella got an abortion, too, which is surprising, considering that her parents were staunch Catholics. I'd have thought she would have done as Lindsay did and have the baby, then give it up for adoption."

"Poor Bella." Rachel shook her head. "April put out in high school because she thought it was the only way to get a boyfriend. I knew she was having sex with several different guys. But Bella having an abortion surprises me. I had no idea she had a boyfriend, that she ever dated for that matter. She was more than a year younger than the rest of us, just a kid really."

"Bella had some severe emotional problems after Jake's murder." Dean laid the three reports down on top of his desk. "It seems her parents put her into therapy for a couple of years."

Rachel heaved a deep sigh. "I don't know what I expected these reports would prove. I guess I hoped something would show up that would point us in the right direction."

"All the reports proved is that nobody's perfect."

"Two nervous breakdowns, one road rage, one illegitimate child, two abortions, one drug addiction, one suicide attempt, one anger management class. Nothing that shouts 'I'm capable of cold-blooded murder.'"

"So what now?" Dean asked. "Dig deeper? Move on to the guys who were closest to Jake or—?"

"You'd be on that list."

"Yeah, I would."

"You didn't kill Jake."

"No, I didn't kill him, but . . ." Their gazes linked, the connection sexually charged. "If he had ever hurt you, I would have."

Chapter 30

As she pulled a small, rusty metal cart behind her, the bag lady with the stringy gray hair hanging down in her eyes came up alongside Rachel. Several people walked between them as they hurried along the sidewalk, and eventually Rachel moved ahead of the pitiful old woman. But it seemed she could not escape. Either the woman was following Rachel or by some odd coincidence they were heading in the same direction. After several blocks, Rachel's instincts warned her that the bag lady was indeed tailing her. The poor thing probably wanted to ask for a handout. Just as Rachel reached the red light where she would cross the street, she paused on the curb and turned to face her stalker.

The woman had disappeared.

Odd.

As she crossed the street, Rachel kept glancing over her shoulder. Sensing that someone was watching her, she felt a nervous foreboding.

When she stepped up on the curb onto Second Avenue, she looked back once again. No bag lady. Instead a buck-toothed redhead in thick glasses, wearing a Stetson and boots, appeared as if out of nowhere, her step quick and agile. The unattractive cowgirl wannabe hurried past Rachel, not even bothering to apologize when she brushed into her in passing.

Shivering with an unnatural fear, Rachel stopped dead still and looked in every direction. Strangers surrounded her. Unknown faces stared at her. Weird-looking women in costumes that hid their true identity gawked at her.

Suddenly a tall, handsome young man came toward her, his

dark hair and blue eyes heartbreakingly familiar. Jake Marcott smiled at her. Rachel sucked in a deep, terrified breath. A deadly arrow stuck out of Jake's bloody chest.

The walking dead.

No, this isn't real. I'm hallucinating.

Rachel woke suddenly, startled for several seconds, uncertain about her surroundings. She lay there, darkness encompassing her, her heartbeat thumping maddeningly inside her head. The residue from her nightmare mingled with reality when she realized she was in the guest bedroom in Charlie and Laraine Young's home in Portland.

It had been a dream. Just a dream.

No, it had been a nightmare. The gray-haired bag lady stalking her. The ugly, rude, redheaded cowgirl. Jake Marcott's smiling corpse. None of them had been real.

She shoved back the covers, slid to the edge of the bed, and sat there for a couple of minutes, allowing herself time to awaken completely. Her mind whirled with thoughts, some coherent, others jumbled and confused. Standing solidly on the wooden floor, she stretched her arms over her head, then down to touch her toes. Awake and slightly shaken by the nightmare, she went into the bathroom, flipped on the overhead light, and turned on the faucet. After dashing cold water in her face, she stared at her pale reflection in the vanity mirror.

Her eyes widened. Her mouth gaped. Realization dawned as the water trickled over her cheeks and seeped down her throat. Oh my God! Dreaming about Jake—about his bloody corpse— wasn't surprising, all things considered. But why a bag lady and an ugly cowgirl?

Because during the past few weeks, she had actually encountered both a dirty old bag lady and an unattractive redhead wearing a Stetson and boots. And there had been a plump blond nanny strolling along with a baby buggy, too. All three of them rather weird.

Disguises!

Each of them had been wearing a disguise. The bag lady, the ugly redhead, and the plump blonde.

Had they all been the same person?

Of course!

Someone was stalking Rachel, keeping tabs on her, playing some sort of sick game.

Rachel dried her face with a hand towel and returned to the bedroom to get her cell phone. She glanced at the digital clock on the nightstand. Five-thirty. Would he be awake at this hour? Probably not.

She flipped open her phone and typed in a text message, then sent it to Dean.

When you wake up, contact me. We need to talk.

Within minutes she received a reply.

I'm awake. Call me. Or come over to my place.

Immediately she called him.

"What's wrong?" he asked the minute he answered.

"Someone has been stalking me for the past few weeks."

"Why are you just now telling me?"

"Because I just now realized it," she said. "I can't believe it took me this long to realize what was going on. Even though she was wearing disguises and changing them to throw me off, I should have sensed something."

"Slow down, honey. You lost me at the word *disguises*."

"My stalker was changing her looks, wearing different disguises when she followed me."

"Are you sure about this?"

Rachel blew out an aggravated breath. "I'm not sure of anything. It's five-thirty in the morning. I had a horrible nightmare in which Jake's smiling corpse appeared to me. I have to go to Mandy's funeral this afternoon and . . ." She clicked her tongue. "I'm just a little scared."

"Want me to come over there?"

"No, you'd just wake up Charlie and Laraine."

"How about I pick you up and we go somewhere for an early breakfast?"

"Give me thirty minutes to grab a shower," she told him. "I'll leave Laraine a note telling her where I've gone. I'll meet you out front."

"Wait inside, just to be safe, until you see me drive up."

"You don't think she's outside this time of the morning, just waiting for a chance to attack me, do you?"

"I don't think she wants to kill you," Dean said. "At least not yet. She's playing with you, tormenting you. And she's bold about it, too. She took a chance every time she put on a disguise and followed you. What if you'd recognized her?"

"I wish I had. I wish I'd realized what was happening, but my mind has been so cluttered with facts about Jake's old murder case and about Mandy's recent murder that I couldn't see what was right under my nose."

"So now you know. You're aware of what's been happening. You'll be on the lookout for her."

Rachel's heartbeat accelerated, the thought of actually coming face-to-face with the mystery woman unsettling.

"Rach?"

"Huh?"

"Are you okay?"

"Yeah, I'm fine. Just a little rattled. Sometimes nightmares have a way of seeming a little too real."

"What are you wearing right now?"

"What?"

"Do you have on a gown or PJs or do you sleep in the raw?"

Startled by his question, it took her a full minute to realize what he was doing and why. "Not very subtle, McMichaels. It's obvious you're trying to get my mind off the stalker."

"Yeah, that and I'm curious as to whether you're naked right now."

"Sorry to disappoint you, but I'm wearing a ratty old Alabama T-shirt."

"I like a woman who goes for comfort in her sleepwear."

"Do you now?"

"In case you're interested, I sleep in my briefs."

"Why would I be interested?"

"For the same reason I'm curious about you."

"Look, let's end this silly game right now." She wasn't good at flirtatious game playing. She was an up-front, what-you-see-is-what-you-get kind of woman. If he came right out and asked her to have sex with him, she probably would. "Pick me up in thirty minutes."

"I'll be there, honey. With bells on."

Dean studied her as she sat there, her small, delicate hands wrapped around a white coffee mug, her gaze focused on the black liquid inside. Just looking at her turned him inside out. He couldn't get her out of his mind. Why didn't he just tell her that he wanted her? The worst that could happen was that she'd say no. And it wasn't as if he'd never been rejected before. But she wasn't just any woman. This was Rachel.

Besides that, she wasn't going to stay in Portland. She was here for only two reasons—the reunion and reopening the Cupid Killer case. For twenty years, he hadn't been a blip on her radar, and truth be told, he hadn't consciously thought about her all that often, so why couldn't he just accept that they were friends and nothing more? Once that had been enough, or at least he'd convinced himself that it was. But he wasn't a horny teenage boy having sex with other girls while he thought about one girl in particular.

The good girl I would have died to protect. Would have killed to protect.

They had eaten the daily special—bacon, eggs, and toast—and discussed Rachel's nightmare and its implications. The bottom line was that neither of them wanted to believe that someone from the old gang had killed Jake and had now resurfaced and was killing again.

"When we get to headquarters, I'll try to find out if one of the girls flew to New York around the same time Aurora did," Dean said.

"And if one of them did?"

Dean grimaced. "Then we find out why she was there."

Rachel sipped on the coffee. "And if none of them were in New York when Aurora was killed and Lindsay was attacked, then what?"

"Then we look elsewhere. Unless . . ."

"Unless what?"

"This woman you've seen wearing various disguises could be not only wearing costumes to hide her true identity, she could use a fake ID," Dean said. "It's not that difficult to get hold of a fake driver's license, and that's all she'd need to board a plane from Portland to New York City."

"Damn! If she did that, then what's the point of checking?"

"I'm just saying maybe she used a fake ID. I'll still check the flights for the time around Aurora's trip."

Four hours and five cups of coffee later, Dean stopped by Rachel's desk at downtown headquarters. "Good news and bad news," he said.

"Let's hear the good first."

"I spoke to Patrick Dewey's son. He's promised to talk to his mother again and see if he can't persuade her to see us. It seems she's selling her house and is in the middle of packing up and clearing out. He's not sure how she'll react when he talks to her again."

"That's the good news?"

Dean grinned. She loved his cocky grin. It made her want to kiss him.

"It could be good news, if Mrs. Dewey will talk to us. We've run into a dead end on the Cupid Killer case, just as your dad did twenty years ago. Without a new lead of some kind . . ." Dean threw up his open palms in a that's-it gesture.

"We're grabbing for straws thinking Mrs. Dewey might be able to shed some new light on the old case, aren't we?"

"Probably."

Rachel frowned. "So, what's the bad news?"

"Both April Wright and DeLynn Vaughn could have been in New York City when Aurora was killed and Lindsay was attacked."

"What do you mean they could have been?"

"April was visiting her sister in Bridgeport, Connecticut, an easy drive to New York City. And DeLynn was in Scranton, Pennsylvania, on a business trip. It would have been a longer drive, but doable."

"Crap!"

"My sentiments exactly."

"I just don't see either April or DeLynn as a killer."

"We could be barking up the wrong tree, you know. Checking to see if any of the reunion committee members were in New York when Aurora was killed was just a thought. It doesn't prove anything that April and DeLynn both just happened to be within driving distance at the time."

"I almost wish you hadn't checked. At least not until after the funeral. I'll have to find a way not to stare at them during the service and wonder if either of them is actually capable of murder."

She cried as many tears as the rest of them did at Mandy Kim Stulz's funeral service. Poor Jeff. He was little more than a zombie, obviously zoned out on medication. His parents flanked him, his father's arm around Jeff's shoulder, his mother holding his hand and weeping softly. And Mandy's parents—such a sad little couple, clinging to each other, trying to be brave for the sake of Mandy's siblings. An older sister and brother were both keeping an eye on their elderly parents.

She would have preferred to skip the morbid service, but if she had, people would have wondered why. No one suspected her, and she intended to keep it that way. She had gotten away with murder twenty years ago, hadn't she? And although Rachel and Dean suspected Aurora's death hadn't been accidental and the homeless man hadn't really killed Haylie, they had no proof that she had killed them.

How absolutely wonderful that Lindsay Farrell was here, on Wyatt Goddard's arm, no less. To think that all these years she had believed the child Lindsay had given birth to had been Jake's. An understandable mistake. After all, none of them had known that Lindsay had been cheating on Jake with Wyatt.

Do you hear that, Jake? All the while you thought Lindsay was yours and yours alone, Wyatt was screwing her.

She had to control the urge to laugh out loud.

And you never knew that I found someone else, too. Someone kind and understanding. Someone who loved me. Someone who didn't judge me harshly and didn't blame me for loving you and hating you at the same time.

If only things could have been different. If she could have kept her baby.

It might not have been your child, Jake. It might have been his.

She let her gaze travel over the mourners. Discreetly, of course. With a damp Kleenex pressed against her cheek, she faked her grief, putting on quite a performance. Nothing over the top. Just a few tears escaping now and then, enough to convince everyone that she was deeply saddened by Mandy's death. She watched the others, especially Lindsay, Kristen, and Rachel, and mimicked their actions. Except she didn't take part in the comforting, caring hugs they shared. Just as it had been in the past, she was close to them, an arm's length from their inner circle. And yet she might as well have been a million miles away for all the good it did her. They wouldn't let her in now any more than they would have back then when she had so longed to fit in.

But soon—very soon—there would be no inner circle, no little clique of popular girls.

They'll all be dead—every last one of them.

And when the bulldozers destroyed St. Elizabeth's, swept away the rubble and buried the remains, she and she alone would be left standing, her thirst for revenge sated, her enemies punished, all the wrongs made right at last.

In the past twenty years, Rachel had made friends in both Chattanooga and in Huntsville, but none of her more recent relationships had been as strong as the bond she had forged in high school with Kristen and Lindsay. Being with them again was like turning back the clock and reverting into teenagers who shared everything with one another. Well, almost everything. Lindsay had kept her pregnancy a secret. God only knew how. Maybe it was because she and Kristen had both known that Lindsay wasn't having sex with Jake and just assumed she was still a virgin.

Rachel made herself a promise—she was not going to lose track of Kristen and Lindsay, not ever again. She was going to stay in touch often.

Mandy's mother had disappeared into the nursery to look after her granddaughter, leaving her forlorn husband in the hands of Mandy's siblings. Jeff continued in remote-control mode, shaking hands with sympathetic friends and acquaintances who had stopped by the house after the funeral. His father stayed at his side while his mother oversaw the refreshments being served by kind neighbors.

As if a gravitational pull had drawn them together, Lindsay and Wyatt stood in the corner talking to Kristen and Ross while Rachel and Dean approached the two couples. After another round of hugs and tearful sighs, the three old friends turned to the men in their lives for support. Ross draped his arm across Kristen's shoulders, while Lindsay clung to Wyatt's hand. As if he sensed she needed his touch, Dean eased his arm around Rachel's waist.

"I don't see how Jeff is making it," Kristen said. "He's lost without Mandy. Those two were so in love."

"He's numb right now," Dean said. "But heaven help him when the medication wears off."

A revolving door of mourners came through the Stulz home in the next hour, most strangers to Rachel. If not for Dean to lean on, she wasn't sure she would have been able to endure this post-funeral affair. When he caught her staring at Bella Marcott, Dean alerted her to what she was doing. She had managed not to focus for more than a minute or two on DeLynn and Martina, but April had caught Rachel looking at her. Rachel had nodded and then glanced away.

As she had studied each woman, she'd asked herself, "Is she capable of cold-blooded murder?"

Bella made her way through the crowd, stopping directly in front of Rachel. "Did you want to say something to me? I noticed you were staring at me."

"I'm sorry," Rachel said. "That was rude of me. I've caught myself wondering which one of us will be next. You, me, De-Lynn, Kris—"

"What do you think, Bella?" Dean asked.

"I'd rather not think about it," Bella said. "It's frightening to believe that someone is killing us off, one by one. Do the police have any idea who killed Mandy and if her death is connected to Haylie's murder or Aurora's death in New York?"

"We have a few theories," Dean replied. "And sooner or later, we'll catch the killer."

"Jake's murderer was never caught," Bella said.

"Not yet." Rachel's gaze meshed with Bella's and she openly studied Jake's sister.

"Do you really think you can solve a twenty-year-old crime?"

Rachel nodded. "Yes, I do, especially if my theory that whoever killed Jake is killing again, murdering the women who were closest to Jake."

"What an odd theory. Why would anyone want to kill Jake's women?"

Such a peculiar thing to say, Rachel thought. *Jake's women.* But she supposed that's what they'd all been in one way or another.

One of the Stulzes' neighbors, a middle-aged lady with blue, Bette Davis eyes came up to Rachel. "I'm sorry to interrupt. There's another floral delivery, but when I told the young man to bring the flowers in and find a place for them anywhere in the living room, he said the flowers were to be delivered directly to Sergeant Rachel Alsace."

A quiver of uncertainty rippled along Rachel's spine.

"Want me to see what this is all about?" Dean asked.

"No, I can handle it." She turned back to Bella. "If you'll excuse me."

"Certainly."

Rachel headed for the door where a twentysomething delivery boy stood holding a large white box. As she neared him, she sensed Dean directly behind her. She glanced over her shoulder and smiled at him.

Focusing on the delivery boy, she said, "I'm Rachel Alsace."

"I was told to deliver these directly to you." He handed her the box, which Dean reached out and took from him. The boy jumped back, startled by Dean's unexpected maneuver. "No need to tip me. It's been covered . . . when the flowers were ordered."

Dean and Rachel looked at each other, neither saying a word. While he held the box, she removed the lid. Inside were seven lilies, each tied with a white ribbon, similar to the lilies and yards of white ribbon used in the spray that had covered Mandy's coffin. Attached to each ribbon was a card, and on each card was written a name. Rachel picked up the first lily and read the card.

"DeLynn," she read.

Hurriedly she laid that lily back down and one by one checked the name tags on the others. April. Kristen. Martina. Bella. Lindsay. And Rachel.

"She's sending us a message." Rachel looked directly at Dean. "She wants us to know that we're all going to die, that she's going to kill each of us, the way she killed Mandy."

Chapter 31

Dean had disposed of the box of lilies while Rachel told Kristen and Lindsay about them, instructing them to let the others know.

This was yet another warning from the killer. They should take every precaution.

"Tell them not to panic, but to be more careful than ever," Dean had advised.

After saying good-bye to Jeff, who probably wouldn't remember who had been there and who hadn't, Rachel and Dean drove straight to the florist, a trendy shop in downtown Portland—the Flower Garden—run by a young couple, Mark and Melanie, in their late twenties. The wife remembered the order.

"Yes, I took the order over the phone," Melanie said. "Four days ago. She said she would send the money before the date of delivery and call back to let me know exactly when to deliver them. And she did. We received the payment in cash, which I thought was rather odd, but she said she preferred dealing in cash."

"When did she call back to give you the details about delivery?"

"This morning," Mark replied.

"Do you recall anything in particular about the woman's voice?" Dean asked.

Melanie frowned. "No, not really."

"Just an ordinary woman's voice," Mark said.

"Would you recognize her voice if you heard it again?"

Melanie shook her head.

"No, sorry," Mark said. "We get so many calls."

"Did you by any chance save the envelope the money came in?" Rachel asked.

"No. I had no reason to save it." Melanie frowned.

"Did the woman give you a name?" Dean asked.

"Yes, of course." Melanie thought for a couple of seconds. "I believe she said her name was Elizabeth Saint."

Rachel groaned.

"Do you recognize the name?" Mark asked.

"Yes, we do," Dean said. "Thanks for your help."

Five minutes later, on their way across town to headquarters, while Rachel and Dean were talking about the name Elizabeth Saint being simply a play on words—St. Elizabeth's—Rachel's cell phone rang.

The caller ID showed Portland, Oregon. Cell number. No name.

Rachel flipped open the phone. "Hello."

"Did you get my flowers?" the disguised voice asked.

"Yes." Rachel motioned to Dean, indicating that the call was from "her."

"Do you want to know who will be next?"

"Do you intend to tell me?"

Laughter. "Of course not. If I did, it wouldn't be a surprise, would it?"

"Is there anything I can say or do that will persuade you to stop? Is there something you want that I—we can give you?"

Silence.

"You're killing for a reason, aren't you?" Rachel wanted to keep her talking. "Tell me what that reason is."

"The only thing I want is the satisfaction of seeing all of you bitches dead and buried with the past."

Buried with the past? "What did we ever do to you to make you hate us so?"

"You know what you did, what all of you did, how all of you treated me."

"What about Jake? Did he treat you badly, too? Is that why you killed him?"

"Jake deserved to die for what he made me do," the voice said.

"What did he make you do?"

Silence.

"Tell me. Please. Help me to understand why you—"

Crying. Soft sobs.

"Please, let me help you," Rachel said.

"It's too late."

Conversation over. Phone call ended.

Emitting a nervous huff, Rachel closed her phone. "She all but admitted that she killed Jake. And she said he deserved to die because of what he made her do."

"Knowing Jake, he could have done anything to this woman, even forced her to have sex with him," Dean said.

A month ago, it would have been impossible for Rachel to believe that Jake had been capable of something so horrible. But the Jake she had come to know through studying the old Cupid Killer files was not the boy she remembered. It was as if he'd led a double life or at the very least had presented a pretty façade to the world to hide the darkness inside him.

"If he raped her, I can understand her wanting to kill him," Rachel said. "But why does she want to kill us? Why Aurora and Mandy and Haylie? It doesn't make sense."

"We've already figured out that this woman is mentally unbalanced."

"And she is one of us."

"Probably."

"DeLynn once had a nervous breakdown and so did Bella. April was into drugs once, and that could have affected her mentally."

"And DeLynn and April were both within driving distance of New York City when Aurora died and Lindsay was attacked." Dean turned his Thunderbird onto SW Second Street.

"I don't want one of them to be our killer."

"But the odds are that one of them is. And if we're right about that, then it means whoever she is, she didn't kill Jake."

Rachel clenched her teeth and cursed softly under her breath. "None of us knew how to use a crossbow, and Jake was killed by someone skillful enough to hit him dead center in the heart."

"Then we either have two killers on our hands or . . ."

"Or we have a man disguising his voice and himself as a woman."

"Or we have a couple working together or—"

"Okay, let's say the killer isn't a woman. What if he was one of the guys at Western Catholic or Washington High?"

"We need to go with the most likely scenario instead of creating a new and less likely one," Dean told her. "And remember that the person wearing disguises who you think has been stalking you is female. The person who ordered the lilies was female. And all of you think the person making the threatening calls is female.

The most logical conclusion is that whoever killed Jake is not our present-day killer."

"I know. I know. It seems the more information we have, the more confused things are. And so much boils down to the fact that I just can't picture one of the old gang as a cold-blooded killer."

"I don't like the idea any better than you do that one of them is capable of murder, but what few concrete facts we have tell me that we need to concentrate on the reunion committee members."

"I guess that rules out our doing a further investigation into the possibility that Marilyn or Patrick Dewey might have killed Jake."

"I didn't say we should rule out anyone. But motivation is the key factor—in Jake's murder and in the recent murders. Patrick Dewey is dead, so he can't be our killer. And why would Marilyn Dewey be killing women she doesn't even know?"

"God, I am so frustrated!" Rachel admitted quite vehemently. "And I feel so helpless. I should be able to do something to stop these murders now, before someone else has to die."

"I suppose your dad felt frustrated and hopeless when he couldn't come up with a viable suspect in Jake's murder. Even those of us in law enforcement can do only so much. If the evidence isn't there—"

"It's there," Rachel told him. "Damn it, it's there. We just can't see it!"

When Kristen and Ross dropped Martina at her house that evening, Ross insisted on walking Martina to her door. And she was grateful for his gentlemanly escort. It wasn't that she was scared, not exactly. Just unnerved.

A lot of that going around lately, she thought as she inserted the key in the lock of her front door, heard the distinct click, and turned around to wave good night to Kristen and her husband. If she weren't all alone this week, with Craig out of town on business and the kids away at summer camp, she wouldn't dread entering her own home. Craig hadn't wanted to leave, but the trip had been planned weeks ago, before Mandy's murder. Martina had insisted that he go, reassuring him that she would be fine for the few days he'd be gone.

She shouldn't be so silly. No one could get inside her house. Not with sturdy locks on all the windows and doors. Not with a security system in place.

As soon as she entered the foyer, she tapped the code into the keypad to disarm the security system, then hurriedly locked the door behind her. Releasing a relieved breath, she walked down the hall and into the kitchen. She had left a table lamp on in the foyer and the over-the-sink fluorescent on in the kitchen.

Using the handy step stool she kept in the pantry, Martina stood on it to reach an upper cupboard. After retrieving the box of candy she kept out of sight and hopefully out of mind, she set the box on the counter, opened it, and chose a piece of caramel nougat.

She knew she shouldn't be indulging this way, but food was her drug of choice. Always had been. That's why now, twenty years after high school, she was fifty pounds heavier.

She shouldn't be doing this. She had stayed on her diet for two months now and lost fifteen pounds so she would look good at the reunion.

But with all that had happened lately—the deaths of three old friends and the constant threat that she or another friend was next—Martina needed the consolation that only candy could give her. If she drank, she'd be downing a glass of whiskey right now. If she smoked, she'd be puffing away on a cancer stick.

Attending the funeral of a dear old friend was reason enough for her to turn to the habitual crutch she could count on for comfort. Food. Especially candy.

Just as she was swallowing the last bite of the sweet concoction, the phone rang.

Startled, Martina cried out and threw her hands up and over her mouth.

Get a grip. It's just the phone. Yes, but what if it's "her"?

But what if it's Craig?

She checked the caller ID. Portland. No name.

Damn!

Just don't answer it.

The phone rang ten times, then stopped.

Martina popped another piece of candy into her mouth, then picked up the box and headed for the den.

The phone rang again.

Unnerved, her hands trembling, she dropped the box and the candy fell haphazardly all over the kitchen floor. Leaving the scattered pieces where they were, she checked the caller ID.

Portland. No name.

The phone rang ten times. Silence. Immediately, it rang again. Ten times. Silence. Then it rang again.

Martina held her hands over her ears. *Stop calling me!*

When the ringing continued, driving her crazy, she finally jerked the portable phone off its base and screamed, "Leave me alone!"

Laughter.

The person on the other end of the line was laughing at her.

"What's wrong, Martina?" the disguised voice asked. "Are you upset that you've blown your diet by eating candy?"

"What! How did you know?" Martina rushed to the windows over the sink and peered out into the darkness.

"You should have answered on the first ring. That way, you wouldn't have spilled your candy all over the floor."

Oh, God! She's out there, watching me. Looking in the window.

But Martina couldn't see anyone. Just the empty driveway, the basketball hoop attached to the front of the garage, and her youngest child's old bicycle.

"You can't see me, but I can see you," the voice taunted.

Martina hung up the phone and immediately dialed Rachel's cell number. The minute Rachel answered, Martina spoke rapidly, fear in her voice. "She's here. At my house. Outside watching me. Please, help me!"

Rachel assured Martina that she and Dean were on their way. Martina hung up the phone, then hurriedly punched in the code and Stay on the security keypad beside the back door.

There. She felt safer. If anyone tried to break into the house, the alarm would go off.

The phone rang.

Martina screamed.

The phone kept ringing. Over and over and over again.

Martina slumped down onto the floor, sitting in the middle of the scattered pieces of candy, and hugged herself as she rocked back and forth.

I'm safe. No one can get inside my house. No one can hurt me.

The phone continued ringing.

Rachel helped Kristen and Ross put Martina in their car.

"Go home with Kris," Rachel said. "You'll be safe there. Dean and I will take care of things here."

As soon as she had received Martina's desperate call for help, Rachel had phoned for police backup, and the closest squad car to Martina's home had been sent out. Then she had phoned Kristen and asked that she and Ross meet them at Martina's.

"She's going to need a place to stay tonight," Rachel had said.

"And I want you to get in touch with Craig and tell him to come home, that his wife needs him."

Martina slid into the backseat of Kristen's car, then reached out and grabbed Rachel's arm. "She was here. In my yard. Looking through the window. Find her, Rach. Find her and stop her before she kills again."

Rachel grabbed Martina's hand and squeezed hard. "I'll do my best. I promise."

Ross shut the door, closing Martina safely inside, then he turned to Rachel. "We'll take care of her and get in touch with her husband, tonight if possible."

Kristen hugged Rachel. "Don't be alone at any time. I know you carry a gun and are able to defend yourself, but . . . We all need somebody to watch out for us. I've got Ross. Lindsay has Wyatt." Kris's gaze crossed Martina's front yard and paused on Dean McMichaels where he stood talking to four patrol officers. The two squad cars had arrived before Rachel and Dean, but Martina had refused to open the door until Rachel arrived. "Dean's a good man. Let him look after you. Okay?"

"Don't worry about me. Just take care of yourself and Martina."

When the Delmonicos left, Rachel walked over to Dean. With her eyes cast downward, she waited until the officers said their good-byes and headed toward their squad cars, then she looked directly at him.

"How's Martina?" Dean asked.

"Frightened to death."

"We found footprints under the kitchen windows," he said. "I've got somebody on their way here to photograph them and make casts. The prints are slightly distorted, as if the person tried to erase them but didn't have time to completely get rid of all the prints."

"So, we wait for your crime scene tech person and in the meantime guard the scene?"

"Yeah, around back," Dean said. "I'll want Hughes to check for fingerprints on the windows, too."

Rachel and Dean spent the next twenty minutes, while they waited for crime scene investigator Phil Hughes, making several phone calls. One by one, they telephoned the members of the reunion committee. The purpose of these calls was twofold. One: to warn them to be extra careful. Two: to see if they were at home. Of course, any one of them could have been here at Martina's and

made it home by now. But they had to check, to make sure everyone was accounted for tonight.

Lindsay was with Wyatt in their hotel room. Bella answered
on the fourth ring. She was home and said she was just stepping
out of the shower. DeLynn didn't answer her home phone but answered her cell phone. She was at her mother's, picking up her
twins. April didn't answer either her home phone or her cell
phone.

"Just because she's not answering her phone doesn't make
April a suspect," Dean said.

"No, but . . . I can't stand this!" Rachel's nerves were on edge.
She had worked quite a few murder cases over the years, first in
Chattanooga and then in Huntsville, but the victims had been
strangers. Everything was different when the victims were people
you knew. Old friends. And complicating matters even more was
the fact that the most obvious suspects were also old friends.

Dean slipped his arms around Rachel and pulled her into a
comforting embrace. At first she stiffened, unsure of herself and
of Dean. It had been a long time since she'd leaned on someone
for any kind of support or counted on someone to be there for her.
When he rubbed his big hand over her back and nuzzled the top of
her head with his chin, she relaxed into him. Loving the way he
held her so protectively, she eased her arms around his waist and
laid her head on his chest.

And that's the way Phil Hughes found them. Embracing in
the dark.

Phil cleared his throat.

Rachel started to jerk away from Dean, but he draped his arm
around her shoulders as he turned her to face Phil. The crime
scene tech carried quite a bit of equipment, which he set down on
the driveway.

"The footprints are under the kitchen windows," Dean said.
"Need help setting up your camera?"

"Nah, I'm fine," Phil replied, a sheepish grin on his face.

"Then get to it," Dean told him. "We don't want to be here all
night."

"Got something better planned?" Phil winked at Dean.

"Get your dirty mind out of the gutter," Dean said.

Phil chuckled as he headed toward the kitchen windows.

"Check the window frames for prints," Dean called to Phil.

"Will do."

Being careful not to disturb the shoe tracks, Phil shined his flashlight on the double windows. He dusted both windows, including the glass panes. When his brush didn't remove enough powder, Phil blew off the excess and studied the dusted surfaces.

"I don't see anything. Either our guy was wearing gloves or he didn't touch the windows."

Finished with the first chore, Phil then placed the frame his camera rested on above the shoeprints, the frame pointing directly down. The crime scene tech used this type of camera because it showed the ratio of the negative to the original. This meant the original footprints could be reproduced in their precise size.

When Phil finished photographing the tracks, he set about making moulages by spraying the ground under the window with a fixative.

"I'll need some water," Phil said. "To mix the plaster. Once that's done, you two can go on. Damp as it is tonight, it could take an hour or two for the plaster to set."

"What's your guess as to shoe size and type of shoe?" Rachel asked.

"Looks like an athletic shoe of some kind. Maybe a size eight or nine. Small for a man. I'd say there's a good chance these are a woman's footprints."

She had waited until after midnight before she drove to St. Elizabeth's, the lure to return here too powerful for her to deny. But it wasn't all that great a risk, was it? Not when no one had any idea that she had created a shrine to the past here at the old school. She always parked behind the building where no one would see her car. Being careful and ever vigilant, she never took her own safety for granted.

She made her way down into the basement. Using a high-beam flashlight with a stand attachment, she illuminated the row of lockers. If things had gone as she'd planned this evening, she would have a souvenir from Martina to place in her locker. But the woman was smarter than she'd given her credit for being.

When she had telephoned her tonight, as she stood in the shadows of Martina's backyard, she had planned on luring Martina outside so that she could kill her.

Are you upset that you've blown your diet by eating candy? You should have answered on the first ring. That way, you wouldn't have spilled your candy all over the floor.

She had been so sure that after she let Martina know she could see her, that she was watching her, Martina would open the back door and search for her. But no, instead of coming outside looking for her caller, Martina had slumped down on the floor and refused to answer the phone again, after she apparently had called Rachel.

You were too smart for me this time. But next time . . .

The reunion was now less than a week away. It would be only days until they all united at St. Elizabeth's. The senior classes from St. Lizzy's, Western Catholic, and Washington High. All the boys and girls now approaching middle age. Twenty years and a lifetime of experience lay between those teenagers and the men and women they were now.

But she would bet her life that none of them had forgotten Jake Marcott or the night he had died.

You're unforgettable, Jake.

But you knew that, didn't you?

I certainly haven't forgotten you. I remember how much I loved you and how much I hated you. And I'll never forgive you for making me kill my baby.

Our baby.

If you'd taken me to a real doctor for the abortion, I wouldn't be sterile. You took everything from me. Everything.

Now I'm going to take everything away from them. Those smug girls who thought they were better than me. Those lucky women who found men to love them and had babies and have lived wonderful lives.

Rachel and Dean sat inside his T-bird, the windows rolled down and the top back, but before he got a chance to start the engine, Rachel said, "Kris wears a size seven shoe, or at least she used to. And I believe Lindsay wears a six and a half."

"I thought you had ruled them out completely as suspects."

"I have. I was just thinking out loud, running over shoe sizes in my mind." She turned in the leather seat, her safety belt unsnapped. "I wear a six."

"Cinderella feet."

"What?" She eyed him quizzically.

"Tiny feet. Glass slipper," he said by way of explanation.

"Oh." Then she charged ahead, still on the subject of shoe size. "I have no idea what size shoes the others wear. We can rule out Martina. She couldn't fake being that terrified. So that leaves DeLynn, April, and Bella." Looking directly at Dean, she asked, "Have you ever paid any attention to their feet?"

"No, I can't say that I have."

"DeLynn is tall and slender. I'd think she'd wear at least an eight. And I seem to recall that April has rather large feet. Maybe a size nine. I have no idea about Bella."

"Why don't we wait until Phil has a definite size for us before we play this guessing game," Dean said. "Once we know a definite size, we can investigate."

"What do you think they'd do if we asked to see in their closets to look at their shoes?"

Dean reached across the console and grasped Rachel's shoulder. "Let it rest for tonight. Phil will call us in the morning. In the meantime, we both need some R&R after the day we've had. I'll take you home—"

"I don't want to go home." The words flew out of her mouth before she gave the implication any thought. "I—I'm not offering or asking for anything more than just not to be alone. Understand?"

He nodded. "Buckle up."

He fastened his seat belt. She did the same. Then he started the engine and zoomed the T-bird out into the nighttime traffic. The wind whipped around them, warm and balmy. When he kicked the sports car into high gear, all of Rachel's senses came into play: The feel of the evening breeze. The sound of the T-bird's motor and the hum of traffic. The mixed and mingled scents of the big city. The blurred lights and buildings as they zipped by at high speed. The taste of desire and fear in her mouth.

Neither of them spoke on the drive from Martina's house to Dean's apartment. Screeching into his designated slot, he parked the Thunderbird in an underground garage. After bringing up the windows and top, he got out, rounded the hood, and opened the door for her. She looked up at him and smiled. He held out his hand.

She put her hand in his and climbed out of his car. "Nothing like death to make you need to prove just how alive you are," she said.

"Is that what you think this is all about?" He raked the back of his hand over her cheek.

She sucked in her breath. "Maybe, at least in part."

"And the other part would be?" He took her hand and led her away from the locked car and toward the elevator.

"Needing sex," she admitted.

He punched the Up arrow button and the elevator doors swung open. Once inside, he hit the Six button, the doors closed, and the elevator began its ascent.

"Nothing personal about it?" he asked, waving his hand between them. "You and me or you and anybody, as long as—"

She put her hand over his mouth. "It's not like that and you know it."

They gazed at each other, the connection between them sizzling. She eased her hand away from his mouth.

"I don't understand you, Rachel. I thought you weren't into meaningless one-night stands."

"You're the one who said we shouldn't mistake need and want for love," she told him. "You're the one who didn't want to get involved."

The elevator stopped and then opened on the sixth floor. Without saying a word, Dean waited for her to exit; then he got out, took her hand again, and silently led her to his apartment door.

He took his key ring from his pocket, unlocked the door, and reached around her to flip on the overhead light in the small entry hall. She felt him behind her, his chest to her back, his breath warm on her neck.

"Come into my parlor."

Said the spider to the fly. Shivering, she hesitated for a millisecond, then when he nudged her into action, she entered his bachelor flat. Nothing fancy. White walls. Wooden floors. Sturdy, masculine furniture. Not overly expensive. Not cheap.

"Come on in and make yourself at home," he said. "Want something to drink?"

She shook her head.

"So how do we play this?" he asked. "Up-front and honest? Or subtle and coy?"

"I'm not good at playing games."

"Honey, you sure as hell could have fooled me. I think you've been playing a game with me for weeks now."

"No, I haven't. Really. I—I—" She turned and walked toward the door. "This was a mistake, wasn't it? I thought you wanted me, maybe even needed me tonight. I guess you should just take me home."

Before she knew what was happening, Dean came up behind her, whirled her around, and shoved her up against the wall. He lowered his head and brought his mouth down on hers, taking her in an all-consuming, conquering kiss that both startled and excited her. With his big, hard body pressing against her, she felt his arousal and knew without a doubt that he wanted her.

And she wanted him. God, how she wanted him!

Rachel pushed against his chest until he ended the kiss. They stared at each other, their lips parted, their breathing ragged.

"We don't have to talk," she said breathlessly. "We don't need to analyze this."

"No, honey, we don't."

He swept her up into his arms, kicked his half-closed bedroom door wide open, and carried her to his unmade bed. They tore at each other's clothes until within minutes they were both naked. Shoes, belts, his slacks, her blouse, and various other items lay scattered on the floor and foot of the bed.

Dean stared at her, visually eating her up as if she were his favorite food. She looked right back at him, appreciating his lean, hard body.

"I knew you'd be perfect," Dean said as he cupped each of her breasts. "I've wanted to see these beauties since I was fourteen."

She smiled. "Better late than never."

He released her abruptly. "Wait right here. I've got a box of condoms in the bathroom."

"Do you think we'll need a whole box?" she asked teasingly.

"Honey, the way I feel about you, we may need more than one box."

Hours later, as dawn light seeped through his apartment windows, Dean rested on one elbow and stared at the woman asleep beside him. Rachel. His Rachel.

Had she meant it when she'd told him that she loved him? Or had she spoken the words in the heat of the moment? Three times! He hadn't thought he still had it in him to go three times, not at the ripe old age of thirty-eight. But by God, he had. And he was hard again. Wanted her again.

He kissed her navel. She stirred. He kissed the musky triangle of blond curls between her thighs. Her eyelids popped open.

"Liked that, did you?" he teased.

She ruffled his hair. "I like everything you do to me. Everything."

"Are you too sore for a little more everything?" he asked as he came up and over her, straddling her hips.

"You know, I could get used to being the object of your desire."

"Permanently?" he asked, but kept his tone light.

She lifted her arms up and around his neck, drawing him

down to her. She kissed him. He rubbed his sex against hers. She sighed into his open mouth.

"What would permanently entail?" she inquired.

Should he tell her that he'd meant it when he had repeatedly told her that he loved her and find out if she really did love him? Should he risk her rejection and ask her to marry him?

"I was thinking—after a proper courtship—we might get engaged and then eventually married and in a year or two after that have a couple of kids and—"

"Why wait?" She spread her legs and lifted her hips, inviting him in, as she pressed her lips against his neck. "I don't need a proper courtship. A few more dates and then you can buy me a traditional diamond ring."

"A diamond ring, huh? How big?" He thrust deeply inside her. She gasped with pleasure. "Really big," she sighed.

He laughed. "I was talking about the ring."

Smiling, she said, "So was I, you arrogant, conceited—"

She gasped when he retreated and thrust into her again as he lifted her buttocks in his hands and claimed her completely.

"Oh, Dean . . . !"

An hour later, Dean's alarm went off, waking both of them. Just as he leaned over and kissed her, his phone rang.

"Who the hell?"

"You'd better get it," she said. "It could be Phil Hughes or even Uncle Charlie."

Dean picked up the phone on his nightstand, not bothering to check the caller ID. "Hello."

"Lieutenant McMichaels?"

A woman's voice. Dean sat up in bed. "Yeah, this is he."

"I'm Marilyn Dewey. I hope I didn't wake you."

"No. No, ma'am, you didn't."

"My son has convinced me that I should talk to you."

"Yes, ma'am, I'd certainly appreciate it if you'd let me drive up to Salem and ask you a few questions about the old Cupid Killer case."

"I—I'm in the middle of moving from my house into a condo near my elder son and everything is a mess here."

He heard reluctance in her voice. And something else. Trepidation?

"Mrs. Dewey, you could come here to Portland, if you prefer. Your son could come with you."

Rachel punched Dean in the ribs and mouthed the name *Marilyn Dewey.*

"No, no, I'd rather not," Mrs. Dewey said. "You come here. Next week."

"Why wait?"

"Why hurry? Jake Marcott was killed twenty years ago."

"The Portland P.D. believes there is a possibility that Jake's killer has resurfaced and recently killed three of Jake's old friends, three girls Jake once knew quite well."

"That's not possible," Marilyn said.

"What do you mean?"

"Jake Marcott's killer is dead."

Chapter 32

The Dewey home, in a suburb of Salem, was in an older neighborhood with well-kept lawns and neat houses, most built in the sixties. A robust, auburn-haired Pat Dewey Jr. met Rachel and Dean at the door and invited them into his mother's living room.

"Mom," he said to the plump, rosy-cheeked lady with sad brown eyes and gray-streaked auburn hair, "Lieutenant McMichaels and Sergeant Alsace are here."

Marilyn Dewey looked up at them from her wheelchair and motioned to the nearby plaid sofa. "Please, have a seat." She glanced around at the numerous stacked boxes that littered the room. "And excuse this mess. You know I'm in the middle of moving."

Putting a pleasant expression on her face, Rachel shook hands with Marilyn. "Thank you so much for seeing us."

Dean nodded. "We really appreciate this."

He and Rachel sat on the sofa facing Marilyn. Her son stood behind her wheelchair, one hand on her shoulder. "Go ahead, Mom. Tell them what you know."

Marilyn Dewey looked down into her lap where she held her clasped hands, her fingers knotted and swollen. "If Patrick were alive, I'd never . . . I've kept his secret all these years."

Rachel scooted to the edge of the sofa. *What secret?*

"Patrick was a good man," Marilyn said. "A good husband and father."

"Yes, ma'am." Dean glanced up at Pat Jr. before focusing on Mrs. Dewey. "Just take your time in telling us what you know."

"Patrick wasn't with me the night that Marcott boy was

killed." The words rushed out of her in one long, run-together sentence.

Rachel and Dean exchanged questioning glances.

Silence hung over the room like a heavy fog.

"Are you saying that when the police questioned you twenty years ago, you lied?" Rachel asked.

"Yes, I lied for my husband. Patrick told me that if I didn't give him an alibi, the police would dig deeper and he'd be in big trouble," Marilyn explained. "I asked him why he needed an alibi, and he said I was better off not knowing, to just do as he asked and everything would be all right." Tears welled up in her eyes.

Pat Jr. squeezed his mother's shoulder reassuringly. "It's all right. You're doing just fine. Tell them the rest of it."

Marilyn swallowed hard. "I was a young woman with two children and no job. I didn't even graduate from high school. I needed Patrick." She paused, sighed heavily and looked pleadingly at Rachel. "And I loved him."

"We understand," Rachel said. She did understand why a woman would lie for her husband. But understanding didn't mean approval.

"I lied to the police about two things. Patrick was not with me the night the Marcott boy was murdered. And the crossbow that he reported stolen wasn't stolen. He—he hid it in the garage, inside this big old toolbox that had belonged to his father."

Rachel tensed. "Do you know why he reported the crossbow stolen?"

Marilyn shook her head. "I asked him, but he wouldn't tell me. We never discussed it—none of it—ever again. Not until . . ." Tears streamed down her face.

Pat Jr. whipped out a handkerchief from his pocket and handed it to his mother. She wiped away the tears and wadded up the handkerchief in her trembling hands.

"Patrick had throat cancer. He'd been a heavy smoker all his life," Marilyn said. "A few days before he died, he told me he had to clear his conscience before . . . He needed to bare his soul to me, to beg me to forgive him."

Rachel held her breath. Dean didn't move a muscle. A deadly soft anticipation filled the room.

"Patrick killed that boy," Marilyn said. "That Marcott boy."

"Did he tell you that he killed Jake Marcott?" Dean asked, his voice sympathetically gentle.

"Yes. He said that he planned it a few weeks beforehand and that's why he reported the crossbow stolen, so that when he used it . . ."

"Why did your husband kill Jake?" Rachel asked.

Marilyn hesitated, then said, "There was a girl, you see. A girl that Patrick had been seeing." She paused as if the truth were too terrible for her to utter aloud. "My husband had an affair with a teenage girl."

Oh my God! Rachel's mind worked at lightning speed, putting together the missing pieces to a twenty-year-old puzzle.

Marilyn Dewey wept, her heart breaking anew because her husband had been unfaithful to her all those years ago. "This girl had been involved with the Marcott boy, too." Marilyn looked up at her son and grasped the hand that clutched her shoulder.

Pat Jr. leaned down and hugged her.

She regained her composure and continued. "Patrick said this boy had been cruel to the girl, that he'd mistreated her badly, that he deserved to die. The only way to stop the boy from continuing to abuse the girl was to kill him."

"Did your husband tell you the girl's name?" Rachel asked, hoping beyond hope that he had.

Marilyn shook her head. "No." She glanced from Rachel to Dean and then up at her son. "Even on his deathbed, he wanted to protect her."

Several days following Rachel and Dean's interview with Marilyn Dewey and a follow-up interview that was officially recorded, the Portland P.D. had permanently closed the cold case file on the Cupid Killer murder. Chief Charlie Young made the wise decision to delay making the news public until after the St. Elizabeth's reunion. And Dean had managed to persuade the powers that be not to press charges against Mrs. Dewey, a woman in her sixties who suffered from crippling arthritis. In Rachel's opinion, the woman had suffered enough, and Dean agreed. It seemed they agreed on a great many things.

If only Mrs. Dewey could have given them the girl's name . . .

Everything made sense now. All except one of the old puzzle pieces had been placed together. Patrick Dewey had been having an affair with a girl Jake had also been involved with, a girl Jake had abused. Patrick had plotted Jake's demise and killed his rival in a spectacular way. The expert bowman had shot Jake directly in the heart with "Cupid's arrow."

But what had happened after Jake's murder? Had the girl turned against Patrick? Or had Patrick ended the secret affair?

Rachel had thought surely someone other than Patrick Dewey and the girl had known about their affair. Where and when had they met? A local motel? Somewhere out of town? Had someone possibly seen the girl with Patrick?

She had racked her brain trying to figure out a way to unearth this girl's identity, but in the end, she realized that the span of twenty years worked against their discovering the truth. Would any motels or hotels still have records from twenty years ago? And even if they did, Patrick would hardly have used his real name. And she certainly couldn't expect any former hotel employee to remember a man and teenage girl who had secret rendezvous in 1986.

As each day had passed, Rachel's frustration level had risen. If not for Dean's wonderful calming effect on her, she wasn't sure she'd have made it through without a major meltdown. As she lay in Dean's arms each night, she wondered how she'd gotten so damn lucky. She could regret not finding love with Dean years ago, but there was no point in looking back. Today was all that mattered. For Dean and her and for their old high-school friends. Jake Marcott's murder case had been solved; the murderer was dead. But the recent murders remained unsolved, the killer still out there, ready to kill again.

Tonight was the night. Everything was in order. Every detail planned. They would all be here, the classmates from the graduating classes of 1986. The alumni from St. Elizabeth's, Western Catholic, and even some graduates from Washington High School. The police had brought in bomb-sniffing dogs and the authorities had done what they thought was a thorough search of the building. But no one remembered the old basement area under the gymnasium. She doubted that there was anyone still alive who knew about that subterranean level that could be reached only through the basement of the school itself and not directly from the gym. The only reason she knew the location was because her great-uncle had once been the custodian, back in the sixties, and he'd told her about it.

If the police had searched down there, they would have found her secret room, the senior lockers, and the souvenirs from Mandy, Aurora, and Haylie. If that had happened, she would have had to formulate a new plan rather quickly, perhaps continue the executions beyond tonight's event. But as luck would have it, she didn't have to change her plans.

After helping the decorating committee set up tables and chairs in the old gym and spread colorful streamers from the bleachers and rafters, she had separated from the others as they left for the afternoon and had made her way into the basement. Several days earlier, she had brought everything she would need for tonight and stored it all down here. And when she reappeared tonight, dressed to the nines, no one would be the wiser.

If no one got in her way, if nothing interfered with her plans, three people would die tonight: Kristen, Rachel, and Lindsay. Whichever one she could get to the easiest would be the first to die.

Giggling happily, she danced around and around in the forgotten cellar beneath the gym, Patrick Dewey's old Beretta in her hand. He had given it to her, all those years ago—an unregistered pistol—to use as protection.

"If that bastard ever tries to rape you again, shoot him," Patrick had said.

Dear, sweet, loving Patrick.

He had truly cared about her. And she'd never had the heart to tell him that although she hated Jake with every fiber of her being, she also loved him.

Patrick wouldn't have understood.

If you hadn't been at my side that night, I wouldn't have had the courage to kill Jake and end the nightmare my life had become. You were my white knight, Patrick, my avenging angel.

Rachel gave herself one final inspection in the full-length mirror on the back of the closet door. Here she was, wearing an ankle-length teal green satin dress that clung to her curves and accentuated her breasts, preparing to attend her twenty-year class reunion. A reunion marred by the recent murders of three classmates and an all-too-real threat that others were in danger. If she'd had her way, they would have canceled tonight's affair, but with so many people actually looking forward to the reunion dance and so many having come in from out of state, the committee had decided they didn't have much choice but to continue with the event as planned.

Checking her watch—six-fifteen—she heaved a deep sigh and picked up the tiny diamond hoops from the dresser and inserted them into her pierced ears. Dean was picking her up at six-thirty, which gave her just enough time to collect her thoughts and calm her jittery nerves.

When her cell phone rang, she gasped. Cursing herself for being so nervous, she flipped open the phone and checked the caller ID.

"Hello, Dean," she said playfully, trying to act as if she weren't worried sick.

"Listen, honey. I need you to get down to headquarters immediately."

"Why? What's happened?"

"I just got a call from Pat Dewey. He and his mother are in Portland and they're about two miles from headquarters. It seems when she finished cleaning out her bedroom closet this afternoon, intending to either pack or trash what was left, she came across some photographs that were in an old suitcase that her sons had brought down from the attic."

"Photographs of what?"

"Of whom," Dean corrected. "She isn't sure who the person in the photos is, but she thinks it could be the girl Patrick had the affair with twenty years ago."

"Holy shit!"

"Yeah, tell me about it."

"Could Pat describe the girl to you? Could you—"

"He couldn't give me a description," Dean said. "It seems his mother won't let him see the pictures."

"What? Why?"

"He thinks it's because the girl in the photos is probably naked. He told me that his mother said she will hand those photographs over only to you."

"Because I'm a woman."

"Yeah, that would be my guess."

"I'll get to headquarters as soon as possible, but in late Saturday afternoon traffic, it'll take me a good thirty minutes."

"Just drive carefully."

"I'll try."

Lindsay would rather be anywhere than here. With the old gymnasium decorated so nicely, it reminded her far too much of the last time this building had hosted a special dance. The Valentine's Day dance of 1986. Only back then, everything had been decked out in red, white, and pink, with paper hearts and fat little

Cupids adorning every nook and cranny. If Wyatt weren't at her side tonight, she would have run out the door as fast as she could and gotten as far away from St. Elizabeth's as humanly possible.

"We didn't have to come here tonight." Wyatt placed his arm around her waist as he whispered in her ear.

"Yes, we did. I did." She turned and smiled at him. A forced smile. "I've been running from the past far too long. I ran from you, from our son . . . and from Jake's memory. I need to do this, so that I can lay his ghost to rest."

"Whatever you need to do to vanquish Jake's ghost and put the past behind us, I'll help you. Just say the word and—"

"Go outside with me," she told him. "I need to go back inside the labyrinth, to the spot where Jake was killed. Where I found him."

"Are you sure?" Wyatt asked. "Why put yourself through that kind of torture?"

"I can't explain it. It's just something I need to do."

"All right. Do you want to go now or wait until later?"

"Now, before I lose my nerve."

As they headed for the exit, they ran into April Wright. "Where are you two going? Not leaving so soon, I hope."

"No, we're just going to get a breath of fresh air," Lindsay lied. "We'll be back before things really get started."

"You'd better be careful out there," April said. "You wouldn't catch me wandering around outside in the dark. Not tonight. Not with somebody out there just waiting to take potshots at us."

"It's not dark yet. There's plenty of daylight left," Wyatt said. "Besides, Lindsay won't be alone, not for a single minute."

"Well, that's good to hear."

Wyatt cupped her elbow and led her out of the gym and onto the school grounds. "I think it's this way, isn't it?"

"Yes," she replied, "right over there."

Hidden deep inside the maze of hedges, the huge oak tree towered high into the evening sky. Beneath the oak, the sculpture of the Madonna still resided in a place of honor. This was where she'd found Jake. The arrow that had pierced his heart had pinned him to the tree.

Suddenly flashes of memory popped into Lindsay's mind, like an accelerated movie clip. She saw Jake's sightless eyes staring at her. The blood on his shirt. The still-smoldering cigarette lying at his feet. She could hear her own screams as she rushed toward him, praying that he was still alive.

But he was dead.

Lindsay shivered uncontrollably.

Wyatt wrapped her in his strong, comforting arms. "Let it go. You're here with me now and you're safe. You've confronted the demons from the past. It's over."

She sobbed against his chest while he soothed her. He allowed her several minutes to recover, then grasped her hand and said, "It's time to get back to the dance."

Marilyn Dewey sat in her wheelchair, a small manila folder clasped in her weathered, arthritis-crippled hands. She looked up the moment the door to the captain's office opened and Rachel walked in. Rachel nodded at Dean, who stood in the corner, then went straight to Marilyn.

Rachel pulled out a chair, dragged it directly across from Marilyn, and sat down facing the other woman. "I believe you have something you want to show me."

Marilyn's dark, soulful eyes lifted, and she stared directly at Rachel. "He took pictures of her." She lowered her voice to a whisper. "Nude pictures."

"You found them today?" Rachel nodded to the envelope in Marilyn's lap.

"They were in Patrick's old suitcase . . . one he hadn't used in years."

"May I see the photographs?" Rachel held out her hand, trying her best not to push, not to be overly eager. But God in heaven, these old pictures could reveal the identity of a murderer and thus prevent any future deaths.

Marilyn lifted the envelope, as careful with it as if it were made of spun glass, and handed it to Rachel. "He—he wrote things on the back of each photograph. Things about her."

Rachel released a chest-tight breath as she clasped the envelope. "Would you prefer that Lieutenant McMichaels and I look at these—"

"No," Marilyn cried. "Not him. Only you."

"All right, only me. Do you want me to look at them in another room?"

"Yes, please."

Pat Dewey placed both hands on his mother's quivering shoulders.

"Stay here," Rachel told Dean as she headed for the door.

He nodded.

Rachel closed the door behind her, went straight to the captain's secretary's desk, sat down, and opened the envelope. With her hands trembling and her heartbeat strumming in her ears, she turned the envelope upside down and shook out the contents. A stack of old Polaroid photos fell into her waiting hands.

Oh, God! Oh, God!

She turned the photos over and groaned when she immediately recognized the naked girl in the first picture. Sitting demurely on the edge of a bed, her index finger stuck seductively in her mouth, she stared at the camera. Wide-eyed, but far from innocent.

Rachel hurriedly looked through the two dozen snapshots of the teenager, each pose slightly different, obviously all the pictures were not taken at the same time. She read a few of the notes on the backs of the photos, then one in particular caught her eye.

Merciful Lord!

That one final missing piece in the puzzle fell into place.

Rachel stuffed the photos back in the envelope, got up, and rushed into the captain's office.

"Put a call in to the patrol cars closest to St. Elizabeth's and send them over to the school," Rachel said. "The killer is there right now. Lindsay and Kristen are in immediate danger!"

Chapter 33

Lindsay excused herself to go to the restroom. Martina and Kristen were coming out as she was going in. When she walked into the locker room, which you had to go through to reach the girls' restroom, she saw several old classmates standing around talking, but once in the restroom, she was alone. A shiver of apprehension raced up her spine. The eerie quiet inside the stall unnerved her. She hurried, relieving herself quickly; then in her haste, she wound up pulling a run in her stockings when her fingernail caught in the nylon. Drat!

If she weren't such a stickler for hygiene, she might have forgone washing her hands and gotten the hell out of this poorly lit, spooky bathroom. But good habits took precedent over a case of nerves. Just as she turned on the faucet, she caught a glimpse of someone in her peripheral vision, someone just entering the ladies' restroom.

"Hello, Lindsay," the familiar voice said. "You look as beautiful tonight as you did the night Jake died."

She whirled around to face the woman who stood only a few feet away, a pistol in her hand.

Dean drove like the proverbial bat out of hell on the trip from downtown to St. Elizabeth's. On the drive over, Rachel had kept in contact with the patrolmen who had been sent to the site of the reunion. Only a few minutes before Dean screeched to a halt in front of the gymnasium, Officer Kyle Williams reported that a woman named Lindsay Farrell was missing and her boyfriend was on the verge of tearing the place apart, brick by brick.

* * *

Lindsay did as she was told, afraid not to, realizing that her would-be killer wouldn't hesitate to shoot her.

"I'd prefer we did this in private, but if you force me to, I'll shoot you right here, right now," she said.

Lindsay realized she meant it and knew that the only way to buy herself some time—and keep herself alive—was to cooperate. But only up to a point. Her abductor was so involved in keeping them out of sight as she led her out a back door of the gym and through the covered open corridor leading into the school building that she didn't notice as Lindsay opened her evening bag and began dropping items. Items that wouldn't make any noise as they hit the ground.

Shades of Hansel and Gretel, Lindsay thought. *But one does what one has to do when in the clutches of a wicked witch.*

Where on earth is she taking me? Lindsay wondered as she was led down a flight of wooden stairs and into the basement.

Not wanting to create a panic that would complicate the situation, Rachel and Dean called for backup, including the SWAT team, then sent the patrol officers off to search for Lindsay while they spoke to Wyatt, Martina, Craig, Kristen, and Ross. Dean told his friends what he'd told the officers: "If you find them, do not try to confront her. Call me and let me handle it."

They separated into groups so they could cover more ground twice as fast. After Dean handed flashlights to the men, Ross and Kristen went in one direction, while Wyatt, Craig, and Martina went in another. As they hunted for Lindsay, the reunion went on as if this unnerving drama weren't happening simultaneously.

Rachel knew that if they didn't find Lindsay soon, it would be too late. If only Marilyn Dewey could have discovered those photographs yesterday instead of today.

"Lindsay found Jake's body inside the labyrinth that night," Rachel said. "What if that's where she's taken Lindsay, back to the scene of the crime?"

"She's just twisted enough to do something like that." Dean aimed his flashlight toward the rows of tall hedges. "Let's go."

As Rachel and Dean started into the labyrinth, Ross and Kristen emerged from the pathway that led into the maze.

"Seems we had the same idea," Dean said.

"Apparently," Ross replied.

"We didn't find anyone," Kristen said. "Now what? I thought for sure that's where she would take Lindsay."

"Let's separate again and continue searching." Rachel did her best to keep her voice calm, despite the growing anxiety she felt.

Lindsay removed the last of the dollar bills—four in all—that she'd placed in her small evening bag. Before she could release the money and allow it to sail softly to the floor, the final clue to mark her trail, the madwoman at her side stopped abruptly in front of a stack of wooden crates and aimed her flashlight straight ahead.

She stuck the gun in Lindsay's ribs. "Move behind the crates." Lindsay did as she was told.

Her abductor forced her forward as she shined her flashlight at an old wooden door half hidden behind the crates. When she reached around Lindsay and turned the doorknob, Lindsay considered putting up a fight. But the feel of the deadly weapon pressing painfully into her ribs made her think twice.

"Where are you taking me?" Lindsay managed to say, fear vibrating her voice.

"Somewhere no one will find you, not until after Rachel and Kristen join you."

Lindsay hazarded a glance at the woman she had known since they were teenagers, and wondered why she had never realized how unstable she was, how unstable she had probably always been.

While her captor concentrated on opening the door and at the same time keeping her gun against Lindsay's side, Lindsay opened her palm and dropped the last dollar bill.

Please, dear God, let Wyatt realize I'm missing. Let him be searching for me.

What was that sound? Was that music she heard? Yes, it was. She couldn't quite make out the tune, but there was music coming from behind the door.

Nudging the gun deep into Lindsay's side, her captor ordered, "Move it. Now!"

Lindsay stepped over the concrete threshold and entered a brightly lit, dank-smelling room. So engrossed in the sight before her, Lindsay barely heard the door close behind her.

My God!

At least a dozen Coleman lanterns, lined up on the floor in front of a row of old lockers, illuminated the cavernous room.

Lockers? The senior lockers from St. Elizabeth's? Was that possible?

"It took quite some effort to move the lockers in here," she told Lindsay. "But it was well worth it, don't you think?" She urged Lindsay forward, forcing her to walk past the lockers to the opposite side of the room.

Lindsay noticed her name on one locker. Rachel's, Kristen's, and Martina's on three others. Those four lockers were open and empty. The others were closed.

"Only four more to go," she said, smiling at Lindsay. "And then it will all be complete. Just in time for the wrecking ball."

"Why? I—I don't understand."

Wyatt, you are searching for me, aren't you? You've called Rachel and Dean. You've told the police that I'm missing.

"All you need to know is that you're going to die."

"Why? What did I ever do to you to make you hate me? What did any of us do?"

"Keep walking until you reach the far wall, then turn around slowly."

Continuing to move toward the wall, her back to her abductor, Lindsay pleaded, "Tell me what we did to make you hate us."

"You and the others were such little snots, excluding me from everything, shutting me out, making me feel worthless."

"But we didn't mean to make you feel that way." *Keep her talking. Buy yourself all the time you can.* "I'm sorry. Truly I am. If I could do anything to make it up to you, I would."

"Did you know that I hated you the most back then? And I still do. I want you to suffer before I kill you. I want you to know just a little of the pain I've felt all these years. Now, turn around and look at me. I want to watch your face when I shoot you."

Lindsay paused, then turned and stared directly at the woman who intended to kill her.

"Will you tell me why you hate me the most?" *Try not to think about her threat to make you suffer. You cannot give in to your fears.*

"Because Jake wanted you more than he wanted me."

Rushing forward, insane hatred marring her facial features, Bella Marcott shoved Lindsay up against the wall, the gun almost touching Lindsay's belly. As her shoulder hit the concrete, Lindsay caught a glimpse of the huge red heart painted on the wall behind her. A morbid reminder of a long-ago St. Valentine Day's dance.

And the music . . . The song coming from the portable CD player on the floor near the lockers was a familiar tune. "Can't Fight This Feeling" by REO Speedwagon. Once upon a time, it had been her and Jake's song.

When her gaze connected to Bella's, she saw malicious anger and sheer madness in her eyes. Eyes so very much like Jake's.

* * *

Kristen and Ross crossed paths with Wyatt twice during their frantic search. The first time he'd been with Martina and Craig, but now he was alone. Alone and angry and blaming himself for Lindsay's abduction.

"You couldn't have gone to the ladies' room with her," Kristen said, doing her best to comfort him.

"No, but I should have insisted that we find you so you could go with her."

Kristen placed her hand on Wyatt's shoulder and rubbed reassuringly. "We're going to find her."

Wyatt covered his mouth as he drew in a deep breath, barely holding his emotions in check. "If we don't find her soon . . ."

Bella will kill her. Kristen knew what he was thinking, what they were all thinking. It seemed unbelievable that Jake's own sister had been responsible for his death, even if she hadn't actually released the arrow from the crossbow and nailed him through the heart.

"Come on." Kristen tugged on Wyatt's arm. "Ross and I are going to search the side entrance into St. Elizabeth's that connects to the gym. Why don't you take a look at the back entrances? I know the police officers have already checked, but they could have overlooked something."

Wyatt stared at her, a crazed expression on his face as if he were on the verge of unraveling, but he nodded, indicating he had understood her. Then he turned and headed for the back of the old school.

"He's half out of his mind," Kristen said.

"I would be, too, if you were the one missing."

Kristen reached out and caressed her husband's cheek. How close they'd come to losing each other, to letting their marriage and their love slip away from them.

"We're going to find her—alive." Kristen pointed the beam of her flashlight straight in front of her, aiming it toward the covered breezeway between the gymnasium and the school building.

Ross kept pace with her, slowing when she slowed, speeding up when she did. As they walked along the corridor between the two structures, Kristen stopped suddenly.

"What is it?" he asked.

"I don't know." She shot a beam of light toward the concrete walkway where something white had caught her eye. "What's that?" She bent over and picked up the Kleenex, then inspected it thoroughly. "Someone blotted their lipstick on this."

"Anyone could have dropped it."

"This is a pink lipstick. Lindsay was wearing pink."

"Kristen, don't—"

"She could have dropped it on purpose, as a clue."

"Okay, maybe you're right. But—"

"I'm calling Rachel." Using her free hand, Kristen flipped open her cell phone.

"How does it feel knowing you're going to die?" Bella pointed the gun directly at Lindsay's heart.

"I'm afraid. Is that what you want to hear? I'm terrified. I don't want to die."

Bella smiled. "Jake didn't have time to be scared, not until the very last minute when he realized I was going to kill him."

"You killed Jake?" *But how was that possible?* Lindsay wondered. Hadn't Rachel and Dean told her and Kris, in strictest confidence, that a man named Patrick Dewey had killed Jake?

"You couldn't have killed Jake." Lindsay spoke without thinking.

Bella glared at her. "What makes you say that?"

"He—he was your brother. You loved him."

"And he loved me."

What would Bella do if I rushed her? Would she shoot me? Could I jump her before she could fire? If I did, maybe I could wrestle the gun away from her. I have to do something. I can't stand here against this big red heart and wait for her to kill me.

Holding the pistol in both hands, Bella kept it aimed at Lindsay. "You thought he loved you, but he didn't. You were as big a fool as the others."

"You're right. I was a fool." *Agree with her. Say whatever you think she wants to hear.* Lindsay clutched her small evening bag, holding it against her waist.

"Too bad you didn't realize that twenty years ago." Bella smiled, the tilt of her lips bordering on a snarl. "I think you should know that I plan to shoot you more than once. I'm going to start with your legs and then your arms and then . . ." Bella's sick laughter echoed in the underground dungeon.

Sour, salty bile rose up into Lindsay's throat. A rush of pure fear flooded her senses. This couldn't be happening. It had to be a horrible nightmare. She couldn't die. Not now. Not when she and Wyatt had reconnected. Not when they had just found their son.

"What makes you think I'll stand here and let you use me for target practice?"

Bella stared quizzically at Lindsay. "Because I have a weapon and you don't."

"If you're going to kill me anyway, what do I have to lose?"

"It's your choice." Bella shrugged. "If you try anything, I'll kill you now. Play by my rules and you might live another hour."

Their tense gazes locked.

"You think maybe someone will find you if you can just buy enough time, don't you? It's not going to happen. No one knows about this part of the basement. It's my little secret. Of course, once the building is leveled, it is possible they'll find your bodies in the rubble. Yours and Kristen's and Rachel's."

This basement hideaway, the row of old lockers, the music from the past all blurred together, the entire scene surreal. Lindsay's mind whirled with thoughts and questions and silent prayers.

When Lindsay shut her eyes as she made a final plea to God— *I don't want to die!*—Bella screamed, "Open your eyes and look at me!"

Shivering, fear clutching her fiercely, she looked at Bella.

"Now, that's better." Bella glanced at the row of lockers. "I think I'll put your evening bag and maybe your earrings in your locker."

It's now or never, Lindsay thought. While she's not looking . . .

Lindsay lunged at Bella, who whipped around, aimed the gun and fired. The bullet barely missed Lindsay's foot, hitting the floor and blasting shards of old concrete across Lindsay's leg. As the pieces scattered, several nipped her foot and leg. Yelping in pain, she dropped her evening bag as she jumped and quickly backed into the wall behind her.

As her heartbeat thundered in her ears, Lindsay waited for the next shot—the one that could end her life.

Rachel stared at the brick school, dark and foreboding, looking exactly like what it was—an abandoned old building. Dean had sent the patrol officers in pairs to the front and back entrances but had heard nothing from them. It would take time to do a thorough search of every room, including the basement.

Rachel's phone rang. She answered on the third ring.

"Rach, come to the side entrance of the school, the one closest to the gym," Kristen said. "We've found something in the open corridor."

Within minutes, Rachel held a lipstick-stained Kleenex in her hand.

"We found it right here," Ross said, pointing to the exact spot, only a couple of feet from the side entrance. "We tried the door and it seems to be locked."

Dean shined his flashlight through the panes of the half-glass double doors. "Rachel, come take a look."

He kept the light pointing straight down on the floor inside the hallway. There lying on the floor was what looked like another tissue.

"We have to get in there right now." Rachel's instincts and training told her that time was of the essence.

Using the end of his flashlight, Dean broke the glass in a lower pane, carefully stuck his hand inside, and released the interior lock. "It was locked from the inside," he said, "which means someone came through this way and locked it."

When Kristen and Ross followed Dean and Rachel, Dean turned to them and said, "Wait here. And call Rachel if you see or hear anything unusual."

The couple simultaneously nodded agreement.

"Where do we go from here?" Dean asked Rachel. "Up or down or forward?"

"You check the up stairs and I'll check the down," she said. "If we don't find anything, we'll move forward into the building."

"I'll contact Officer Williams while I'm checking out the stairs," Dean said.

Rachel opened the door that led into the basement, shined her flashlight on the wooden staircase, and took several steps downward. There lying on the fifth step was what looked like a credit card. Rachel stooped to pick it up, took a good look at it, and hurried back up the stairs. After closing the door, she called out to Dean, who rushed down from the top of the upper staircase.

"Take a look. It's Lindsay's driver's license."

With her back against the wall and her foot and leg bleeding, Lindsay tried to think rationally. But how was that possible? She was in the clutches of a crazy person, someone who had already killed three other women.

"Bella, you don't have to do this. You aren't yourself," Lindsay said. "You need help."

Bella's serene smile unnerved Lindsay.

"I needed help twenty years ago," Bella said. "If someone had stopped Jake . . . if they had kept him from hurting me . . ."

"How did Jake hurt you?" *Keep talking. Buy time. Pray that someone finds you before it's too late.*

"Patrick knew. He cared when no one else did."

"Who was Patrick?"

Bella's smile widened. Her eyes glazed over. "Patrick loved me. When I told him about Jake . . . I should have told Patrick first when I found out, not Jake. Patrick wouldn't have made me do it. He would have let me keep my baby."

"Baby? You were pregnant? You had a child by this man named Patrick?"

"I wanted my baby, but Jake said I couldn't have it. He made me have an abortion. Patrick said that was wrong. That's why he killed . . . no, that's not right. Patrick wanted to kill Jake for what he did to me. But I wanted to kill Jake myself. I remember touching the bow, watching the arrow fly through the air. Jake couldn't believe what I'd done. He just stared at me."

"Bella, you didn't kill Jake. You couldn't have."

Bella shook her head. "You're wrong. Don't try to confuse me."

"You might have wanted to kill Jake, but you didn't."

"I did! I killed him!" Clutching the gun in both hands, Bella walked toward Lindsay, stopping less than three feet from her. "I killed Jake. And I killed Haylie and Aurora and Mandy. And I'm going to kill you."

Lindsay's legs shook so badly that she could barely stand. Sweat peppered her face and seeped through her bra and panties.

I don't want to die.

I'm not going to die!

Dean called in the patrol officers and gave them instructions, then he and Rachel went down into the basement. They followed a trail of items, scattered ten to fifteen feet apart. Another tissue, then the empty tissue pack. A credit card, and then dollar bills.

Good girl, Lindsay. You didn't panic. You used your head and left us clues.

When the final clue ended near a solid block wall, Rachel clenched her teeth. "This doesn't make any sense. It's as if they disappeared into nowhere."

Dean waved his flashlight all around the area, searching for an opening of any kind. He nudged Rachel when the light fell on the top of what appeared to be a door half hidden behind a stack of mildewed wooden crates.

While Dean kept the door spotlighted, Rachel inspected it, then pressed her ear against it. "Listen."

Dean leaned against the door. "It's music."

"Do you know what song that is? It's Lindsay and Jake's song."

"Son of a bitch!"

Dean handed Rachel the flashlight, then tried the door, which opened without any trouble whatsoever, without him exerting an ounce of extra pressure. And the old door didn't creak, made hardly a sound.

"Someone has been using this door fairly often," Dean said quietly, then motioned to Rachel as he pulled his regulation Glock from his shoulder holster. "Stay behind me."

They moved slowly, cautiously, into another room of the basement, the area illuminated by a dozen lanterns placed in a row in front of a line of old lockers. *My God, those are our lockers from senior high,* Rachel thought. *How is that possible?*

A portable CD player lay on the floor, the popular tune from the mid 1980s filling the air with sweet music and words of love.

Standing at the far end of the long, narrow room was Lindsay, her trembling body outlined by a huge red heart painted on the block wall directly behind her. Bella stood a couple of feet in front of Lindsay, her back to Dean and Rachel, a pistol pointed directly at Lindsay

"Jake didn't love you," Bella said. "He didn't love any of you."

"You're right," Lindsay said, her voice quivering. "He he didn't love any of us."

"He loved me," Bella shouted. "But he made me kill my baby and he didn't make you kill your baby. Tell me why! It wasn't fair!"

"Why—why did Jake make you kill your baby?" Lindsay asked.

"Because he knew it might be his."

Lindsay gasped.

"We'd been lovers since I was twelve years old. I didn't want to do it with him, not at first. It hurt. But he forced me. He told me he loved me. He promised me . . . But he lied. He kept making me do it. Over and over again. And then he made me kill my baby. He took me to some quack doctor who cut my baby out of me and ruined me forever."

Dean crept closer and closer to the madwoman with the gun, one slow, nerve-wracking step after another. Rachel held her breath when she realized that Lindsay saw Dean.

"That's why I had to kill him," Bella said. "He had to be punished for what he did to me. Patrick said that he was going to kill Jake, but I told him that I wanted to do it, that it was my right to kill him."

Don't let on that you see Dean, Rachel thought. *Please, Lindsay, don't give him away. Your life depends on it. She's insane. She'll kill you, just as she killed Haylie and Aurora and Mandy.*

"I didn't realize that you knew how to use a crossbow," Lindsay said, her gaze fixed on the gun less than twenty-four inches from her heart.

That's it, Linds, keep her talking, keep her distracted until Dean can get closer. Just a few more feet.

"I didn't know anything about crossbows," Bella admitted. "Patrick was an expert bowman. He knew how to kill Jake."

"I thought you said you killed Jake."

"I did. I hated Jake."

"How did you kill him?"

"You know how. With a bow and arrow. I was there, hidden in the hedges, waiting and watching. Jake was leaning against the old oak tree, smoking a cigarette. We caught him by surprise. Patrick had his crossbow and . . . No, that's not right. I had the crossbow. I killed Jake." She shook her head. "But Patrick cocked the bow. I watched him. I was hiding, and when Patrick aimed and fired at Dean, I did it with him. No, that's not right. I was watching when the arrow hit Jake in the heart. But I killed him." She screamed the final words as she grasped the gun with both hands. "And I'm going to kill you. All of you."

"Bella!" Dean called her name.

She whirled around and fired. The bullet zoomed past Dean and cracked a chunk out of the wall behind him. Bella Marcott snapped back around and aimed the gun at Lindsay.

"Don't!" Dean cried. "Put the gun down."

A second shot rang out in the dank, cavernous room. Lindsay screamed. The music from a long-ago night continued playing. Rachel rushed forward as Bella crumpled to the floor, facedown, a single bullet wound in the back of her head.

Rachel wrapped her arms around a nearly hysterical Lindsay. "It's all right. You're safe. Bella's dead."

Gulping for air, Lindsay wept as she asked, "She was crazy, wasn't she? She thought Jake raped her. And she kept talking about this man named Patrick. Jake didn't rape her, did he? He wasn't the father of the child she aborted, was he? Jake wasn't like that. Was he?"

"Hush, now," Rachel said soothingly. "I'll explain everything later. All that matters is that you're safe. And this nightmare is finally over for all of us."

Epilogue

Wyatt and Lindsay Goddard hosted a New Year's Eve party in the penthouse apartment they rented overlooking downtown Portland. Lindsay had wanted a second home here in Oregon so that she could visit not only her family but her dear friends, Kristen and Rachel, as often as she liked. The couple had been married in November, a small, elegant wedding, with Kristen and Rachel as attendants and Leo as Wyatt's best man. Their relationship with their son was building slowly, and although he had spent Christmas with his adoptive family, he was here now with Lindsay and Wyatt for New Year's.

Kristen and Ross seemed truly happy, Rachel thought, almost as happy as she and Dean were. Amazing how a person's life could completely change—for the better—in less than a year's time. Actually, in a little over six months. When she had returned to Portland for the twenty-year class reunion, intent on finding Jake Marcott's killer, she'd had no idea how everything would turn out in the end. She certainly hadn't counted on falling madly in love with the bane of her teenage existence. And neither she nor any of her classmates would have imagined that Jake had begun raping his younger sister when she was only twelve and had forced her have an abortion at sixteen. Poor Bella. Poor crazy Bella. To the very end, she had truly believed that she, not Patrick Dewey, had killed Jake. In her delusional mind, she had hated Jake so vehemently and wanted him dead so badly that somehow, over the years, she had convinced herself that she had actually shot him.

Nothing could change the past. No power on earth could give back Haylie and Aurora and Mandy to the people who loved them. And that fact alone was reason enough to celebrate life, to make a toast to the bright and happy new year that lay ahead. Life was for the living. Savor every precious moment.

"Am I the only one who feels just slightly guilty to be so happy?" Lindsay asked.

Kristen and Rachel had joined their hostess in the kitchen to help her replenish the snack trays that their husbands and the two teenagers had wiped clean.

Kristen sighed. "I know what you mean. Here we three are with so much to be thankful for and several of our old classmates are gone. Aurora will never see her grandchildren, and Mandy won't be around to see her daughter grow up. And poor Haylie."

"If only we had known twenty years ago what Jake was really like, what he was doing to his sister." Rachel shook her head. "Maybe we could have helped Bella and prevented what happened this past summer."

"We can't change the past," Kristen said. "All we can do is appreciate how lucky we all are and not waste precious time on regrets."

"Hear, hear." Lindsay removed a sheet of mini quiches from the oven.

"I know one thing for sure—Ross and I will never again take each other and our marriage for granted," Kristen said. "We know that from here on out, we're going to have to work at it every day and find ways to compromise. But it's worth whatever we have to do because in the end all that matters is that we love each other."

"You're right about that." Rachel had not gone into marriage with Dean believing everything would be perfect. But Kris was right—in the end all that truly mattered was that they loved each other. "I gave up my job in Alabama and moved here permanently to be with Dean and I know I'll never regret making that decision."

Lindsay removed the warm mini quiches from the baking sheet onto the serving tray. "My being married to Wyatt seems like a dream. When I think about how many years we wasted, how many years I—"

"No regrets," Rachel said. "We all made mistakes in the past, the biggest one being the fact that we were all infatuated with Jake

Marcott. Let's just chalk up our stupidity to having been young
and foolish."

Kristen and Lindsay smiled sadly and nodded.

"Leo is going to spend his spring break with us," Lindsay said.

"That's wonderful," Kristen and Rachel responded simultaneously.

"I know we will always have to share him with his mother—
and yes, she is his mother in all the ways that truly matter—but
Wyatt and I are just grateful to have him in our lives."

"Have you and Wyatt thought about having another child together?" Rachel asked.

"I've thought about it," Lindsay admitted. "But I haven't discussed it with Wyatt."

The distinctive chimes of the grandfather clock in the foyer
announced the three-quarter hour.

"It's almost midnight," Kristen said. "We'd better join our
men if we want a New Year's Eve kiss."

Leaving the mini quiches in the kitchen and leaving all the un-
happiness and tragedy in the past where it belonged, the three old
friends walked into the living room and into the arms of the men
they loved.

As those final countdown moments drew near, the small, intimate group of old friends came together, champagne and
sparkling grape juice glasses in their hands. Rachel noticed Kristen's daughter, Lissa, nonchalantly making her way closer to Leo,
whom she'd been flirting with all evening. *Now, that would be a
pair,* Rachel thought.

Dean leaned down and whispered in her ear, "That is grape
juice in your glass, isn't it?"

"Of course. You know I wouldn't drink anything else, not
now."

"What are you two lovebirds whispering about?" Kristen
asked. "I can understand Lindsay and Wyatt acting like newlyweds since they just got married last month, but you two have
been married since September. Really, now!"

Everyone laughed, happiness filling the room.

Rachel looked to Dean for approval before sharing their wonderful news. He nodded. She took a deep breath, exhaled, and
said, "We're pregnant."

The women shared hugs and kisses. The guys shook Dean's
hand and slapped him on the back. The two teenagers stood side

by side and smiled at each other. Then they all lifted their glasses and made a toast—to Rachel and Dean, to good friends, and to the future.

The clock struck midnight. A new year dawned.

Leo turned to Lissa and kissed her on the cheek. She threw her arms around his neck and planted one right on his mouth, then hand in hand they walked to the windows to watch the fireworks bursting brightly in the dark sky.

Dean pulled Rachel into his arms. "Happy New Year, Mrs. McMichaels." He laid his hand over her still-flat belly. "I love you and I love our little rug rat."

Then he kissed her passionately as the other two couples followed their lead.

Dear Reader,

How great is it that you picked up a copy of MOST LIKELY TO DIE? I hope you enjoyed the girls of "St. Lizzy's," and their love stories set in a background of tense suspense. I was more than thrilled to write my portion of the book and to be able to set the bulk of the story in Portland, Oregon. Portland is special to me as it was the closest "big city" to the small logging town where I grew up, so I felt right at home introducing you to the area!

I've got lots of great news on the horizon. For those of you who didn't get a chance to read the hardcover edition of SHIVER last year, the paperback will soon be available. In March 2007, you can visit Our Lady of Virtues Hospital, an abandoned mental hospital that puts the weird goings-on at St. Elizabeth's to shame. SHIVER is Detective Reuben Montoya of the New Orleans Police Department's story. You remember Montoya. He was first introduced in HOT BLOODED and has popped up in my New Orleans books ever since. Now, the cocky, brash detective gets his own tale, one that involves a twenty-year-old mystery and a beautiful, spunky woman, Abby Chastain, who is ultimately tied to the old hospital. I think you'll like it.

In April 2007, right on the heels of the publication of the paperback edition of SHIVER, is my next hardcover novel, ABSOLUTE FEAR, the sequel to SHIVER. If you finished SHIVER, then you know there were some loose ends left at the end of the book. ABSOLUTE FEAR answers those questions and brings in some new characters: Defense Attorney Dennis Cole and Eve Renner, his lover, the woman who claims he tried to kill her. He's been incarcerated and now he wants the truth and vengeance, not necessarily in that order. ABSOLUTE FEAR is an edge-of-your-seat thriller, a tense story of lies, deceit and betrayal. I think it's the perfect follow-up to SHIVER!

Also, I've got a special surprise for all of you who loved IF SHE ONLY KNEW. I have a new novel, ALMOST DEAD, that brings back some familiar faces from San Francisco. Remember Cissy Cahill, Marla's daughter in IF SHE ONLY KNEW? Well, it's ten years later and Cissy's back with a sexy husband and an innocent baby. Once again Cissy's life is turned upside down. Everything she holds true turns out to be false. Her marriage is a sham. Both she and her child are in life-threatening danger, and people around her start dying. Fortunately Anthony Paterno of the San Francisco Police Department is on the case, but he might just be too late. ALMOST DEAD is a bizarre, twisted tale that's guaranteed to keep you up late. Look for this original paperback in August 2007! In the meantime, please turn the page for an excerpt of SHIVER!

Again, thanks for picking up a copy of MOST LIKELY TO DIE. If you want to contact me about any of my books, you can do so through my website: www.lisajackson.com.

In the meantime, keep reading!

Lisa Jackson

Twenty years earlier
Our Lady of Virtues Hospital
Near New Orleans, Louisiana

She felt his breath.

Warm.

Seductive.

Erotically evil.

A presence that caused the hairs on the back of her neck to lift, her skin to prickle, sweat to collect upon her spine.

Her heart thumped, and barely able to move, standing in the darkness, she searched the shadowed corners of her room frantically. Through the open window she heard the reverberating songs of the frogs in the nearby swamps and the rumble of a train upon faraway tracks.

But here, now, he was with her.

Go away, she tried to say, but held her tongue, hoping beyond hope that he wouldn't notice her standing near the window. On the other side of the panes, security lamps illuminated the grounds with pale, bluish light, and she realized belatedly that her body, shrouded only by a sheer nightgown, was silhouetted in their eerie glow.

Of course he could see her, find her in the darkness.

He always did.

Throat dry, she stepped backward, placing a hand on the window casing to steady herself. Maybe she had just imagined his presence. Maybe she hadn't heard the door open after all. Maybe she'd jumped up from a drug-induced sleep too quickly. After all, it wasn't late, only eight in the evening.

Maybe she was safe in this room, *her* room, on the third floor.

Maybe.

She was reaching for the bedside light when she heard the soft scrape of leather against hardwood.

Her throat closed on a silent scream.

Having adjusted to the half-light, her eyes took in the bed with its mussed sheets, evidence of her fitful rest. Upon the dressing table were the lamp and a bifold picture frame; one that held small portraits of her two daughters. Across the small room was a fireplace. She could see its decorative tile and cold grate and, above the mantle, a bare spot, faded now where a mirror had once hung.

So where was he? She glanced to the tall windows. Beyond, the October night was hot and sultry. In the panes she could see her wan reflection: petite, small-boned frame; sad gold eyes; high cheekbones; lustrous auburn hair pulled away from her face. And behind her . . . was that a shadow creeping near?

Or her imagination?

That was the trouble. Sometimes he hid.

But he was always nearby. Always. She could *feel* him, hear his soft, determined footsteps in the hallway, smell his scent—a mixture of male musk and sweat—catch a glimpse of a quick, darting shadow as he passed.

There was no getting away from him. Ever. Not even in the dead of night. He received great satisfaction in surprising her, sneaking up on her while she was sitting at her desk, leaning down behind her when she was kneeling at her bedside. He was always ready to press his face to the back of her neck, to reach around her and touch her breasts, arousing her though she loathed him, pulling her tightly against him so that she could feel his erection against her back. She wasn't safe when she was under the thin spray of the shower, nor while sleeping beneath the covers of her small bed.

How ironic that they had placed her here . . . for her own safety.

"Go away," she whispered, her head pounding, her thoughts disjointed. "Leave me alone!"

She blinked and tried to focus.

Where was he?

Nervously she trained her eyes on the one hiding place, the closet. She licked her lips. The wooden door was ajar, just slightly, enough that anyone inside could peer through the crack.

From the small sliver of darkness within the closet, something seemed to glimmer. A reflection. Eyes?

Oh, God.

Maybe he was inside. Waiting.

Gooseflesh broke out on her skin. She should call out to someone, but if she did, she would be restrained, medicated . . . or worse. *Stop it, Faith. Don't get paranoid!* But the glittering eyes in the closet watched her. She felt them. Wrapping one arm around her middle, the other folded over it, she scraped her nails on the skin of her elbow.

Scratch, scratch, scratch.

But maybe this was all a bad dream. A nightmare. Wasn't that what the sisters had assured her in their soft whispers as they gently patted her hands and stared at her with compassionate, disbelieving eyes? An ugly dream. Yes! A nightmare of vast, intense proportions. Even the nurse had agreed with the nuns, telling her that what she'd thought she'd seen wasn't real. And the doctor, cold, clinical, with the bedside manner of a stone monkey, had talked to her as if she were a small, stupid child.

"There, there, Faith, no one is following you," he'd said, wearing a thin, patronizing smile. "No one is watching you. You know that. You're . . . you're just confused. You're safe here. Remember, this is your home now."

Tears burned her eyes and she scratched more anxiously, her short fingernails running over the smooth skin of her forearm, encountering scabs. Home? This monstrous place? She closed her eyes, grabbed the headboard of the bed to steady herself.

Was she really as sick as they said? Did she really see people who weren't there? That's what they'd told her, time and time again, to the point that she was no longer certain what was real and what was not. Maybe that was the plot against her, to make her believe she was as crazy as they insisted she was.

She heard a footstep and looked up quickly.

The hairs on the backs of her arms rose.

She began to shake as she saw the door crack open a bit more.

"Sweet Jesus." Trembling, she backed up, her gaze fixed on the closet, her fingers scraping her forearm like mad. The door creaked open in slow motion. "Go away!" she whispered, her stomach knotting as full-blown terror took root.

A weapon! You need a weapon!

Anxiously, she looked around the near-dark room with its bed bolted to the floor.

Get your letter opener! Now!

She took one step toward the desk before she remembered that Sister Madeline had taken the letter opener away from her.

The lamp on the night table!

But it, too, was screwed down.

She pressed the switch.

Click.

No great wash of light. Frantically, she hit the switch again. Over and over.

Click! Click! Click! Click!

She looked up and saw him then. A tall man, looming in front of the door to the hallway. It was too dark to see his features but she knew his wicked smile was in place, his eyes glinting with an evil need.

He was Satan Incarnate. And there was no way to escape from him. There never was.

"Please don't," she begged, her voice sounding pathetic and weak as she backed up, her legs quivering.

"Please don't what?"

Don't touch me . . . don't place your fingers anywhere on my body . . . don't tell me I'm beautiful . . . don't kiss me . . .

"Leave now," she insisted. Dear God, was there no weapon, nothing to stop him?

"Leave now or what?"

"Or I'll scream and call the guards."

"The guards," he repeated in that low, amused, nearly hypnotic voice. "Here?" He clucked his tongue as if she were a disobedient child. "You've tried that before."

She knew for certain that her plight was futile. She would submit to him again.

As she always did.

"Did the guards believe you the last time?"

Of course they hadn't. Why would they? The two scrawny, pimply-faced boys hadn't hidden the fact they considered her mad. At least that's what they'd insinuated, though they'd used fancier words . . . *delusional . . . paranoid . . . schizophrenic . . .*

Or had they said anything at all? Maybe not. Maybe they'd just stared at her with their pitying, yet hungry, eyes. Hadn't one of them told her she was sexy? The other one cupping one cheek of her buttocks . . . or . . . or had that all been a horrid, vivid nightmare?

Scratch, scratch, scratch. She felt her nails break the skin.

Humiliation washed over her. She inched backward, away from her tormentor. What was happening to her was her own fault. She'd sinned somehow, brought this upon herself. She was the one who was evil. She had instigated God's wrath. She alone could atone. "Go away," she whispered again, clawing more frantically at her arm.

"Faith, don't," he warned, his voice horrifyingly soothing. "Mutilating yourself won't change anything. I'm here to help you. You know that."

Help her? No . . . no, no, no!

She wanted to crumble onto the floor, to shed her guilt, to get away from the itching.

Fight! an inner voice ordered her. *Don't let him force you into doing things that you know are wrong! You have will. You can't let him do this to you.*

But it was already too late.

Close to her now, he clucked his tongue again and she saw its pointy, wet, pink tip flicking against the back of his teeth.

In a rough whisper, he said, "Uh-oh, Faith, I think you've been a naughty girl again."

"No." She was whimpering. There it was . . . that horrid bit of excitement building inside her.

"Oh, Faith, don't you know it's a sin to lie?"

She glanced to the wall where the crucifix of Jesus was nailed into the plaster. Did it move? Blinking, she imagined Jesus staring at her, his eyes kind but silently reprimanding in the semidarkness.

No, Faith. That can't be. Get a grip, for God's sake.

It's a painted image, that's all.

Breathing rapidly, she dragged her gaze from Christ's tortured face to the fireplace . . . cold now, devoid of both ashes and the mirror above it, now an empty space, the outline visible against the rosebud wallpaper. They said she broke the mirror in a fit of rage, that she'd cut herself. That her own image had caused her to panic.

But he'd done it, hadn't he? This devil whose sole intent was to torture her? Hadn't she witnessed the act? She'd tried to refuse him, and he'd crashed his fist into the looking glass. Mirrored shards sprayed, hitting her, then crashed to the floor like glittery, deadly knives.

That's what had happened.

Right?

Or not? Now, feeling the blood beneath her nails, she wondered.

What's happening to me?

She stared at her bloodied hands. Her fingernails, once manicured and polished, were broken, her palms scratched, and farther up, upon her wrists, healed deep gashes. Had she done that to herself? In her mind's eye she saw her hands wrapped around a shard of glass and the blood dripping from her fingers . . .

Because you were going to kill him . . . trying to protect yourself!

She closed her eyes and let out a long, mewling cry. It was true. She didn't know what to believe any longer. Truth and lies blended, fact and fiction fused, her life, once so ordinary, so predictable, was fragmented. Frayed. At her own hands.

She edged backward, closer to the window, farther from him, from temptation, from sin.

Where was her husband . . . and her children, what had happened to her girls?

Terror burrowed deep into her soul. Confused and panic-stricken, she blinked rapidly, trying to think. They were safe. They had to be.

Concentrate, Faith. Get hold of yourself! Zoey and Abby are with Jacques. They're visiting tonight, remember? It's your birthday.

Or was that wrong? Was everything a lie? A macabre figment of her imagination?

She took another step backward.

"You're confused, Faith, but I can help you," he said quietly, as if nothing had happened between them, as if everything she'd conjured was her imagination, as if he'd never touched her.

Dear Lord, how mad was she?

She spun quickly, her toe catching on the edge of a rug. Pitching forward, she again caught her reflection in the window and this time she saw him rushing forward, felt his hands upon her.

"No!" she cried, falling.

Glass cracked.

Blew apart as her shoulder hit the pane.

The window broke, shattering. Giving way.

With a great twisting metal groan, the wrought-iron grate wrenched free of its bolts.

She screamed and flailed at the air, trying to reach the windowsill, the filigreed barricade that hung from one screw, the bricks, anything! But it was too late. Her body hurtled through the broken panes, pieces of glass and wood clawing at her arms, ripping her nightgown, slicing her bare legs.

In a split second, she knew that it was over. She would feel no more pain.

Closing her eyes, Faith Chastain pitched into the blackness of the hot Louisiana night.

Dear Reader,

Lisa Jackson, Beverly Barton, and I have more in common than the *New York Times* bestseller list and a passion for spine-chilling suspense fiction. We happen to share one of the most creative editors in the business: John Scognamiglio. It was John's idea to team us up for this novel, and I wholeheartedly welcomed the chance to collaborate, under his wing, with two of the industry's foremost romantic-suspense writers. I'm honored to have known Lisa and Beverly for many years. Not only am I a longtime fan of their writing, but I adore them both as down-to-earth, generous, and genuine women . . . who just happen to be famous authors!

So I had definitely been looking forward to this collaboration, and was particularly inspired when we settled on a class reunion theme, because it rang true to my own life. To this day, I remain close to a tight-knit circle of high school friends back in my hometown, and I could envision myself in these characters' shoes as they reconnect with each other and their past. In fact, I happen to be facing a milestone class reunion myself this year . . . but I'm not saying which one!

Living in the New York City area, I could easily relate to Lindsay's character in particular. I thoroughly enjoyed making her—and my favorite city—come alive within these pages. My loyal readers will recognize some of my trademark elements in her segment, including an unexpected twist and a couple of secondary characters who aren't quite what they seem to be.

One of them is Isaac Halpern, Lindsay's ex-boyfriend who, we learn here, is obsessed with a mysterious woman named Rachel. Of course, there is far more to Isaac's obsession—and Rachel's absence—than Lindsay suspects. Isaac will resurface this May in my upcoming suspense novel DON'T SCREAM. Set primarily in a small town in the Berkshires of western Massachusetts, the novel features a group of sorority sisters who swore one another's silence about the terrible truth behind a shocking tragedy. Now, ten years later, they're approaching their thirtieth birthdays and have long since gone their separate ways to pursue careers, motherhood, marriage, and money. But three of them are about to come together again . . . for the funeral of the fourth.

And so it begins. Someone knows the sisters' darkest secret. Someone who will see to it that each in turn gets what she deserves: a private surprise birthday party . . . drenched in her own blood.

Turn the page to read an excerpt from DON'T SCREAM. And be sure to visit my website at www.wendycorsistaub.com to learn more about my other thrillers, or e-mail me at corsistaub@aol.com. I love to hear from readers!

With warmest regards,

Wendy Corsi Staub

September
Ten years earlier

". . . and I do solemnly swear that I will never ever tell another living soul what happened here tonight . . ."

"And I do solemnly swear that I will never ever tell another living soul what happened here tonight," the female voices echo dutifully; none without a quaver.

Brynn's is most tremulous of all, barely audible even to her own ears. She prays Tildy won't notice and single her out to repeat the pledge solo. If that happens . . .

What will I do?

What can *I do?*

She'll just have to go along with it, the way she's gone along with all of this, right from the start. Against her better judgment, against her conscience, and, ultimately . . .

Against the law?

Tildy says no. Adamantly. She insists that they haven't broken any laws.

"It's not like we've murdered someone," she hissed when Brynn balked at the proposed plan. "Anyone in our situation would do the exact same thing."

Brynn highly doubts that, but she can't bring herself to say it.

There was a time when Brynn Costello—apple of her daddy's eye, valedictorian of her high school class, dean's list candidate for her first four semesters at Stonebridge College, Zeta Delta Kappa pledge—would have stood up to all of them. Even Matilda Harrington.

So why didn't you?

Why are you standing here in the woods in the middle of the night being sworn to secrecy?

This can't really be happening. If anyone ever found out . . .

But nobody will find out.

They're not going to tell.

Anyway, Tildy was right when she pointed out that what happened isn't their fault.

Still . . .

I just want to get out of here, go back to the sorority house, and forget this ever happened.

Or, better yet, just go home.

Home.

Swept by a wave of nostalgia, Brynn swallows hard over a lump in her throat. She longs for worn oak floors, oval braided rugs, chintz slipcovers. The savory aroma of fresh-brewed coffee and onions frying in olive oil. The radio in the background, sock-hop standards and sixties anthems of the local oldies station. Clutter, and laundry, and people coming and going . . .

Home.

But the seaside, blue collar household on Cape Cod is two hundred miles and a world away from the campus nestled in the Berkshires, the mountains of western Massachusetts.

And there's no going back—not the way Brynn yearns to do.

Before her thoughts can meander down the fateful path that ultimately led to Stonebridge College, she's dragged back to the present. Tildy, apparently deciding their oath needs something more to make it official, solemnly declares, "So help me God."

"So help me God," the others obediently intone.

Not Brynn. She just moves her lips, refusing to invoke God. Not under these circumstances.

"Now we'll sing the sorority song," Tildy commands, lifting her hand to push her blond hair back from her face. Her sorority bracelet, a silver rope of clasped rosebuds, glints in the moonlight. They're all wearing them—including Rachel—and each is personalized with dangling silver initial charms.

Brynn manages to join the others in singing. The ingrained lyrics she secretly always considered embarrassingly hokey now seem bittersweet as she forces them past the lump in her throat.

We'll always remember
That fateful September.
We'll never forget
The new sisters we met.
We'll face tomorrow together
In all kinds of weather.
ZDK girls, now side by side
May travel far and wide.
But wherever we roam
Sweet ZDK will be our home.

The sisters' voices give way to the hushed nocturnal woodland descant: chirping crickets, a rushing creek, and the September breeze that gently rustles the maple boughs high above the clearing.

Then another sound reaches Brynn's ears . . .

The faint, yet resonant crack of a branch splintering underfoot.

She clutches her friend Fiona's arm, asking in a high-pitched whisper, "Did anyone hear that?"

"Hear what?" Tildy's tone is sharp.

"Shhh!" Standing absolutely still, afraid to breathe, Brynn listens intently.

They all do.

There is nothing.

Nothing but crickets, the creek, a gust stirring the leaves overhead. Just like before.

After a long, tense moment, Cassie says, "I don't hear anything, Brynn."

Brynn doesn't either. Not now.

But someone is there.

She can feel it.

Someone is lurking in the shadows among the trees, listening.

Perhaps even watching . . .

And recognizing.

It happened ten years ago this week, just after Labor Day . . . and just a few miles from here.

In fact, if one knows where to look one can pinpoint up in the greenish-golden Berkshires backdrop, beyond the row of nineteenth century rooftops, precisely the spot where it happened.

And I know where to look . . . because I was there. I know exactly what really happened that night, and it's time that—

"Oh, excuse me!" The elderly woman is apologetic, having just rounded the corner from Second Street. "I didn't mean to bump into you . . . I'm so sorry."

She looks so familiar . . .

It takes just a split second for the memory to surface. Right, she used to be a cashier at the little deli down the block. The place that always had hazelnut decaf. Yes, and she was always so chatty.

What was her name? Mary? Molly?

What is she doing out at this hour? The sky is still dark in the west, and none of the businesses along Main Street are open yet.

Don't panic. She probably doesn't even recognize you. Just smile and say something casual . . .

"Oh, that's all right, ma'am."

Good. Now turn your back. Slowly, so that you don't draw any more attention to yourself.

Good. Now get the heck out of here, before—

"Excuse me!"

Dammit! The old lady again.

What can she possibly want now?

"You must have dropped this when I bumped you." With a gnarled, blue-veined hand, she proffers a white envelope.

"Oh . . . thank you."

Could she have glanced at the address on the front before she handed it over? If she did, could she have recognized the recipient's name?

"It's going to be a nice day today." She gestures at the glow in the eastern sky, above the mountain peaks. "We needed that rain, though, at this time of year."

"Mmm hmm." Just nod. Be polite.

"Well . . . enjoy the day."

"I will." *But not as much as I'll enjoy tomorrow.* "You, too."

With a cheerful wave, the woman turns and makes her way down the block.

The post office is just a few doors in the opposite direction. These last two envelopes—the ones to be delivered right here in town—must go out in this morning's mail.

It's important that they be mailed from here, so that the recipients will realize that the sender is nearby.

The timing is just as crucial. All four cards need to arrive at their destination tomorrow, on the anniversary.

The others went out first thing yesterday morning—one to Boston, one to Connecticut. That excursion was uneventful. It was raining, and there were no witnesses . . .

Unlike today.

Now isn't the time to start taking chances. Not after months of painstakingly laying the groundwork. Not when it's finally about to begin at last.

Millie.

That's her name.

The post office can wait. The first pickup won't be for at least another hour.

What a shame, Millie.

What a shame you weren't more careful.

Dear Reader,

When our wonderful editor, John Scognamiglio, asked me to participate in writing a novel with fellow writers Lisa Jackson and Wendy Corsi Staub, I couldn't say yes fast enough. After all, who wouldn't want to collaborate with two of the most talented suspense/thriller authors in the business? Lisa came up with the basic idea and created the background for the story and the characters. She wrote the first third of the novel, telling the story from St. Elizabeth's alumna Kristen Delmonico's point of view. Then Wendy took the book from Portland, Oregon to New York City, and gave us Lindsay Farrell's story. I came in for the final chapters, taking readers down South where Rachel Alsace lives in Huntsville, Alabama, and then back to Portland for the twenty-year reunion that brings these old friends together for the first time since high school.

Police detective Rachel Alsace once worked for the Chattanooga P.D. with another female officer, Lindsay (Lin) McAllister, and now Lindsay is a private detective for the Powell Agency in Knoxville, Tennessee. Rachel takes note of a serial killer case making headlines in many area newspapers—The Beauty Queen Killer case—because she knows her old friend has been personally involved in tracking this vicious murderer.

When Chattanooga millionaire Judd Walker's wife, a former Miss Tennessee, was murdered, Lindsay assisted the lead detective on the case. During the investigation she found herself falling in love with the victim's husband, a man on the edge of self-destructing. Filled with agonized grief and a mad thirst for revenge, Judd hired the Powell Agency, headed by his long-time friend Griffin Powell, to conduct an independent search for his wife's killer. Four years and numerous murders later, the Beauty Queen Killer is still on the loose, and Judd has still not come to terms with the death of his wife.

Look for Lindsay McAllister and Judd Walker's story in my next romantic thriller, THE DYING GAME, April 2007. And for those of you who have been clamoring for Griffin Powell's story, I have good news. You will get the chance to learn more about this to-die-for billionaire P.I. and his mysterious past as he works with Lindsay and Judd to track down a killer who has outsmarted not only the Powell Agency for four years, but also local law enforcement and the FBI. All of Griff's secrets will be revealed as he's drawn into a very deadly and a very personal new game of murder in his own novel coming in February 2008.

I always love to hear from readers. You can e-mail me at *bbarton@beverlybarton.com*. For more information about my books and me or to sign up for my e-mail newsletter, go to my website at *www.beverlybarton.com.*

Thank you for reading MOST LIKELY TO DIE. Now, take a sneak peek at the prologue of THE DYING GAME!

Warmest regards,

Beverly Barton

The intensely bright lights blinded her. She couldn't see anything except the white illumination that obscured everything in her line of vision. She wished he would turn off the car's headlights.

Judd didn't like for her to show houses to clients in the evenings and generally she did what Judd wanted her to do. But her career as a realtor was just getting off the ground, and if she could sell this half-million-dollar house to Mr. and Mrs. Farris, her percentage would be enough to furnish the nursery. Not that she was pregnant. Not yet. And not that her husband couldn't well afford to furnish a nursery with the best of everything. It was just that Jennifer wanted the baby to be her gift to her wonderful husband and the nursery to be a gift from her to their child.

Holding her hand up to shield her eyes from the headlights, she walked down the sidewalk to meet John and Katherine Farris, an up-and-coming entrepreneurial couple planning to start a new business in Chattanooga. She had spoken only to John Farris. From their telephone conversations, she had surmised that John, like her own husband, was the type who liked to think he wore the pants in the family. Odd how considering the fact that she believed herself to be a thoroughly modern woman, Jennifer loved Judd's old-fashioned sense of protectiveness and possessiveness.

When John Farris parked his black Mercedes and opened the driver's door, Jennifer met him, her hand outstretched in greeting. He accepted her hand immediately and smiled warmly.

"Good evening, Mr. Farris." Jennifer glanced around, searching for Mrs. Farris.

"I'm sorry, something came up at the last minute that delayed Katherine. She'll be joining us soon."

When John Farris raked his silvery blue eyes over her, Jennifer shuddered inwardly, an odd sense of uneasiness settling in the pit of her stomach. *You're being silly,* she told herself. Men found her attractive. It wasn't her fault. She didn't do anything to lead them on, nothing except simply being beautiful, which she owed to the fact she'd inherited great genes from her attractive parents.

Jennifer sighed. Sometimes being a former beauty queen was a curse.

"If you'd like to wait for your wife before you look at the house, I can go ahead and answer any questions you might have. I've got all the information in my briefcase in my car."

He shook his head. "No need to wait. I'd like to take a look around now. If I don't like the place, Katherine won't be interested."

"Oh, I see."

He chuckled. "It's not that she gives in to me on everything. We each try to please the other. Isn't that the way to have a successful marriage?"

"Yes, I think so. It's certainly what Judd and I have been trying to do. We're a couple of newlyweds just trying to make our way through that first year of marriage." Jennifer nodded toward the front entrance to the sprawling glass and log house. "If you'll follow me."

"I'd be delighted to follow you."

Despite his reply sending a quiver of apprehension along her nerve endings, she kept walking toward the front steps, telling herself that if she had to defend her honor against unwanted advances, it wouldn't be the first time. She knew how to handle herself in sticky situations. She carried pepper spray in her purse and her cell phone rested securely in her jacket pocket.

After unlocking the front door, she flipped on the light switch, which illuminated the large foyer. "The house was built in nineteen-seventy-five by an architect for his own personal home."

John Farris paused in the doorway. "How many rooms?"

"Ten," she replied, then motioned to him. "Please, come on in."

He entered the foyer and glanced around, up into the huge living room and to the right into the open dining room. "It seems perfect for entertaining."

"Oh, it is. There's a state-of-the-art kitchen. It was completely gutted and redone only four years ago by the present owner."

"I'd like to take a look," he told her. "I'm the chef in the family. Katherine can't boil water."

Feeling a bit more at ease, Jennifer led him from the foyer, through the dining room and into the galley-style kitchen. "I love this kitchen. I'm not much of a cook myself, but I've been taking gourmet cooking lessons as a surprise for my husband."

"Isn't he a lucky man."

Jennifer felt Mr. Farris as he came up behind her. Shuddering nervously, she started to turn and face him, but suddenly and without warning, he grabbed her from behind and covered her face with a foul-smelling rag.

No. No . . . no, this can't be happening.

Had she been unconscious for a few minutes or a few hours? She didn't know. When she came to, she realized she was sitting propped up against the wall in the kitchen, her feet tied together with rope and her hands pulled over her head, each wrist bound with individual pieces of rope that had been tied to the door handles of two open kitchen cabinets.

Groggy, slightly disoriented, Jennifer blinked several times, then took a deep breath and glanced around the room, searching for her attacker. John Farris loomed over her, an odd smile on his handsome face.

"Well, hello, beautiful," he said. "I was wondering how long you'd sleep. I've been waiting patiently for you to wake up. You've been out nearly fifteen minutes."

"Why?" she asked, her voice a ragged whisper.

"Why what?"

"Why are you doing this?"

"What do you think I intend to do?"

"Rape me." Her voice trembled.

Please, God, don't let him kill me.

He laughed. "What sort of man do you think I am? I'd never force myself on an unwilling woman."

"Please, let me go. Whatever—" She gasped, her mouth sucking in air as she noticed that he held something shiny in his right hand.

A meat cleaver!

Sheer terror claimed her at that moment, body and soul. Her stomach churned. Sweat dampened her face. The loud rat-a-tat-tat of her accelerated heartbeat thundered in her ears.

He reached down with his left hand and fingered her long, dark hair. "If only you were a blonde or a redhead."

Jennifer swallowed hard. *He's going to kill me. He's going to kill me with that meat cleaver. He'll chop me up in little pieces . . .*

She whimpered. *Oh, Judd, why didn't I listen to you? Why did I come here alone tonight?*

"Are you afraid?" John Farris asked.

"Yes."

"You should be," he told her.

"You're going to kill me, aren't you?"

He laughed again. Softly.

"Please . . . please . . ." She cried. Tears filled her eyes and trickled down her cheeks.

He came closer. And closer. He raised the meat cleaver high over her head, then swung it across her right wrist.

Blood splattered on the cabinet, over her head, and across her upper body as her severed right hand tumbled downward and hit the floor.

Pain! Excruciating pain.

And then he lifted the cleaver and swung down and across again, cutting off her left hand with one swift, accurate blow.

Jennifer passed out.